'Be upstanding in court,' the usher called as the double doors behind the bench opened and the purple-robed judge stepped through and took his seat without looking anywhere but ahead of him.

Everyone in the courtroom except the prisoners and escort sat with the judge and waited with a sense of expectation.

Lord Justice Ernest Kinahon slowly opened his large notebook in which he meticulously summarised all aspects of the trial in his neat round hand and glanced over the pages, then lifted his head to look from beneath his pale, hooded eyes at the two defendants. He remembered thinking earlier how if the security of the state was dependant on such frail emotions as they had displayed, then God save it – as he had no doubt He would.

'Two policemen, both with hitherto unblemished records, stand before this court accused of the most heinous crime of murder, a killing that took place in the course of a particularly dangerous duty.'

Also by G. F. Newman in Sphere Books

SET A THIEF
THREE PROFESSIONAL LADIES

THE
TESTING
GROUND

G. F. Newman

SPHERE BOOKS LIMITED

A SPHERE BOOK

First published in Great Britain by Michael Joseph Ltd 1987
Published by Sphere Books Ltd 1989

Printed and bound in Great Britain by
Richard Clay Ltd, Bungay, Suffolk

Sphere Books Ltd
A Division of
Macdonald & Co. (Publishers) Ltd
66/73 Shoe Lane, London EC4P 4AB
A member of Maxwell Pergamon Publishing Corporation plc

Prologue

H E HAD CONTRACTED AIDS. How, he didn't want to think about, but he was convinced he had the disease and was terrified of seeing his doctor to confirm this. The annual medical he was obliged to submit to was still six months away and doubtful as the means of detecting this disease, as it was mostly concerned with the volume at which the heart circulated the blood, rather than its quality, and whether one took drugs that might impair judgement.

Judgement was essential in his work. Unless it remained finely gauged, he and any number of the people who operated on his instructions might die; the propaganda battle might be lost; the government seriously embarrassed, or even fall. The responsibility wasn't something he treated lightly, nor let weigh heavily upon his shoulders. Daily in his work he dealt incisively with life-threatening situations, in the certainty of the rightness of his actions. There his judgement proved faultless, and even if it weren't so, there were many means of disguising mistakes, and few people to openly challenge them.

Where his judgement could be considered lacking, were it generally known, was in his increasingly frequent visits to King's House Community Home for Boys. The principal of the school for delinquent children and those placed in local authority care out of broken homes was one of the few people who understood his need, arising out of the terrible pressure he worked under. It was an expedient confidence, not one brought about by mutual respect; Maurice Humphreys was a man with a recent past which if revealed could easily cost him his life in certain corners of Northern Ireland. Sir Michael Newfield was someone who had exploited such vulnerability for the benefit mostly of the state; latterly such weaknesses were exploited for his own gratification, which made him increasingly vulnerable and which he in turn despised himself for.

What would he do if it was confirmed that he was carrying the

AIDS virus? The question was like that perennial playground favourite: Who would you prefer to die, your mother or your father? – he had never any doubt about the answer. The prospect of celibacy, until his suspicions were maybe confirmed, hadn't occurred to Sir Michael Newfield. Certainly he wasn't about to confide in Maurice Humphreys, for such information would have given him moral superiority, if not exactly power, over him. Nor would he tell any of the boys. In other circumstances he might have rushed about getting back at ex-wives and lovers; there were none. He had never been married.

But someone was going to pay for his past suffering, and the physical suffering he would doubtless experience as the diseases of the syndrome manifested themselves. The sullen, working-class boys of King's House were the ones being made to pay. But for them, he told himself, he wouldn't have this vulnerability, this weakness that might be discovered and used to destroy him – assuming anyone was brave enough. The thought of it made him sick most mornings; it was either that or a symptom of the physical disease. Those wretched boys deserved nothing less than the time bomb he was bequeathing them. He hated them, their sly ways and deceitful looks; their faces burred both from the harsh climate and the daily struggle to exist; their dulled, unseeing eyes, so eager to please and gratify the weaknesses of the adult world in some expectation of favours.

Precisely how the head teacher procured the services of the most amenable boys he didn't inquire, but Maurice Humphreys had an odious talent for it. It seemed somehow poetic that he should exploit him as Humphreys exploited those given to his charge. Those boys would, he knew, eventually go off into the world and exploit those they subsequently had sexual contact with. He hated them more each time he drove out to the school in Sydenham, East Belfast. Having infectious sex with them wasn't simply a sad and sordid way of having the last word, it also served to block off the truth, as currently perceived, about the state of his body.

By coming out to King's House like this, Sir Michael was breaking all the ground rules on security that he had established since taking up office as Ulster Security Co-ordinator at the request of the Prime Minister. He was a likely target for any one of the terrorist organisations. Should they get to know his movements, he would be liable to some sort of attack, either from a bomb or an ambush, especially as he travelled alone and went unarmed; should they get to know the purpose of his visits, he would be just as dead. But lately he was taking more risks; he was someone for whom time was running out, against which knowledge the risks seemed relatively unimportant.

The main precaution he took was giving the head teacher only scant notice of his arrival, and never once using a car that could be traced back to him. The blue Metro City was one of dozens of cars at the disposal of the Secret Intelligence Service, which in Northern Ireland was answerable to him, along with its rival MI5. No one under him was put unnecessarily at risk through the over-familiarity of the vehicles they used.

He parked on the gravelled sweep outside the main school entrance. The building was a pleasant red-brick structure, built by the Victorians for a happier purpose, but made ugly by the subsequent grafting on of annexes and metal fire escapes. The odour of cheap disinfectant permeated the place. The smell of it was something he carried with him from his own schooldays and was as much an object of hatred as his reason for being there. As he hauled his large, round frame out of the low car, he suddenly felt sick and giddy; he held on to the roof of the car for fear of falling over. His stomach was clamping; waves of nausea overcame him and he wasn't sure he could hold on to his bowel movement. Incontinence was the thing he most feared; total dependence on a stranger would be an humiliation too awful to bear – there was no one close to him who would undertake such an onerous chore. Suicide would be the only way out; but there was the fear that the decision would be left too late.

A hot flush followed another wave of nausea as his stomach clamped again. His fingers tightened on the edge of the door. He wouldn't fall, but didn't know how long he could remain there before someone came out to see what the trouble was. To bed with a hotty on the tum, that was the solution matron at Lady Manners School always offered. It relaxed the stomach and stopped the clamping. Sir Michael wondered if he shouldn't heed the advice of the dead matron and return to his office and the day-bed he kept there, or to his apartment on the top floor of Stormont Castle, rather than the sullen mouth of whatever boy would be provided. But he was free from his prison now and clear of his protecting shadows, and relatively safe. He would have to make further arrangements for another visit and didn't know when that might be. The thought of being taken ill here and of a doctor being called wasn't encouraging.

3

There was no telling what secrets might escape then, or how this head teacher and his wretched charges might react. Humphreys would telephone the duty officer at Stormont if he were to collapse here, so it was silly to allow this stomach upset to deny him his needs in this way, he told himself; he wasn't, after all, allowing AIDS to inhibit him.

Tensing himself, Sir Michael swung the car door shut and let go of the roof, but as he turned to cross to the steps he felt the world spin and put his hand out on the car again. He wouldn't make those ten paces or so. He glanced up in panic and caught sight of a young face at an upstairs window. He felt suddenly angry at being spied on. He would complain to Maurice Humphreys. He wouldn't have the boys watching for his arrival. He knew that particular boy would be the one the head had arranged for him to go with, for on notice of his visits Humphreys sent all the other lads on a cross-country run, and most of the staff with them lest they absconded.

He took a deep breath, then another, hoping his sick feeling would pass. Finally it did, and he crossed from the car unsteadily, mounted the steps and entered the main hall through the double oak doors. He was met by that awful, familiar smell of disinfectant and wax, while the decor of orange and grey affronted him as it did each time he came here. He approached the long table before the minster fireplace which had received paint like everything else in the building. He didn't reach for the bell but used the table to steady himself.

As if from nowhere Maurice Humphreys was at his side. He was shorter and fatter than his visitor, but had the much-practised ability of custodians of such institutions of moving in total silence in order to catch whichever miscreant up to whatever sordid trick. He was an obsequious authoritarian, whose hands made a faint sighing noise as he rubbed them together.

'Hello, how nice to see you again so soon.'

Sir Michael didn't respond but examined the words for the hidden meaning. He knew that this procurer of young boys was reminding him of his increasing weakness.

'Most of our young souls are out cross-country running. It does them the power of good. Jonathan is the only one left, but he'll be pleased to have a visitor. He will so.'

Tall, with a slender, down-covered body; high cheekbones painted red with excitement, and a rosebud of a mouth, was as Sir Michael Newfield imagined the boy as he was led up the narrow stairs that were out of proportion to the hall. Halfway along the ill-lit

4

corridor Jonathan waited in one of the rooms that overlooked the drive. He was an attractive thirteen-year-old, all that Sir Michael had come to expect, but he seemed far from pleased to see him.

'You've not met Jonathan before,' Humphreys said with a sly, knowing smile. 'Jonathan's one of the attendants on the Boy Bishop at the Cathedral. He is so.'

Sir Michael didn't wish for such personal details, he didn't want to know anything that gave him any sort of identity. Such details intruded, forced him to acknowledge things he didn't wish to acknowledge. They were like the intrusion of múndane domestic details at the scenes of terrorist violence, those familiar labels inside cheap clothes, a hole in a sock, a button missing from a shirt cuff. Details that terrorists never considered important disturbed Sir Michael profoundly. They suggested a chaos that he had spent a lifetime trying to order, but more than that they made those figures in a war game people instead of objects.

'Hello, Jonathan,' Sir Michael said stiffly.

'Hello, sir,' he replied, without looking at him.

'I've some reports to catch up with, I have so,' Humphreys said. 'The runners will be about an hour.' He departed, preceding his sighing hands backwards out of the door, which he closed.

There was an awkward silence. Sir Michael Newfield knew not what to say to the boy. He never knew what to say to them, so invariably he said nothing. He looked the lad up and down, then quickly averted his eyes. He was attractive – the head teacher always found the most attractive and willing boys – but somehow Sir Michael wished they would smile some of the time, as if this were giving them pleasure too. That was ridiculous, of course, and he stopped himself pursuing such thoughts.

He sat on the edge of the narrow bed with its blankets drawn drum-tight and watched the boy move closer to him with a familiarity that precluded the need to say anything. All he wanted to do was stroke his smooth, downy limbs, fondle the boy's small genitals, feel his hard, vibrant prick. But it wouldn't stop there. It never did. He would go on until he reached his own nadir of disgust; only then would he stop, clean himself with the meagre facilities the room provided and rush away. For days, sometimes weeks afterwards, he rattled around in a miasma of self-loathing and guilt, telling himself that was the last visit he would make, that he would find the strength not to go through this degrading business again. Then a soft yearning as random and as insidious as cancer would begin to swell in him until he was forced to contact Maurice Humphreys again.

When he had finished dressing Sir Michael stole a glance at this attendant to the Boy Bishop and thought about the possibility of the AIDS virus he had left with him. He found his whole demeanour offensive, that nasty little mouth full of filth, those weather-burned cheeks, cold eyes, full of resentment; unlike himself forty-six years ago, this lad seemed without remorse. This was a solemn and symbolic act of revenge for a lifetime of suffering.

He left the school quickly without saying goodbye to the head or seeing another soul. He was glad of that. He felt safe when he climbed back into the small blue car, started the engine and drove back along the rutted drive. As he pulled out of the gates, the strung-out cross-country run was returning, but none of the runners noticed him. Nor had they noticed the man in the trees near the fence that surrounded the school grounds, either going out or coming back. He had a Canon 500 with a telephoto lens and motor wind. He shot thirty-six photos of Sir Michael Newfield's arrival at the school, and twenty-nine of his departure forty-six minutes later. Time, date, car, the clothes he was wearing, were neatly logged, as was the matter of him breaking the cardinal rules of security, despite the fact that Sir Michael had written those rules.

Quite why he was collecting the information on his boss, the observer didn't know, and hadn't questioned Laurence Payne, his immediate superior. He sensed it was for something a lot more dangerous than simply revealing this man's double standards, or gaining ascendancy in their continuing squabble with SIS. People had died to keep Sir Michael Newfield's secret, and it might have been easier to keep had the visits to King's House been confined to him, and not involved high-ranking members of the judiciary and Orange Lodges. Possibly Laurence Payne would tell him when he reported back, possibly he wouldn't, but almost certainly he would be safer not knowing.

1

THE FORD GRANADA that threaded its way across Westminster Bridge and through the tail end of the rush-hour traffic that spread through south-east London like some chronic disease was almost as obvious as a police car with a klaxon. But it had no such facility for speeding through the congestion. The man in the back took the opportunity to read intelligence reports prepared by detectives from C11. When he wasn't using car time to work, Commander Jack Bentham would travel in the front next to his driver.

He always felt a little conspicuous in the back, especially when travelling through the decaying inner cities. He had never been pelted from the roadside, or even gestured at, but he was aware of the deepening rift between himself and the ever-expanding under-class. Their looks held anger and resentment, which people in positions of privilege and power had but a few years ago mistaken for respect. The reports he was reading, in order to avoid the real reason for this trip out, concerned politically motivated black criminals, and also left-wing students at London University who were trying to foment violence from general dissatisfaction. There were areas he was being drawn into more and more. This sort of thing had at one time been dealt with exclusively by Special Branch, but they were pursuing the fatter political subversives as defined by MI5.

Jack Bentham never knew whether the threats the reports identified were imagined or real, and suspected the former; the Security Service spent far more time than seemed healthy watching fairly innocuous movements like CND, Animal Rights, trade unions. The Criminal Intelligence department at Scotland Yard, C11, which he ran, often found itself dealing either with the overspill from those operations or the shortfall they created, and pushed him further and further from policing recognisable crime, where policemen of his generation felt most comfortable. The generation below him who had been conditioned to public-order policing

7

experienced no qualms about wading in. For them anyone on whatever demo was in the wrong and so was fair game; they acknowledged no social, moral or ethical mitigation. There would come a time when there'd be a generation of policemen who would be able to do little other than respond to any given situation with boot and baton, or whatever weapon politicians gave them. That worried Jack Bentham, as he knew it did some of his contemporaries. But few seemed to want to take action to check this slide. Perhaps they just didn't know how to check it as the political demands of the job increased.

The process by which policemen slipped from being thief-takers to policemen with a political bias as they rose in rank was as imperceptible as the gut you suddenly found hanging over your belt, Bentham thought. Both were something you always intended doing something about tomorrow. He was only five foot eight, the bare minimum height acceptable in the Metropolitan Police, and couldn't easily disguise his extra weight; his university education helped him to pick his way through the political bias when he found it hemming him in.

'Something going off there, guv,' the driver said, interrupting Bentham's thoughts. They were passing a police van parked not a hundred yards from the local police station, amid spools of litter that suggested a street event had passed. The street event was now, as three uniformed policemen laid into a black man, only none of the street people stayed around to witness it. They knew that they could be too easily brought up on charges for getting involved.

'Pull up, Joe. Let's have a look.'

Why he wanted to bother with a familiar street stop, he didn't know, but he assumed it was because of the reputation the police station had. The locals avoided going there for any reason, especially members of the large black community. The close proximity of the stop to the station made Bentham curious. He wound down the window to try and hear what was being said. The car had stopped a few yards past the police van.

'I'm not taking my fucking clothes off in the street, man! Fuck you!' the black man protested. This stopped when one of the policemen sank his fist into the suspect's chest.

Bentham couldn't hear what the policeman said, but the suspect was shouting again when his breath returned. 'You mother-fuckers! You can't do this to me. You can't, you dirty fuckers!'

Not surprisingly, the shouting brought no one to his assistance.

Black faces peered angrily from Asian newsagents and grocery stores with their dusty and faded windows displaying the goods inside.

Calm was almost instantly established by the reassuring presence of a uniformed sergeant who finally came from the station to investigate. 'Look, you black bastard,' he said. 'You either do what they tell you or do it at the nick.'

That was no choice at all for the suspect; his clothes came off in the street. He hesitated at his Jockey shorts.

'What's that all about, guv?' the driver asked.

'I expect they're searching him for drugs,' Bentham replied, recognising at once the excuse he was making. Suspicion may have been the reason for the stop, but he guessed humiliation was the purpose of the exercise. That sort of scene was becoming more and more frequent under the Police and Criminal Evidence Act, which gave policemen the right to stop and search anyone on a reasonable suspicion. Blacks were stopped most frequently, and unless there was a genuine willingness at the top to change things the situation would get worse.

He nodded to his driver and the car started along the road. The local police station was a grim, four-storeyed brick building that dominated a grim landscape, although not by its physical presence, for it wasn't the biggest building in the area and the surrounding neglected flatblocks towered over it. Bentham climbed out in the pound at the rear, leaving his driver in the car. He punched the digital keys at the top of the rear steps to gain access.

The first person he met inside was one of his detectives, who was there with other C11 detectives working with the local intelligence units. Detective Inspector Bill Senior had been waiting around for his arrival, following the call to him at the Yard.

Bill Senior showed a reluctant, unsure manner, which was unlike him. He glanced around the corridor.

'What's the problem, Bill?' Bentham asked. That was why he was there.

'Could we talk in private, guv?' Conversations about C11 were mostly secret.

Bentham opened a door. The room was empty, and he motioned Senior inside. The DI heistated again.

'The thing is, guv, I had word that Superintendent Horsfell was at it – selling our intelligence to villains we've been collecting it on. That haulier out of Bermondsey is one. It's what I heard' – he spoke almost apologetically, certainly reluctantly. Most policemen disliked blowing the whistle on other policemen, especially those they were currently on a job with. Those that didn't usually joined the professional whistle-blowers in CIB-2, which conducted the investigations into complaints about dishonest policemen.

'Where did it come from, Bill? A villain?'

'Not really – a DI out of Chelsea nick. He's been suspended for putting villains into a Post Office.'

'Have you talked to Alan Horsfell?' That was the most logical move to Bentham's way of thinking. He had done a number of internal investigations, and didn't particularly like doing them.

'I may be out of order, sir,' DI Senior said, with an edge creeping into his voice, sensing his boss didn't want to know. 'I thought I'd best mention it. I mean, you never know when you're being set up these days. That DI who's been suspended might be trying to claim a body to trade for his liberty with CIB-2.'

That might have been going on here, but Jack Bentham refused to give in to such paranoia. 'I wouldn't be surprised. What's the name of the suspended detective inspector?'

'Pyle, guv. Fred Pyle. Word is he's a right wrong 'un. He's out to save himself.'

A smile tugged at the corner of Bentham's mouth. He knew DI Pyle to be a right wrong 'un, having been instrumental in his suspension, along with that of a number of other fairly senior policemen. He'd imagined CIB-2 had got the case against Pyle sewn up long ago, and wondered again if he wasn't being led into something that might trip him up. But still he refused to believe such a move.

'Why would he put his hands up?' He stood off the edge of the table bringing the meeting to a close. 'I'll deal with it, Bill.'

Visits out from his department on the fourth floor at the Scotland Yard building weren't a frequent occurrence. If higher authority were needed for a particular action, it sought him. Having come down here at DI Senior's request, he knew he'd have to do something about Detective Superintendent Alan Horsfell. He found him in the interview room where two detectives from the local criminal intelligence unit were interviewing a black suspect. He had known Alan Horsfell about eight years, first meeting him when he was a DI on the Flying Squad. He didn't doubt he was capable of doing what Bill Senior had suggested, but knew Horsfell to be a hard-working detective; and such moves were counter-productive. Perhaps he was being arrogant in his belief that a senior detective under his command would not behave in that way. He knew all policemen were capable of wrongdoing in certain circumstances; it was naive of him to believe otherwise. What he knew he should do was try and discover the circumstances here and then make a judgement. But that would have meant his doing CIB-2's job, and he wouldn't do that, nor pass this information on to them.

The cries that followed the suspect being slapped in the face by the young detective sergeant conducting the interview penetrated his thoughts.

'What were you storing the petrol bombs for, Floyd?' The question was put to the young black man time and again.

'I don't know how they got there, I don't,' came the familiar reply, tiredness and fear increasingly apparent in the boy's voice.

No daylight ever penetrated the small, pale green, featureless interview room, which was within the jurisdiction of the front office on the ground floor; the harsh neon light was never off. Standing by the door of the room which smelled of the detectives' anti-perspirant and the suspect's stale sweat of fear, Commander Jack Bentham watched as the suspect was struck around the head and knocked off the chair. He was a little surprised that his presence in no way inhibited these detectives. His thoughts, like theirs, were about the damage those petrol bombs could do, especially to riot policemen who went into the predominantly black ghettos.

The detectives carrying out the interview hauled the youth off the floor and back into the chair. The DS hit him again, repeated the question, and received a similar answer.

'How much more of that is he going to take?' Bentham asked, seeing this interview getting nowhere. He would have taken a different approach, but wasn't about to intervene. Without doubt, violence worked in the right circumstances, but with more and more suspects complaining about police brutality their credibility was inevitably suffering in spite of, and possibly because of, internal investigations too often finding no case to answer.

'Depends how good C11's info was, sir,' the young detective sergeant replied, and then, as if realising he had gone too far, 'We'll crack him, sir. He's almost there.'

Detective Superintendent Alan Horsfell glanced anxiously at his boss, half-expecting some sort of explosion from him. If these two detectives didn't get a ballocking now, he thought, he might later for allowing their physical interrogation in this way.

When Bentham nodded and went out, Alan Horsfell quickly

11

followed. 'Whatever happened to reasonable force in policing?' he said, trying to anticipate his boss. Jack Bentham was a bit of an unknown quantity. Sometimes he'd support his men kicking and screaming right up to the deputy commissioner, then at other times he'd add to their troubles himself.

'It disappeared along with reasonably behaved suspects, I suppose, Alan.' The picture of the naked black man on the pavement outside the police station came to Bentham's mind, bringing a fleeting doubt. 'This lad's definitely involved?'

'For sure. There's a riot of some kind waiting to go off. For sure.'

'As long as we don't spark it with that.' Almost any sort of treatment of suspects or any kind of corner-cutting was justified by the right sort of result. Few policemen ever questioned who it might be right for. 'They're quietly shitting themselves on the sixteenth floor about something popping here. The truth is they don't know whether to let it happen and bring in gas and baton rounds, or try and head it off. Either way, we need information.'

'They'll get a result, guv.' Horsfell followed his boss out to the yard where his car was and waited as Bentham paused.

The wait puzzled Alan Horsfell. He knew then he wasn't going to get a ballocking because the result they needed was too important. But he sensed there was something else.

Bentham half-turned and looked at him. 'There's a rumour that you're earning off villains we've been looking at.'

Horsfell laughed but saw at once it wasn't a joke. 'Some fucking chance. What cunt gave you that?'

Continuing to fix him with his stare, Bentham said, 'If it's true, I'd like to know where my whack is.'

A moment followed when neither of them moved, as each considered the other, trying to anticipate and jump the right way. This was a doubly dangerous moment for Detective Superintendent Horsfell. On the one hand he could put this senior officer into the earner; but he could risk exposure with such an offer by acknowledging he was at it. The traditional way when caught bang to rights was to deny everything. He's heard stories about Jack Bentham, but had no evidence that he was a part of the firm within a firm. He made his decision. 'It's ballocks, guv. I haven't had a decent fucking earner since I've been on C11.' To have said he had never had one would have been to take his boss for a fool.

'I should dig out a suspended DI from Chelsea by the name of Pyle,' Bentham advised him. 'He's putting you in.'

'Pyle?' Horsfell shook his head as though never having heard of him.

'Mind how you go, Alan.'

Bentham smiled grimly and opened the car door. His driver had remained behind the wheel. He hoped that that was the end of the matter. Better it was sorted out like this than that yet another policeman was suspended while yet another internal inquiry got under way. He had had enough of internal inquiries, even though the last he had conducted for the Deputy Commissioner had helped him get promoted to Commander. He had expected that more policemen would stand in the frame, but it mattered less now that they hadn't. He was learning expediency in high office, and had managed to all but ignore the hand of Freemasonry that had reached in. Although not a Mason himself, he understood the self-interest that guided most policemen; they were human too, and only wanted to survive like everyone else.

2

COMING TO NORTHEN IRELAND felt like coming home; even the icy blast of sleet across the tarmac as he walked with his partner from the 8.30 shuttle.

They passed, along with ninety-one other souls, through the airport security screen. Unnoticed in their cheap business suits with their cheap attaché cases full of brochures about central-heating boilers. He hadn't been here for over two years. Then the circumstances were entirely different – he had been here with his regiment doing their tour of duty keeping the peace. He was still with the 5th Battalion of the Parachute Regiment, but, seconded to the RUC Special Branch, he and his partner were here now to create the peace.

They took the bus from the airport to the bus station on Glangall Street and walked the half mile to their bed and breakfast digs on University Road. Their first-floor rooms overlooked the YWCA, which Sergeant Adam Birchfield thought absolutely perfect. The truth was he preferred looking at and talking about sex to actually doing it, but he'd managed to get a sound reputation within his company as a real dagger.

Any opulence the Edwardian house had once had was gone, and it had run to seed, as if the owners suffered the disease of vanished tourists since the troubles. It wasn't the sort of place to attract any attention. Two post-graduate students from Queen's University lived on the top floor. Birchfield and his partner, Sergeant Lenny Stone, would change their accommodation at least three times, perhaps more, before they were pulled out.

The phone rang on the landing outside Birchfield's room and Stone watched through the open adjoining door as he lowered the small telescope he carried everywhere and crossed the room. He didn't identify himself when he lifted the phone and his replies amounted to no more than monosyllables. In a final burst of loquacity he said, 'I know where it is.'

14

A black taxi took them to the car park on Great Victoria Street, behind the Europa Hotel. It was the business section of the city and had a depressed look about it: buildings empty and lots vacant, looking for developers; security fences that collected some of the litter.

As they rode silently, watching the back of the driver's thick red neck, Birchfield thought about the piano wire threaded into his belt. He considered reaching through and putting it around the cab driver's neck. The black cabs were run by the Provisional IRA, supposedly, and Adam Birchfield's closest friend had been taken to his death in a black cab on their last trip over here.

Without looking at the driver, a habit he found hard to break and one that meant you were less likely to be remembered, Birchfield paid the fare at the entrance to this busy car park and made a note of the expense, including the tip. He didn't have seniority over Stone, who was four years older, but tended to be self-assertive.

Two men waited in a dark blue Austin Montego at the back of the car park. As Birchfield and Stone approached, they glanced about them, alert to any sort of ambush, even though there was no possibility here.

Through the off-side mirror the man behind the steering wheel saw them come along the side of the car. He rolled down the window about an inch as Birchfield leaned into it.

'You're waiting for us,' he said, surprising the driver.

The passenger leaned across and studied Birchfield. Like the driver, he showed little concern for the disguised quasi-uniform under Birchfield's coat. Ironically, when they did wear full uniform it was as a disguise, so they'd be taken for regular RUC officers.

'Would you be Mr Stone?' the passenger inquired.

'Birchfield.' He nodded to his partner who was watching the car park. 'He's Stone.'

'What's the password?'

The two SAS men looked at each other surprised.

Even at this late juncture Birchfield managed to say the words with a straight face – passwords were never taken less than seriously: 'Paddy can't make the match tonight.'

'Why's that then?'

'His father just died,' Stone said impatiently. He felt exposed, no matter how safe they said it was. 'Let's get the fuck out of here.'

'Fair enough,' the passenger said as he reached over and pulled the door plug. 'You can never be too sure.'

Stone might have thought Chief Inspector Brian Paisley was parodying himself, had he no experience of the Northern Irish. Paisley was red-faced and slightly overweight, either that or he wore slightly undersized clothes. He was quick-tempered, and as quick to forget the whole incident that caused it. He was perfectly foiled by the man who drove them out of the car park. Sergeant Terence Keeper had a quiet, thoughtful manner. Of the two Stone instinctively trusted the sergeant, despite his shock of red hair, which reminded him of his old man.

They were driven out to Knock, the security-laden headquarters of the Royal Ulster Constabulary which had spread like some terminal disease in planning outwards from an inelegant stone-built gentleman's residence. The building they were taken to was a somewhat less salubrious Nissen-type hut, which stood in the extensive if crowded grounds sheltered under the main building, linking that and the new Communications offices. There was nothing special about the green-painted prefab, only what it contained once you passed through the only entrance via the main building. The range of firearms spread along steel shelving in the small armoury was impressive even by SAS expectations. Little of it was standard, but had either been captured from terrorists or brought in clandestinely, and kept that way. Stone and Birchfield moved along the shelves picking up weapons and handling them with an affectionate familiarity.

'We can choose anything we want to use?' Stone looked at Paisley and Carson and picked up an American-made Ingram sub-machine gun, checking the magazine release. This was an SAS preferred weapon, but there were difficulties getting it nowadays; under pressure from Irish Americans, who saw it being used on the wrong side in Northern Ireland, the State Department had slapped on an effective embargo.

'Whatever it is you're preferring. We find these handy.' Chief Inspector Paisley reached down a Remington 870R pump-action shotgun. It had a folding metal stock and a pistol grip; concealment and ease of use were further aided by the sawn-off barrel.

Adam Birchfield took down an Armalite 18, a weapon he had a lot of experience with and a superstitious faith in. He would be less happy going out with anything else, but not necessarily less effective. 'Have you got a scope for this?' he asked the armourer, whose face was striped with a thick band of broken capillaries that stretched from one cheek, through his nose, to the other.

Stone's choice was the German Heckler and Koch MP5A3, with an extending stock which he would remove altogether to use as a two-handed pistol. That gave him maximum movability.

'Something for the hand?' Chief Inspector Paisley said.

Birchfield laughed, thinking about his dick, but didn't share the joke. He chose a Walther PP .32. His partner took an S & W .38 Special.

The armourer came back with a scope sight for the Armalite. 'Get one of the wee bastards for me,' he said with a smile.

'I'll get you, any more talk like that,' Chief Inspector Paisley responded sharply. He didn't think the Special Support Unit benefited from the secondment of SAS officers, but now they had them he didn't want them to think that the Unit comprised of gun-happy bigots out for revenge.

Sergeant Keeper winked at the chastened armourer as the Chief Inspector turned out. He was more in touch with the feelings of the rank and file in the Unit, and although he knew that discipline was important in keeping the Unit tight, camaraderie was the essential cement to the loyalty that kept all of its secrets. Lately that sort of loyalty was seeping away, like dry sand through fingers, slowly, almost imperceptibly, and, no matter how tightly you squeezed, still it disappeared. Terry Keeper wasn't quite sure why this was so, but it worried him. Maybe they had been operating too long with relatively too few successes, but he didn't know whether bringing in outside people was the answer, especially now when the Unit was entering such a dramatic and dangerous phase.

The end section of the Nissen hut farthest from the headquarters building was used for most purposes by the forty-odd men in the Special Support Unit. It was a barracks with cot beds for those working the night relief, which a lot of their operations called for; a mess with a makeshift kitchen for microwaving or frying food; a briefing room where Chief Superintendent Johnston, who had operational command of the Unit, or Assistant Chief Constable Peter Eglington, laid out their next operation, or debriefed them after the previous one.

Birchfield and Stone had attended the briefing which led to the roadblock on the back road to Armagh outside Millmount. Dressed in an odd assortment of clothing, they were both among the eight-man team.

The road block was put in place after a radio signal from an MI6 operation across the border. They had no business being there and would put more strain on the Anglo-Irish Agreement if discovered. The Ford Escort that appeared with three men inside, as MI6 advised, slowed as it approached the roadblock, formed by the familiar grey RUC Land-rover. No encounter with any part of the RUC was welcome to anyone with other than deep Loyalist feelings and possibly a role in the criminal justice system, but such stops weren't automatically expected to prove fatal.

The three men in the Escort, the eldest of whom was twenty-four, were edgy but responded to the signal to stop given by Sergeant Keeper. He was wearing the regulation dark green RUC uniform. No one in the car spoke, but they had a single thought, hoping this was a random stop and that they'd soon be on their way.

They had been to a known Provo bar across the border; there had been a lot of talk about the eternal problem in the North, a problem that was doubtless going to get worse as a result of the Hillsborough Accord, seen by them as the perfect instrument to unite the Loyalists, who, up until the point when the British and Southern Irish governments had decided to co-operate in certain areas, and particularly across the border, were in disarray and fighting among themselves. There was fine talk of what actions might be taken, but none tonight. One of the men, Frank Kennedy, had been with the Provisional IRA since before he was born – it was almost like being put down for Eton. Although he was on the Security Forces' computer and had been lifted on many occasions, none were as menacing as that last time he had been held at Castlereagh interrogation centre. There people from MI6 had worked on him to make him, in their parlance, a Charlie Tango, to go back among his kind as a converted terrorist and tout for them. He had found the pressure they had applied hard to resist. He had thought at one point they were going to bury him. But too many people knew he was at Castlereagh.

The three men had taken the back roads to Armagh as a matter of habit and each wondered briefly if it wasn't a bad habit they were getting into. There had been only one police vehicle and two policemen so they assumed there couldn't be any kind of heavy operation, even though there would be two more taking cover somewhere.

The car came to a halt almost precisely where Sergeant Keeper indicated. Confident that this was a casual stop, the young driver started to reach for the handbrake. He didn't make it.

Birchfield and Stone appeared with two other RUC men from the hedge, none of them in regular uniform. Birchfield saw the movement from inside the car. His first shot slammed into the driver. It was difficult to tell who killed the second and third men as shots peppered the car from the off side. Everyone on the Special Support Unit opened up, as if this was something too good to miss. Unlike the two SAS men, they emptied the magazines of their Ingram sub-machine guns. They had been for special training with the SAS at Bradbury Lines in Herefordshire, both in the Killing Room and out on the Brecon Beacons, but none of them learned their lessons as well as the SAS men, who always left a shot or two in the clip or chamber – in case of an emergency. There was no question of an emergency arising here, but almost as a reflex action, like the last breath issuing from collapsing lungs, Frank Kennedy let the clutch in and the car shot forward, slamming into the Land-rover. The engine raced briefly and died as if in sympathy.

Silence hung in the air until a dog answered the faded gun reports. Probably it had responded to the first but no one had heard.

Chief Inspector Paisley stepped forward and opened the driver's door. The sight that greeted him was like the St Valentine's Day Massacre. The interior light had been smashed and he was almost reluctant to put on his torch. He let it play briefly over the suspects, long enough to decide they were dead.

There was nothing else of interest inside the car, certainly no weapon, nor in the boot which Sergeant Keeper searched. Some arms would later appear beneath the car seat after the car was towed in to divisional headquarters for forensic examination. No one at this party would question that they had been there all the while.

'Looks like someone slipped up', Sergeant Keeper said to no one in particular. He would have been happier had these men tried to shoot their way out.

'I'd say we can count ourselves lucky they weren't armed. One of us might have got it.'

The debriefing session back at Knock Road was a tense affair, most of the tension being generated by the Security Liaison Officers, one of whom had supplied the information about Frank Kennedy. The Security Liaison office was on the top floor of the main headquarters building along with that of the Special Branch. There, intelligence and security was collated for Special Branch units of the RUC and the army, and briefings prepared for the Ulster Security Co-ordinator.

Neither of the Special Branch chiefs who were present could reconcile either of the Security Liaison Officers. This hostility was part of a long-running struggle for ascendancy. MI5 as the domestic end of security saw Northern Ireland as their exclusive domain, despite the fact that the more flamboyant Secret Intelligence Service, which usually operated externally subverting foreign government employees, had been brought in during the early seventies.

Dominance of the intelligence system changed between the two branches according to who occupied the Co-ordinator's office. Currently the influential job of Ulster Security Co-ordinator belonged to the former head of the Secret Intelligence Service, Sir Michael Newfield, which effectively put MI5, Special Branch and Military Intelligence under MI6. Neither Laurence Payne nor Mark Howellett, his opposite number in MI6, had been around in the seventies and knew little of the basis of the original inter-service rivalry. At that time MI5, Special Branch and the Army Intelligence were considered amateurish and incapable of achieving substantial results; while MI6 were thought too dangerous to have free rein in Northern Ireland, the fear being that they would penetrate the IRA, the INLA, the Loyalist organisations, as well as the Garda Siochana across the border, and so blur the lines in an already confused situation. This was something they had subsequently done under Sir Michael Newfield, with devastating effect. Despite their lack of historical perspective, both Payne and Howellett performed a dance for their predecessors, similar to the unreasoning jig both Republican and Loyalist boys did to their grandfathers and great-grandfathers. In private, each neither wanted his rival to succeed nor was prepared to trust the other, while in public they tried to appear to co-operate fully. Only when the glue came undone, such as with the operation tonight, did the tension surface fully.

'There was a failure on the part of SIS to get us the right fucking information,' Laurence Payne said angrily. 'Those three men were expected to be armed.'

He was sitting at a large briefing table made up of four oblong oak tables pushed together in the pale green painted room with its lightly closed blinds.

'I expect they were, Laurence. Where the breakdown occurred is in properly searching their car for weapons,' Mark Howellett countered. He saw no problem. If the arms weren't in the car when it was stopped they soon would be after his people examined it. He was twenty-five and had been recruited to MI6 straight from Cambridge, where he'd spent more time with the Footlights Review than he did reading English. Unlike MI5, who preferred to recruit older people who established themselves in a career, SIS liked young men with dash. Mark Howellett never doubted he had that.

'We are agreed,' Assistant Chief Constable Eglington said sarcastically, 'that we got the right people in the car?' He was getting weary of the point-scoring between Security and Intelligence and was beginning to wonder if the RUC had made the right choice aligning itself with SIS instead of maintaining its more traditional link with MI5. At fifty-three, he was a year from retiring with maximum pension, unless he decided to stay on, but either way he wanted the end of his time as head of Special Branch to bathed in glory, not as part of a dragged-out street brawl.

'That would appear to be borne out by the fact that they tried to ram the roadblock,' Laurence Payne said graciously, realising this open hostility was benefiting no one. He was patient, having learned all its virtues. He would wait for the right moment to strike back.

The debriefing concluded that the car accelerating into the RUC Land-rover was trying to run the block, despite there being one hundred and twenty-two bullet holes in it at that point and the occupants very dead. The whole operation was marked down as a success, especially by MI6, as it had rid the Province of a middle-strata member of the IRA, one who was particularly dangerous as they had been unable to turn him. Chief Inspector Paisley, who was in charge of the operation, would write a report explaining how these men came to be shot. There would be no mention of this being part of anyone's official plan. The superintendent who ran E4, the operations department of Special Branch which oversaw the Special Support Unit, would carefully check the report to make sure the official hand of state didn't appear by design; Chief Superintendent Johnston, the Branch's deputy head, would finally initial the report and send file copies to both MI5 and MI6. The latter would summarise it for Sir Michael Newfield.

That wasn't the end of the matter as far as Laurence Payne was concerned. He saw the means of compromising MI5, through the response that would come from members of the community who would see these killings as an outrage. One of the most vociferous was a priest from Armagh who knew one of the victims, Frank Kennedy, and was compiling a dossier on victims of the RUC and Ulster Defence Regiment, with particular reference to those who were unarmed. Father McMichael's initial response to the killings was kneejerk. He hadn't known that the occupants of the car were unarmed and probably wouldn't have known had not Laurence Payne leaked the information to him.

It appealed to Payne's sense of humour that he did this in the confessional at St Patrick's Church in Armagh.

'What is it you wish to tell me, my son?' Father McMichael said. He was twenty-eight and had been a priest for three years and still felt awkward and more distanced than he would have liked in that form of address. He waited, wondering if the man on the other side of the curtain had changed his mind.

'I wish I could tell you I have sinned, father,' Laurence Payne said, suppressing a snigger, 'but the truth is, I haven't.'

'You're an amazing man then, you are so,' Father McMichael said, unable to let this affront go uncommented upon. Despite his calling, he had an ego and enjoyed the high profile his protests about the Security forces were giving him. 'What is it I can do for such an amazing person?'

Laurence Payne laughed quietly. 'I have some information about the shooting outside Keody you might find useful.'

In fact it appeared more useful than it was. For although Father McMichael went out shouting about the three young men of his parish being unarmed when they were shot, he couldn't prove that they didn't have the guns MI6 put in the boot of their car. What his information served to do was keep the pressure on MI6.

Undeterred by protests from Catholics within the community, MI6 briefed the SSU on its next target: a house in Ballymurphy, a predominantly Republican district of West Belfast. The information about the occupants of this 'safe' IRA house in Westrock Drive, almost opposite the new Roman Catholic Church of St Thomas's, was supplied by the SIS, along with a key to the front door, provided by one of their Charlie Tangos. The pieces of information Mark Howellett didn't divulge about the two men they'd find here were that one was a converted terrorist who was no longer giving them useful information – possibly because he had changed loyalty again;

and that the other was an explosives expert with friends in Pennsylvania who had refused SIS's overtures.

Evening mass at St Thomas's was over and poorly attended. The five men from the SSU waited in the parked 'Q' car for the last of the congregation to hurry away through the cold, wet night. The PP paused on the steps to light a cigarette after locking the doors, then he disappeared too. An army personnel carrier came by and turned into Springhill Avenue heading for Springfield Road. Silence followed it. Too silent to go in straightaway after it. They waited another fifteen minutes, their hands sweating on the metal stocks of their guns despite the seeping cold in the car.

Finally it was time to go, and Chief Inspector Paisley touched Birchfield's shoulder, then slipped out of the car with a case to approach the rear of the house through a service alley at the side. He took one man with him.

Birchfield and Stone approached the house under cover of the bad early evening light and the slanting rain. Each of them wore trainers and carried his easily concealed firearm beneath his loose-fitting coat. The key wouldn't turn in the lock.

'The fucking snib must be on,' Birchfield said, with tension in his voice.

'Let me try.'

The key was newly cut and catching, but worked for Stone after some difficulty. They froze as the door creaked open. All they heard was the TV. Inside the tiny terraced house the two men who were watching television froze in a stark tableau when Birchfield casually opened the sitting-room door and levelled his gun. No single word was exchanged, not protest, exclamation or plea for mercy. Both men were shot dead.

Accompanying the information on the occupants of the house in the report that followed were details of bomb-making equipment found there. No one was taking any chances on being upstaged by Father McMichael or anyone else. Chief Inspector Paisley unpacked the equipment from the case he had brought and planted the evidence for the scenes-of-crime officer from the RUC to find.

3

THE MURDER OF a politician, albeit a local politician, was sufficient to make the police more than usually active. But the fact that he was black and had been waging a vociferous campaign against the police in an area of London where there was a large black population and where the police could appear to be implicated in the killing, if only by their lack of results, was enough to set alarm bells ringing on both the sixteenth floor of Scotland Yard and the seventh floor of the Home Office. Phone calls had been going back and forth from the offices of the Commissioner of Police and the Home Secretary, and neither one had found any sort of comfort in the acrimonious exchanges. Some sort of black retaliation was expected – street demonstrations, leading to riots, leading to looting and arson – to which the police would have to respond in force. The Home Secretary knew what that would mean politically. It would almost certainly be interpreted as another sign of their law and order policy failing.

Jesse Jarman was a popular figure in that part of the world, one the police had tried unsuccessfully to placate. Every complaint made by a black person to the local police monitoring unit ended up on Jarman's desk at the local council; he pitched into the police furiously, petitioned local Labour MPs and the Home Office.

Jack Bentham almost prayed that the killing wasn't political, but knew it was going to be hard to prove. Even if it were somehow shown to be apolitical, that wouldn't necessarily head off a riot.

The report that C11 had been compiling on black activists in and around south-east London would get a lot of attention at the conference Bentham was heading for with his boss, DAC 'Doc' Holliday, but in the circumstances it was wholly inadequate, he thought. That opinion wasn't shared by the DAC, but then his application was a lot different from Bentham's. 'Doc' Holliday worked at minimum mental level and often supported maximum physical response.

24

The DAC was the old-fashioned type of copper and, even though his department wasn't one that ever made arrests or went to court with suspects, C11 always stayed in the background collecting intelligence for others to action. Bentham wasn't sure how the man had survived as head of the Intelligence Unit, especially as he had been heavily involved in major corruption. The internal investigation that Bentham had recently concluded had resulted in the abrupt resignations of a number of senior officers at the Yard, including an Assistant Commissioner. It was rumoured that Doc Holliday's Masonic connections had saved him. Bentham had been affronted by that result, but was now less concerned, having found a more realistic approach and come to the view that policemen were inevitably part of the corrupt process, if only by virtue of the fact that the good ones did nothing about the bad.

Doc Holliday never mentioned their past relationship, but as if by way of an apology he always let Bentham do things how he wanted. That way their department produced results. Which was how it would be with black activists in south-east London, and with the animal rights activists who were another area of concern on the agenda of this morning's meeting. Doc Holliday approached them as he would ordinary criminals, but Bentham knew from close experience that animal activists weren't ordinary criminals and trying to deal with them as such was a waste of time.

Bentham fleetingly thought about Helen Daniels as he crossed the fifth-floor bridge between the Victoria Street block and the tower block at Scotland Yard to take the lift to the sixteenth floor. He had only caught her on television a couple of times since their relationship had ended. He wondered if she had given up animal rights activities to concentrate on her acting career. But doubted it.

'There have been ninety-two break-ins to laboratories or similar establishments this month alone,' Doc Holliday was saying as they stepped into one of the four lifts. He paused to light a cigarette from his stub, threw it on the floor and coughed. 'Animals were either set free or equipment was smashed and papers stolen. Mostly rats were taken. Can you imagine what sort of fucking idiot wants to liberate rats?'

'If it eats, breathes and excretes, they don't distinguish between them,' Bentham said. He knew that to be the case. 'What's needed, Doc, is a serious change in police tactics. We ought to make a conscious effort to change their image.'

The DAC drew deeply on his cigarette and waited.

'If we treat these people as terrorists rather than animal liberators, we can change the entire public perception of them,' Bentham said, thinking tactically.

At the weekly planning conference which was chaired by the Deputy Commissioner, Harry Streeter, in the large conference room, Doc Holliday quoted Jack Bentham almost verbatim, and without crediting him. 'If we were to find the ringleaders in the Animal Rights Movement with explosives or incendiary devices,' he said, 'that would undermine their romantic image completely.'

'*Knowing* that some of them are prepared to stop at nothing, Doc,' AC Roy Genders observed, 'and *finding* them with explosives are two different things entirely.' Roy Genders was head of Specialist Operations with overall responsibility for all policing functions in the Met which were carried out through centrally organised units, and was boss of both Doc Holliday and Jack Bentham. He was a higher authority rather than an operations organiser, but he needed to see how policy was going to be applied. He was made uneasy by abstract ideas about policing ventured by university graduates like Bentham – he knew that all the ideas from C11 were Jack Bentham's.

DAC Holliday glanced at Bentham to provide the answer. When it wasn't forthcoming, he said lightly, 'We'll plant it on them, like we usually do, Roy.'

Laughter erupted around the room.

Deputy Commissioner Streeter glanced at his watch. He wanted to move the meeting on and not let it get bogged down in the details that Roy Genders liked. He could get those from one of his own meetings with C11. He liked the idea of changing the thrust of police operations against the Animal Rights Movement. He had had conversations with Jack Bentham about the difficulties of policing that area because of the moral high ground the offenders held. But the police interpreted and upheld the law as it was enacted; it was hardly their fault that moral right was at the vanguard in their society.

'Can you take that one on, Doc, get some information organised?'

'It looks like I talked myself into it,' Doc Holiday said, lighting a fresh cigarette. He was the only person who was smoking. 'But I'll willingly be talked out of it.'

'It would be better,' Bentham said, 'if it was given to Special

Branch. They're pretty much involved already, as MI5 have been keeping a watching brief.'

Martin Golding, the Special Branch DAC, didn't respond, knowing they had been doing more than keep a watching brief. They had formed the Animal Rights Militia to undertake acts such as planting incendiary devices in department stores' fur departments and poisoning meat to totally discredit the Animal Rights Movement. Golding was closer than anyone to AC Genders – who was his boss too – and did most of his petitioning in private. Special Branch was considerably influenced by the Security Service, for whom they acted as the operational arm, and so liked to do everything in private.

The only other assistant commissioner present was Peter Henderson, who oversaw territorial operations relating to all the divisions. 'What the fuck are MI5 doing looking at the pussy-cat brigade?' he wanted to know.

Martin Golding shot a pissed-off look at Jack Bentham for raising this. 'It's a mistake to think of these people as sentimental cat lovers, Peter. There are a lot of lunatic criminal elements among them. Others would welcome our scientific research programmes being set back, no matter what it costs.'

'How active is MI5 in this area?' Peter Henderson asked.

'They keep a watching brief.'

'Can the Branch take that up with C11?' Deputy Commissioner Streeter said. 'I'd like to move on.'

'It'll be a problem unless we get some help,' Martin Golding said.

'C11 will give you some help. They'll pass on what intelligence they get.'

'We gather our own intelligence,' Martin Golding responded defensively.

'What we need,' Roy Genders said, 'is more bodies drafted into the Branch. I know the problem, of course. But it can only eventually be solved by finding more manpower. Perhaps the anti-terrorist squad should pick it up.' That was his area of responsibility also, but the commander who ran that squad within Special Branch wasn't present to argue against this extra work being shoved his way. These meetings inevitably touched on police resource, as senior officers tried to duck new areas of responsibility.

The meeting finally moved on to the question of possible race riots following the death of Jesse Jarman.

'What's the progress there?' the Deputy Commissioner asked, glancing across the large oblong table at Peter Henderson, who with a glance referred the question to Geoff Halesowen, the Deputy Assistant Commissioner from No 3 Area, where the murder took place.

'If effort ever produced a result, Harry, we'll have whoever did it very soon.' It was his way of saying they were no further along than when the body was discovered. 'We've got more policeman on the ground than we had on our swamp operation' – that particular policing tactic had led to the Brixton race riots. 'It's really a question of how far we push these people. Too much pressure and they'll pop. Before we know it, we'll have a riot on our hands.'

'I thought that was the prospect with too little police response.'

'As usual the police are caught between the devil and the deep blue sea,' Geoff Halesowen said. 'My own feeling is if we're going to get a riot anyway, then we may as well go in hard and lick a few black heads, have it on our terms from the off. We've been taking a lot of rubbish from them, particularly in that District.'

Listening to this DAC Bentham clearly understood why racialism among the police was diminishing. He was a long-time subscriber to the belief that all attitudes at the sharp end reflected the leadership, whether it was racism or corruption. Geoff Halesowen was the walking proof of what he had seen on the street outside that local police station.

A discussion followed about the best approach to the situation that was building up in the area. No one had any real solutions, for yet again the police were being asked to deal with what was primarily a political problem; it was safe to assume that the politicians had no just or humane solution or they would have run it up.

Bentham's contribution to the discussion was, 'If we've got a riot coming, and from our intelligence that seems likely, then what we should do is try to gain some advantage from the situation. Our only gain is going to be worthwhile propaganda. The left-wing press will blame us immediately if we put so many into those ghettos that we provoke an explosion – regardless of the operational necessity of such a move. We might benefit more from a fairly low profile with a lot of hard work on finding Jesse Jarman's killer.'

'Fuck me! That's what we've been doing, Jack,' Geoff Halesowen said, 'but where's it getting us? These people are not human, they get doped up, get their heads full of reggae music; you can't reason with them. At the end of the day you're gonna get a riot anyway – we've caused it by being seen not to have done enough. What's the advantage?'

'Make sure the right sort of journalists are given some access to the investigation. Because of the importance of Jesse Jarman, make it the biggest murder hunt ever mounted.'

'We've got forty detectives working on it, plus every uniformed officer in the District. We're not exactly idle. The truth is,' Geoff Halesowen added rashly, 'I couldn't have wished for anything better.'

'A lot of policemen feel that way,' Bentham said. 'I'm sure a lot feel the same about most politicians. But since when do our feelings count? We're impartial policemen, after all,' he added with his tongue in his cheek, but still found solemn nods from some of these senior policemen.

'What is your practical proposal, Jack?' AC Roy Genders asked, digging in his ear again. 'Based on C11's involvement on the manor.'

'We weren't looking at Jarman's murder,' Bentham said. 'But seeing the cultural problems we're up against, someone is needed down there to work undercover.'

'Perhaps one of my lads should black up,' Geoff Halesowen said.

That brought laughter around the table.

'They might get a quicker result.'

'They might fucking well get themselves topped.'

'Find a black policeman who can duck and dive there.'

'Jarman wasn't universally loved. It wasn't just the policemen who were pleased to see the back of him. The dope dealers had a long-running vendetta against him. So did the National Front. He really pissed off a lot of brothers when he walked into the local police station before Christmas with the three blacks who mugged that old-aged pensioner and killed her. I must admit he even went up in my estimation then.' That from Geoff Halesowen, and served to remind those around the table what a potential ally the police had lost with the death of this adversary.

'Let's look at Jack's suggestion', Harry Streeter said. 'It won't be easy finding the right policeman to work undercover, but it might keep the Home Office quiet. They're worried about swamping the manor, and waiting for the explosion. Don't get me wrong, Geoff. We'll do that soon enough if it's the right move tactically. We must have someone somewhere in Division who will fit the bill, Peter.'

'We'll give it a go,' Peter Henderson said. 'We can second someone from outside the Met if necessary.'

The third item on the agenda concerned the proposed visit by the Home Secretary to London University Students' Union to speak to the Conservative Students Association. But because of the opposition that was expected from other students, the police would be taken out of the traditional consensus role into confrontation policing.

The solution was simple as far as AC Roy Genders was concerned: 'Let's ask him not to speak at this meeting or any like it.'

'You'd do as well to ask him to stop breathing, Roy.'

'Politicians don't seem to realise what these confrontations are doing to police–public relations.'

'Don't they?' Bentham said. 'Most of them know only too well. Especially government ministers. The more partial we're forced to become, the more we inevitably become an instrument of the government.'

'That's bullshit, Jack,' AC Peter Henderson said. 'The government designs the legislation, gets it enacted into law, and we enforce that law. Nothing more. The government changes, they repeal some laws and bring in new ones, we enforce those. That's democracy.'

Bentham could have asked what laws ever get repealed with a change of government, but it wasn't in his interest to challenge senior colleagues at every turn. At times like these he had to remind himself that he was a senior policeman with a political perspective, the one of the government of the day, and no longer a warrant card-holding policeman who related to the interests of the man immediately below him. It was difficult to court popularity from the rank and file and at the same time maintain a realistic political overview. Perhaps he should not have accepted promotion, but that was something he found hard to resist. He was not only as ambitious as the next man, but considered himself more able.

'We're having more and more problems enforcing those laws,' Harry Streeter said, 'in purely physical terms. Whatever we think of a politician or his views, if he can't be persuaded from expressing them when we know it'll bring trouble, we have to be prepared to go in hard and in force.' He glanced at Jack Bentham, knowing he was entirely right in his views. Politicians were forcing a wedge between themselves and the public, and there was nothing they could do about it but respond with more and more manpower and equipment until the day arrived when it was no longer recognisably the police force any of the men around this table had joined.

30

'The Home Secretary is refusing to abandon his speaking engagements, despite the reaction he got from students in Manchester. He's speaking next at Exeter University Students' Union. Maybe it'll get so out of hand he'll cancel his visit to London University.'

'It's a raggle-taggle of students we're talking about,' the DAC from Special Branch said. 'Are these left-wing agitators going to dictate public order? Between us, Jack's people and Special Branch we can identify the ringleaders, and have them out.'

'We'll try again to persuade the Home Secretary to slip in the back way, make his speech, and leave the same way,' Streeter said. 'I don't suppose he'll change his mind.' He got up and took his half-full cup of coffee to refill it. Everyone knew he was moving away to fart.

'This is a public order event, Harry. One that might be resolved by discussion with the Student Union executive,' Roy Genders said, addressing his back.

'With respect, Roy,' Bentham said, modifying the familiar form of address to his boss, 'this is a trial of strength. Otherwise the Home Secretary would go in the back way. Whatever anyone thinks of the particular law or his right to speak, we have to win this trial of strength if we can't avoid it. Basically, it's a private meeting, we're not invited. But I suggest the officer liaising with the Students' Union persuades them to concede the Union building and its precincts as a public right of way, just for the day.'

'To what purpose, Jack?' the Deputy Commissioner asked, returning to the table, sulphurous traces filling his wake.

'Then we'll have the right to go in in strength, in anticipation of trouble,' Bentham responded. 'It's an opportunity for the Home Secretary to see what it's like for policemen in the front line. It'll impress him more than a month of negotiations with the Home Office over extending police powers.' He shot a glance at AC Henderson, who was nodding approvingly. He didn't mind how clever the footwork was provided the end result went towards increased police resource.

That was what each of these men were about. They were senior managers of police resource that they had convinced themselves was inadequate to meet policing needs and they never once considered that approach might be wrong. More and more, to his increasing concern, Jack Bentham found himself treading the same path.

4

DESMOND O'DONNELL PEERED anxiously over the sill of the slightly open window into the poorly lit area below. Nothing stirred that he could see, and he heard nothing that disturbed him. He had tried over and again to tell himself that he was being edgy for no reason: he was holed up in a safe flat, in a traditionally safe area, even though old loyalties were eroding as people became tired of this struggle with no end in sight. Anyone of them might have had the RUC's emergency number and touted. Waiting was, he felt, like waiting for death, but when finally he convinced himself that it was crazy to stay any longer, his nerve failed him. Why would he be any safer outside? He'd be liable to random stops. He could feel the damp cold air from the window against his face and he shivered, but it made no difference to the trickles of sweat that were running down his back. A distant sound of a prised-off corrugated sheet from a boarded-up flat as the wind caught it made him tense. He looked behind him into the darkened apartment, expecting the RUC to burst in. Why was the estate so quiet? An answer came in an instant: People preferred not to be out on the street on cold February evenings when warm homes and hot dinners and television were the alternative. But he wasn't reassured. The RUC caused people to disappear also, as if by magic. The light was off in the area below, and in the alleyway beyond.

God, they were there waiting for him.

Stop! he told himself. Think.

He tried to remember if the light had been off yesterday. With the level of vandalism on the estate nothing lasted. The lamp at the end of the alley, which turned at a right angle to follow the line of the next block, was still on. That had survived the vandals, if vandals had put this one out, and not the RUC.

An indistinct noise somewhere in the building caused him to start; his heart raced, his mouth went dry. He tried to moisten it. There was no moisture to be had. He thought about the jumbo bottle of

Coke in the fridge, but was afraid to move and get it. The sound of a neighbour's television reached him. He wondered why he hadn't heard it before. Had they been made to turn up the volume to mask the noise of the flat being entered? O'Donnell tried to identify the programme, and decided it was *Good Evening, Ulster*, the news and current affairs programme.

His attention darted back to the area around the block. Still nothing moved. He wasn't convinced it was safe for him to climb from the window. He hesitated, lost to anxiety, fear paralysing him. The flight reflex suddenly engaged, adrenalin spurted into his system as the flat door was lifted off its hinges. What started as an irrational fear that he hadn't dared mention to his comrades had become a reality. The death squad was here.

He threw open the window and sprang through it almost in one movement. There was no time to think what he might be jumping on to. The ground was littered with debris, his foot hit a piece of rubble and as he went down his knee struck another piece, breaking the skin. It pained him badly as he got up and forced himself to run. He daren't look to see what he had done. He didn't look behind him as he clambered over the fence that sectioned off the semi-derelict block and dropped into the alleyway, grateful now to the hooligans who had broken the light. Someone was shouting at the window, but he was below the line of the corrugated iron fence and ran towards the light at the corner, knowing the opposite way led to the front of the flat block and towards Divis Street, where the RUC would be in force.

He stopped ten yards from the end of the alley as two figures stepped around the corner, both in paramilitary clothes but not complete uniforms. And in their hands they carried guns. They weren't intending conversation.

Fragments of a prayer ran through O'Donnell's mind. He was unable to remember the whole prayer. If only he could say it in its entirety he would be saved. He turned back. Men with guns at the other end were running towards him. He threw himself at the corrugated fence, but this was the smooth side and there was nothing to pull himself up by. He tried to jump again and just caught the jagged top of the fence with one hand and hung there despite the spiked iron cutting into his fingers. Someone gripped his ankle. His instinct was to kick out, but the thought that they would treat him more harshly if he did stopped him.

'OK, OK, I'm giving myself up,' he whined as he dropped from the fence. His injured knee wouldn't support him and he went down.

Carefully, so as not to be seen or heard from the open balcony of the flat block that overlooked the lit section of the alleyway, Stephen McFadden raised his rifle and cocked a shell into the chamber. There was barely a sound from the smooth, well-oiled mechanism. He drew a bead on the man on the floor of the alley and steadied his aim. Other men joining them moved through his line of fire and he waited. They had guns too, he noticed, and they were pointing them at the man on the ground. As he waited, Stephen let his finger relax on the trigger guard so there was no chance that the gun would go off accidentally. Suddenly his line of fire was clear. Gently he curled his finger around the trigger.

The explosion startled Stephen. Three more shots followed quickly. He stared down into the alley at the man lying in a crumpled heap, wondering if he had done that, but then realising he hadn't. It was those men with the real guns. Something was happening, he wasn't sure what, but thought it might have been one of those dreams he couldn't easily wake from. Despite believing it wasn't his fault, he somehow feared it might be on account of his being there. He had seen people killed on television, but he knew this wasn't the same.

A small, involuntary whimpering noise came out of Stephen, and he was shaking when he pushed himself up off the parapet wall. As he turned to run he crashed into uncollected milk bottles that were spreading outside a door, and cried out louder.

The noise drew eyes to the first-floor balcony and the fleeing figure.

'Someone's seen us!'

'It's another one of them.'

Half the detail sprinted along the alleyway towards the flat block, their weapons armed ready to fire from any position.

Stephen ran in panic, and only instinct saved him – he had seen situations similar to this a hundred times on television. He went into a crouch to keep below the parapet, and up the stairs and along the walkway of the next floor to where his mother's flat was. His fingers scrabbled through the letterbox, grabbing the key his mother left hanging there on a string. He thrust it in the lock and let himself into the flat. Neither his mother nor his two sisters were home from their aerobics class and the flat was dark. He didn't attempt to put on the light as he leaned against the door. The light that normally swept away his fears, would, he sensed, bring greater danger to him. He slid along the floor on his stomach and into the sitting-room, getting between the back of the sofa and the wall below the window that overlooked the balcony. There he knew, from distant games of Hide and Seek with his sisters, that he couldn't be seen. The police wouldn't find him if they shone their torches through the window. But they would hear the noise he was emitting and he bit hard on his top lip to stop himself.

Alert and straining for any sound of their approach, Stephen waited, holding his breath to try and keep from making any noise. He sensed rather than heard their approach.

They came swiftly up the stairs, spreading above and below Stephen, their guns preceding them along the walkway. Trained eyes searched every crevice of that walkway for the second IRA man. But he had disappeared, and no one knew what they would do with him anyway now, with people from the surrounding flats starting to appear.

'Your nose back inside!'

The woman who peered from her doorway didn't need telling twice. Her anger was mute, expressed in a look that had worn deeply into her face by years of tension and resentment.

Seeing the key in the lock caused Birchfield a sudden flutter of excitement, but he tried not to give himself away, as he was directly in the firing line from the flat window. If the IRA man was in there and armed, he would be the first to get it. The thought was fleeting and not inspiring as he went past and approached the door using the wall for a shield. Cautiously he reached out to turn the key.

'Anything?' a voice demanded from the floor below. There were too many people around now to do anything practical about the second man, the witness to the killing.

'Come away. We'll seal the block and put the army in, they'll find him.'

The Ulster Defence Regiment was despised and reviled along the Falls Road, being seen as the home-grown force of the Protestant Loyalists. It was set up as a more tolerable non-sectarian part of the British army based in the province, but had failed in whatever good intentions it may have started with. It fostered the same mistrust as the now disbanded B-Specials, the RUC's reserve force that dated from partition in 1921; that had been seen as little more than a gang of armed Protestants led by local Unionist politicians as they went about terrorising the Catholic population. The UDR failed to be non-sectarian by recruiting ninety-eight per cent Protestants, and over fifty per cent ex-British military personnel who had previously served in Northern Ireland.

The UDR went through the flat block with the proverbial fine-toothed comb, turfing everyone out of their flats, making them identify themselves, including Stephen McFadden, his mother and sisters who had by then returned. They didn't find who they were looking for because they didn't know who they were looking for.

Stephen trembled as he held on to his mother where they stood on the walkway while the soldiers went through their flat. These were only the notorious Divis flats, these were only the treacherous Catholic Divis flat-dwellers.

Maureen McFadden held her son, not understanding his fear. It wasn't the first time this had happened, but she wondered now if she shouldn't try and make it the last. She was coming to think that she had held on here out of no more than perversity, rather than the belief that if people left rather than stayed to care about their community, there would be no community. Her staying had made no noticeable difference other than to put pressure on her children and her.

The RUC scene-of-crime officer had been by this time, photographed and taken full details of the body and its immediate environs, and allowed it to be removed. The SSU had slipped away back to Knock for debriefing, which descended into acrimony and recrimination, mostly on account of the witness. The UDR eventually pulled out also, leaving a palpable hostility among the community. After such visits they felt like rape victims, not necessarily damaged physically, but certainly violated; angry and confused and not knowing what to do with their feelings, and, as all too often happened, they turned on the estate itself, wreaking more havoc and destruction, resulting in yet more flats becoming uninhabitable.

As she watched the acrid smoke from the burning tyres that had been thrown into the windows of a flat in the block opposite, and stood with her arm around Stephen's thick waist, Maureen McFadden came a little nearer to her decision to leave. She had been offered a flat on the outer edge of the city and before now she had thought if they moved it should be away from Belfast, away from Ulster altogether.

Stephen, who had followed every detail from the shooting in the alleyway to the search by the UDR to the arrival of the fire brigade to put out the burning flat opposite, found none of what he had seen corresponded to the news he watched on the television in his bedroom as he ate lunch on a tray the following day. Stephen often had his meals in his room in front of his own television. He liked watching, especially cowboy films. The walls of his room were covered with pictures of cowboys from films on television; mostly they were pictures of Clint Eastwood. There were pictures of horses too, and guns, but Stephen wasn't allowed to have a gun, not even a toy one and didn't quite understand why, especially not when so many other people had guns. Stephen would dearly have loved to own a gun, but his mother, who gave him anything else his heart desired and her finances could run to, was quite firm in refusing all his requests for such a toy.

Maureen McFadden smiled as she pushed into the bedroom and found Stephen staring at the television, grateful that it kept him occupied and so out of trouble. There was little else for him to do in Belfast, save wander the streets. He would watch anything that had a simple story and identifiable stereotype characters. The soap operas were great for that, only he'd get the stories mixed up as there were so many different ones on television now.

Her response to Stephen was that of a mother to a young child, for that's what Stephen would remain, despite his expanding physical size. Her instinct was to protect him the whole time, and defend him, whatever the circumstances. She was becoming more and more actutely aware of the fact that he was a seventeen-year-old with a mental age of half that. Physically he would get older and his needs would change and increase, but mentally he would never develop beyond eight. At the health centre she had attended with Stephen she had been advised to place him in a special school; friends and relatives alike had offered the same advice. Only a priest at St Comgall's, where she sometimes went to mass, on the Falls Road, was brave enough to say she would be depriving herself of a loving soul if she were to shut Stephen out of her life in a home for the mentally retarded. There were few visible signs of love in Belfast, and Stephen putting his arms around her and telling her he loved her more than compensated.

'Is there no good news, Stephen?' she said, identifying the news item before he could reply. 'Didn't we have enough of the real thing last night?'

She sat on the edge of the bed, caught up briefly with the news broadcast.

'Officers from the RUC returned fire from Desmond O'Donnell,' the newcaster was saying, an earnest expression glued to his face. 'The warning to lay down his gun was ignored by O'Donnell. A middle-ranking member of the Belfast Brigade, who acted as paymaster on raids on banks and sub-post offices, he was armed with a Russian-made Kalashnikov machine gun. A similar weapon killed two RUC men last month. He fired several rounds at the police before being shot himself. The UDR later conducted a house-to-house search in Divis flats for a second suspect. He was thought to be Martin Doherty, who the police want in connection with the killing of a postmistress in Londonderry last year . . .'

Frustration followed confusion in Stephen and he clenched his knife and fork and shook his head over and over. He tried to speak, but couldn't get the words out. This was television; they had got it wrong; he didn't understand; things were right on television, how could they not be? They had to tell the truth. Stephen was getting angry and tears were springing to his eyes. Why did they get it wrong? 'Wrong,' he finally managed. 'Wrong. I seed them, Mum. He didn't. I was outside, I seed them. He didn't have a gun. He didn't.'

A cold hand of terror reached out and touched Maureen, preventing her responding. This was what she was most scared of: her son caught up in the troubles that she had managed to steer her family clear of these past seventeen years. Stephen wasn't a baby to be led by the hand any more. He enjoyed going out on his own; he took buses, talked to strangers, was easily tricked. Maureen knew that the spell which had so far protected him was now broken, and realised that if Stephen truly knew anything, it wouldn't be long before he told someone. And with the province riddled with informers, it wouldn't be long before the police got to hear of it. If the police had done something wrong, as rumours suggested, then Stephen was in trouble.

She put her arms around him and held him, adding to his confusion. 'Oh Stevie, Stevie,' she said, using a name she rarely called him by, making him even more confused. 'You didn't see anything. Dear God in heaven, you didn't.'

'I did, Mum', Stephen insisted, thinking she was doubting him. 'I was down on Kit's walkway calling for him. I seed him. They shooted him, honest.'

The earnestness in his face could not but presage the truth. This wasn't one of the cowboy fantasies he often evoked. She tried to hold back the tears that were pushing at her eyes. 'How am I ever going to keep you from telling?' she said, almost to herself, never questioning the truth of what he was saying. She had no idea how she would do that. She couldn't keep him in the whole time.

Her daughters, Angela and Kathleen, were fifteen and sixteen respectively, and two of the prettiest and most mature around, even allowing for her bias. They had grown up without a father, who had departed for England to work after the birth of the youngest, never to return. After many years of bitterness at the desertion, Maureen had decided he had been unable to cope with a young family, especially with one being retarded, or with the tension in the province. At first she had blamed him and hated him and hoped in vain that he would come back; she had offers from other men in those days, but had waited instead for her children's father to return or send for them.

Then, when the weeks of waiting turned into months and finally she heard he had gone to America, she became angry and hurt, but still harboured some faint hope that Joe McFadden would come back. She was a long time letting go that hope, and then no offer from any man would do. She managed without them. She had also made a conscious effort to compensate the girls for any emotional deprivation by giving them all the freedom and support they needed, letting them share the adult world at an early age as her father had let her share his world of trade union politics at Harland and Wolf shipyard where he was a welder. He'd been sacked soon after the troubles and dead not long after that, having given up the fight to bring about small changes, so overtaken by events as he was. Part of the adult world that Maureen gave her daughters was their decision-making when there was anything major to decide. It was only ever done after first talking things through, without her vetoing any decision the two girls might come to which didn't coincide with her own.

'I think we should tell the police, Mum,' Angela said at the supper table in the compact, tidy kitchen, after Stephen had returned to his room to watch television. She knew the police were sectarian and weren't to be trusted, but felt the witnessing of such a killing was too big a burden for the family. Stephen could be in real danger.

'It's themselves he said did it,' Maureen reminded her.

'Tell someone, at least. I don't know. Someone. Maybe Father Corrigan.'

'How do we know what Stephen said's true?' Kathleen demanded. She was the more cautious of the two girls, taking after her mother. 'He makes up such fantastic lies.'

'He does, I know, Kathleen. But didn't the UDR come looking for someone? He wasn't after making that up. Perhaps we should get out. Just go.' It would be a rash move and cause all sorts of problems. Fleetingly her husband in America came to mind – he only ever did in crises – and with the thought came the resentment she still found she harboured towards him for taking the easy way out. For all she knew, he was dead.

'Mum, I'm doing my CSE this summer,' Kathleen said. 'I'm right in the middle. I can't go, I'd fail.'

'I know, of course.' She knew how much the girls wanted to do well in their exams and go on to university maybe. She wanted the same for them. It was the only hope of some sort of future. 'God, what would happen to our poor Stevie if the police were after questioning him?' She knew she was putting unfair pressure on them, and knew at times that she favoured Stephen too much. Getting out would mean England, and she was not sure if Kathleen would go. Nor Angela come to that. They both had a life here, apart from school; an increasingly active social life.

'We've got to tell someone,' Angela said with a slight quake in her voice, 'in case they find out.'

Seeing that as the means of not leaving, Kathleen agreed, and Maureen was outvoted.

However that didn't solve the problem of whom to tell. Not the police obviously, yet it needed to be someone with an official or semi-official role. The priest was the best she could come up with having spent an evening agonising over whether to approach Father Corrigan at St Comgall's. At one point she started out to visit him, even though she had barely any contact with the man. But finally she decided against speaking to him because he was sectarian, and anyway Catholic priests weren't thought much of by the state, which seemed to consider them all potential subversives.

The solution came from a woman in one of Maureen McFadden's aerobics classes. She had a cousin who was a solicitor and she believed he could advise Maureen – whether she took the advice was something for her to decide. Not having ever had need of a solicitor, Maureen regarded the profession with respectful distance and accepted that a solicitor would have sufficient weight of authority. They certainly had a semi-official role in society. They weren't emotional and therefore, Maureen assumed, weren't partial. She didn't consider whether he was Catholic or Protestant, as being a solicitor after all made him automatically neutral. He had offices in the non-sectarian commercial district.

Stephen was dressed in his best clothes when they went to keep their appointment with Edward O'Dwyer of Cromer and O'Dwyer. Looking at his broad back where he sat in the front seat of the bus near the driver, Maureen imagined Stephen a sixth-form student in his dark blue blazer and grey trousers. Only the fact that he was dribbling when he turned to make sure she was still behind him shattered her illusion. She smiled and indicated for them to get off at the next stop. Stephen jumped up and rang the bell, then again and again, causing the driver to glance round. Maureen reached out and took her son's hand.

Edward O'Dwyer's office had a shabby look to it where it sat on the first floor overlooking shops on North Street. The shops beneath looked as if they were having difficulty surviving too. There were hundreds of manilla bag files stacked on shelves all around the reception room, over which pervaded the faint smell of sweat acting on the acid in the paper. The same smell was to be found in the solicitor's own office. It may have emanated from O'Dwyer, who had the slightly dulled look of a drinker, with smiling eyes that would never sparkle. He didn't respond at all when she told him what Stephen had witnessed and what her fears were.

He pulled at the cuffs of his shirt as he considered the problem, easing them out over the edges of his jacket sleeves. Maureen noticed they were grubby, as if it were yesterday's shirt. She felt curiously let down by this man, especially as she and Stephen had taken trouble with their appearance.

'You shouldn't hold quite such a jaundiced view of the police, Mrs McFadden,' he said. 'They're probably more decent than most give them credit for. But I understand your misgiving.' He adjusted his cuffs again and looked over at Stephen, who was picking at the stuffing through a hole in the fabric of a captain's chair. 'You like to play cowboys and indians, is that so, Stephen?'

'Just cowboys,' he replied. 'I don't play indians. I don't let girls play neither.'

'Then I'd say you'll keep your money and your good looks.' The lawyer smiled, amused at this. 'You shoot all the baddies.'

'I do so, sometimes.'

'You saw the baddy being shot in the alleyway behind your flat? Is that so, Stephen?'

Stephen glanced at his mother, and when he got no signal from her he hung his head to hide his confusion. She had said he wasn't to tell anyone about that, and didn't know why she didn't nod if she wanted him to tell. He glanced at her again, not understanding that she was avoiding giving him any sort of lead.

'Were you after seeing what happened, Stephen?'

Slowly Stephen nodded. 'It wasn't like on the telly,' he mumbled. That continued to upset and confuse him more than anything. He had seen one thing, they had said another. He didn't know what to believe on TV anymore.

At the end of the interview and after only brief deliberation Edward O'Dwyer said, 'I share your concern, Mrs McFadden, but in the circumstances, in view of Stephen's . . .' He hesitate and pulled at his grubby cuffs again. 'The difficulty he would have relating this coherently to the police – whether they would be after believing him. Perhaps it would be better altogether if nothing more were said about what Stephen thinks he saw. That might be better altogether.'

Although she found little that was reassuring about Edward O'Dwyer, she was grateful to hear those words. To have had this solicitor advise her to do nothing meant that her civic conscience was clear. But to receive that advice was one thing, to make Stephen understand it and so avoid putting himself in danger was quite another.

5

WEARY OF GOING backwards and forwards across the Irish Sea to this godless province to do a thankless job, a job he'd been doing for far too long, and desperately wanted a change from, Timothy Faligot, the Minister of State for Northern Ireland, would rather have been going to Hell than back to Belfast.

Sometimes he thought he was going to Hell when he boarded the plane for yet another trip. Sometimes he went back and forth three times a week, depending on what was going on both there and in the House of Commons; some business detained him all week. If he only had to go there once a month he would still long for a change of job, and couldn't understand why the PM didn't give him something more congenial. Being the minister with responsibility for law and order, he sometimes felt physically sick at having to meet with the bigots and bully boys from whose very pores aggression oozed, who carried violence on flecks of spittle as they spat out their demands across the conference table in his office in Stormont Castle.

He was thought to be good at his job, well informed – which was true, as he had been doing it for nearly five years, but there were none the less things that he still didn't understand, and wouldn't be able to penetate, even if he stayed in the job another five years. He had no comprehension of why people would go on fighting and killing for some abstract principle, the winning or losing of which would make no apparent physical difference to anyone. Whether Unionist Protestant or Republican Catholic, and regardless of where their ancestors hailed from, they were all Northern Irish now. One day they'd all simply be Irish when the North was re-integrated with the South, as logically, if not economically, it should be. The truth was that Eire wasn't making it as a trading nation, and possibly that was part of the Unionist politicians' resistance to integration. The Hillsborough Accord was a step towards integration, as Timothy Faligot saw it, the exchange of civil servants from Dublin working in Hillsborough House outside Belfast on policies such as cross-border policing and trade. A move in the right direction which he had been trying to effect was the complete integration of Catholics into the RUC, the UDR and all areas of civil service in NI, but that was as difficult as getting black people into racist institutions like the police on mainland Britain. At times Timothy Faligot wondered if they would ever progress, and at times he didn't care.

The sense of futility that accompanied him more and more on these trips slipped off the plane with him now. How he would be able to effect calm and reassurance in an atmosphere of increasing hostility to what was being seen as an RUC shoot-to-kill policy, he didn't know. Those making the allegations were dug in, and were in no mood to be reassured that no such policy existed. He wasn't entirely convinced himself, but hadn't been told that there was; he had heard similar proposals put forward as the answer to NI sectarian troubles, such as moving the SAS in and letting them wipe out every IRA cell that existed – the security forces knew who they were and where they were. The authors of such proposals obviously never considered the legacy of hatred that would leave, to say nothing of how Dublin would respond, or what the various Tammany Halls in America still capable of putting pressure on their government would do. Perhaps they would mount a Grenada-style assault on the province. The thought caused him to smile as he came off the plane, sandwiched between his two detectives, to be met at the end of the portable concourse by Brian Churchward, the civil servant who ran his private office in Northern Ireland.

Timothy Faligot had hoped there would be a helicopter to ferry him out to Stormont; that way he would avoid contact with the squalor of Belfast. Despite the security, the closed-up businesses and burned-out houses amidst the spools of litter were a depressing legacy to the failure of successive governments to find any meaningful solution to the troubles.

'Good trip, Minister?' Churchward asked, mistaking his smile for good humour.

'No better than usual, Brian.' He didn't explain the smile. He knew his presence meant no helicopter ride out to the green and pleasant environs of Stormont.

'The press are out in force, Minister. I anticipated you'd want to see them here rather than call a press conference after your briefing.'

'Are the answers to the questions going to change at all, Brian?'

'Good Lord, I hope not, sir.'

Timothy Faligot preferred not to talk to the press; in fact he preferred not to do anything in public, which was a handicap to a public figure who had speaking engagements every week of his political career. An impromptu address was just tolerable, but a pre-planned meeting found him feeling nauseous hours before, especially if it was likely to be difficult or hostile.

His armed detectives stayed close behind him in the VIP lounge where Brian Churchward had the press assemble. The civil servant kept close to hand, ready to prompt him should he need additional information; or curtail the meeting should it get out of hand. But this Minister rarely made silly remarks to the press or anyone else.

There were fifteen or so reporters and photographers, plus a television news crew, and few could be counted on to give him an easy time, least of all those from the Dublin papers. One slip and they might lay British government policy bare to the bone, though not necessarily to the comfort of the Dublin government.

'If there's no such policy being operated officially or unofficially here in the North, Minister,' a reporter from the *Sunday News* asked, 'can you comment on the fact that none of the six men who have died recently at the hands of the RUC was actively being sought? They were alleged to have been only middle-ranking members of the IRA. None was armed.'

'That doesn't accord with my information,' the Minister said sharply. 'I believe they all had arms or access to them. To be a member of any proscribed organisation here is a dangerous thing. But their deaths are no more than a coincidence.'

'Is that a warning to other members of the IRA, sir?'

'The security forces have a duty to take all reasonable precautions to protect both the public and themselves.'

'The priest from Armagh, Father McMichael, has compiled a dossier on similar killings in the province over the past five years. There have been nearly a hundred such deaths, sir.' The reporter from the *Irish Times* spoke quickly to avoid being interrupted. 'He claims there's an RUC death squad –'

'Absolute rot,' Timothy Faligot said angrily. 'It's irresponsible and, I believe, malicious. There is no such policy, never has been nor will there be. Such a policy would not only be criminal' – he was aware of Brian Churchward's cautioning glance – 'it would mean there could never be hope of reconciliation here.'

'Are you in touch with the Dublin government over this, sir?' a woman from the *Unionist Newsletter* asked slyly.

'We're in touch with the Dublin government about a great many things these days.'

'Are you dismissing Father McMichael's accusation?'

Timothy Faligot might have hoped the floor would open and swallow the *Irish Times* reporter. His whole object seemed to be to cause trouble. He smiled at him tolerantly.

'Father McMichael compiles any number of reports. He sends them to my office with unflagging regularity, and I do him the courtesy of reading them. So too does the Director of Public Prosecutions and the police. But as yet there has been no substance to his accusations, none that the DPP can take action on. These killings as far as I understand are no more than a coincidence. I believe that is the Director's view.'

The press conference ended, and Timothy Faligot went quickly to the grey Ford Granada that was waiting at the door. His detectives went in the front and the civil servant in the back with him. He always felt on edge in the car, no matter what part of the province he was travelling through and despite the carload of armed police behind. As soon as he heard that central locking system engage he felt trapped behind the bullet-proof glass. He tried to put his thoughts to the matter of the recent shootings by the RUC. He believed there was no more to them than coincidence. He also believed that would be his conclusion following the various meetings he would have over the next twenty-four hours with the Chief Constable, the DPP, Sir Michael Newfield and civil servants from Dublin; knowing it couldn't be otherwise.

'Your last operation was a complete fucking shambles,' ACC Peter Eglington said without prelusive niceties as he came to the top of the briefing room and faced the forty men who were standing there. Each accepted part of the corporate rebuke for what had happened over the killing of Desmond O'Donnell, though all weren't present. He paused briefly and glanced over the body of men; not one single one of them was dressed in a complete uniform. 'The only thing that redeemed that operation is the fact that you got the target. Sit.'

He sat himself and passed the briefing over to Chief Superintendent Johnston.

'There seems to be a bit of confusion in the reports, following that operation,' Chief Superintendent Johnston, the deputy head of

Special Branch, said, 'Particularly with regard to the witness to the shooting.'

'Did the UDR get any sort of lead on O'Donnell's confederate?' the ACC asked.

'They did not,' Johnston responded.

'Well, unless he's found he's only going to fuel rumours currently going around.'

'I know you men weren't chosen for this unit because of your way with writing reports. But unless we get the facts right, after the event, we look like a bunch of fucking cowboys. What we most definitely are not is cowboys. Check your facts with other members of the unit so you can remind each other what happened. Make notes as soon as you can afterwards. Show each other what you're writing. This is important, especially when troublemakers are sounding off about our being trigger-happy. Those reports will be our alibi.'

Laurence Payne, the MI5 security liaison officer, saw through this ploy immediately when he read the rewritten debriefing reports. His department had emerged as the villain without ever once being named. To him it was a yet lower ebb in their relationship with the RUC, and it needed no Cassandra to suggest who was responsible: Mark Howellett's dirty tricks department in MI6 had resented MI5's prospering relationship with the RUC, one that resulted in their will being done. The tide was definitely running in MI6's favour currently, but it wouldn't always be so.

What he plotted in secret wasn't signalled in any way by his declared response. He went along the second-floor corridor at Knock to Johnston's office. Chief Superintendent Johnston had stepped out, the secretary told him. Payne waited, picking up papers from the desk to read. He didn't have to wait long.

'I don't like the implications in those debriefing reports, Neville,' Payne said, rocking back on two legs of the desk chair as Chief Superintendent Johnston came into the office.

Johnston stopped and looked at the young man sitting at his desk as if he owned the place. He had known him to put his feet on other people's desks. That was how he was frequently to be found in his own office. What he had once seen as commanding and confident, and had admired in him, Johnston now saw as arrogance and decided Payne's manner was developed to disguise his shortcomings. 'It wasn't our fault that O'Donnell did a runner.'

'He should never have got outside of the flat. You wouldn't have had this problem with the witness then. Your people were controlling the operation.'

'Your people were controlling my people, Laurence.'

A smile crept across Laurence Payne's fresh boyish face. He looked about thirteen when he smiled, instead of thirty-three. 'What would you like me to tell Control, to recommend to the Co-ordinator that we cut the Special Branch free to operate on their own?'

'Of course not,' Johnston said weasellingly, and moved past the younger man and into the narrow space behind his desk. He smelled Payne's cologne, which rose off him in a nauseating cloud. At this time of year everyone smelled a little while the supply of Christmas aftershave and anti-perspirant continued to hold out, but Laurence Payne had it all year round, and Johnston now decided it was a symptom of an inferiority complex. But unlike the man at his desk, he wasn't engaged in questioning why the change in him was coming about. 'Maybe MI5 should conduct the operations in the field, as they seem to be making all the noise elsewhere.'

'Why not go across to the house and tell that to your Chief Constable, Neville?'

'I prefer practical suggestions to criticism – from you or anyone else,' Johnston retorted. 'What those debriefing reports were is practical after all.'

Laurence Payne nodded and smiled again, but didn't ask if the SIS had any hand in them. He suspected they did and planned to pay them back.

'Record the next operation,' he said, knowing Johnston would be uneasy about this, and that MI6 would be even less easy about who had control of such tapes in the event. Payne would be wary of there being any such record, but would be less concerned if SIS made it, and they would certainly try to once Johnston reported the plan to them. 'There'll be no argument about who did or said what then. You can make your debriefing reports from the tapes.' He let the chair drop back to rest on four legs and stood decisively.

Chief Superintendent Johnston didn't argue, but thought it a daft idea, notwithstanding the rightness of their actions. He didn't trust what Laurence Payne might do with any such tapes, and would discuss the matter with Mark Howellett before the next operation.

6

THE DERELICT FARM buildings out on the Glencairn Road on the north-west side of the city were an eyesore and of no benefit to anyone apart from the children who sometimes played there, dossers who sometimes slept there or birds that nested there. But they were on no one's priority list for tearing down and tidying up, along with the broken, rusting farm machinery and the rotting cars and junk that had been collecting there. Ownership of the barns and surrounding piece of land wasn't clear. The house that formed part of the yard had long since fallen in, and had been so reclaimed by nature that even in the starkest of winters it was difficult to make out the outline of the buildings through the leafless brambles and lifeless brown nettles, waiting to be overwhelmed by spring's new growth. The locals used it as a tip for anything they were throwing out, and met few objections, least of all from other locals.

Dawn awoke to find unusual activity among the litter in the yard. RUC men from the Special Support Unit were moving in, not to search for suspected terrorists, but to lie in wait for them. As on all such occasions, suggestions made by MI5 were taken for the directives they truly were, so microphones were being placed in the barn on the rotting oak trusses to record what went on below when the suspects found the guns the RUC men were hiding among the straw. There were two Ingram machine guns with empty magazines and a couple of Smith & Wesson .44 Magnums, which would stop an armoured personnel carrier, they were so powerful.

'Are you after hearing me OK, Jimmy?' an RUC man asked, looking up at the mike that was concealed in the rafters.

Out in the yard in an abandoned panelled van with its wheels missing and windscreen shattered two men were setting up the receiver and recording equipment. One was a field officer from MI6, who was there to see that this was done properly. He knew little of the reasons for their getting involved here like this, but assumed it was to do with MI5's decreasing efficiency. They certainly weren't

49

incompetent like in the bad old days that the dead-heads talked of, but they sometimes seemed not to have their heart in their work.

'Tell him to turn his personal radio off,' Roger North the field officer said to the RUC man who sat in the fetid-smelling van with him. It smelled like someone had crept in there and relieved himself, but he wasn't about to hunt around in the half light for turds, and hoped he didn't step in any, or worse, in the confined space where both would remain concealed until after the operation.

'Did you hear that, Gary? Put your radio off. Move around a bit, see if we can hear you from other parts.'

The RUC man did as he was told, moving to various parts of the barn, checking if he was coming in loud and clear. After doing this a few times he said to Sergeant Keeper, 'How do I know if they can hear me, Serge?'

'I daresay they'll be letting you know.'

He was finishing covering the guns, making a poor sort of job of hiding them. How the suspects had been given the information he didn't know, but guessed the dancing boys from MI6 had made sure of that. They would all be outside within easy striking distance when contact was made.

How long they would have to wait no one could say. It might only be a matter of hours, or it could be days. Though Terry Keeper hoped it wouldn't be that long because his position crouched with Constable Maurice Peters beneath a piece of decaying canvas under what looked like it might have once been a harvester was none too pleasant. It was damp and cold, and he could smell a faint odour of fear in Peters, or perhaps it was even coming from himself.

Occasionally their wait was interrupted by bursts of whispered conversation, the unending silence yawning before them sometimes proving too much. The topics reached such dizzy heights as, 'Did you see *The Price is Right* this week? That woman who guessed exactly right every time. She weren't a penny out, she weren't. You'd think they told her.'

'My missus is good at that. She ought to be on there,' Sergeant Keeper said. His wife had written in several times to go on the TV quiz show.

'Got it dead right every time,' Maurice Peters said incredulously. 'Won a sewing machine, a steam iron and a holiday for two in Spain. She got the price exactly right.'

'My missus should be on that,' Sergeant Keeper said again, before they lapsed into silence once more.

As the sun poked briefly through the low cloud over the Falls and Springmartin, it highlighted the ugliness that imprisoned the people who were condemned there decades ago, and refused to stay long enough to help spark an existence out of that cycle of deprivation. Further west over the abandoned farmyard it was lost forever in a bank of cloud that threatened rain. Nothing was seen to move in the yard. However, the stillness itself might have presaged danger to the wary as it did to the birds and rabbits, who would otherwise have been about there.

Late on in the morning, an old man appeared with two thin dogs. Then later a van pulled off the narrow lane and the driver threw some bags of rubbish out down the escarpment into the litter-clogged Ballygomartin River.

It was early afternoon before anyone of interest appeared and only two of the nine men hiding about the place had brought anything to eat – the habit not being encouraged on such operations. Sergeant Keeper had a bar of chocolate, which he shared with his partner. Both men would sooner have had a smoke.

Although still growing, Stephen McFadden rarely thought about food, and wasn't a bit hungry, recently having eaten the lunch his mum had made for him and his friend Kit McMahon. Kit was Stephen's only friend and often ate food at his flat. He was eight years younger and although in most ways much smarter, he deferred to Stephen because he was strong and made people afraid of him. Kit had been bullied and bashed by family or state in one form or another for most of his nine and a bit years and found it reassuring to be with Stephen. Even his dad, who shouted and threatened everyone, avoided giving Stephen an argument when he came to call for him. It would have been grand to have had him in that community home where he had been in care when the aunties pinched and slapped him for bedwetting and the uncles did worse. They wouldn't have done that if his best friend had been around.

Raising his left hand to halt the posse he was leading, Stephen reined in the dark chestnut horse and came to a stop. The other horses stopped behind him. Kit was at his side, Kit was the only person he told about the secret rendezvous they had at the old barn. Kit knew there was going to be a showdown and would stand by him all the way. He liked the loner image that was personified on the television by Clint Eastwood, but wouldn't have been without his sidekick. He was the outlaw Josey Wales and had seen the film eight times. Kit wanted to be an outlaw too, but a good one, and decided to be Billy the Kid.

'That's where they're holed up, Kid,' Stephen said in a low, urgent voice trying to give the situation the gravity it deserved. 'We just have to get down there and flush them out.' He glanced behind him at his gang and raised his hand with his index finger slightly protruding and jerked it forward. 'Let's go.'

None of them noticed the loop of snot that hung from Stephen's nose as he kicked his chestnut into the gallop American quarter horses were schooled to. Kit never mentioned about Stephen frequently having a snot-nose – and his da wouldn't have dared to call him that to his face – for Stephen never said anything when he pissed his trousers.

They swooped down from the ridge up near the road, running in a sideways gait like cantering horses, heading for the barn that lay down near the Ballygomartin River – it wasn't but a stream that rose out of the nearby hills. Their horses suddenly forgotten, they ran behind the piles of litter on reaching the yard, using different pieces of machinery for cover as they approached the barn. They got there unseen and without a single shot being fired, but that didn't mean they were out of danger. There was nothing between the broken-down railway wagon where they took cover and the barn. The last fifteen yards would have to be crossed in the open, but Stephen had no fear of being hit by the hail of bullets that the baddies let fly because of who he was. He had never seen Clint Eastwood killed. He signalled his partner and set out for the barn, running zig-zag at a low crouch. Kit did the same and jumped straight through the narrow opening of the broken barn door after his friend. They scrambled across the damp straw away from the open door, and checked about the place, deciding it was safe.

'Whoever was here has let out,' Stephen said, turning a full circle with his carbine held at the ready.

'Where are the guns, Josey, are they after being here?' Kit McMahon asked.

'Sure, that was the deal. How are we gonna rob the bank without them? That half-breed said they'd be in the old barn down by the creek. You search over there, Kid. I'll check in back here before anyone shows up.'

Kit did as he was directed. He thought it was grand the way Stephen could talk like cowboys on the television and wished he could. It somehow never sounded right when he tried. It would be grand if they found the guns and robbed the bank and got enough money to go off to America, just him and Stephen, and bought the ranch they always talked about. That was Kit's dream, to get away from the harsh realities of home life and the perpetual threat of going back into the community home. He hoped and prayed the promise that this excursion held would come true as he sifted through the wet straw that was littered with weeds, crisp packets and old Durexes. That it wasn't just another game. His heart stopped when his hand came up against the cold, steel barrel of a Smith & Wesson .44 Magnum and for a moment he couldn't speak as one thought tumbled after another through his head in confused excitement. They could rob a bank and go to America and have a ranch. 'Stephen!' he called, forgetting his cowboy persona now. 'We can rob the bank!'

'Jesus fucking hell, would you look?' Stephen said in the same excited moment. 'Would you look at this, would you?' He had found an Ingram sub-machine gun. Not exactly his favoured Winchester 73, but he wasn't complaining. 'I've found them. I've found the guns.'

'You have contact,' Roger North said quietly from the 30-cwt van hulk. His voice hissed through each of the personal radios the men were carrying; it wouldn't go on to the tape of the scene inside the barn.

Contact was all Stone and Birchfield needed to hear. They didn't emerge from cover but took sight of movement inside the barn through the broken sheeting and peppered the walls. Firing came from the direction of the old combine harvester, then from the third and fourth and fifth positions further round on an arc. They emptied their magazines, removed them, slapped another in place, and held the firing position. All firing had stopped now and Sergeant Keeper emerged, then Chief Inspector Paisley appeared from across the far side of the yard.

Cautiously the SSU men moved in on the barn, their guns drawn. Paisley was the first to reach the doorway and peer in. There was no room for more than two to see in at once and others crowded behind. They stepped inside singly and approached Stephen McFadden where he lay in the straw, his eyes open. A bubble of mucus coming from his left nostril was getting bigger and bigger and galvanizing the onlookers until finally it burst with the last cubic centimetre of air being expelled from his body. Only then did they seem to notice the holes that had cut a bloody swathe across his diaphragm; a bullet had smashed his left hand where it had clung to the metal stock of the Ingram. No one said anything. Or moved. Only Adam Birchfield's eyes flicked about the barn seeking out the second man. He doubted if he was still alive but would only be sure when he saw him.

They all heard the sound at once and turned as Kit McMahon let out a faint cry. It was as if the sound came from a tortured mind rather than a pain-wracked body.

The seven men moved almost as one across the barn to where Kit lay in a crumpled heap between some bales of rotting straw and the far barn wall. The impact of the bullets hitting him had thrown him there. He moaned again.

'God, he's no more than a wee boy', an operations-hardened constable said, having difficulty holding on to his stomach. 'What are we going to do?'

He directed his question at no one in particular, and there was no immediate response. After a moment Birchfield drew the Walther from its holster and glanced at Chief Inspector Paisley, not for an order but thinking he might challenge him. Paisley said nothing.

It wasn't going to happen, it couldn't, Sergeant Keeper decided, but wasn't entirely convinced the Chief Inspector would stop it. A sense of panic spread through Keeper, not at the thought that Birchfield might shoot this boy in cold blood but that he would do nothing about it. He was frozen for a second, unable to take any actions other than to look at Paisley. Finally he made a move and reached out instinctively and pushed Birchfield's gun away as it came round to the piss-stained lad.

'Get an ambulance,' Sergeant Keeper said.

His words were neither a request nor an order, but served as a brief stay of execution while Birchfield looked to Chief Inspector Paisley to countermand what the Sergeant had said. It was a decision the Chief Inspector didn't want to make nor be heard not to make. He turned and quickly went out.

Sergeant Keeper laughed, as if assuming Birchfield's gesture was a joke. He dearly hoped it was, but wasn't convinced, so avoided stepping between Birchfield and the wounded boy. This business wasn't finished and there was no telling whether someone like Birchfield would finish it through him. Not having an overview of the situation in Northern Ireland, Sergeant Keeper didn't always understand quite what they were doing, but none the less knew it was right. There were few things he drew the line at, but this was one of them. If this was the shape of the future in the SSU it was time he got out, he decided.

Finally he broke from the younger man's mesmerising stare and glanced at the microphone in the rafters, as if seeing it was necessary to making himself heard. 'Jimmy, get an ambulance. One of these wee lads is still alive and badly hurt. Get an ambulance in here urgently.'

Crises were nothing new in the political workaday of Northern Ireland, and certainly nothing unusual in Timothy Faligot's life. Sometimes when they were anticipated and forestalled he felt particularly effective; sometimes they were allowed to emerge into the public domain before being dealt with so that he was seen by his colleagues at Westminster to be effective; mostly they involved the IRA on a bombing rampage or a prison hunger strike which brought martyrdom, but lately it was the Loyalist factions. They were so deeply opposed to any sort of co-operation with southern Ireland that they responded with violence when their strikes, political gatherings and demands for complete isolation from the South were ignored.

Crises within the security forces were much rarer; they had existed, resulting out of jealousies and infighting over ascendancy, but basically they had all been resolved because the forces were all going in the same direction, seeking the same objective.

But the current crisis they found themselves in with the RUC Special Support Unit and its so-called shoot-to-kill policy was deepening as more and more mistakes were made. The latest was the shooting of two young lads out at Glencairn Park. Pressure for some kind of inquiry was being mounted from outside, led by irresponsible elements of the media and leading members of the clergy with a vested interest in undermining an effective anti-terrorist force. How long such calls could be ignored, and whether they finally could be, was the purpose of the meeting he had summoned in his first-floor office in Stormont Castle with Sir Norman Hateley, the Chief Constable of the province, the head of Special Branch, and the Security Co-ordinator, Sir Michael Newfield. The latter was one of the few people whose opinion and judgement Timothy Faligot truly trusted here, and he was the most unopinionated, unassuming man imaginable. He trusted Brian Churchward, the undersecretary responsible for security and operations at the Northern Ireland

Office, and to a much lesser extent the second undersecretary, but both had been in their posts too long and had started to go native.

'This clearly was a case of mistaken identity,' Timothy Faligot said to the small gathering in the ornately furnished room with its gold-painted reproduction Georgian furniture and pale green upholstery. This, along with the real antiques and washed Chinese rugs, gave the place an elegance he was reluctant to leave for the starker existence of a comparatively threadbare Whitehall.

'It clearly was, Minister,' Brian Churchward responded. 'But that doesn't lessen the overture calling for the officers responsible to be prosecuted.'

Minor explosions were going off inside Sir Norman Hateley's head as he listened to this, his face getting redder than it normally was beneath the broken capillaries. He expected nothing more of Faligot, a minister with no real investment in this province, but Churchward had overall responsibility for the police and law and order divisions at the NIO and shouldn't even consider blame attaching to policemen.

'There is no way I am going to let any of my men face prosecution for these shootings, Timothy,' he said forcefully, as if needing to mow down legions. 'Absolutely no way. You'll have my resignation before that happens.'

That wasn't a threat he made often, but he believed there was no chance of his being challenged. His resignation over such an issue would cause a real crisis. The symbiotic relationship he had with the leader of the Loyalist factions significantly helped make the province governable. It came about through shared perceptions of life in Northern Ireland and the fact that they belonged to the same Masonic lodge.

'This is a desperate situation, Norman,' Timothy Faligot said, 'but it hardly calls for such a drastic response.'

'It was a regrettable incident,' ACC Eglington said. 'But we mustn't lose sight of the fact that these two youths were clearly seen holding weapons that were awaiting collection in that barn, and talked of robbing a bank.'

'They actually said that?' the Minister asked.

'It's on the tape recording of the whole incident.'

The Minister seemed satisfied.

'One of them was only ten years old, Peter,' Brian Churchward reminded him.

'He was so,' Sir Norman Hateley said, 'armed with a .44

Magnum, possibly the most powerful handgun in the world. You're just as dead when shot by a ten-year-old as you are when his father or older brother shoots you. Although we can't in any way condone the shooting of young people, we are facing the real danger of having this element creeping in here.'

The Northern Ireland Minister wasn't sure that an armed threat from children was real as of that moment, but knew the security forces could make real anything they chose to. There was nothing he or any of his colleagues could do to disprove such a circumstance, even if they dared, other than to appoint a judicial inquiry headed by someone as independent as Lord Scarman, and they knew that could resurrect more problems than it might solve.

'Were these two youths from families with known IRA sympathies?'

'It very much looks that way, Timothy', Sir Norman Hateley said, covering his policemen, regardless of the paucity of evidence; the father of Kit McMahon had a criminal record for violence, while a Special Branch tab attached to his police file carried the information that he had threatened IRA reprisals against the police who had arrested him.

'We still have to deal with the mounting pressure this whole incident is causing. I don't know what to suggest, short of the public inquiry that's called for.' He glanced fleetingly at Sir Norman Hateley, then on to let his eyes settle on the round figure of Sir Michael Newfield sitting quite relaxed on the eighteenth-century ormolu chair. 'Could I take your mind on this, Michael?'

Sir Michael Newfield smiled, enjoying being deferred to as he was by the Minister. He suspected it was probably more on account of his close friendship with the Prime Minister than any penetrating insight he might have to guide them through this mess. 'Quite clearly, until Norman's people have completed their initial investigations, it's difficult to decide what course of action to take. You might find difficulty resisting some form of inquiry. Indeed it seems only right that there should be one. Two people of very tender years were shot and killed. We shouldn't be seen to take this lightly – indeed, I know of no one who's treating it so, but the trick is to be seen.'

'You clearly feel there should be some sort of inquiry sooner rather than later.'

Letting his round eyes settle on the anxious minister, Sir Michael said, 'That might be advisable, Minister.' This belied his true feelings for the man. Although he believed him able in an unremarkable way, he had twice ventured the opinion that Faligot was the right man for the job when the Prime Minister had asked him. Timothy Faligot was malleable, and that made him tolerable as far as Sir Michael Newfield was concerned. In his flat at the top of Stormont Castle, he kept modelling clay; all of his models were from memory and none for public showing. 'Perhaps if Norman got started in anticipation of increasing public disquiet. Whether any prosecutions should result is another matter.'

'I've asked my deputy to make provisional inquiries,' Sir Norman Hateley said, seeing the way out for the RUC without loss of face. 'I'll ask him to beef it up to a full inquiry into the circumstances surrounding the shooting. But I feel it's only fair to warn you, Timothy, that if that were to result in RUC men being prosecuted for what amounts to protecting life and making this province liveable, we could be heading straight back to the bad old days before the "normalisation", when the army was in complete control of security.'

'Of course no one wants that, Norman,' the Minister said, knowing the insuperable difficulties such a backward step would cause in parliament both in London and Dublin. 'Let's cross that bridge after your deputy completes his inquiry.'

He smiled at Sir Michael Newfield, thankful for his clear judgement and pleased to have forestalled another crisis. The Ulster Security Co-ordinator opened his wet lips to return a half-smile. He was thinking how Kit McMahon had at one time been in care at King's House Community Home. He was too young for them to have had any contact, but still he felt as if a ghost crossed his grave, and he began to feel slightly sick. He excused himself and returned to his own office in the west tower, thinking about the dangerous game he was playing by recommending an inquiry, wondering if it were a final destructive act on his part.

M AURICE KNIGHT FELT the need to pinch himself to prove that
the journey he was making wasn't a dream. The train from
Plymouth was real enough and the people in it. The black ticket
collector gave him no sign of recognition; Maurice purposely didn't
notice black people doing fairly lowly jobs and so didn't get angry
about their lot. He was aware that there were few black policemen
and knew that was because culturally and emotionally they weren't
suited to the job. He had been brought up in a predominantly white,
lower-middle-class neighbourhood by lower-middle-class parents – a
district nurse and a carpentry teacher – and had acquired the white
values of those around him.

The clipped ticket was real, so too was the buffet car coffee, which
had the distinction of being worse than that in the police canteen; his
trombone case on the seat next to him and his small grip bag with his
clothes in were also real enough. So too the countryside they were
now passing through that was increasingly showing signs of light
industry. But still he wasn't entirely believing this journey.

The day before yesterday he had still been a community
policeman in the Devonport sub-division in the West Devon
Division of Plymouth, talking to primary school children about
neighbourhood watch schemes. He supposed he still was, even
though the divisional superintendent had informed him he was being
seconded to the Met to work in plain clothes. It was something he
would have given his right arm to do. He was twenty-three and had
been a policeman for four years – a career choice which had a lot to
do with the fact that second to the army the police had the best
training facilities around, and Maurice took full advantage of them.
He boxed, though had no desire to do so professionally, but he
boxed well enough to help the Devon and Cornwall Constabulary
win a number of cups and shields.

Having joined the police, Maurice soon decided that he wanted to
be a detective. He had applied for the CID three times, and was still

waiting. This offer was one he couldn't refuse, especially as it meant transferring to London. His visits to date had been as a tourist. The district he was going to was a name on a map, and he knew no more about the area than Brian Horsfell, the detective superintendent from C11, had told him when he came to see him yesterday. He was to work undercover on a murder investigation. It was all too exciting for Maurice to pay any regard to Detective Superintendent Horsfell's warning that it could be dangerous; that the murder of the left-wing black politician Jesse Jarman almost certainly touched the drug trafficking that went on in the area.

The brightly polished shoes on the floor were real enough – he'd been brought up not to put his shoes on seats. His father had cleaned the shoes for him, and his mother had pressed his best uniform, and was disappointed when he told her he wouldn't need it. You couldn't work undercover in a uniform. This was promotion, his parents assumed, and Maurice shared that assumption, along with his friends, most of whom were cousins, when they came to the house for an impromptu party yesterday evening. He had been chosen after all; the fact that the Divisional Superintendent had told him that he was doubtless chosen simply because his name popped up on the computer didn't dampen his spirits.

Reality was about to prick Maurice's euphoria like a shard of broken glass. He was met at Paddington station by Detective Superintendent Horsfell and the Divisional Chief Superintendent, Mike Barclay. He was anything but welcoming. Even Maurice's sparky, easy-going humour couldn't wrap itself about Barclay's hostility. He hated the notion of any outsider being brought in like this.

'What the fuck have you got there?' were his opening words when he saw the trombone case.

Maurice looked at his trombone slightly incredulously, wondering if, despite the Chief Superintendent's tone, this wasn't a joke. He started to smile. 'It's a trombone, boss.'

'Even someone straight off the fucking boat ought to know better.'

Somehow Maurice had thought he was one of them, but this wasn't comradeship. Detective Superintendent Horsfell said nothing.

With an expectant glance to Horsfell, Maurice said, 'They told me to come as I normally travel – so I brought my trombone, boss.' He extended the mouthpiece that was on a silver chain around his neck to validate his words.

'Don't call me boss, or you'll be on the next train.' With that he turned and strode across the concourse towards their parked car.

'He always this happy?' Maurice asked, defensively slipping back into his Devonshire accent with its long vowel sounds.

'He badly needs a result,' Horsfell said as they started in the same direction. 'Even the Home Secretary is up his daily. You'd better try sir or guv when you address a senior officer. You're not in the country now.'

Maurice gave a toot on his mouthpiece, but got no more than a look from Horsfell. He wondered if the senior detective was dim or blind, but didn't risk pointing out that Plymouth was a city.

Driving through south-east London in the front of the Triumph Accord with Detective Superintendent Horsfell at the wheel and the Chief Superintendent in the back, Maurice felt like a child on a visit to a fair; his eyes didn't know where to stop. Little of it was colourful or eye-catching, but not one bit less exciting for all that. In other circumstances, Maurice would almost certainly have been depressed. The decay and poverty of the inner city, with such an obvious hostility to the environment as shown in the assault on property and the litter in the streets, was a direct contrast to where he lived in Plymouth.

'I used to dream about being taken out of uniform and put on a murder investigation,' Maurice said, oblivious to the atmosphere in the car.

'If you've got any illusions about cracking this or becoming a fucking hero,' Chief Superintendent Barclay said irritably, 'forget them.' He was still smarting from losing his argument with C11 about bringing in an outside black. It suggested a failure on their part to get on top of this murder investigation. The Area DAC had backed him over not bringing anyone in, least of all a black. They had used the argument that it was morally dangerous to ask a policeman to associate in that way with criminals, and possibly engage in criminal activity himself. But Commander Jack Bentham had argued more cogently, backed by the Assistant Commissioner. Even if he had brought the Home Secretary to the meeting to argue his corner, Mike Barclay still wouldn't have been happy about that decision. He hated the pressure he had been forced to work under, as much as the black who had caused it. Now he had to suffer this tint from the sticks bouncing around like he could solve all his problems. 'You might get lucky, get a whisper on our black suspect. But you're not going to crack any murder case.'

61

'Yes, bo . . .' Maurice checked himself. 'I'll do my best, sir.'

Mike Barclay stared at the smiling black face as it turned towards him. The mouth seemed to have far too many teeth. 'You're here because the fucking computer spewed you up. If there was a fucking chimpanzee in the computer we'd have probably drawn that.'

Taking his future in his hands, Maurice Knight said, 'And you probably couldn't have told the difference, boss.'

Detective Superintendent Horsfell held his breath, wondering how the young black had the front for that.

Suddenly Mike Barclay laughed. He would tolerate a self-deprecating black. 'You're going to fail,' he said. 'When you do, we'll pull you out, wipe your arse and put you back on the train. At least then the Home Office will have seen I was right.'

'I'll do my best not to disappoint you, boss.'

Horsfell knew the black policeman was pushing his luck with his double-edged replies, and felt inclined to tell him to shut his mouth. But the truth to tell, he had little time for Barclay himself.

'You get flash with me, Sam, you'll be in more trouble than you'll ever find on this manor.'

The car drew up behind a parked Ford Sierra, its driver sitting there. Mike Barclay climbed out without a goodbye or good luck and got into the car in front and was driven off.

'Friendly soul,' Maurice said.

'Real charmer,' the detective said, and put the car in gear.

Now Maurice had no doubt about the reality of this. He had learned it was easier to be the black clown than carry the burden of his tribe.

They drove out to Greenhill Farm Estate, which Maurice soon discovered was a euphemism for a depressed, prison-like black ghetto. The only remnant of green was the bald, littered sward between the concrete blocks. There were no hills as such, and it was as far from a farm as only the hemmed-in inner city can be. But it was teeming with life as they drove through. The only white/black cross-over point was between kids too young to be victims of conditioning.

They didn't stop anywhere, but Detective Superintendent Horsfell filled him in on the background to the Farm: what the level of crime was; how it was policed by confrontation because the residents wanted a no-go area, and by and large that's what they got, despite the Commissioner's public declarations to the contrary; how Jesse Jarman was killed. The black local councillor had been the single biggest object of hate for the local police, because he was keeping dossiers on all the reported incidents of police brutality and corruption affecting blacks. 'He had a whole pile of dirt apparently,' Horsfell added.

'How did you feel about him, guv?' Maurice asked.

'I expect I'd have been as pissed off as any of them if this was my manor. Mind you, I think what Jarman was doing was right – we don't want the boot boys in on the job, do we, no matter who they happen to be kicking.'

Maurice glanced sideways at the man, suddenly impressed by him. He was always impressed by policemen striking such noble attitudes.

As they continued their journey, Maurice became chastened by what he saw and compared it to the surroundings he was brought up in. Then dealt with it by telling himself that this was largely of their own making – there was, after all, an abundance of opportunity for members of the black underclass to improve themselves. It depressed him that so many blacks turned to crime or wallowed in deprivation, waiting for the state to solve their problems.

'People live here from choice or get sent by the courts?' Maurice asked to disguise his feelings.

Horsfell laughed as they turned away from the Farm. 'You'll do well to breathe in that atmosphere, much less submerge in it.'

It wasn't long before Horsfell stopped the car, and reiterated the details of how Maurice was to operate. He wasn't to go near the local police station for fear of having his cover blown. Instead he would work through Detective Sergeant Brian Tait, who ran the local police intelligence unit. Horsfell was faintly amused by that, as Tait was known to have a persuasive way with blacks.

'How reliable is Detective Sergeant Tait?' Maurice asked.

'He's a diamond. A hundred and ten per cent.'

'How do I contact him?'

'Tait puts himself about a lot – he'll contact you. Don't even try to contact him unless it's a dire emergency or your cover's blown. Give me your warrant card.'

'My warrant card?' Maurice was surprised, his Devonshire accent more pronounced. 'I want to do this, but why have I got to give you that?'

'You don't have to do it. You're found with this,' Horsfell said, slipping it into his pocket, 'what's that gonna get you? Tait'll be your lifeline.' He nodded him out of the car, without wishing him luck.

The truth was his expectation wasn't so different from Barclay's.

'Well, good luck, son,' Maurice said self-mockingly. 'We're counting on you.'

'The Chief Superintendent expects you to fail, but the problem is he needs you to succeed. Either way, you won't get much thanks.'

'Great! What about the Queen's Police Medal?'

On the street, grip in one hand, trombone in the other, Maurice felt very exposed as he moved past shops that were either shuttered or closed up with corrugated sheet metal. It was as if he had his uniform on still, and he felt like he had when a black guy approached him.

'You wanna score, man?' he asked. He had a dog on a lead which looked as wasted as he was.

'Dope?' Maurice asked. 'You mean dope?' He'd have been on the streets of Plymouth a long time before that happened, and there was no shortage of stuff there.

'You a cop or just come in from the country?'

Maurice's heart sank at the thought of this first contact blowing his cover. He could almost see other policemen gloating.

'I got cow shit on my boots?'

'You talk funny. You wanna score this dog or what?'

'What sort of dog is that?'

'An alsatian,' came the reply.

Alsatian the dog most definitely wasn't. It waited patiently, looking up at them. But Maurice didn't think it would help his cover.

'You want to buy a kettle drum?' Maurice proffered his trombone. The man with the dog considered the proposition for what it was worth, not for what it was. 'Ain't got no money. S'why I'm selling my dog.'

'Do you know Del Lindo?' Maurice asked impulsively. That was the prime suspect in the murder investigation. He had disappeared and was believed to have been hidden by someone on the Farm.

'Does he want an alsatian?'

'Probably. Here.' Maurice fished some change from his pocket and gave it to the man. 'Get your dog a bone.'

He hadn't been on the street five minutes when a car eased alongside him and the two white men in it studied him. Maurice continued walking with difficulty as tension crept through him. He tried not to look at the men. Had he done so he might have recognised them for detectives, instead of thinking they were whites out to cause trouble.

The car paced Maurice for a few yards, then stopped and the two men leaped out. Other young blacks on the street recognised what these men were and lengthened their stride.

'What's in the bag, Sam?' one said.

'Hey,' Maurice responded boldly, 'you knew my name.'

'I know everyone. Open the bag.'

The other man searched his pockets without asking Maurice. Suddenly he slammed Maurice against the fence, while his partner took his luggage.

'Where d'you get the trombone, Sam? Nick it?'

'No, of course not. When I was a kid I worked hard and was thrifty, very soon my pennies were pounds – '

The detective sank his fist into Maurice's stomach, causing him to double over, as much with surprise as pain.

'You're nicked.'

Things got no better for Maurice at the local police station, where he had the audacity to ask the station sergeant why he had been arrested.

'How about for being a fat-mouthed coon?' was the reply.

'I'd better call my solicitor then – a serious charge like that.'

'Where the fuck did you find this joker?'

'In Ryeland Road – trying car doorhandles, skip.'

'Hey, man, didn't your Mummy tell you what happens you tell lies?'

'Suspicion of having stolen property will do, skip,' the detective said. 'This trombone.'

'This is a joke, right? Right? S'joke? I just got here, I came looking for a job. I didn't steal the trombone.' He was fairly relaxed. He was a policeman. This couldn't get too serious.

Until the second detective, who had been searching his grip on the charge-room table, reached into his coat, produced a small parcel and palmed it, not very skilfully, into the bag. 'Hey-ho!' he cried. 'What's this I've found?'

In spite of his protests that he saw the detective plant the dope, Maurice found himself charged with possession of a hundred and twelve grams of cannabis, and held in cells for the magistrate's court the following day.

At any moment throughout the seventeen hours he was in custody he expected someone to turn up and say it was a joke, or at least a mistake. At first he resisted asking for DS Tait, believing that the next set of footsteps he heard on the cell-block corridor would be his. The flame of hope was rekindled every time only to splutter out like a guttered candle.

Finally, when the prison van took him to the magistrates' court and he was placed in a cell below the court, he cracked and asked for DS Tait to be contacted. He heard the purposeful stride of the jailer at the court as he approached. Maurice pressed his face to the bars of the window in the door – it had no shutter. 'Did you phone Detective Sergeant Tait like I asked?'

'I certainly did, sunshine,' came the chirpy reply. 'He's never heard of you.'

That was the end of the conversation. Later, when Maurice was taken up the steps, he decided that none of this was real, it was a bad dream, that he'd wake up, put on his uniform and go back to being a community bobby in Plymouth. He may as well for all the sense he was making of working undercover. This wasn't how he imagined he'd be treated and he told himself he wouldn't get this sort of treatment if they knew who he was. Slowly it began to dawn on Maurice that perhaps some of the brothers who complained about the police might not have been all wrong. But he came to no real conclusion about that because he couldn't quite put himself in their position.

Brought into the dock, where he stood between two uniformed custodians of the law, Maurice was about to announce that he was not only innocent, but a policeman working undercover, when he was galvanised by the man who stepped into the witness box. He identified himself as Detective Sergeant Tait.

'The police are offering no evidence in this case, Your Worship,' Tait said.

'None at all?' The magistrate seemed disappointed.

'No, sir.'

The authority Tait had was impressive, Maurice found, especially considering he was little older than himself, guessing about twenty-seven. And a detective sergeant who made things happen. Maurice didn't think that it was a white man's world, but rather that that was where he would be at that age.

'You might consider yourself lucky, *Mr* Knight,' the magistrate was saying. 'Very lucky indeed. Far too many of you people are involved in drugs. If you take my advice you'll get a plane back to where you came from.'

'I was born in Plymouth, sir,' Maurice explained. 'Plymouth, Devon.'

'Don't push your luck, Sam,' the warder whispered as he opened the dock gate. 'He'll do you for contempt.'

In the discharge room above the cells, DS Tait was waiting as Maurice was brought up for release and given back his possessions. He was small and compactly built and moved on the balls of his feet, Maurice noticed. His grey suit looked as if it wasn't bought from Burton's – which was where Maurice only ever bought his.

'Maurice – I'm Brian Tait.'

'Oh, DS Tait? DS Tait?' Maurice said. 'Never heard of you!' He noticed he had one green and one brown eye.

A grin broke over Tait's rock-like face. He rarely smiled. 'You'll do, uncle.'

As they walked away from the court, Tait produced the packet of grass that Maurice had been fitted with. 'You'd better have this back. It'll give you street credibility.'

'Those detectives planted it on me. They planted it.'

'Detectives might do that sort of thing in Plymouth – not around here,' Tait said without trace of irony. They stopped at his car, and he opened the boot and pulled out Maurice's grip and trombone. 'Bringing that wasn't very bright.'

'I'm beginning to think that about this whole assignment.'

'There are plenty of trains back to Plymouth. Say the word – we'll find some other way of digging out Jesse Jarman's killer.'

Maurice held his look, recognising the challenge. 'If I stick around I might have a chance of running across those two detectives again. I'd like to see them arrested.'

Tait gave him a grim smile. Two in a day was something, and it wasn't even midday. He liked this black cop, believing he had to be someone special to have kept his sense of humour, despite the shit he doubtless took, from the public and especially the black public. He had been tested, and had passed his test.

Detective Superintendent Horsfell was pleased when Tait reported to him about how Maurice Knight had shaped up. But not as pleased as Commander Bentham when the Detective Superintendent reported to him in turn.

Putting the black undercover officer on test as they had was a far more sensible approach than trying to train him in such a short period. This way there was no danger to him other than hurt pride if he failed. Bentham was given only brief details of the black constable's test, but he was getting to find out enough about DS Tait lately to know he was an unorthodox detective, and probably a bent one too. But he was also an effective thief-catcher. In this man he recognised the embryo of another effective thief-taker who was currently awaiting trial on major corruption charges resulting out of the investigation he had carried out for the Deputy Commissioner. The more recent investigation Bentham had conducted involving DS Brian Tait was informal, done as a favour to CIB-2, the branch of Management Support that investigated complaints against police-men. Bentham knew the Bureau was so swamped with complaints that they were barely keeping their heads above water, and because increasing its strength meant more and more experienced detectives were being taken out of the front line the Commissioner was avoiding increasing the size of CIB-2. As he got out of the lift at the fifth floor to cross the bridge for the Tower Block lifts to yet another sixteenth-floor planning meeting, Bentham was joined by DAC Ron Hazell, the DAC who headed the Bureau. He was going as far as the tenth floor.

'Jack. Just the man I wanted to see.'

'I haven't drafted a report yet – if that's what you're after.'

'Did those two detectives from the Intelligence Unit torture those two blacks?'

'Torture's a bit emotive, Ron. Just taking a suspect to the station could be torture for him.' Bentham hesitated and looked directly at the Bureau director, who seemed to believe he was doing him a favour by asking him to look informally into the complaints against DS Tait and DC Lines by two black suspects. Bentham had seen part of the interview of the suspects that had resulted in the complaint, but even so recognised that the action often wasn't as bad as the subsequent investigation sometimes suggested. 'What my inquiries show informally is that they used a lot of force to get the information they needed. I don't think it was excessive in relation to the situation down there. What it did reveal was that Floyd Springer and Boyse Brownjohn are black supremacists who'll accept no sort of compromise. It's that little mob who are thought to be involved with the killing of Jesse Jarman.'

'You're recommending no action be taken against Tait and DC Lines?'

'For what it's worth, Ron. If Springer and Brownjohn don't go down for at least conspiracy, we should consider prosecuting them for wasting police time.'

That was a policy suggestion Bentham had put to the Deputy Commissioner out of desperation when asked to do more and more of CIB-2's work, believing that if there were consequences attached to complaining against the police there might be less complaints and therefore less internal investigations. The policy had been taken up but there was no sign yet of the theory taking effect; the smarter victims of the police were tending to sue now rather than complain, and out-of-court settlements were rising alarmingly.

'I'll have a word with Jonathan Entwistle, see what he wants to do. Thanks, Jack.' He stepped across the threshold of the lift, letting go of the door.

Bentham continued up. He knew Jonathan Entwistle, the deputy chairman of the Police Complaints Authority, and doubted he would do other than proceed with a supervised investigation. He was a man out to make a name for himself and believed that establishing the PCA's independence was the way to do this. If his investigation had been official, his conclusion would inevitably have been different.

The meeting in the Deputy Commissioner's office totalled only eight senior officers, who sat around in easy chairs, imitative of meetings held by the Commissioner in his much larger office. There was coffee in a jug machine on a warmer. Jack Bentham helped himself to a cup and brought it across to the circle. Not for the first time, he glanced at the Deputy Commissioner's private secretary, who was, he guessed, fifty and had a smile that made her beautiful. Bentham thought how he would like to invite her to dinner and make love to her afterwards. It had been a while since he'd been with a woman, and he had never been with an older woman. But he let the thought go to concentrate on the meeting.

'The Home Secretary is adamant about addressing the Union at London University,' the Deputy Commissioner said. 'The Commissioner asked him if he'd consider slipping in and out by the back door, but was told in no uncertain terms to fuck off.'

'Nor should he be forced to slip in like that,' argued the DAC in whose Area where the students' union building was. 'It would make life easier for us, wouldn't it just. Or better if he didn't talk to them at all. Fuck me, is a bunch of hairy left-wing students going to dictate public order? Not on my manor. We've done as Jack suggested. We negotiated with the Union president and the senior administrator to concede that the steps into the building, and the stairs up to the first-floor lecture theatre, will be a public right of way for the nonce.'

'They didn't see any problem with that?' Bentham asked, surprised that it had been effected so easily. He imagined they would have had more tactical savvy.

'No. They don't see any problem at all,' the DAC said. 'They think he's just going to talk to the Conservative Students Association, which invited him. Then be on his way. They think he might get a bit of verbal from the non-invited students.' He smiled at that.

Bentham smiled too at such optimism.

'Do we have any firmer information on what's planned, Jack?' the Deputy Commissioner asked. Frequently he wouldn't chair such a meeting, but was there on behalf of the Commissioner, whose job he was expected soon to get. 'What numbers are likely to turn out, what action are they planning?'

'There are so many unknown quantities – the weather being the biggest. If it's raining, we're likely to have a result. It would be a good idea, Roger, to have some men sweep through the area beforehand with council workers and remove anything unattached or loose that could be used as a missile or weapon.'

'Good idea,' the Deputy Commissioner said. 'Anything found on them we'll know they took there. We don't know what numbers will turn out, so we don't know what manpower is needed. Are we guessing?'

'About six hundred students turned out against the Secretary of State at Exeter.'

'If that's what we saw here we'd contain them with two hundred men,' the local commander said. 'If we had the District Support Units in reserve to lick heads, if needed.'

'Two hundred with tactical back-up is a lot of men to put on the street,' the Assistant Commissioner said, thinking of the overtime involved and where those men would be drawn from. That wasn't his only worry. 'We're sure to be accused of pre-empting violence by over-policing.'

'On the other hand, Peter,' Harry Streeter argued, 'we don't want to be under-policed and put the Home Secretary at risk. There's no way to firm up these figures, Jack?'

'Not short of a crystal ball. Going on previous turnout, weather and current feelings among the students is the best we can do.'

'What is the current feeling?'

70

'They seem generally pissed off with their lot, and this government in particular.'

'So what's new?' The observation brought a laugh around the room.

'If the manpower can be found without depleting every other policing operation in the Area, fine,' the AC said. 'But it might be wiser to have a smaller force visible, and a larger force to go in hard if need be.'

'With respect, Peter,' the DAC said, 'we might be more effective for being seen in this situation than for being available. I don't subscribe to the view that so-called over-policing prompts violence. People either go to these demos with that in mind or they don't. Those who don't are glad to see a strong turn-out.'

'You may be right.' The AC avoided arguing too forcefully with his policy-makers at Area level. They had to bear responsibility for the men and women who put policy into operation.

Sitting in this high office, letting his thoughts drift towards the Deputy Commissioner's attractive secretary, Jack Bentham realised how pointless this discussion was in policing terms. Two basic elements mattered: having the right intelligence that told of the kind of demo to expect and the violence it could bring, and having sufficient manpower to arrest the violent elements. Whether politicians, or anyone else, were allowed to give provocative lectures to potentially volatile bodies was a matter for political judgement. It wasn't a policing matter, despite the police more and more allowing themselves to be caught up in the debate, and suffering in public esteem as a result.

'It's becoming increasingly obvious,' he said before the meeting closed, 'that we're getting some bad advice from the Home Office in the way we handle political situations. If it had been otherwise, we might have better kept our distance, instead of effectively operating as an arm of government, and suffering their misfortunes. The situation is unlikely to change with a change of government unless the police decide to change it. What the police are good at is pressuring – some might even say panicking – politicians into acting on our behalf. The apparently spiralling breakdown in law and order is always a strong lever to gain increased powers, arms, even raise our numbers. But I seriously believe that's where we should draw the line.' Bentham glanced around at the silent faces. Some agreed, but others weren't up to debating the issue and he wasn't sure why he'd raised it. He was planning to deliver a speech along similar lines to the Association of Chief Police Officers as a representative of the Commanders' Association. Whether such declarations would do his career any good was another matter. Possibly it was no more than intellectual pride that made him speak out as he did. But at least he was able to deliver the goods on a practical level too.

As he was starting out of the conference room with DAC Doc Holliday, Bentham excused himself and went back to the table where the secretary was collecting up the notepads. 'Planning to make graphite impressions?' he said.

'No. No, of course not, Commander.' She seemed a little flustered.

Feeling his pulse race and nerve-endings tingle at the proposition he was about to make, Bentham was amazed that this still happened. He decided a similar reaction was going on inside her. 'Would you like to have dinner tonight?' he asked.

She smiled, and simply said, 'Yes.'

That smile would have made it worthwhile even had she said no, Bentham decided.

8

SEEING SOME OF THE smartly dressed young barristers as they sauntered out to lunch reminded Sir Cyril Shelldrake, the Northern Irish DPP, that his wife always bought his clothes. She budgeted carefully and he knew that when he retired they would be comfortably off. But he sometimes wondered if it was worth it when they lived as they did, with their five-bedroomed house out on Massey Avenue in East Belfast near Stormont only heated to a temperature two or three degrees below what was comfortable. His clothes, although always neatly turned out, were from chainstores – John Collier and Marks and Spencer – and had the look of cheap suits and shirts. If he had said anything to his wife, she would have told him it was a pointless waste to spend four or five hundred pounds on a suit, even though he knew that a suit of that quality would stay looking good for many a long year. Jilly, his wife, frequently shopped for herself in jumble sales, and he wished she wouldn't.

He recalled how a long time ago, soon after they were married, when he was a young barrister hanging up his hat in the law library at the Royal Courts of Justice and she a legal secretary, they were saving for their first house. He had expressed a desire to buy an expensive suit, like one worn by a young barrister over from London, only to be chided by Jilly, who had asked, Did he want the new house or to look like James Bond? The truth was he had wanted to look like that QC, but hadn't the courage to disappoint his wife.

Sir Cyril noticed the suits of his two detectives as they climbed into the grey Ford Granada with him, and he felt slightly depressed to think that his clothes hung on him no better than theirs.

Going to lunch with the Chief Constable, as he was, usually dredged up similar recollections, for although not having the sartorial elegance of that young barrister Sir Cyril so long ago envied – his shape was wrong to begin with – Sir Normal Hateley was obviously a man who was never mean to himself.

Meetings with the DPP made Sir Norman Hateley think more about what he would wear than he did on any other occasion. He knew how Cyril Shelldrake lacked the courage to pay decent prices for his clothes, and it amused him. And that his bean-stick of a wife who did good works for poor Catholic kids picked through the jumble for herself first. In the office of Chief Constable, Sir Norman was required to attend many official and ceremonial functions, and so received an allowance for his uniform, one within which he knew he could have reasonably kitted himself out, had he chosen to. He spent far more than his uniform allowance, despite the fact that the Grand Master of his Masonic lodge was a master tailor who gave him a special rate. He enjoyed clothes and had no intention of ever being seen to be inferior in any degree to contemporaries on the mainland, or the politicians, civil servants and state dignitaries he met in office.

Lunch with the DPP or civil servants at Knock was easily arranged in the privacy of his flat adjacent to his headquarters office, but he liked to come into the officers' dining room on the first floor of the main building to show that he was in touch with his men on all levels. He felt isolated as it was, living in for security reasons.

He believed himself a *bon viveur*, and found it a high price indeed not to be able to freely frequent the restaurants in the city, to say nothing of suffering the near-indigestible meals he was obliged to eat here. The volume he put away he felt no need to justify, but it was a lot to do with the emotional and physical deprivation he had sometimes experienced in early childhood. He was thought by some to drink too much, though never to such a degree that he was incapable of making anything other than sharp decisions. Three or four gin and tonics a day made almost no impression on his large frame, and certainly helped him cope with some of the pressures; the bottle, and sometimes two, of wine that he drank at dinner was little more than a pleasurable aid to digestion and he remembered clearly particularly fine vintages.

He was drinking his second schooner of sherry when the DPP came into the dining-room, as if hounded by some spectre of scandal. The lawyer searched around to identify him among the senior officers and civilian staff eating there, then hurried anxiously across the room, his cheap chalkstripe suit worn like the uniform it was.

'Sorry I'm late, Norman,' Sir Cyril said, pulling out a chair and bumping the table, causing the tall sherry glass to rock. 'I tried to persuade the Minister to join us as I couldn't get him to close the meeting.'

'I have enough problems digesting this food as it is,' Sir Norman said, and emptied his glass to start again on a par with his guest. He disliked the Northern Irish Director of Public Prosecutions for being weak and vacillating over evidence that to his mind could put terrorists in jail; he disliked Timothy Faligot the Northern Ireland Minister more. Neither he, the Secretary of State nor any of his Cabinet colleagues were contributing anything to a lasting and honourable peace in the province.

Certainly the Hillsborough Accord, which provided joint working of civil servants from both the north and south of Ireland, wasn't going to. They would eventually hew that peace out of the violence and hatred that was the daily staff; it would be won inevitably by the bullet and the bothersomeness of Unionist political intransigence, and not by so-called balance and fair-mindedness that the Anglo-Irish Agreement was supposed to usher in. Sir Norman saw no way of being balanced and fair-minded with a pit of Catholics, and nothing of Shelldrake's weak reasoning would change his view. He was obliged to listen to his views, and those of the Northern Ireland Minister, but operationally he was in charge, and believed his position unassailable. Weak politicians weren't about to kick the police sideways in favour of the army, not when it was fairly obvious to all that they wanted to get out from under.

'I suspect the Minister's no stomach for this,' Sir Cyril conceded. He hadn't himself, knowing any sort of confrontation with the Chief Constable was an unpleasant experience; this one was likely to be head-on. 'He's adding to the already intense pressure on my office to prosecute the officers who shot and killed the McFadden lad in that barn.'

'That wee terrorist bass, Cyril', Sir Norman Hateley corrected. 'And what would be needed of course is evidence.'

The DPP's smile barely got past his lips. 'Lack of action is fuelling the rumours of a shoot-to-kill policy. Father McMichael has approached my office about starting a private prosecution.'

'Hasn't the Deputy Chief Constable conducted an inquiry and found nothing that those officers are answerable for?' He shot his shirt cuffs forward aggressively, and Sir Cyril noticed how well made they were, a finely woven Egyptian cotton with neatly finished-off buttonholes. Sixty to seventy pounds from Jermyn Street, he guessed. 'This pressure's from Dublin,' Sir Norman continued. 'There's no doubt about that. The Northern Ireland office puts it through all sorts of screens to mask it. But they're the fuckers we're dealing with here, we are so.'

'It won't do, I'm afraid, Norman,' Sir Cyril argued carefully, wanting to walk out of this meeting with his skin intact. The Chief Constable's tongue could strip the proverbial paint. He glanced over to where the Deputy Chief Constable was lunching and lowered his voice. 'We really need a more impartial inquiry. Oh, I don't say Donald didn't do a thorough job. But we'd need to satisfy both London and Dublin, whether we like it or not.'

Sir Norman sat and considered the man opposite, wondering if there was something going on that he didn't know about that he came here like this. 'I'd have to think carefully about who I called in if there was to be an external inquiry,' he said cautiously, holding down the anger he could feel driving the blood into his head. 'I'll talk to some of my colleagues in the Association – surely not even Dublin could question the absolute impartiality of the Association of Chief Police Officers.'

'The Police Complaints Commission will want some say in it,' Sir Cyril ventured, believing they might prove less partial. He knew of the connection between ACPO and Freemasonry through its members, and although there was nothing sinister in that, old loyalties were difficult to ignore; this he knew from his own experience as a Freemason.

Anger was getting the better of the Chief Constable. 'We'll have no one unless I approve him. This is not the cosy fucking mainland. We're barely holding the line against these maniacs.'

'I'm aware of that. I argued as much with Timothy Faligot. But if action of some sort isn't taken, Norman,' the DPP cautioned, 'I might be forced into a position I'm reluctant to take.' He hesitated, not wanting to spell out the consequences.

Sir Norman Hateley climbed slowly out of his chair, trying to control what he was feeling. He threw his napkin down on the table. 'I'll not be responsible for what happens here if my men are charged with murder. Just so long as everyone from Michael Newfield to the Prime Minister knows the nature of the beast we might be unleashing.'

This ultimatum didn't want a reply. Sir Norman lumbered across the dining-room to where his deputy was entertaining a journalist from the *Belfast Newsletter*. 'When you've finished, Donald,' he said, 'join me in my office.' Even though this was a safe Unionist journalist, he said no more, but moved on out, more angry for being lunchless.

As he rose, lunchless also, aware that most of the senior policemen in the room were looking at him, Sir Cyril realised how much he disliked the Chief Constable. He was a bully and a bigot who ran the Six Counties as though they were his own personal fiefdom, with no gesture of consensus with the law officers, much less large sections of the population. He knew what the man was hinting at by raising Sir Michael Newfield's name, and the scandal that was waiting to burst out and touch everyone in high office in NI. At that moment he almost didn't care if it were to spill out, and almost hoped it would.

When he had calmed down back at his office where he had had a sandwich, the cost of which came well within his lunch budget, and the excess he held in his secret horse racing fund, Sir Cyril knew a scandal such as that which was always threatening couldn't be risked by an uncontrolled outside investigation. Had circumstances been other than they were, he might have held in the line, ignored the protests and sent back the papers on the Stephen McFadden killing marked 'insufficient evidence for prosecution'. But the RUC decided otherwise when the SSU stopped and shot two suspected terrorists near the Donegal border.

Almost as if in defiance of a direct order of the Chief Constable's, but certainly against his wishes, the DPP sent the papers on the Stephen McFadden killing back to the Deputy Chief Constable, stating that in the opinion of Treasury Counsel there was a better than even chance of securing convictions for murder against two principal constables involved. Further, that in the interests of justice being both done and seen to be done these men should be charged. He also sent a copy of this opinion to the chairman of the Police Complaints Commission in order to make it more difficult for the Chief Constable to ignore.

Sir Cyril regretted his move almost as soon as he had done it, and was more than a little scared that he may have put the whole province on a course that would end in disaster. And all for the sake of a Chief Constable didn't know how to consult.

The case having gone the route the DPP sent it on, the matter was out of the Chief Constable's immediate control. The Deputy Chief Constable, who was responsible for all complaints and discipline against officers, had no option but to proceed with charges. These were laid by the chief superintendent who ran G Department, which handled the day-to-day complaints and matters of discipline. Both constables were formally charged in the presence of their solicitors and suspended from duty.

The move sent out shock waves, not only through these two men and those serving in the Special Support Unit, but the RUC itself. Not because men hadn't been similarly charged before, but because they were never seen to be as vulnerable as they were over the McFadden killing.

'My client doesn't wish to say anything at this stage,' the solicitor acting for Constable Maurice Peters informed the Chief Superintendent.

Ignoring the previously received advice, Constable Peters said, 'Oh yes he bloody well does. Why me? Why pick on me and Gary?' He was sniffing and struggling against tears. All of which served to make other policemen in the charge room feel bad.

'Steady on, lad,' the Chief Superintendent advised. 'Don't say any thing you'll regret.'

'I know, but it's not fair.'

The Chief Superintendent nodded. Life was rarely that. He glanced at the two solicitors, not daring to say any more himself to these two young policemen. 'We intend taking them to court this afternoon for a Section One remand. There'll be no objection to bail.'

Nor was there from the magistrate who bailed both men in their own recognisance.

The entire episode left Sir Norman Hateley seething. Seeing any of his men, soldiers too, come to that, charged with doing a difficult and dangerous job, was to him an act of betrayal, and one he had to bear some responsibility for as he hadn't been able to stop it.

He wasn't sure what Cyril Shelldrake's position had been in this, but suspected he was bowing to pressure. It never occurred to him that he might be doing this to get at him in some way. Either way, he didn't want to see the shabby wee man, and suspected that what he wanted to tell him at this meeting he had requested wouldn't be good news.

'Charging my men with murder is no way to police the Six Counties, Cyril,' he said across the desk in his ground-floor office at Knock.

'It might be regrettable,' Sir Cyril said in a conciliatory tone, 'but I'm thinking it's necessary, Norman. There is pressure on my office to re-examine some of the shooting incidents in the recent past.'

'How long is it to be before Dublin is after telling us directly what to do? Before the terror boys have it all their own way? Fuck me, they're killing RUC men and I hear no similar cries of outrage.'

'I know it makes life difficult, but the alternative is a judicial inquiry,' Sir Cyril said, trying to exonerate himself.

The Chief Constable fixed the senior law officer with a stare, despising him for the weaseling wretch he was. 'I'd say we can have any kind of inquiry those cowardly renegades in Whitehall want,' Sir Norman said evenly. 'I'll tell you, and whoever wants to hear it, I have absolutely nothing to hide and even less to fear. Nor have any of my men. So don't come here with your hints at skeletons in cupboards. There are none in mine.'

The boldness of that statement surprised the DPP. He knew there had been a number of complaints to the RUC about pederastic activity at a community home in East Belfast, involving the judiciary and civil servants, which hadn't been properly investigated. But he didn't challenge the Chief Constable now.

'I expect those two officers to be completely exonerated by the court. We'll know them for what they are – innocent men. Then perhaps we'll be allowed to get on with the job.'

That belief for Sir Norman Hateley was an inviolable truth, and one he wouldn't be shaken from. For him the end justified the means.

9

MAURICE KNIGHT'S FORAY into the underside of South London wasn't a success, nor an experience that left him feeling that he was even half streetwise. He found a room in a flop which catered for Social Security recipients. The owner charged five pounds a night extra for a receipt for the Social Security office. The place reeked of stale vomit, sweat and disinfectant; the doors to the rooms were barely secure they had been hammered down by the police so often. The sheets weren't particularly clean, and the communal bathroom looked as if it had never been clean, but Maurice supposed the place gave him some sort of street credibility. Until the first time he left the room and had all his gear stolen. His few items of clothing were replaceable, the dope he didn't care about, but his trombone was a real loss. It was a family heirloom, though probably not worth much on the open market. His grandfather, whom he had never known, had played it in a band in Barbados; his father had played it for a while in the St John's Ambulance Band in Plymouth and had given it to Maurice when he taught him to play.

Risking blowing his cover, Maurice went to the local police station to report the theft. The policemen on the front desk weren't even superficially polite as they were in Plymouth. The desk sergeant had a laboured forbearance about him, but the edge to his manner was palpable.

'How did you come by this instrument, sir?' he asked.

'I brought it with me from Plymouth. I was hoping to get a gig or two here.'

'You bought it, did you? In Plymouth?' the sergeant said deliberately, correcting him.

'No, I brought it up here.'

'Oh you *bought* it in London?'

'No. It's old. M'dad had it.'

The desk sergeant nodded. 'So you don't have a sales receipt.'

Maurice was having difficulty understanding what was going on, but none in understanding the hostility towards the police other black people here felt. Most didn't want anything to do with them, least of all with this station. He'd assumed they were all making their living on the street from dealing.

'Look, Serge,' Maurice said, feeling frustrated and letting slip the universal familiarity, 'I came here to report a theft, all you do is treat me like a criminal. Why would I report a theft of something I'd stolen? It's stupid.'

The sergeant leaned on his knuckles and put his head closer to Maurice. 'Get flash with me, Sam, you'll lose your teeth as well as your trombone.'

Eventually Maurice had his details taken, but was told not to hope for much. He knew that the reality of over-stretched policing meant little effort would be put into it. To Maurice this was an emergency, and as such he contacted DS Tait. He didn't ask for him at the front desk but rang his number.

Tait wasn't pleased, first that Maurice arrived late, having taken the wrong tube train, then to learn why he had called him out.

'You brought me away from important work to tell me you'd lost your trombone?'

'Everything went – including that dope you gave me.'

'That won't have done you any harm. Did you find anything on Jesse Jarman's death – like a lead on Del Lindo?'

'Not yet. I did meet a dope dealer called Benny Soares. He was dealing openly in a pub.' Maurice had been shocked. 'No one took any notice.'

'What, you mean no one was buying?' The DS was surprised.

'No one called the police or anything.'

'Perhaps they knew you were there. What did Benny say?'

'Nothing much. I helped him out. He was being mugged.'

'What did you do, arrest the muggers?'

'No,' Maurice said, a little surprised. 'I didn't think you'd want me to break cover.'

DS Tait looked at him, and nodded slowly. 'Maurice, my son, you have the makings of a very corrupt policeman.'

'You didn't want me to break cover,' Maurice said, worried now.

'Don't worry about it. Stick close to Benny Soares if you can.'

'I'm seeing him this evening, at the youth club on Greenhill Farm Estate.'

'Good. All that's bent or subverted passes through there. Your face'll fit all right. They won't even think twice about you. Especially not if you're with Benny Soares.'

'I want my trombone back. Can you do anything?' Maurice asked.

'No problem. I'll call Scotland Yard, get the Serious Crime Squad to give it a look.'

His sarcasm flipped right back at him when Maurice simply said, 'Thanks.'

'Try the second-hand shops,' the DS advised. 'Everything ends up there. Here' – he passed him a new parcel of marijuana – 'it's good grass. Don't lose it this time.'

Maurice considered the dope in a plastic bag with a press seal at the top. 'How d'you get these supplies?'

Tait laughed. 'Busting dope dealers. How else – put in a request to the Receiver?' He saw the black policeman's puzzled look. He hoped it was simply because he didn't understand the role of the Receiver for the Metropolitan Police District, who was responsible for all police property in the Met and was probably the second most important person to the Commissioner.

However it was come by, whatever official right he had to it, the dope made Maurice uneasy and he thought about depositing it back at his flop, hoping it too would be ripped off. But that was also risky, as his room was as likely as not to be raided by policemen who wouldn't know he was in the job.

Short of throwing it away, he didn't quite know what to do with it, as he didn't smoke himself.

The answer came as if by divine guidance as he was heading for the youth club on the Farm.

'You got anything, man?' a black kid at his side asked as he walked across the bald sward on the estate, heading for the block that housed the club.

'What d'you want?'

'What you got?' He was about eleven years old.

'Only grass.' Maurice offered him a lid, but didn't know how much for. He had heard what the street prices in Plymouth were and tried those. The youth didn't baulk at shelling out twenty pounds for what Maurice gauged to be an ounce.

Only one or two heads turned when Maurice pulled open the double glass doors in the youth club, but he still felt all eyes were on him. Kids existing on the street had the ability to look without being seen to look, like smart detectives operating in crowds, on the look-out for those always looking.

Maurice bought himself a mug of coffee at the bar where two kids were selling familiar food: sweet potatoes, yams, green bananas; there were also crummy meat pies being warmed in a microwave. He took a plate of yams; meat pies he could get anywhere. No one challenged him as he wandered around watching the action. The really cool guys who thought themselves 'street' were playing pool, or cards, and screaming abuse at each other on account of the luck or skill of another player. Others sat and talked. There was talk of police and street politics, and Maurice would have liked to have joined in, but didn't know how to do that casually. So instead he found himself being drawn to the more seriously intended members, who wanted to get out from under and were looking to the traditional routes. Some were boxing in a fit-up ring that looked as if it would collapse if anyone were slammed into the ropes with any force; others were working out on weights; some were doing some kind of break-dancing to the heavy rock beat coming through speakers high in the wall. Maurice couldn't make out if the kids were simply looking to have fun or for a way out of the underclass. One kid did a sort of pirouette on the top of his head on a table. It impressed Maurice more than the boxing display.

'He's good,' he observed to an older youth nearby, as he settled at the side of the ring to watch a couple of fifteen-year-olds and eat his food. One was better than the other and had promise.

Maurice couldn't sit still and simply eat. His food wasn't halfway finished when he was wriggling around, ducking and diving from the blows the boxers should have been landing. He was good enough himself to turn pro and generous enough to help anyone else who might wish to. He began calling out advice. Not long after that he was at the ringside giving pointers, whether they were wanted or not. There seemed no one else around to do it.

Emerging from the office that gave directly on to the servery, Roberta Ford paused and looked the long length of the L-shaped room. She suddenly felt guilty for having promised Robertson that she'd try and get them a boxing coach, and was curious now at the man who was there doing just that. She didn't know who he was, but if he could hold the attention of the boxers like that and a few more besides, she would welcome having him around.

Roberta stepped up to the coffee urn standing on the counter to pour herself another cup, when the young man in dreadlocks working there took her mug. 'Roberta – I'll do it,' the youth said willingly. 'The tap's sticking. Coffee goes everywhere.'

That was another problem for her to deal with. The majority of the committee that ran the youth club and negotiated with the local council and anyone else for finance and facilities used their position primarily as a talking shop to air their grievances about everything from bad housing to police corruption to lack of adequate public transport. Practical details were a low priority. Coffee out of the urn was foul, but they couldn't afford a proper coffee machine.

'Who's the fella showing them boxing?' Roberta asked.

'Dunno. He came in about half an hour ago and had some grub.'

Roberta wandered across saying hello to people as she went. She was around here as often as her anthropology course at London University would allow, but most of her time here was spent fighting for the club's survival in committee, with little left for socialising. Remaining the chair of the committee and in full-time study as a third-year student was difficult, and a while back she had seriously considered giving one or the other up. Her tutor had advised her to give up the youth club; but she felt that would have been a betrayal, not only of these people, and what they represented, but of her own commitment to the underclass and their aspirations of elevating themselves even to the meagre level of working class.

She knew that there were a lot on the estate and a part of the club who had no such aspirations; they were happy to do a little dope, do some dealing, collect their Giro and stay right where they were. Jesse Jarman, who had helped her into the committee chair, told he not to bother with that trash; it wasted everyone's time and wouldn't go any place, told her to concentrate on those who wanted to be part of life's progress. She took this advice almost to the letter, and valued it more than ever now he was dead. She didn't even concern herself much with the dealing she saw, not because she approved but simply because there were more worthwhile things to worry about. She missed Jesse Jarman, more than she would have guessed. He had been someone to call up whenever there was a problem in the club, or at college come to that; a friend who would give you the time of day whenever you called on him. She shut off those thoughts to avoid crying again. She hoped his murderer would soon be found, if only because of the pressure it was putting on this community, pressure from the police that it couldn't withstand indefinitely.

'Keep your right up. Keep it up,' Maurice said to one of the boxers in the ring. 'You're letting him in.' He was inside the ring with them. They were hungry for instruction but seemed unable to grasp it quickly. 'That's better, don't let him in. It's a door, that right, when he's on the attack. Keep it closed. Feint. Let your left out. Yes.'

He climbed out of the ring to find Roberta there sipping her coffee and watching the sparring match over the top of her mug.

'Robertson's very good,' she said. She thought he had elegance in a world of street brawlers.

'He shows promise,' Maurice replied, conscious of how attractive this woman was and refusing to look at her too much. 'His reach could stop anyone getting near him.' He turned – 'Keep that right up! – he doesn't listen.'

'He's win-hungry, but no one wants to come to the Farm to help them.' Her words were left hanging.

Maurice recognised an offer when he heard one, but refused to pick it up.

'You've done boxing?'

'Some.'

Roberta found him hard going. She introduced herself and told him what she did, but could barely drag his name out of him. 'Are you going to be around?'

He turned and looked at her. 'You ask a lot of questions. You a cop?'

'I'm sorry,' Roberta said, stepping back slightly as if to avoid giving offence. 'Are you wanted by the police? I'm sorry.' She smiled apologetically, determined to press him into doing some coaching.

'It's not difficult if you're black – to be wanted by Old Bill.'

'No.' She watched, curious now. He sounded like a young black with a grudge, but didn't have the body language to go with it. Few knew better than her the problems young blacks had with the police, even though she was immune herself because of her position, the fairly high profile she kept and the fact that she was articulate. Despite that, the local police had no liking for her, and considered her politically dangerous because of the friends she kept: Jesse Jarman and the left-wing majority of the local council; the black supremacist element she supported. Also, she knew about the dealers who were paying the police and trading with them in both dope and smaller fishes.

'I 'spect I'll be around, if there's any work.'

'A lot of people are trying to crack that,' Roberta said, thinking maybe he would stay around if he was seriously interested in working. 'You could help out with their boxing, if you like – it doesn't pay anything.'

'Great. Who pays my rent?'

'Social Security – pays everybody else's.'

Maurice looked at her, deciding that her position here might be useful to his purpose. He said, 'I'm waiting for someone. He said he might have some work for me. Benny Soares.'

Instinctively she took half a step back, not even wanting to be associated with acquaintances of Soares. She couldn't believe that she had read this man so wrongly, to find he was in with someone who represented everything that was negative to the kids around here. 'You with that trash?' She couldn't keep the shock out of her voice.

'It's work.'

'Getting nine- and ten-year-olds to make dope deliveries and take all the risks!' Roberta spat the words out.

'They're below the age of criminal responsibility.' That wasn't what Maurice wanted to say. He wanted to say he was on her side, that he would help bust Benny Soares and all the other dealers. That he was a policeman, as if hoping that might impress her – it didn't too often impress black people, not even in Plymouth. 'Why don't you call the police on him?'

Roberta laughed. 'They supply him half the time.'

Maurice didn't say anything, but thought of the ready supply of dope DS Tait had.

Roberta glanced at her watch, knowing she had to go, to get back to the Students' Union to obtain some tickets for the talk the Home Secretary was giving. She wanted to ask him again to stay on and give some help, but ignored her instinct that told her he was basically all right and might be brought round. Instead, she followed her head and decided if he was with Benny Soares he wasn't really worth bothering about.

There seemed to be a lot of policemen about the Students' Union building and she had difficulty getting in, even though it belonged to the students! It was more like preparations for a swamp raid on the Farm than a talk by a senior politician to a group of students. Some would obviously protest against his visit, and might even try to have it stopped, but she hadn't heard of anything being planned to warrant this police presence.

The Union building was in a wide and institution-lined street, with a stolid appearance. The most disturbance it saw was when students got drunk after their finals and ran across the tops of parked cars, and so Roberta found it unsettling to see so many police, more so than when they appeared on the Farm where their presence was the norm.

'Goodness, are you expecting an invasion by the WRP or someone?' Roberta asked an earnest-looking girl with spots. She was putting out plastic stacking chairs in the small theatre on the first floor.

'You never can tell, can you? Some people will try to spoil anything. It is the Home Secretary.'

'Are you Amanda Bryant? – I was told you had spare tickets for tonight.'

'They are for students, aren't they? We don't want yobs getting in.'

'Oh yes, they're all students,' Roberta lied without any conscience, knowing that two of the tickets were for two members of the local council's Police Advisory Committee, who wanted to ask the Home Secretary some difficult questions. They didn't share her optimism about the meeting being orderly, and might even contribute to its disorder.

'The police are going to throw anyone out without a ticket.'

'Can they do that?' Roberta was surprised. She thought they might have the power to stop people on the street, but not eject them from their own building.

'Yes – they've been invited in by the president and the administrator,' the spotty girl confided as she gave Roberta the tickets.

Roberta was shocked at that. At a Students' Union Council meeting she had attended, no such question had been raised, much less approved. She went off in search of the president or the administrator.

'Anything that resembles yobbish behaviour we will squash before it gets out of control,' their section commander had said at their briefing earlier that afternoon. He in turn had heard it at the strategy meeting earlier in the day. PC Gareth Jackson squeezed his grip expander and thought about the words. He was feeling good about the whole operation. This was his first outing as part of the Mobile District Support Unit and somehow he had expected to be more excited. Instead he was very calm.

'There are going to be a lot of policemen there. More than enough to deal with a bunch of students,' the section commander had said. 'If we have to go in, go in hard, but don't fuck around. Lick a few heads. We don't want a bunch of poxy longhairs embarrassing the Home Secretary.'

'Can we embarrass him by asking for more money, guv?' one of the lads had asked the serials inspector.

Everyone had laughed. Most had felt relaxed then.

'One other thing, there'll be a lot of Branch detectives mingling with students both inside and outside the building. Make sure you don't go whacking any of them. Or nicking them.'

'How will we know, guv?'

'They'll all have Special Branch written on their anoraks.'

Everyone had laughed again. Trouble was still a couple of hours away. When the order to move out came, the atmosphere changed instantly.

Inside the locker room at the Mobile District Support Unit's station, where PC Jackson was based, there was a tense, expectant air as his colleagues ritualistically donned their protective clothing, examined each strap and zipper for security. The room was full of excited macho and sexist banter that tumbled out with nervous laughter. The experienced men had learnt that every excursion was different, they never knew what they would meet, from an armed siege to football hooligans with too much ale in them, to the overtly political demonstrators whose ends justified any means.

Not knowing what to expect was part of the excitement which attracted a lot of these officers to the job. Feeling the adrenalin pump into the system, and sometimes finding an excuse to release it was great. Sometimes officers left the Units suffering from adrenal exhaustion as a result of prolonged adrenal stimulation; they'd get run down, debilitated by a series of minor infections, irritable, liable to explode, a danger to themselves and the colleagues they served with.

'You'll do all right here, Gareth,' a constable said to the new man to the Unit. 'Forget those old plonks you usually pull. You can feel up one of these students.'

'More than one, I hope, man,' Gareth Jackson responded. He was ready to go. In his hand he had his grip expander, which he worked as he sat on the bench pumping up his forearms.

'You want to watch they don't bite you,' another policeman cautioned. 'You might get AIDS.'

They all laughed, knowing how disease-ridden most students

were. Even the graduates among their own ranks were approached charily.

They were dressed and ready, but for one more thing – a personal weapon, or maybe two or three. Some preferred the standard pick-axe handle, baseball bat or brass knuckles, which could be taken into the crowd and used surreptitiously; one took a small axe, another took a sap. Most of these weapons were left in their vans, within easy reach, and only reached for in extreme provocation. On the whole long staves and shields did the job nicely.

Outside the Union building only about a hundred students had gathered by six-thirty and with the Home Secretary due to arrive to speak at seven the police began to relax slightly. Clearly with the sort of numbers they had around and about they could deal easily with the students outside; the Conservative students on the inside would represent no sort of problem. They were on the same side, more or less; supporters of the status quo.

Despite feeling more relaxed, they didn't relax the rules they had laid down to maintain order. The sergeant and three constables who stood on the double steel and glass doors at the top of the steps were letting in only the chosen few. Approaching students were challenged with a brusque, 'Where do you think you're going?'

That was how Stanley Scone, a third-year sociology student, was greeted. He wasn't particularly interested in the meeting, or in politics, having at twenty-one found most of the answers and decided that none of the political parties were worth supporting owing to their obvious inability to tackle most of the problems that confronted modern society. All Stanley Scone wanted was a decent degree to secure his place on the career ladder at the finish of his course. He was the first person in his family to have a university education and he intended making the very best of it. He wasn't interested in dramatically changing society, and of the fifty-seven thousand students belonging to the university he believed the majority were exactly the same. When challenged by the policeman on the door, Stanley told him that he was going to the first-floor bar. He often went there to socialise, and the beer was cheaper than in the local pubs.

'It's closed,' the sergeant told him. 'Are you a student?'

'Of course. It can't be, it's only six-thirty.'

'That's what I've been told – till after the Home Secretary's gone. We all have to suffer these hardships.'

'Well, I'll go into the sitting-room then,' Stanley tried. He didn't really want to be out here waiting, for he'd feel obliged to join the protesting students.

'You can't go inside – I've just told you. Not unless you have a ticket for the talk.'

'But it's our building,' Stanley said in vain.

'Why don't you fuck off,' the sergeant said quietly, 'before you find yourself nicked?'

That surprised, affronted and threatened Stanley Scone. He had had little contact with the police, and from a distance had found them to be attractive, even admirable in the way they did a difficult job. He had at one point thought about joining them, knowing that they were welcoming graduates with offers of secure, well-paid employment and rapid promotion. Had he been taller and not already decided to become a social worker, he might have been put off a police career by this experience. He looked around as if to appeal to the other students who had joined them, but they seemed not to have heard the abuse and were more concerned that they were not allowed in; two students with tickets were let through, and went quickly, keen not to be associated with those who were barred.

Stanley withdrew with the other students, with whom he commiserated. After this shared experience he had no option but to join the crowd on the pavement, which had grown in size. He didn't want to be there and was determined to get into the building. He went round the block to try and enter by the back door. He was shocked to find what seemed like hundreds of policemen filing into the building, dressed as though they were expecting trouble. He hurried back round the building to tell other students, feeling he couldn't simply walk away, despite himself.

Word spread quickly, painting a blacker picture of police intentions with each mouth it passed through. Tension increased among the students as more and more arrived. As seven o'clock approached there were an estimated six hundred gathered outside, more than were inside waiting for the Home Secretary. A lot of them had ended up there by accident, as Stanley had; others had come with more serious intentions. They started chanting, 'Why are we waiting?' 'Two, four, six, eight, who is it we all hate?', and a lone voice through a megaphone: 'What do we want?' 'Freedom from oppression,' came the chorus, along with a few personal options. 'When do we want it?' asked the girl with the megaphone. She was drowned out by a roar in unison of, 'Now, now, now!'

Caught up in the uniting energy of the cause, students were

oblivious to the Special Branch detectives decked in grubby anoraks, jeans and running shoes as they moved among them marking out the likely leaders, ready to pass back details on them to the uniform branch for when they went in to sort out the troublemakers. Life was easier if they were identified beforehand.

Lefty Morgan who had been in the Branch for about a year was invariably picked for this sort of operation on account of his relative youth and the fact that he had himself been a student at Swansea University – a real hotbed of radicalism – hence his nickname. It wasn't a name he would have chosen for himself, even at his most ironic, but he knew that the more you kicked against such pricks in the police force the more you were made to suffer. He had been made to suffer on account of his bad skin that became inflamed when he was under stress, and for the fact that he was a history graduate. The day would come when he would convert Lefty to Lofty, even though he wasn't especially tall in a tall profession.

The student with the megaphone was an obvious target for many of the policemen on duty, if only because under her nylon mac she had big tits. She also had a big mouth. Lefty Morgan couldn't stand women with big mouths. He ignored her. His interest was taken by a girl who was passing out eggs. His inclination was to step in and arrest her, but he knew better. Instead, he moved to the edge of the crowd and found a police inspector he could approach unobtrusively, and indicated the girl with the eggs.

'Did they search you?' Stanley Scone asked, as Lefty Morgan moved back into the crowd.

'Yeah, the bastards,' he said vehemently. 'They ought to get some stick as well as the Home Secretary. We ought to break one or two paving slabs for them.' He smiled to himself, his identity secure.

A series of updates about what was happening outside the Union building were reaching the DSU serials in the adjacent street, but the policemen who formed up outside their reinforced trucks could hear the chanting and were keen to start. PC Gareth Jackson was feeling excited and a little apprehensive. They had reports of the Home Secretary's progress from Parliament. He was running fifteen minutes late and tension was mounting. They should have been halfway done by now, and some of the men had already gone slack as if after sex, only without an orgasm; others were left feeling as they felt when hyped up to an event only to be let down at the last moment, not knowing where to put their energy and often venting it on the first unfortunate to cross their path.

'Come on, come on, where the fuck is he?' one of them said. 'Let's get the soapy sods sorted.'

Gareth Jackson said nothing to his neighbour at this outburst, but instead continued working his grip expanders, first one hand, then the other. The muscles in his forearms had a hardness and definition like iron when he closed his fingers into a fist. He was as impatient as his colleague to get stuck in, but working the expanders kept the energy nicely moving rather than boiling over.

'He's just coming into the square.' The information came over the Superintendent's personal radio, and ran quickly around the eighty or so men. They stirred as one.

'Right,' the Superintendent said. 'We're going in to clear those steps. We go in hard, get those students back from the steps and we keep them back.' He used the royal 'we', but he wouldn't be going in himself at all.

The four inspectors had their serials form up, ten men under each of the eight sergeants, who all ran to it when the order to move out was given.

The students didn't know whether to put their attention on the black Daimler as it turned into the street with police outriders, or the menacing blue wedge suddenly driving at them.

With two of the DSU serials forming the sides of a thick arrowhead, the police drove into the students who were blocking the three wide steps and the pavement in front of the Union building; the forty-odd men from the other two serials filled the centre of the wedge, grabbing the students and pulling them through their ranks; other officers dragged them off to the waiting police vans. As the police pushed in harder towards the double doors, the students could go only two ways: down the steps, manhandled by the police, or over the stone parapets at the side of the steps to fall twenty feet into the basement area, but either way the steps were taken. The police had surprise on their side. The students were unorganised as such and didn't expect these antics, nor such violence. Some were punched indiscriminately, kicked or dragged out by hair or clothing; some gave the police extreme provocation by shouting out or protesting; few fought back; the most foolhardy landed ineffectual blows on the thick padding the officers were wearing.

PC Gareth Jackson had put his grip expander away when he went in as part of the right flank, and drove his fists into whoever was in front of him and making the most noise. He punched a woman in the chest and saw her fall back in pain. He could anticipate what would happen as his colleagues pushed from behind and the students immediately behind the front line pushed the other way – the woman would be trampled. He didn't want that. He reached down and pulled her up. Her huge breasts more than filled his large hands as he took her from behind and dragged her out. He squeezed those breasts through her clothing, causing a stirring in his groin. Reluctantly he passed her to a colleague behind him, then turned back to punch his way further up the steps.

'Move or get your fucking head kicked!' he bellowed at a student in front of him. The student couldn't move, he was compressed into the crowd as the police continued to force them back.

With sharp jabbing movements from his elbow, PC Jackson hit a student in the face several times, casuing him to drop his placard and lose his glasses. 'Sorry,' he said, 'I didn't see you there.' He grinned at a colleague by his side.

'This one'll go,' the colleague said, and grabbed a girl by the crotch and collar and swung her round to drive her behind him and down the steps, not taking his hand off her crotch until he had to.

Policemen filling the wedge were no less harsh in their treatment of the student, throwing them backwards with punches and kicks. One black student had his glasses ripped off, then stamped on.

The steps were secured in about a minute, just as the black Daimler stopped at the kerb. But the students were undeterred and hurled what abuse they could find at the man who had the highest level of responsibility for the police. Whatever intention there might have been for constructive barracking was lost to unco-ordinated, violent name-calling. Stanley Scone had never been on a demo before and was shocked and angry that the authorities could behave in this way, that the Home Secretary was prepared to have this done in his name. He joined the name-calling.

The Home Secretary cowered under every barb from 'racist bastard' to 'dirty cunt' as he was propelled without dignity or grace from the car and through the police bodies. There was a moment's panic at the top of the steps when the doors were found to be locked and this very senior member of the government was left stranded like some frightened misbegotten whale.

Even Roberta, with fewer expectations of the police than most, was startled by their tactics. She hadn't been able to find her friends to give them the tickets. She assumed they couldn't get through, and she wasn't going to risk leaving the building for fear of not being able to reenter it. There were questions she would like to put to the

Home Secretary herself. As she was thought a responsible person, even by the CSA – despite being directly opposed to them politically – Roberta was asked if she'd distribute unclaimed tickets to other students wanting them. She did, but not very responsibly, finding as many students in the building as she could who she believed would give the Home Secretary a hard time. The theatre was not going to be packed with government supporters, if that was what the organisers hoped for. After what Roberta had witnessed from the police outside, there was no way the Home Secretary would be guaranteed any sort of platform, if she had anything to do with it.

An angry buzz about what was happening outside went round the four hundred students jammed into the small theatre; some rushed out to see for themselves. The students' anger increased as the Home Secretary entered the room and made a dash with his police escort for the rostrum that had been set up. The heckling and name-calling started at once.

'Fascist! Fascist! Fascist! Fascist! Fascist!' came from a group of Asian women at the back of the hall, and Roberta felt instinctively and ethnically drawn to them. Even some members of the Conservative Students' Association joined in.

The small, round figure of the Home Secretary looked comical alongside the beanpole chairman of the CSA, and desperately vulnerable as they stood at the microphone. He produced a tight smile for the young people before him, but it scarcely concealed his fear. Only outwardly was he calm. Inside there was a storm of anxiety. The thought of having to pass back through those students made him feel sick, while the thought of slipping out the back way like a thief in the night made him feel worse.

The chairman of the CSA stooped to the microphone, tapped it and started to introduce the Home Secretary. She got nowhere. She tried again. 'If the yobs who have managed to get in despite everything would just shut up for two minutes . . .' That was all she managed to say.

The Home Secretary smiled again, deciding to employ his long experience as a public speaker. On many occasions when he had been shouted down in the House by the Opposition, or on the hustings by hecklers, he had found the best approach was to speak through them. 'Public order . . .' he said into the microphone. And hearing his voice boom back at him he smiled, reassured. '. . . Public order is not only a fact of life, this government is determined to make it a way of life. The rule of intimidation by the mob is over.

Freedom of speech on any subject within the law, by any law-abiding subject of the United Kingdom is inviolate –'

It was at that point that a black student sprang on to the rostrum, causing it to rock, the Home Secretary to pull back in panic, and nearby police officers to leap forward. They didn't move fast enough to stop the microphone being wrecked.

The arrest of the black student by the half-dozen white policemen dressed in blue caused a lot of other students to see red. Students of all colours of skin and politics rushed the stage and the Home Secretary abandoned his speech.

The actual as well as the symbolic defeat of this senior politician in their presence was a potent catalyst for the police. They couldn't be seen to be in any way responsible for his going out with his tail between his legs, the freedom of speech he proclaimed being so obviously denied to him. They had to win back something of his dignity, restore a little of his pride.

The local Chief Superintendent who approached him was not best advised by anyone for his suggestion: 'Sir! It might be better if we take you out the back way, sir.'

He was withered to an ash by the politician's look. 'You obviously fail to appreciate the significance of our policy on public order if you imagine I'm going to slink away.'

That was all the Chief Superintendent wanted to do at that moment, as the Home Secretary marched down the terrazzo stairs towards the front entrance, a dozen policemen, his two personal detectives and a number of Special Branch officers with baseball bats at his flank.

His descent of the wide front steps was no more dignified than his brief ascent, and he chose not to see the way the students were dealt with. He was put into his car and driven away.

With the Home Secretary safely gone, there, in theory, the police action should have ended. But there was something to win back after that frontal assault on their credibility.

The order was given to clear the street and DSUs set about it with a vengeance, backed up by local policemen and ably assisted by those in plain clothes who brought forward the troublemakers. After the climax of the Home Secretary's flight, the students were for the second time that evening found to be unprepared. The last thing they expected was a police operation more violent than the previous.

Students scattered with no reason to stay, but many didn't move fast enough and they were either struck or arrested, often both.

Eleven people were arrested prior to the Home Secretary's arrival, not including the black student at the meeting. Thirty-seven were arrested after his departure. The prison van taking them to the various charging stations wasn't going fast enough, and one of the last to be arrested was put into a maroon Austin Montego belonging to the Special Branch and taken in by PC Gareth Jackson. She was Roberta Ford.

She had pursued the Home Secretary out of the lecture theatre, still intent on tackling him, but hadn't been able to get near him. She wasn't surprised by the violence from the police that erupted in the wake of his departure – that was something citizens on the Farm frequently suffered – but she was sorry to see the students on the receiving end.

Seeing the flamboyant Claud Fentiman, the students' governing council's vice-chair, in his pink jacket, where he stood on the top of the steps remonstrating with police officers about their violence, she had gone to give him her support as a council member.

'It's done now,' Claud was shouting angrily. 'It's done. Just get out, get out! Clear the building. Don't come back, any of you, ever again. Get out!'

Policemen looked at him as if with no immediate comprehension of this outburst. Finally one of them grabbed him by his buttoned-up shirt collar and crashed him against the visor of his helmet, having had just about enough of students for one night without this one, who they thought was on their side, abusing them. Other students tried to intervene and they were bundled down the steps and arrested along with Claud Fentiman.

'You can't do that,' Roberta had said, coming through the doors at the policemen. 'Stop that!'

'Shut your mouth, you black cunt,' PC Gareth Jackson had told her and punched her on the collar bone, knocking her down the steps into other policemen at the bottom.

He had followed her and grabbed hold of her, noticing how good looking she was for a black. He'd decided to arrest her for assault.

The sergeant in his section told him to take her around to the van. The van was missing, but a car was offered by Lefty Morgan, who said he thought she was political. He'd see her there later. He had other political agitators to collect.

10

A STATE OF DEEP SHOCK settled over Roberta Ford when she found herself alone in a police cell. Being in a cell wasn't a new experience, she'd been arrested before on demonstrations and had also visited police cells to speak with young black people who'd been arrested and wouldn't speak to anyone but her. But being alone in a cell was new to her.

Arriving here when she had done nothing more than tell a policeman to stop hitting a fellow student councillor undermined her confidence. Perhaps she wasn't immune to police harassment after all. She tried to tell herself that the constable who had arrested her didn't realise who she was; that all she needed was a more senior policeman to arrive and she would be released, or at least dealt with decently. Perhaps that was too much to expect. She was black after all, and knew from her experience on the Farm that that oafish constable who had punched her and called her racist names was only typical. Policemen who worked the streets responded like that every day, despite senior policemen saying it didn't happen, or politicians saying racialism was being eradicated from the police institutions. Too many senior policemen either tolerated racism or were racists. From her studies she understood the fear people had of other cultures, and only when times were good, when society was stable and secure, would people tolerate the alien, whether by speech, colour or habit. Now, as times were getting harder, society less stable, the hopes she had once held weren't as buoyant.

She would complain about the constable for what he had called her, she would make a note of his collar number when she saw him again. She had forgotten to ask his name when she was arrested. She reminded young blacks of that hundreds of times, only to forget herself when it mattered. She began to feel angry with herself for being so stupid. She didn't even know what police station she was at. She hadn't noticed the route they had taken but thought that they hadn't gone far. She had been unconcerned at first about where she was, assuming she would be with other arrested students. In fact she had seen no one. That was strange. Where was Claud Fentiman? He had been arrested ahead of her. He should be here somewhere.

She didn't know what was happening, but whatever it was meant that they weren't receiving any attention. She had her finger jammed on the call bell in the clean, bare modern cell but the custody officer didn't respond. Usually a thirty-second blast was enough to get them running.

Knowing that to antagonise the police by continually ringing the bell was risky, Roberta nevertheless still had faith in her immunity and clung to the vague notion that no harm could befall her. But despite this, she withdrew to the back of the cell when finally she heard someone outside the door. The shutter opened and a policeman she hadn't seen before looked in.

'You try'na break that fucking bell, Cind?' he said, and slammed the shutter without waiting for a reply.

Roberta instinctively pulled back into the corner of the cell on the bed bench and drew her knees up to her chest, then wrapped her arms about herself as if to make the smallest target possible.

The bolt was drawn and the door opened. The constable stepped inside with the one who had arrested her. PC Kevin Pratley was smiling as though the young black woman was doing something funny. PC Gareth Jackson was scowling as if expecting trouble. He was. Special Branch had said she was probably a member of the Black Supremacists. That lot were trouble for any white person, much less a white policeman.

'Why am I here – am I being charged?' Roberta asked.

The two policemen shot each other looks. There was an excited gleam in their eyes; adrenalin from the demo had yet to leave their bloodstream.

'I need to see a doctor – my shoulder hurts.'

'We'll get you a doctor,' PC Gareth Jackson said.

'S'a nice-looking black girl like you doing hanging around that white student trash?' PC Pratley wanted to know. He laughed; so did PC Jackson.

'I'm a student – I'm reading anthropology.'

'Trying to find out when you climbed out of the trees, Cind?'

The more they could wind her up the better they liked it. Some prisoners responded like epileptics if enough pressure was put on them. Roberta's mouth went suddenly dry when she noticed that

98

neither policeman was wearing a collar number. They were sometimes instructed to take them out to avoid being identified.

'You fucking students think you can behave as you like. You're a Black Supremacist, right. Want to cut off the balls of all the little white boys and shove them in their gobs. Isn't that right?'

Roberta started to shake her head, but shut her eyes instead, as if to stop this altogether.

'That's what they want to do, a guy in the Branch told me.'

Courage deserted Roberta and she couldn't make any sort of reply.

'Undress, we'll search you in case you're concealing anything.'

Roberta pulled her knees closer to her body, and said, 'I'm not – I don't have to – I don't.'

'You most certainly do, you black cunt. Get them off or we'll take them off.'

PC Jackson stepped up to her, followed by PC Pratley.

Roberta suddenly burst into tears and felt ashamed of herself. Why it happened she wasn't sure; not because of the verbal assault – she had heard worse in equally threatening circumstances. Tears didn't come easily to her. She had cried when she had learned of Jesse Jarman's death, and thought perhaps these tears were to do with that. Jesse had given her strength, as he had a lot of black people; he'd made them feel proud of what they were, never to think of themselves as an underclass or a criminal class. He had always been prepared to bring his actions into line with his mouth, and it was his passing, his absence, she realised, that made her feel so vulnerable.

'Please. I don't want to. I need to see a doctor . . . There should be a policewoman present,' she said, despite having little faith that a WPC's presence would change anything.

'Know all the rules, don't you, Cindy,' PC Gareth Jackson said. 'You're right, of course.' He turned to his colleague. 'We may as well do it properly. Get a couple of plonks. They can hold her.'

The two WPCs, both of whom were little older than Roberta, stood and watched with their hands on their hips while she undressed painfully slowly. 'Can you go a little faster? We're very busy tonight.' Then when Roberta hesitated at her bra and pants, 'All the way. You've got to have a proper body search.'

They were faintly amused by this, and faintly resentful of the black woman having advantages they didn't have; she was good-looking, able to go to university, where people learned among other things to be articulate and not be afraid of the police.

On the cell-block corridor there was silence apart from the faint buzzing from one of the call bells in the custody officer's empty room, plus the quickening breathing of PCs Jackson and Pratley as they jostled one another out of line with the viewer in the door. Both were getting an erection as if by a shared thought, and both knew what they would like to do to this black woman, but neither quite knew how far the other was prepared to go, especially not with the two WPCs present. The chances were they would see it as a bit of fun too. Neither of them quite understood the sexual arousal they felt in situations like the one earlier that evening, feelings that grabbing the odd breast or crotch could ever satisfy.

Still not quite believing this was happening to her, Roberta stepped out of her pants and glanced to the door in panic as the two constables walked towards her, smiling from ear to ear. She covered herself with her hands and hunched herself forwards.

'Come on, don't be shy, Cindy, let's have a look at you,' PC Pratley said, stepping forward to examine her, as he would goods in a bazaar. 'I bet you're not shy with all those students. Let them go through you, do you?'

Unable to think of a coherent reply, Roberta backed away until she was against the pale green painted brick wall. She wanted to scream some protest, but her throat and mouth remained dry and tense and she couldn't swallow.

'We have to make an intimate body search. You don't mind that, do you?'

Roberta started shaking her head to indicate that they couldn't, but realised that was quite the wrong gesture when both men closed on her. 'Please . . .' she managed. 'A doctor . . . please . . . get . . . a doctor . . .'

'We haven't got time, Cind, a dangerous drugs dealer like you. You've obviously stuffed them.'

Pushing against the wall, Roberta became aware of a pain near the small of her back a wet sensation where the pressure had broken the skin and caused her to draw blood. By continuing to press back and concentrating on this pain she was able to blot out the policemen, until they grabbed hold of her. She struggled to push the small of her back against the wall and re-establish contact with the pain. It was preferable to the violation they had in mind.

'Hold her,' PC Pratley told the WPCs. They took Roberta firmly by the wrists and pulled her on to the hard bed shelf which had no mattress.

Suddenly a sound emerged from her throat, startling Roberta as much as the police officers. It was a scream. She went on screaming. PC Jackson quickly shut the cell door, and one of the WPCs slapped her face, shocking her momentarily to silence.

Then she sobbed with a suppressed hysteria while she struggled against the hands that were restraining her. One of the constables had his face close to hers and was breathing heavily. He had bad breath. That more than anything else inexplicably made her give up the struggle. 'No,' she hissed on all but the last of her breath. 'No.' Then it was gone, and she retreated into herself. She felt something penetrate her vagina and her anus almost simultaneously. The pressure on her caused the small of her back to dig into the concrete bed shelf and she made contact with that pain again and clung to it.

'Where the fuck have you been?' the sergeant from his DSU serial said when he returned. 'We've been waiting for you. We thought you'd got buried.'

'Not quite, skip,' PC Gareth Jackson said as he climbed into the van. There were only seven other policemen there. 'Had to escort a prisoner.'

'Do any good, did you?' one of the constables said. There was an electric feeling in the van, like they were all charged and ready for action rather than being stood down.

'They all look like they need a bloody good wash,' PC Jackson said. 'They don't learn that at university.' He settled with his grip expander and began to work it as they waited for the last two men to turn in, which they did soon afterwards.

As they drove back to base none of the policemen were ready to stand down, and were either bragging about their part in the demo, who they'd hit or felt up, or were on the look-out for new action.

PC Gareth Jackson was silent as he continued to work on his grip. He was one of the first to see the two black youths in a car which they looked as if they shouldn't have been in. But the policeman next to him was the first to articulate the single thought they shared. 'Look at the tints! They need a tug.'

Everyone's attention was on the two young black men in the 2.6 Rover that was stopped at traffic lights in the Edgware Road. Even the police driver was watching. He automatically slipped the van into gear and was ready to pop the clutch in if he got the word.

Anxiety rose high enough in the two youths to ring an alarm bell at this sort of attention, even though they were only driving around looking for girls. Tension caused the car to go away from the lights too fast.

The DSU driver needed no order; it was in the air. He roared after the car, overtook it and cut across its path, forcing it to stop.

Policemen leaped from the van and dragged the two youths out of their car with body punches that left them helpless. They found this as bad as their worst nightmare, which was having armed policemen burst into your Mum's home in the middle of the night.

'Where's your driving licence, you thieving bastard?'

'Where d'you nick the car?' – no one had bothered getting on to the station to check with the Police National Computer whether the car was stolen. They would have had an answer back before the lights changed.

'I gottit, I gottit, sir.' The driver didn't slip his hand into his pocket quickly enough. The policeman pulled it away and ripped open the pocket. He was disappointed to find a current driving licence.

'What you coons up to? Delivering dope?'

'No, sir. No! Jes' driving around.'

'Looking for what you can nick?'

Without warning, Jackson's helmet crashed against the youth's head as if it were a football. Then, taking hold of him, he dragged him towards the DSU van and banged his head against the door. There was a roar of approval.

Seeing the possibility of this getting out of hand, even though there weren't too many people around in the Edgware Road at that time of night, the sergeant stepped in. 'All right, all right, that's enough.' He glanced over the driving licence. The details were in order, the age fitted. 'These are only working lads, not students,' he added as if to placate his men's blood lust.

'We ought to nick this coon, skip, for damaging police property,' said one, pointing to the dent in the side of the police van.

Everyone laughed, but the laughter was more restrained. The men had let out some of the steam, now they were coming down. The problem of tension which most policemen felt after demonstrations and riots, and which DSU policemen felt most acutely, wasn't easily resolved. Sometimes they travelled the streets for hours looking for trouble, and too often they found it.

*   *   *

No one knew who had brought Roberta Ford to the police station or what she was to be charged with, if indeed she was to be charged. So, after his provisional inquiries when no one claimed the collar, the station officer decided to let her go. They could have charged her with obstruction or disorderly behaviour like most of the other students, but if the arresting officer couldn't be bothered, the duty sergeant saw no reason to chase him, especially not when it could have been any of three hundred men.

'You are not going to be charged at the present,' the sergeant said, as if to leave the option open.

Roberta stood in front of the desk in the charge room where she had been brought by a WPC and stared at the ragged splinters at the edge. She didn't respond, not because she couldn't think of anything to say, but rather because she couldn't push the words up and over the barrier of shock.

The sergeant glanced at the WPC, as if for some explanation. None was forthcoming, so he said, 'Would you like us to phone anyone to have them collect you?'

After a long moment Roberta slowly shook her head.

What had happened in the cell had rendered Roberta numb. The shock of the assault had left her without a thought of complaining or trying to identify the policemen. She could barely function physically; her thoughts refused to reach out and probe the violation; it had robbed her of all the confidence she once had. It was as if a sluice gate had been suddenly opened and a reservoir emptied. She couldn't get on a bus, and the thought of hailing a cab terrified her. She started to walk southwards towards her home. When she got to Blackfriars Bridge and stopped and looked at the inky water dotted with reflected lights, she found herself attracted to it.

She could submerge herself in it, hide until the fearful numbness had gone away, until she had recovered. No one would believe what had happened, so she couldn't tell anyone. She scarcely believed it herself. All she had to do was slip over the parapet and let herself float down into the water, submerge with all those thoughts and feelings that were pushing against the barrier of numbness. Only a debilitating lethargy that had descended upon her stopped her mounting that parapet. There was nowhere to hide from the world back at her flat, or at college or at the youth centre at the Farm. Perhaps if she stayed there long enough she would overcome her lethargy.

The car that crept along the kerb to halt opposite Roberta had gone past once, turned at the end of the bridge, come back and turned again. Before leaning across the front passenger seat and winding down the window the driver made certain there were no policemen about. He had had that sort of trouble before.

'Do you want a lift, dear?' He gave a little laugh. This was a real bonus, finding one to pick up out here. Blackfriars wasn't a regular patch for prostitutes.

There was no immediate response from the girl, other than her turning and looking at him. The driver wasn't deterred. He glanced around again in case the police had crept on to the scene. He wasn't prepared to wait too long.

'Do you want to do any business, dear?'

'Leave me alone.' The words emerged from Roberta like a deep and painful moan. Then louder as anger fountained out of her, pushing her towards hysteria.

The driver pulled back into his seat without shutting the window, let in the clutch and the car roared away.

Roberta started along the pavement in the same direction. She kept running, believing she could run away from what was behind her, if she couldn't submerge herself in the water. She didn't stop running until she reached her flat.

There were lights on in the flat, but Roberta managed to avoid Sally Hedley, her flatmate, and fled to the bathroom where she locked herself in and pulled off her clothes and climbed into the bath and ran the shower. She couldn't bear the idea of lying in the bath water but wanted to wash away all trace of that violation; she let the shower run and run. How long she stayed there she didn't know; it seemed like hours but still she didn't feel clean. Finally she heard Sally banging on the bathroom door. There was concern in her voice as she asked if she was all right. Roberta didn't answer, but couldn't help thinking how such a thing could never have happened to Sally, simply because she was white.

Three days passed before Roberta was able to say anything about what had happened to her, three days during which she confined herself to her bedroom or the bathroom, unable to answer anyone's concerned inquiries about her. She made no response to comments about the awful treatment some of the students had received at the hands of the police. She couldn't reply to questions from other committee members at the Farm youth centre when they telephoned about problems. If she was on her own she didn't answer the phone or the doorbell. As she rattled around the flat, all the right thoughts about what to do about what had happened started to seep into her mind, but she couldn't put them into effect. Everything was too much of an effort. Nothing seemed worthwhile any more. This wasn't a case that had been reported to her, that she was going to fight on another's behalf. This had actually happened to her, and as a result she felt somehow she had failed all those people she had struggled for in the past. It was as if by the very fact of her inviolability she had been saying to them that they too could achieve that state, but now they couldn't.

When she finally told Sally what had happened, there was an air of disbelief that yawned like a chasm between them.

'They did, Sally,' Roberta insisted. 'The two of them while two policewomen held me.'

'Oh my God. What did you do?' Sally didn't know how to express her feelings. She had been to rape-counselling sessions organised by the Students' Union, where practical advice was given for just such a contingency, but she realised those giving the advice had never been raped. She didn't actually know anyone who had been raped before, and a room-mate was about as close as you could get. Advice at those seminars had been to involve the police, who were learning to be more sympathetic! But what did you do when it was the police who had committed the rape?

'You've got to make a complaint against the police,' Sally said. 'You've got to. Lots of the students are, after the demo.'

'I don't know. I don't . . . Who's going to believe me?' Roberta burst into tears. The one person who would have believed her without question was Jesse Jarman. It was almost as if there was nothing worth fighting for any more.

Sally was a tower of strength and remembered all the right moves to make: first, get a medical examination. There was no likelihood of semen still being present in the vagina, but the college doctor was sympathetic and found an equally sympathetic psychiatrist. Then Sally found a helpful solicitor – Roberta knew any number, but didn't want to go to a politically motivated lawyer.

Martin Potter operated out of two shabby rooms above a betting shop in The Cut, Waterloo. He was young, enthusiastic and patient and listened carefully to all the details Roberta gave him from the moment she arrived at the Students' Union.

'I think a complaint against the police in these circumstances is going to be impossibly difficult, Roberta,' he said finally. 'Not least because you waited three days before you sought medical help.'

Roberta nodded, as if accepting the hopelessness of the case. 'I couldn't do anything afterwards. I felt paralysed.'

'I understand. The psychologist made that perfectly clear in his report.' He glanced at the typed document in his hand which stated that both her physical and mental states were consistent with someone who had been raped, as indeed did the report of the rape counsellors who also saw her. 'Despite all the difficulties we're likely to encounter, I feel we should proceed with the complaint, Roberta. Even if at the end of the day it's not upheld it might make other policemen think twice. I don't know if you're prepared for that sort of martyrdom. I don't know if you're prepared to go through all the suffering you will doubtless go through, telling and retelling your story, but if you can find the strength to do it, you should.'

Roberta didn't respond immediately, but somehow she knew she would find the strength from somewhere to act.

11

'WHAT'S THE STORY, Jack?' Deputy Commissioner Harry Streeter asked as he came through the ante-room of his office.

This was one of the few occasions Jack Bentham enjoyed waiting for a meeting to start. He was enjoying talking to the Deputy Commissioner's secretary; she was desperately shy, he had discovered at dinner with her the other night, and far more intelligent than her job of senior policeman's secretary would suggest. He hadn't tried to make love to her, and wasn't concerned to now, even though he still found her very attractive. If it happened, it happened. 'I'll speak to you later.' He smiled at her and followed her boss into his office.

Among his many duties, the Deputy Commissioner had overall responsibility for discipline and complaints, and the number of complaints that had come in resulting from the policing of the Home Secretary's visit to the Students' Union was disturbing, most especially the alleged rape.

'You might be better off asking Ron Hazell to investigate it,' Bentham replied. 'He runs CIB-2, not me.'

Streeter dismissed the notion with an impatient gesture. 'I'm asking you. There's no one got his ear closer to the ground. There's no one I'd trust more to give me straight answers. Do you think that black girl was raped?'

'I'd hate to think so, but we have to take her complaint seriously. It's happened in the past, in different circumstances.'

'Yes. A policeman getting carried away after taking details from a rape victim. But if this is true, two plonks held her down.'

Bentham smiled to himself at the Deputy Commissioner's section-house description of WPCs, as if trying to prove he was one of the boys. 'Roberta Ford's not someone you can dismiss in any circumstances. Being black, and from her background, she'd know the kind of problems she'd have making a complaint like that. Fuck me, it's not something she's likely to have invented, Harry.'

'She is very political. She'd know the sort of damage it would do us, whether it was proven or not.'

'She's more than political. She was actively involved with Jesse Jarman.'

The Deputy Commissioner sighed, as if it were all too much to cope with. 'It begins to look like some sort of police plot against them.'

'There's a chance it is.'

'You've been penetratingly right about things in the past, Jack. But this is something I hope to fuck you're wrong about. Any chance that lad who's under cover on the Jarman murder inquiry can do a bit on the Ford woman? See if he can't find out something, if it was a get-up on her part?'

'It's worth a go,' Bentham conceded. From the reports he'd received so far, not too much was expected of the undercover policeman, but possibly that was both to do with his being from an outside police force, and being black.

'This could be what sparks off that whole black community.'

Seeing the level of concern the situation was causing, Bentham was finding it difficult to resist the Deputy Commissioner's next move.

'I'd like you to investigate this one, Jack – only the circumstances surrounding the alleged rape. Not the other complaints. I've talked to the deputy chair of the Police Complaints Authority. They're happy for you to do the investigation. Jonathan Entwistle's going to supervise this one personally.'

'What about Ron Hazell?'

'He thinks the Bureau is well out of it. The PCA wants an outside force in to investigate all the complaints by those students. I've asked Merseyside.' He paused and let his small round eyes settle briefly on Bentham. The Deputy Commissioner rarely looked anyone straight in the eye. 'I know you'll go right down the middle, Jack, being fair to everyone. But we're on a hiding to nothing here. This complaint is about as nasty as you can get . . . What I'm saying is, Jack, if our position can be retrieved . . . I mean, fucking hell, it'll get so not even a white person will go near a policeman, much less those fucking blacks.'

Everyone was racist, Jack Bentham had decided a long while ago; well, almost everyone, except for that unique minority who lived he didn't know where. He knew himself to be racist at times, if only for not doing something more about those he worked with. He felt he was being asked by the Deputy Commissioner to somehow mitigate the corporate racism of the Met, if not every police force in the British Isles. The alleged rape of a black woman in a Divisional police station wasn't simply a local issue affecting only those who worked there, it was a national issue that would put the police on trial until it was brought to a conclusion one way or the other, and it was fairly obvious what was expected of him.

Bentham simply nodded, but didn't like himself for doing so.

'Cheeky fuckers!' was Bentham's conclusion when he was told about students at a Union meeting demanding the showing of membership cards, which obliged C11 detectives who were present to leave.

He laughed, deciding it was more gracious than showing the irritation he felt. More and more he was conscious of the image he presented to the world. His irritation arose less out of what the students did than the fact that Branch officers who were furnished with Student Union cards by MI5 had remained in the meeting. The Union meeting was called to discuss the actions of the police at the demo against the Home Secretary, and the complaints that had resulted. Any inside information might have been useful, but he'd be hard put to get much out of the Branch or MI5.

'How did those students sus our people, Frank?' he asked Detective Superintendent Burroughs in the back of the Ford Granada as they were driving away from the Yard across to Great George Street to a meeting with the deputy chair of the Police Complaints Authority. It would have been quicker walking.

'Sounds like someone marked their card, guv.'

'They're behaving like real villains. Perhaps we'd better take a closer look. Especially at those making complaints against the police.'

'I thought that's what Merseyside were going to do.'

'No harm in us having some information.' He glanced over at the Superintendent, but gave nothing away in his expression. 'Do we know what they decided at their Union meeting?'

'Up until our people were thrown out, they planned to collect statements of their own. Some of the students were organising that.'

'What about after our people left?'

Detective Superintendent Frank Burroughs was an infinitely practical policeman who had recently been promoted from DCI almost solely on Bentham's recommendation. He was a policeman who disliked the police involvement in politics and for that reason

Bentham avoided politics with this man, even police politics, but liked working with him for his shrewd eye and gut feeling for a job. There were few policemen he could rely on more than Frank Burroughs, even when he didn't quite manage to articulate what was on his mind. Bentham knew Burroughs had more information about what had happened at that meeting than his detectives had gleaned. He was well respected and had friendly contacts in the Branch.

'They picked the four students who were going to collect statements from all the others. None of them have any sort of record.'

'Not even in the Branch computer?'

'Not that they're telling me about, guv.'

'I suppose it's something that they're not political.'

Traffic was solid up through Storey's Gate where a scaffolding lorry was unloading. Bentham and Burroughs got out of the car and walked into Great George Street.

Jonathan Entwistle was waiting in his first-floor office, which showed little of the comforts accorded a senior civil servant. There was a threadbare feel about the place that suggested it was starved of funds and showed lack of commitment to its purpose. Everywhere the PCA proclaimed its independence, as if not quite believing it itself.

The deputy chair, who had a permanently lugubrious expression, was a tall man with a pronounced stoop that was causing his back to slightly hump. Being short, Bentham had to look up to him, but this caused no subsconscious resentment in him; he tried to avoid looking down on anyone. He introduced Frank Burroughs.

'Superintendent Burroughs is going to act as my staffing officer. He will conduct the investigation when I'm not around.'

Entwistle glanced over at the voluminous detective who was spilling out over his chair, and quickly looked away. 'I understood the Deputy Commissioner asked you to conduct this investigation personally, Mr Bentham.'

'So I shall, Mr Entwistle. And when I'm not around, Frank will.' That was a firm declaration that brooked no argument; a resignation perhaps, or a dismissal. The function of the Police Complaints Authority was to oversee the police investigation itself. One of its powers enabled it to dismiss the investigating officer if not satisfied with the way he was conducting the investigation. For a moment Bentham thought that might happen here.

It didn't. The deputy chair nodded curtly.

'I intend to supervise this case personally, Mr Bentham.' Again he gave a quick glance at Burroughs, as if not trusting people that large. 'I intend to stay closely in touch with all developments, however trivial-seeming. Rape is such an odious crime.'

'If it happened,' Bentham pointed out.

'Yes, of course,' Jonathan Entwistle said quietly, as if not even wanting to consider that possibility. 'How do you intend conducting this investigation?'

'It should be fairly straightforward. First we have to identify the policemen she alleges were in the cell with her.'

'And the policewomen!' Entwistle pointed out.

'That's what makes it more than a little suspicious,' Bentham said.

'I think that whole dimension makes it fascinating, Mr Bentham.' He gave another quick glance at Burroughs, as if to assess whether he might share this fascination.

When they were leaving the building to look for their car that was going to take them on across the river, where he was examining another complaints investigation, Bentham turned and glanced at Burroughs, whose face was unmoving.

'What do you think?'

'About the investigation?' He knew what his boss was asking. 'To be perfectly honest, guv, I think he's turned on by the whole prospect. I'd say he'll be more than a bit disappointed if it goes the other way.'

Bentham nodded. He thought that a pretty shrewd assessment.

Whenever he was visiting divisional stations, Jack Bentham made sure he knew the key code to the computerised back doors, to save announcing his presence at the main entrance. He liked wandering in and seeing the people doing the job; it told him far more about the state of the police than ever a written report commissioned by a senior officer did. Sitting unobtrusively in a station canteen while policemen on relief cooked their greasy sausage-and-egg put him in touch with the mood of the men.

He wouldn't pick up much this afternoon in the police canteen, where he'd arranged to meet Detective Superintendent Horsfell, and even wondered if Alan Horsfell hadn't cleared the place on purpose. Perhaps it was just as well, as he didn't want it generally known what he was pursuing Horsfell about. He was under pressure from the Police Complaints Authority to make official his informal report to CIB-2 on the two detectives who had allegedly beaten up black suspects at this nick. They were pursuing their complaints through the local council advisors to the police sub-committee, and demanding an independent inquiry. That was easier to put into effect than the consequences might be to live with, for one of the detectives, DS Tait, was involved in the undercover operation to investigate Jesse Jarman's murder. The same could be said of most policemen who had to be suspended, pending an inquiry: often their work, especially criminal intelligence work which was probably peculiar to them, simply stood still.

'Off the record, Alan,' Jack Bentham said, glancing from the detective as if the question wasn't important and letting his gaze settle on a constable who had wandered in to get a pre-prepared meal from the coin-operated cabinet to pop into the microwave oven alongside, 'what sort of coppers are DS Tait and DC Lines? You've had a chance to get to know them here.'

'With the clear-up rate falling like it is, guv, you'd be sorry to see them taken out with a complaint from a tint.' He knew Tait to be an effective policeman, but owed him no special loyalty, even though they had done business together. 'They're a bit out of control at times, but then who isn't? Brian Tait's a good thief-taker.'

'Did they beat up that black suspect? – we're not talking about a cuff round the chops in interrogation, Alan. The medical report says there's a ruptured spleen and renal damage.'

Detective Superintendent Horsfell thought carefully, seeing that this looked like becoming heavy. He knew he couldn't bullshit Jack Bentham and change tack and say he didn't think those two detectives touched the black suspects. He believed Bentham wanted to give them some help, which was why he was here, and would only do so if apprised of the facts. 'Is this strictly off the record, Jack?' He didn't often use the Commander's first name. He glanced at Frank Burroughs, wondering why he was here, but decided it was for a no more sinister reason than to provide another shrewd brain to look for an out. 'They probably did, but then I'd say that particular black bastard deserved all he got, and more. He was making petrol bombs. They were gonna come raining down on some poor fucking woodentop's neck when he walked through the Farm.'

'Part of his complaint is that they were put on him,' Bentham said. 'There's not a policeman here who hasn't had those sort of complaints.'

'Sounds like an active station,' Detective Superintendent Burroughs said.

'You're not kidding.' Horsfell paused, and glanced between the two detectives. 'We've all been in those situations where blacks have got lippy and aren't allowed to get away with it.' He grinned.

Bentham thought about this statement, then nodded solemnly before moving on to other matters, mainly that of getting Horsfell to expand on the Jarman murder investigation. It was going in the direction he wanted it to go in, if not fast enough for members of the police hierarchy closest to the political pressure. They were always aware of the possibility that black ghettos like this could explode into a race riot, and believed this could be forestalled by the local police finding the murderer; however, they seemed to ignore the possibility that the thoughtless heavy-handedness of their visible presence might be enough. But they couldn't ignore the possibility that the more active and vociferous blacks locally might not like the result the police turned in.

A great deal of the information Maurice Knight was passing back via DS Tait Detective Superintendent Horsfell chose not to pass on to his boss. A lot of it related to police involvement in dope dealing, some of which Jesse Jarman had been logging. Maurice Knight hadn't supplied the names of policemen dealing, and until he did Horsfell was letting it ride.

'What do you know about Roberta Ford?' Bentham asked, getting to the final purpose of his visit.

'She's a lot of trouble, guv. Whatever way you book it. I'm not surprised she came to grief.'

'Is that the word around here, that she was raped?'

'She could say Big Ears himself raped her,' Horsfell said, referring to the Commissioner; 'people around here would believe her. Why wouldn't they? She and Jesse Jarman were going to lead them to Zion.'

'You think she's lying?'

'It's a pretty bizarre thing to lie about, but there's a better than even chance she is. It's her way of paying the police back over Jarman's murder. It could bring all sorts of trouble. Their sort always manage to make political capital out of those situations.'

A weary smile wrinkled in the corner of Jack Bentham's mind at that but appeared nowhere on his face as he thought about the political capital the police made out of riot situations. The Commissioner's detailed reports following the last two riots were used to stampede Parliament into amending the Criminal Justice Bill to include the increase of police powers by law and manpower on the ground, while adding also to its expanding arsenal. He made no such observation here, preferring to save those arguments for any opportunity he would have to speak at public forums. That gave him the reputation of being radical, but he knew in reality that even the tiniest pebble thrown into that rather stagnant, reactionary, often racist pool in which the police were slowly drowning, was considered radical.

From the little he knew of Roberta Ford, Bentham guessed that there probably weren't many points of agreement he'd find with her, but even so he had a sneaking admiration for her, for the courage she showed in being prepared to fight the police, despite what must appear insuperable odds. He thought he would like to help her even out those odds – no more than a pebble – and was determined that if policemen had raped her as she claimed, he would make sure they were prosecuted.

'I feel in a bit of a bind, Frank,' Jack Bentham said as he climbed back into his car in the station yard, to drive to The Cut to interview Roberta Ford at her solicitor's office. It was to be their first meeting. 'I feel like recommending that Tait and Mills are suspended pending an independent investigation.'

'You get Tait pulled, you could put our undercover lad at risk. Tait's his only contact.'

'But even so, I'm not prepared to leave Tait here indefinitely as if he were no problem. I'd like to see Alan Horsfell moved out of here to a less sensitive area too.'

'We'll have a bit of a problem there, guv,' Burroughs said. 'We're over-extended as it is. What do we drop and who do we put down here?'

'There are too many fronts for us to fight every black person in the area. This little lot aren't about to deal with their racism. All they seem to want to do is mitigate it by causing bigger and bigger confrontations.'

They rode in silence for a while. Then Bentham said, 'Put Bill Senior back down here to keep an eye on the situation.'

'You want him to be a grass, guv? You'd be better with someone from CIB-2.'

'You find that objectionable, Frank?' Bentham said sharply, but didn't wait for his reply. 'Fuck me, we're encouraging the entire nation to be informers with television programmes and neighbourhood watch schemes. I'd like Senior to help them move the investigation along, and avoid too many incidents like the beating-up of that black lad.'

He believed DI Bill Senior to be a fair-minded policeman, and began to think perhaps Frank Burroughs was racist. Maybe it wasn't a good idea to take him to the meeting with Roberta Ford, but he wasn't about to ask him to wait outside. He couldn't do all the interviewing himself personally, and he couldn't exist without delegating and relying on his superintendents.

In a flat, almost detached voice, Roberta Ford told her story to these two senior policemen. She had lost count of how many times this made so far.

Her solicitor had warned her that she would have to go over it time and again, and with enough warning she managed to prepare herself so that the words affected her hardly at all. She refused to allow them to evoke either the mental anguish or the physical and emotional pain she had experienced. Her life had found some level of normality. It had to; too many people worse off than herself needed her help, and she found her way through the distress by concentrating on the action she was taking to prosecute the police. That was an anchor. In addition, although she couldn't admit it, Roberta Ford almost enjoyed being a martyr.

Neither of the policemen who came to interview her impressed her much. The more senior of the two seemed to her uninterested, while the larger man seemed not to believe her; then, that was no more than she expected of policemen.

Bentham's questions were easy on her. As if by way of initiation, they simply solicited the facts as she recognised them in chronological order. He was a bit surprised at how unemotional she was, and wondered how long she would be able to maintain that position, especially when the questions at later interviews would become interrogative, challenging, threatening. He hoped she would maintain this equilibrium, for emotion was no ally of the truth in an investigation of complaints against policemen.

As if to test the calm, almost detached position she took, Bentham said, 'I don't believe a word you say, Miss Ford.' His statement startled both her and the solicitor.

'Why would you? You're a policeman.'

'Do you know anyone better to investigate the complaint? Were you Jesse Jarman's lover?' That startled her too.

'I don't think that has any relevance,' the solicitor said.

'Doesn't it?'

'Yes. Yes, I was,' Roberta said, looking directly at him, almost defiantly.

Bentham held her look. He had every reason not to believe her story, but curiously, even reluctantly, he sensed what she said was true, or at least that she believed it was. He would do his best to uncover the truth, however painful.

12

BELFAST CROWN COURT on the Crumlin Road was a solid, porticoed building that had the look of an institution that would never, could never, be shaken. But this drab, cream and orange painted edifice had been shaken in the past, both by bombs and offensive miscarriages of justice, and was left in no way impervious to such affronts in future, despite the wired-in protection of anti-mortar fences and the armed RUC.

Ronald Hartman was a barrister from a long line of lawyers, most of whom had practised in Ulster, some in the whole of Ireland before partition. Others had gone to America to make their fortunes and had done quite nicely, and one was quite a well-known judge in the days before Diplock Courts. That particular member of the family had on retirement spoken out against Lord Justice Diplock's notion of any trial with political connotations in Northern Ireland being given a fairer hearing without twelve of the defendant's peers. He had clung to the romantic notion that justice was safe in the hands of random fellow citizens taken from the electoral registers. Ronald Hartman thought the notion both romantic and unreliable. He had been called to the bar since Lord Diplock had bestowed upon the people of Northern Ireland, with the blessing of the UK government, his system of justice, and it was, he thought, infinitely more reliable than any they had on the mainland. A single judge heard the case and pronounced guilt or innocence without a jury. Hartman was unshakeable in his belief that that was a deal safer than a bunch of old women with their heads filled with television jingles or laughing boys with their heads full of IRA propaganda.

Being one of the chosen in Ulster, Ronald Hartman had his pick of prosecution briefs and any number of law firms queued at the law library for him to take on their cases. Long before the start of the trial, the DPP had asked if he had been briefed for the defence on the case. Hartman wasn't too sure whether Sir Cyril Shelldrake was sounding him out in order to know what gun to field against him, or was wishfully thinking that he might take on the case for the prosecution. He had in fact been approached on behalf of Constable Maurice Peters, soon after he was charged. Hartman was never too sure what the DPP's position was politically at any given time, but liked to assume he was on the side of the angels. He sometimes vacillated over prosecuting cases when it was clearly his duty and in the public interest to do so, and less occasionally pressed on recklessly with cases where there was no public interest in prosecuting.

In taking the case, Hartman faced something of a dilemma. Both intellect and gut feeling told him to accept the brief, but political instinct sounded more strident alarms the deeper he looked into it. The case was open and shut, and initially he doubted the judge would let it go all the way. His client was clearly a pawn, a foot solider in a complex game played by brigadiers and generals. But it seemed he might only free him from the barb of criminal culpability over the shooting of Stephen McFadden by pulling them into it. The question was whether he should sacrifice the client for the greater good, and, if not, how much damage might be done to the fabric of the society he lived in and enjoyed.

But legal pride wouldn't allow him to dump his client, and so instead he set a damage-limitation course. More had come out about the operations of the RUC's Special Support Unit and its involvement with MI5 and MI6 across the Irish border and its penetration of the Garda Siochana than the media dared to write about, but nothing like as much as could have emerged had he pressed senior officers about those operations, or called members of MI5 and 6 as witnesses. Lord Justice Kinahon, who had been brought out of retirement for this case, was as politically shrewd as he was legally astute and didn't press questions that the defence left unasked and the prosecution had no interest in pursuing.

Yet still as he bounced up the steps of the court building, leaving his cigarette-smoking junior gasping behind him, Ronald Hartman worried that he had revealed too much. There wouldn't be a visit to his office from the dancing boys in MI6, or their more stolid counterparts in MI5, but there might be a socially chill wind blowing his way. He would know soon enough, as this was expected to be the last day of the trial.

Security was getting slack on the cell block below the court – habits became difficult to maintain at pitch – and Ronald Hartman was simply waved through to his client.

Maurice Peters, who was immaculately attired in his RUC uniform – he chose not to appear in civvies – rose from the bench as Hartman stepped into the cell and curtly extended his hand, with a grip now familiar to them both. Nothing was ever said by way of recognition other than the ritual they went through each morning they met.

'Mr Peters,' Hartman said quickly, matching his movements, 'a day we all hoped would never arrive. But there you are.'

'Not just with me and Gary in the dock, sir.'

'Not with anyone in the dock, not for shooting the McFadden lad.' He smiled reassuringly at the drawn, anxious face opposite him. Although veiled threats had been made by the defendant about the other RUC men present, along with MI6, who had been mentioned in court but not called, he hadn't, as far as Hartman knew, taken them any further. Neither Peters nor his co-defendant struck the barrister as martyr types, and he wondered what strange hold his colleagues had over him to secure his silence. Hartman found his restraint truly admirable. 'I have every confidence in the judge letting you leave the court a free man, Mr Peters. And without a stain on your character. You've been a hostage to manufactured public opinion, and now it's about to turn on your side.' He smiled tightly and extended his hand again. 'Good luck.'

As he sat in the dock of Number One court, Maurice Peters suddenly felt ill and prayed to God he wouldn't be sick and make a fool of himself. He'd avoided breakfast to prevent that happening, but it was no guarantee. He could hear Gary Hinton's stomach rumbling; the whole court must have heard it. Gary was a real glutton and just thinking about the food he would tuck away on duty worsened Maurice Peters' feeling of nausea. He felt his stomach heave, and he let out a low moan as he opened his mouth to suck in a deep breath.

'Steady, lad,' said the elderly prison officer at his side. He reached out and gripped his arm to help steady him. 'Yous two'll be OK.'

Just to hear those kind words was enough for Maurice Peters. They brought more comfort and reassurance than anything said to him since the time of his suspension. Not his solicitor nor the cocky barrister with one of the best reputations in the Six Counties, not his wife, nor his father-in-law, who was an Orange Lodge drummer, had comforted him as much; his colleagues had been supportive but silent lest they be dragged into the frame; senior colleagues in the RUC's Special Branch had reminded him that he had signed the

Official Secrets Act, and that admissions even under oath in court could carry severe penalties. When he had raised the possibility that he might be asked questions they wouldn't want him answering, he had been told to lie; the reassurances that the Chief Superintendent had given him about emerging from this as everyone wanted him to, that it was a formality to placate Westminster and Dublin, hadn't been comforting. He had reasoned that if what they had been doing had approval all the way from the top, and his understanding was that it had, why were people in Westminster in need of placating, and why give a fig about Dublin? His argument hadn't brought him to any conclusion, and his silence was secured for fear of consequences far greater than the threat of prosecution under Section 2 of the Official Secrets Act.

But now his jailer, the personification of all the state had come to represent, had told him he'd be OK. A cloud had suddenly lifted.

'Be upstanding in court,' the usher called as the double doors behind the bench opened and the purple-robed judge stepped through and took his seat without looking anywhere but ahead of him.

Everyone in the courtroom except the prisoners and escort sat with the judge and waited with a sense of expectation.

Lord Justice Ernest Kinahon slowly opened his large notebook in which he meticulously summarised all aspects of the trial in his neat round hand and glanced over the pages, then lifted his head to look from beneath his pale, hooded eyes at the two defendants. He remembered thinking earlier how if the security of the state was dependant on such frail emotions as they had displayed, then God save it – as he had no doubt He would.

'Two policemen, both with hitherto unblemished records, stand before this court accused of the most heinous crime of murder, a killing that took place in the course of a particularly dangerous duty.' He paused.

Ronald Hartman scribbled across his notepad 'We have it' for his junior to read – a futile gesture so close to the judge's deliberation, but the barrister enjoyed the feeling of accurate anticipation.

'After careful deliberation and weighing of the evidence before this court, I find Gary Hinton not guilty . . .'

A sort of breathless laughter tumbled around the beige- and mushroom-painted courtroom as air held too long under tension was released from lungs. The judge didn't wait for the usher to call for silence, but ploughed through the understandable euphoria to pronounce Maurice Peters not guilty also.

The warders in the dock shook hands warmly with the defendants, who turned like the political contestants they undoubtedly were, and smiled to friends, relatives and supporters on the public benches. The armed RUC guards in court reached into the dock to shake their hands. One rushed out to tell the RUC men securing the doors.

Lord Justice Kinahon wasn't finished, but gave these men their moment; it was little enough to recompense them for what they had been put through. He had no difficulty in arriving at his decision. He rarely had difficulty with any of his judgements, having worked out everything there was to work out about life when in his late teens. There had been a brief hiccough while at Keble College, Oxford, reading law; he had become emotionally involved with another student, a member of the British Union of Fascists. The homosexual liaison was transient and completely unsettling, but finally he had broken free by pushing himself like crazy; he not only got himself back on the tracks, but found himself with a double first. He had stayed with the British Union a good deal longer. The major question that arose during this trial, and one that was only touched upon but briefly and not pursued, was why more members of the RUC's Special Support Unit weren't in the dock. Recognising the pressures on the state, the difficulties of those basically decent, responsible men and women who struggled to hold it together in the face of persistent terrorism, Lord Justice Kinahon had refused to pursue those questions. He knew what the RUC was made of from his contact with the officers who constantly guarded him.

When the court quietened, the judge said, 'Before the defendants are released, without stain on their character, I would like to take this opportunity to commend them for the courage and dignity they have displayed throughout this ordeal. It brings much credit to the force in which they serve. Courage, fearlessness, determination have become the bywords of the RUC as they have brought political bandits to justice, and in some cases, at no small risk to themselves, the final courts of justice.'

The jubilation of those around her on the tiers of seats in the public gallery was something Maureen McFadden could understand, if not appreciate or share. The two men in the dock were doubtless someone's sons. She had had small hope of the trial being fair, or of the two men being found guilty if it was; not that it would make any difference to her, her two daughters or her murdered son if they were. But the judge's words were more offensive than she could imagine. To praise the RUC for that killing was intolerable, and she thought how it would have been too easy to dismiss the judge as mad. He wasn't. Not a bit, or certainly no madder than everyone else who either participated in running the province or sought its downfall. If in all the weeks after his murder someone had had the decency to approach her and say sorry, that they hadn't known it was a wee simple soul who had gone into that barn with his wee friend, then she may have been more forgiving. No one from the RUC or the state had said sorry to her, they had only been interested in first accusing her son of being a terrorist, then of finding terrorist connections within her family. Not even when they had found none could they say sorry. Maureen felt herself as close to the point of running away as she had ever been. All the effort she had put into living there and trying to check the inexorable deterioration of life suddenly seemed pointless. She wondered again for whose benefit she was staying there, and what purpose it served.

She rose unsteadily and, gripping her two daughters by the hand tighter than she needed to, she edged along the narrow row of seats and out of the court, out of the building, where at last she felt she could breathe. The area immediately surrounding the court house was a high-security zone where grim-looking RUC men with machine guns grouped at strategic points stood grinning. It was almost as if they were mocking her. How she longed for normality to touch her, and wondered what it would be like to live other than in the atmosphere of hatred and fear which she pushed to one side, pretending it wasn't affecting her, but which like fine sand in the cogs of machinery was, through an almost imperceptible process of attrition, wearing away sharpness, lightness, quickness of response, spontaneity. It had been such a long while since there had been anything different and she, like most people, assumed that this was the norm.

In an effort to make life appear as normal as possible, Maureen went to the city centre to shop with Angela and Kathleen. They all bought a summer dress each in Next, as if in anticipation of the summer that never seemed to want to come. They went across Donegal Place, the wide main shopping thoroughfare that was closed in with security like a prison compound, and bought new bodysuits in Primark; then back to Marks and Spencers for underwear.

'Mum, can you afford all this?' Angela said with some concern, as they came out of the store loaded with carrier bags.

'Not really. But what does it matter?' She smiled as best she could. 'It's only money.'

This was a kind of delayed displacement activity, and a means of avoiding going back to the flat now that the chapter on Stephen was closed. Somehow the tears and memories wouldn't allow it to close.

They went on to a café to get some tea. The place had a pall of cigarette smoke hanging over it, and a rank smell of burnt fat. But there was nowhere else. As she sat there looking at other customers with grey and harassed expressions on their faces, people weighed down with their own troubles and oblivious to who they were or what had so recently blighted their lives, Maureen questioned what the purpose was of going on, if this was all that life amounted to – a carrier bag full of distractions and stewed tea in a stinking café.

She thought again about moving away from Belfast. The disruption to the social and academic life of her two daughters aside, she recognised that people wouldn't necessarily be more caring elsewhere. That was what she needed, she realised, someone to care about her for a change; that was what she missed most with Stephen's departure, his putting his arms around her and holding her. She wanted to find someone for herself, someone to touch her, stir her, even make sparks fly inside her. That was something that had never happened and had remained a distant expectation. She didn't even find the priest taking her hands after mass at St Comgall's comforting. Her prospects of finding someone, she reflected, were as bleak as those for Belfast itself.

The contact Mrs McMahon made spontaneously when they returned to their flat in Divis Street moved Maureen more than anything in a long while. Mrs McMahon caught them on the stairs – the lifts were out of order.

'I heard the news,' she said. 'It's shocking. They let them get away with murder. That's all it is.' She put her arms around Maureen as a mother might. She was probably younger, but looked older, a mother of seven who didn't cope well ordinarily but was at times capable of great affection. She too had lost her son, for Kit, who was shot with Stephen, was still in hospital, not having spoken two words since the incident.

'He was the nicest thing about this place – our Kit thought he was just great, your Stephen. I'm glad you stayed on, Mrs McFadden. Though God alone knows why anyone would want to live here.' She smiled and said, 'Thank you', as though Maureen had done her a great kindness.

123

It was then that Maureen burst into tears. She fled into her flat and cried and cried, for the loss of Stephen, for Kit and his mother, her runaway husband, and not least of all herself.

Wellwishers saw to it that it was a long time afterwards that Constable Maurice Peters finally left the court. Surrounded by family and friends, he gave an impromptu press conference, where the inevitable trite questions were asked about his future and how he felt. Peters said he felt grand and smiled a lot.

'Do you feel aggrieved that you were the only two officers in the dock?' an Ulster TV news presenter asked.

'Aggrieved?' Peters said, giving himself time to think. 'No. Justice has been done here. It's a great day for the RUC.'

He meant it. He had kept his mouth shut and the RUC had been vindicated, or so he assumed until he walked into a row which started immediately about disciplinary hearings. He was dumbfounded at the thought of having to go through another ordeal, and left the angry Police Federation representative to fight it on his behalf. They had been apprentice boy drummers together, and although there was no one Maurice Peters would sooner have fighting on his side, the disciplinary process that was to be started by the Police Complaints Commission left him feeling depressed.

With anger and anxiety was how the rank and file greeted the news in Ulster. Even though few expected any real trouble from the RUC's complaints and discipline department, and even less from the Police Complaints Commission, it was the principle that offended those in the job.

The grumbling discontent of RUC men wasn't something that worried Sir Norman Hateley. He knew his men and knew what they were able to endure. A more worrying aspect of discontent over the whole episode came from the SDLP MP Marcus Toomey, mostly because he could and did command air time on both local and national news with his angry attacks on the bastions of Ulster Unionism.

The Chief Constable was at a dinner being hosted by the Industrial Development Board when the MP went out on the BBC's *Nine O'clock News*; unlike Toomey, Sir Norman and the Secretary of State, as well as most other state dignitaries, were trying to persuade foreign capital that NI was a safe place to invest in. Fortunately, potential investors were at the dinner at Stormont

Castle when the broadcast went out, but Sir Norman had it recorded and watched it soon afterwards with the DPP, and became no less angry.

'. . . There is no doubt in my mind, nor in that of a great many people both in the north and south of Ireland,' Marcus Toomey was saying forcefully, looking directly at the interviewer, 'that the RUC has been operating a covert shoot-to-kill policy. Now, that's little different from the death squads that operate in El Salvador. Or if it is, I'm sure you'll point out the difference to me.'

'But the difference here, Mr Toomey, is surely,' the interviewer argued for the sake of balance, 'that those accused of the killings are taken before the courts?'

'A trial in the Diplock Courts is a trial by the British government. They're not being judged by their peers,' Toomey pointed out. 'Why would the British government find its agents guilty?'

'Are you saying that if a shoot-to-kill policy existed, then the government knew about it?' The interviewer wasn't disguising his excitement.

'I'm saying it does exist, and of course they knew about it. Someone has to formulate that policy, then task it. Only a public inquiry might get to the truth. Why is such an inquiry resisted? If the government in Westminster has nothing to hide, then, like the RUC, it should have nothing to fear from these questions. Public disquiet will only increase all the while such an inquiry is actively resisted . . .'

At the end of the interview, Sir Norman Hateley jumped forward to the TV set in the undersecretary's first-floor office and angrily ejected the video cassette. He waved it agitatedly at the DPP, blood pumping into his arteries faster than they could distribute it.

'It's fucking sickening that politicians like Toomey are given air time for malicious propaganda. What in God's fucking name does the BBC think it's playing at letting that go out?'

Sir Cyril Shelldrake sighed, hoping he wasn't going to be around when this man had his inevitable stroke. He felt superior in that he kept his temper and didn't resort to bad language. It was the only advantage he believed he had on this man. 'I imagine their line is the usual "grave public concern" over the issue. But it appears they might be more concerned to fuel it rather than quieten it.'

'How many times must the RUC go on trial? Perhaps it's time we reassessed our relationship with the fucking BBC.'

Knowing the risks involved in such retaliatory measures, Sir Cyril chose to say nothing as he watched the Chief Constable stamp around the room. His uniform was immaculate and so well cut that he could have slept in it and still it would look immaculate. His own dinner suit hadn't even looked that good when he had bought it twelve years ago; then he assumed they had worn trousers off the shoes.

'Is that actionable, Cyril?'

'Mr Toomey's statements were made outside of the House of Commons – wouldn't such an action fuel rumours of an RUC cover-up?' He believed it would but didn't wish to push the headstrong Chief Constable into a yet deeper bunker over this. He was holding down a lot of anxiety and could feel the top vertebrae in his neck locking with tension. He wished he stood at a greater distance from law-enforcement in the province. But no way could he do that now without resigning. 'My feeling is that public disquiet will continue to be aroused by the likes of Toomey and Father McMichael until such time, God forbid, as we've had an independent inquiry.' Having said the words he was dismayed at the thought of such an inquiry ever taking place and, if it did, of the possibility of the soft underbelly of Protestant Unionism being left exposed. There were things that went on that Sir Cyril denied to himself he ever heard about, but things that woke him up in the middle of the night all the same.

'The public's perception of an independent inquiry is often a resolution in itself,' Sir Cyril said circumspectly. 'It can take the steam out of the situation and focus attention elsewhere.' He didn't want to go further, not even in this most private of offices. He had no difficulty with the notion of the type of public inquiry which merely served to catch loose ends and tuck them into the weft, while making a display of public accountability. Questions thrown up by the trial, but now answered, such as who gave the order to shoot and why only two policemen were charged, and questions about the security forces' clandestine involvement across the border might be of no concern to anyone, compared to what could come out if the rumours he had heard about the involvement of some senior members of the bench in ungodly acts at a certain boys' school were true. None of them here would survive if that were leaked, and possibly there would be heads rolling in Westminster too.

Sir Norman was silent for such a long moment that the DPP began to think he had had the expected stroke and lost the power of speech. Finally, he said on a reasonable note, 'I don't want outsiders with no understanding of the province coming here, Cyril. If I have someone, he'll need to be carefully chosen.'

That brought nothing but a feeling of relief to the DPP. 'The choice is for you. You'd find the right person. If this pressure is allowed to build up, the Secretary of State might be forced to impose some sort of inquiry on you. It'll become a matter of political expediency. I doubt if he quite appreciates what's at risk.'

Slowly and not a little reluctantly, Sir Norman Hateley nodded, knowing that he had to take the initiative and set out the ground rules. 'I would have to be extremely careful about who I let loose here. It would have to be the right man.' He glanced at the DPP. 'Someone who was seen to do a thorough job, Cyril.'

'Yes indeed,' Sir Cyril said, the tension in his neck beginning to ease.

13

THE ATMOSPHERE OF SECRECY that hung over the eleventh floor at Scotland Yard where the Association of Chief Police Officers had their offices always impressed Sir Norman Hateley whenever he came over to the mainland, and sometimes made him a little envious. He was never able to achieve that sort of secrecy back at the Knock headquarters of the RUC. Information was always leaking out somehow, endangering someone; they could rarely achieve the level of secrecy that surrounded the North-east Regional ACPO meetings he more often attended. This meeting had been scheduled, and he had called the president and had Northern Ireland added to the agenda.

The president, Roger Gannett, the Chief Constable of Kent, was very good at keeping the meeting to the agenda. He started on time, finished on time, and covered every item, albeit in a truncated form at the end. The RUC's difficulties were taking up a lot of time and Sir Norman was grateful that sufficient discussion was allowed.

'Northern Ireland has proved an invaluable testing ground for police methods that have eventually been introduced here,' the president was saying. He lifted his round rump off his chair and unself-consciously scratched his anus through his trousers. It was well known he suffered from piles and scratched them relentlessly when under stress. 'Most of us have good reason to be grateful to Norman Hateley for his hospitality when men have gone over to observe new techniques or to be trained.'

There were echoes of agreement, which Sir Norman Hateley sat through in silence, his eyes slightly lowered as if unaware of just how grateful they were to him.

'It would be a pity to lose such a testing ground, as we rely on these policing methods more and more. That might be the case if the army were to resume the role of policing over there.'

'There's no way the army can effectively police the Six Counties,' Sir Norman said. 'Didn't they try it before and fail?'

'Presume they learnt something from experience, Norman,' Harry Streeter, the Deputy Commissioner, said, 'Look at Cyprus – I was out there as a DC when the police were an aid to the military. It worked.'

'Some of us seem to forget we're talking about a part of the United Kingdom,' Roger Gannett observed, 'not wog-land. There's a bit of difference, Harry.'

Harry Streeter didn't press the point. He wasn't planning to argue against what the Northern Ireland Chief Constable had come to the meeting for. Far from it.

Everyone's attention went briefly to the lady in the blue checked overall who rolled a coffee trolley in. There were Danish pastries too. Almost in unison, the men around the conference table reached into their pockets for artificial sweeteners for their coffee, but none refused the sugary pastry.

Sir Norman glanced at the lady in the blue overall and wondered briefly if she was Irish, but had no anxiety about her, not in the atmosphere on the eleventh floor. 'It's the front line out there,' he said, bringing the meeting back to Northern Ireland. 'The lives of my men are at risk every day. They get little thanks, but they're holding on, despite morale being pretty low. If I thought the army could do a better job, they'd be welcome, I'd say. But they can't, because all the other policing functions that are needed here are carried out there just the same. It's not wog-land, Harry, that's what makes it so bloody difficult. I'm going to have to put the Northern Ireland Office and the Home Office on notice. If any kind of public inquiry gives the RUC a hammering, then we might as well hand over the province to Dublin.'

'I thought that was the government's plan,' the outspoken Chief Constable from Merseyside said. 'With the Anglo-Irish Agreement.'

'It'll be over a lot of dead bodies, Keith.'

'I don't think there's anyone who believes those allegations of a shoot-to-kill policy are anything but rubbish,' the president said. 'I'm sure that between us we can find the right man to conduct an investigation, and prove it to everyone's satisfaction.' There was no sense of irony in this.

'Whoever he is he'd better be dead right, Roger,' Sir Norman said, and added, without any concern about being repetitious, 'these are not ordinary policing circumstances, nor are they ordinary policemen. We've more reason to be grateful to them than we realise. They should be supported from the highest level.'

'They will be, Norman, I'm sure.'

Those policemen who had experienced rioting in their regions knew just what Sir Norman was saying. But none could help much with a senior policeman who was immediately acceptable. Names were put forward. None were rejected out of hand, but none were automatically shortlisted. Some were recognisable for their Masonic connections. But DAC Doc Holliday, who was at the meeting, argued that as such they wouldn't let membership of the Freemasons influence their judgement as policemen anyway and, although the meeting agreed in principle, the consensus was that it might be misconstrued or used in the wrong way politically, as it had Northern Irish Orange Lodge connotations.

Finally the meeting broke up without deciding on a suitable candidate, only a short shortlist. Sir Norman wasn't best pleased about that. He would ponder the names during his two-day visit, but was determined to go back having settled on the right man. Now that he had agreed in principle to have an external inquiry, he wanted the matter done with.

Harry Streeter caught him in the corridor as he was on his way up to pay a courtesy call on the Commissioner.

'Norman, there's a policeman in the Met I'd recommend to carry out this inquiry for you,' Harry Streeter said. 'Jack Bentham.'

'He's not on the list.'

'No. It was for purely selfish reasons that I didn't put him forward. I wouldn't like to lose him for too long. There'd be no problem with the Association endorsing him if you decided he was right. He's thorough, highly efficient, and nobody's man but his own. There'd be no way anyone would say you bought him off.'

They stopped at the lifts and Sir Norman looked at him directly. 'Would he do what would be expected of him?'

Harry Streeter smiled at this blatant assumption. Sir Norman Hateley interpreted the smile as acquiescence.

'I've been taking a personal interest in Jack Bentham. A few more like him would be handy. He's ambitious, and acutely intelligent. I expect one day he'll have my job. He could go even higher.' He wasn't going to say the words for the Northern Irish policeman, but he thought Bentham a shrewd enough policeman to know what to deliver there.

Sir Norman thought about the offer, then said, 'I'd like to meet him.'

*   *   *

Just how far he was to become involved in criminal activity Maurice Knight wasn't sure, and felt uneasy about his deepening relationship with Benny Soares, the dealer. He had been given no guidelines for working undercover other than being told to use his common sense. That wasn't a useful guide, as common sense also told him that the more deeply involved he became with the dope dealer the more he would be trusted and made privy to the secrets of this world that he had entered. But the more involved he was, the greater his criminality, and common sense told him that he shouldn't break the law in order to uphold it; within the closed and secret workings of the police, the opposite view might seem acceptable, but if seen from the outside, perhaps with him ending up in court, he couldn't imagine a judge or jury taking the same understanding line.

Maurice had actually dealt drugs for Soares, delivered them, collected money, and had taken some of it. He had also learned a lot about the neighbourhood and its relationship with the police. It would have needed no genius to know that the local people didn't like them, but he had sorely underestimated by how much. Black policemen they hated even more. That wasn't an experience he had had in Plymouth. He had met hostility before for being a policeman, but not especially for being a black policeman. He didn't dare contemplate how the black community he was in contact with here would react if they found out he was a black policeman working under cover.

There were a lot of stories about police corruption, and at levels that Maurice found hard to believe. Not only were policemen taking bribes, they were also running drugs. Maurice remembered the ready access DS Tait seemed to have to dope. But that wasn't the extent of criminal activity by the police. According to legend, they had even killed a dope dealer for not paying his dues. There was talk in some quarters that they had burned Del Lindo, the suspect he was looking for in the Jesse Jarman murder investigation. That made no sense to Maurice. If they had killed Del Lindo, why bring him here to work under cover? He was assuming that all the police right up to Chief Superintendent Barclay would be involved, in the event, rather than it being a street operation by the local CID. For the present he chose not to believe, but was left feeling uneasy.

While waiting for Benny Soares at the youth club, Maurice involved himself with the boxers. The interest in boxing had grown at the club, and he wasn't sure if it was because there was now someone to show them or because he benefited from the reflected glory of Soares. Most of the kids saw the dealer as Mr Successful, with his good clothes and flash motor. That, not an education or a job, was what attracted most of them, and Maurice saw it as a bad reflection on both the educational system and the housing system that black kids were still relying on boxing or dope to take them out of the ghettos.

When he had talked to Roberta Ford about that, she had responded to him as if he was a human being, if only briefly, forgetting for the time being his relationship with Benny. He had a fantasy about telling her, Hey! I'm not a dealer after all, I'm one of the good guys. But he wondered if that was how even she would see him. He'd heard about the trouble she'd had in a police cell, and the couple of times he'd seen her since then her moods had taken great swings. So he wouldn't bet on her seeing him cast as a good guy. Especially not if there was any truth in what he had heard; there was bound to be some truth, but he refused to believe that two policemen would rape a woman in police cells.

Under his guidance, some of the boxers were shaping well. Two were nearly ready to enter some of the ABA competitions. They'd lose, but competing was the only way they were likely to gain the right attitude. As he couldn't be around the whole time, he had shown the non-participating boxers how to watch each other and help correct each other's faults. It had led to arguments initially, lads not wanting to be told by no greater mortals than themselves.

'You the bloke what wants a trombone?' a voice said at Maurice's side where he stood at the edge of the ring watching the boxing.

Maurice turned and looked at the lad, who was about fifteen.

A lot of what went missing locally was fenced at the Farm youth club, mostly – it was claimed – by policemen, who rarely if ever went there. Maurice wasn't hopeful that his trombone would show up here. He felt excited, but tried to remain cool. 'How much?'

Word was he was looking to buy one, not recover a stolen instrument. He had tried the local pawn shops and second-hand stores without success.

'Twenny quid.' The kid opened the case to display his goods.

It was his trombone and Maurice reached in for it, happy at this reunion.

The young lad watched him in anticipation. ''S in perfect nick.'

'It's got a bit missing.' Maurice indicated the mouthpiece.

'Yeah,' the kid conceded, as if it were of no importance. ''S only a small bit. You can easy get that.'

Pulling out the mouthpiece that hung inside his jacket on a chain, Maurice fitted it and blew a couple of bars. 'Twenny's a bit steep for my own trombone. What about the dope you nicked out of my room? How much d'you get for it?'

Realising his predicament, the kid at once started assessing his chances of running.

Maurice anticipated him. 'I bet I can run faster. Where's the dope?'

With a nervous laugh that amounted to an admission, the kid said, 'It was fucking easier to get rid of than that. I know where you can score some more.'

Once accepted, Maurice was shown all manner of crime, offences he found difficulty not responding to as a policeman and arresting someone. His numbers, an important aspect of any policeman's promotion prospects, would have shot up.

The young black kid took Maurice to a nearby shopping precinct, where shops, like those in the Farm, were permanently boarded up or covered with close wire mesh as if under siege. There he pointed out a couple of ten-year-olds hanging around some vandalised phone boxes. They were sherpas – they led the customer in safety to the dealer.

After a while one of them made contact, and Maurice and the kid followed them to the litter-filled service road behind the shops. They watched the dealer and dopehead come together and negotiate.

'All we got to do is nick the dope off him.'

Before negotiations were complete a Ford Escort swept along the service road and two men jumped out. Maurice recognised one of them as one of the detectives who had picked him up when he first got to town. The kid announced that it was the police and slipped away, as the two detectives laid into both the dealer and the dopehead. They arrested neither of them; instead they took the dope, got back into their car, and were gone.

'How d'you know they were detectives?' DS Tait asked as he travelled on the underground with Maurice. 'Did you see their warrant cards?'

'Of course I didn't. But they were. I recognised one. He was one of those bastards who arrested me. I knew I'd find him.'

'Sounds unlikely,' DS Tait said in a tone as expressionless as his face. 'But I should be able to find out easily enough. Meanwhile, stop pissing around dealing and concentrate on finding out something about Jarman's murder. They want a result back at the nick.'

'There's a demo being planned about the lack of action. They're going to picket the local station.'

'That'll give too many of the thugs on our side too many excuses.'

Maurice was impressed by this concern, and as a result let slip the doubts he was beginning to have. What he failed to appreciate was that such concern didn't come from the effect a black demo probably leading to a riot might have on the community, but what it would do to the business within the community.

'You'd better dig up some more info about that. That woman at the youth club, she's bound to be involved. A political activist like that, she can't be off. What did you hear about her? She say anything to you about what happened in that police cell?'

'No, it's hard to talk to her about that.'

'It would be handy, Maurice, if you found out she was just making trouble for the police. You'd have a lot of friends up here, wouldn't you just. I heard half the Farm has fucked her.'

Maurice didn't respond to that, but felt annoyed that this detective had said it. He didn't believe it was true for a moment.

The sort of dilemma Maurice feared would confront him when he got involved with Benny Soares was about to appear. The dealer had been ripped off by a trusted distributor; trust had broken down somewhere along the line and neither the distributor nor the money came back.

'You'd better find Bobby Sterling, Maurice, and teach the fucker a lesson,' Benny Soares said, when he dropped Maurice off at the Farm after a delivery.

'What if he's got the money?' Maurice said hopefully.

'I still want that fucker getting hurt.'

Word soon went round on Bobby Sterling, and that Maurice was looking for him. No one on the Farm doubted that Maurice could do the business, and, because of his association with Soares, that he would.

Although in no way condoning what Bobby Sterling was into, Roberta felt responsible for him as one of the underclass who used the club, and didn't like to think what might happen to him. She felt doubly responsible for allowing Benny Soares air space there, and letting his henchman get involved with the boxing. She was still puzzled by Maurice Knight, and assumed he was weak rather than wicked, for he was talented and didn't need to do what he did. She wanted to help him change his ways; believed she could.

'He's long gone,' she said, approaching Maurice at the pool table. 'I know you're after Bobby Sterling.'

Maurice looked at her, then played his shot.

'What happens if you find him? Will you beat him up?'

Instead of saying to her what he wanted to say, Maurice found himself acting out the role she expected of him. 'Something like that.'

'Why don't you let Benny do his own dirty work?'

'Still gets done.' He made the shot, clearing the last ball and winning the game, taking fifty pence off his opponent.

He moved over to the counter of the café. Roberta followed him. 'You don't have to do it,' she said. 'You have a way with these kids.'

'You leaving?' Maurice asked, seeing her bag and briefcase. 'I'll walk you to the bus.'

Roberta only barely stopped herself asking whether he would mug her. Before the incident in the police station, she had no fear of walking anywhere on her own, day or night; it wasn't muggers or rapists she feared now, but policemen.

As they were going down the dark, narrow, graffiti-scarred steps through the centre of the block, Roberta said, 'I know kids a lot worse off than you who wouldn't stoop as low.'

He rounded on her, angrily. 'You know nothing about me. Not why I do this, what the circumstances of my life are.'

'You think anything excuses what you're doing?'

That brought Maurice back to his basic dilemma, his role as a policeman participating in crime, but no nearer to resolving it. He felt frustrated at not being able to tell her what he was doing, clinging obstinately to the belief that she would understand. 'Where are you going?'

'To the police station to identify some policemen.'

'The ones that held you in that cell?'

She didn't reply, and Maurice felt bad about pursuing this, trying to catch her out. How he might do that he didn't know. A part of him hoped he wouldn't.

'Would you go with me?' she asked suddenly, after walking in silence.

'What for?' He didn't mean to respond in that way.

'I'd feel easier going to the police station with a friend.'

Maurice's spirits soared at the thought of being considered her friend. Maybe he was getting closer to her than he imagined. He took her arm now as they walked towards the bus stop, his thoughts in a turmoil about what he wanted of her and why. She didn't flinch or react in any way to the gesture, and he thought maybe she hadn't been raped. Not that he had any first-hand experience of rape victims, but he assumed they would all recoil from subsequent contact with another man. But then, he argued, perhaps she realised instictively that he was all right, and perhaps, given a little time, he would win her confidence.

'There seem to be a lot of beards in your division,' Bentham observed drily to the uniform superintendent next to him.

They were in the muster room at Tottenham Court Road police station where twelve policemen, all in uniform, and all showing their collar numbers, were being paraded for Roberta Ford. She moved slowly along the line watched by a chief inspector who had organised this batch of men, along with the two other batches of twelve. Thirty-six were as many as anyone could reasonably be expected to look at in one session.

The superintendent looked at the Commander, wondering why he had come out to the station, even given the fact that he was overseeing the rape complaint investigation. They had even had the deputy chairman of the Police Complaints Authority at one of the parades! 'I can't ask them to shave, sir,' he said, knowing some of the beard growths were but a few days old. 'Perhaps it's their genitals she should be looking at.' Both he and the inspector with them chuckled.

Bentham didn't respond.

'This is the eighth parade we had her to. She's identified no one.'

'She'll see every man and woman on duty in the entire area that night if need be,' Bentham said. 'And those from outside.'

An anxiety attack came over Roberta as she walked slowly up the line and then back down to look at a policeman who she was sure was in the cell that night. She didn't know what to do for a moment, and couldn't speak or remember what the inspector had told her to do if she recognised anyone. Finally she crashed him around the face with her open hand, and would have hit him again but for his pulling back and the chief inspector stopping her.

Immediately she realised what she had done. She had hit the wrong man. She felt terrible about that. She had no liking for the police, but didn't want the wrong man to get the blame.

'I suppose we could nick her for assault,' the superintendent said.

'Let's have a look at his duty sheet for the night in question.'

'Do you want us to go on with the parades, sir?'

'Until she's eliminated everyone who could have been in that station with her. Calm her down, give her a cup of tea, and go again with her.' Bentham glanced at the black man with the trombone as he went out, having no idea who he was.

If the station superintendent was surprised to see a commander visit the identity parades, he was staggered by the arrival of the Deputy Commissioner, even though Harry Streeter had a habit of looking in at police stations unannounced and talking to the policemen running them.

'Guv,' was how Bentham greeted him when he was shown into his temporary office. 'A long way from home.'

'I used to walk a beat from this nick, Jack.'

Bentham didn't say anything, but knew his visit wasn't for the sake of nostalgia.

'Different sort of coppering then. Now so much depends on your political perspective.'

'It would be nice to get back to that sort of villain maybe,' Bentham said obligingly.

'Not much chance, even if we were given the manpower. How's this inquiry going?'

'No one saw anything or heard anything. No one remembers who dealt with Roberta Ford, or who arrested her. The duty officer was dealing with too many other problems. And I have the deputy chair of the PCA calling me every day. He wanted to know what colour pants she had on.'

'What, today?'

'I think the day of the alleged rape, for the difference it makes.'

'What colour were they – did you find out?' Streeter asked.

'I don't think she had any on. Most black girls don't wear them.'

'Is that right?' The Deputy Commissioner was surprised. He hoped Bentham would expand on this, uncertain if he was joking, but didn't want to ask. 'You probably won't be thanked, whatever you turn up. This looks like one of those thankless bastards you'd wish you hadn't heard of. I've another one like that – you'll be owed a favour if you take it on, but you'll probably get even less thanks.'

Bentham wondered how many more investigations he was going to be asked to conduct that CIB-2 should be doing. There weren't too many possibilities that sprang to mind as Bentham waited for the Deputy Commissioner, and Northern Ireland wasn't even near.

'Norman Hateley wants someone to go over and investigate the alleged shoot-to-kill operations by the RUC. You'd be made up to acting Assistant Commissioner to give you the authority the job requires.'

That was immediately appealing to Bentham, but it wasn't enough. 'And when it's over?' he inquired.

Harry Streeter smiled. 'That might depend on the result, Jack.' He enjoyed the bargaining and was good at it. He had come to the notice of the Home Secretary as a possible Commissioner when as Chief Constable of Essex he had personally negotiated with some Middle Eastern terrorists who held customers hostage in a restaurant, threatening to kill them. The siege had ended peacefully without a shot being fired. Afterwards, he had said it was no different from negotiations with the police authority for manpower and resource.

'Is it a job I could turn down if I chose?'

'Is it one you'd want to turn down, Jack? The right sort of result here will get you noticed.'

Without responding immediately, Bentham thought about what the Deputy Commissioner was saying to him; he was implying there was an easily arrived-at option in the result. There always was, of course, in the way information was gathered and presented; it could be done in such a way as to leave but one conclusion. Only he didn't like having the ground rules set out in that way. 'This begs the question, what is the right result, Harry? I expect Sir Norman wants no case found to be answered, the RUC exonerated.'

'I'd say that's what the government wants,' Harry Streeter said, and smiled, showing a line of neatly capped teeth with gold crowns beyond those – the expensive dental work had been done since he'd taken high office. 'That's what you'll probably find too, Jack. But what you find is what you find. I told Norman Hateley you'd do it your way or not at all, that you'd come to your own conclusions, not his. He wants to meet you.'

'What about this inquiry?'

'No less important, Jack. Jonathan Entwistle wants you to keep this one running. It might spark something across the water if we're not careful. Though I'll tell you' – he glanced about as if to make sure there was no one else listening – 'there are some in ACPO who are waiting for that, so the riot squad can go in with gas and baton rounds. Fucking depressing, isn't it?'

All Maurice Knight had had to do to find Bobby Sterling was knock on the door of his mother's flat. He had gone there after taking Roberta back home. His plans had suffered a setback as a result of her reliving the trauma of her police experience. But he had seen inside her place briefly and wanted to be drawn further into that world of students and learning and decent behaviour, instead of the jungle he was thrashing around in. But she hadn't invited him, her mood had changed; he was a man, he was unwelcome. But he would go back there. He would devise a way to see her for herself, because he wanted to.

Bobby Sterling was dead, having OD'd on the heroin he was supposed to have sold. His mother thought he was sleeping. A pathetic, wasted nineteen-year-old lying in a tip of cigarette packets and beer cans and burnt tin foil from dragons long since chased. On the wall were three framed certificates of merit he had earned for swimming. They looked incongruous. This youth's entire potential amounted to three pieces of paper. Maurice felt angry at first and wanted to hit out at Benny Soares, but when he calmed down he realised there was no more point in blaming him. No one was really to blame but the dead boy himself.

Finally Maurice's anger became sadness, but it wasn't released, not even by the sad notes he found himself blowing out the park late at night. He had purposely avoided the youth club or any of the pubs where he may have run into Benny. He sat against a fat old plane tree and blew, not loudly, but loud enough for the sound to carry against the roar of heavy lorries on the bordering trunk road, the neighbouring housing estate and the adjacent empty hospital. The notes were like a muted cry that couldn't help but affect those who heard them. Maurice felt alone, isolated, a little afraid. He wanted friendship and acceptance and love, but saw no easy way to those, none if he turned back and quit, and possibly none if he went ahead and succeeded.

The three uniformed policemen who climbed the tall wrought iron gates at the entrance to the park weren't moved by the sounds from the trombone, other than to irritation. They assumed whoever was playing was drunk. Drunks were a pain. The policemen left their van parked outside the gates, the engine running, none of them sure how they'd carry a drunk back over.

They were surprised to find the young black man playing; more so that he continued without missing a note, and not a little envious that he played so well.

'What the fuck are you doing? It's one o'clock.'

Maurice continued his piece. Neither the policemen nor the world existed.

Stupefied expressions fell over the policemen's faces. They looked at each other.

'Hey, Sambo, I'm speaking to you.'

Still Maurice ignored them, not because he thought it clever but because his emotions were exposed and random. Then one of them caught hold of the trombone slide as it came towards him and bent it.

'I was enjoying my right to go freely about my business,' Maurice said a little too formally.

The morning was decidedly brightening for these three policemen. They laughed as Maurice stood up and patiently tried to straighten the bow out of the trombone slide.

'He must've just come down outta that fucking tree.'

'All right, turn your pockets out.'

'You bent my trombone, man,' Maurice said, and put it away in the case. He clipped the mouthpiece on to his chain.

'I'll bend your black fucking head, you don't turn your pockets out.'

The policeman made a serious mistake in grabbing hold of Maurice at that point, for Maurice had screwed down a lot of anger. He got it full in the face from Maurice's forehead, a move Maurice regretted as this was a brother officer, someone of the calling he had decided to give a lot of his life to. The uniformed policeman's nose split open bloodily. Maurice hit the one nearest to him with his trombone case and went straight for the third, savagely raining blows on him. Maurice could feel his knuckles stinging as he kept hitting him until he went down.

The third backed away from Maurice and pulled his truncheon. The last thing he expected was a kick in the ballocks, or the second and third, any one of which would have left him breathless with pain. Maurice grabbed his trombone and ran. He had an excuse now to go back to see Roberta.

Sliding into the bench-type seat opposite Maurice Knight in the greasy spoon near the Farm DS Tait grinned like a Cheshire Cat. He assumed the black constable was getting what he wanted. Without greeting he reached over and helped himself to a piece of toast and chewed it.

'The eggs are good,' Maurice said. He glanced around, but assumed Brian Tait wouldn't approach him like this unless it was safe to do so. He didn't know how he had found him; he could never find people that easily.

All was suddenly made clear when Tait said, 'It was as well you avoided your flop last night. Every Old Bill around is looking for a spade trombonist.'

'Short of a body for a group are they?'

Brian Tait laughed and dipped the remainder of his toast into one of Maurice's eggs. The local detective who was on observation at Roberta Ford's flat reported seeing the black trombonist the local police were looking for, but to DS Tait, not the uniform branch.

'D'you do anything about those two bent detectives?'

'You might be right about them,' Tait conceded, 'but there's fuck-all I can do about it at present, I mean, I can't stick you up as a witness.'

'I want to see them nicked.'

'Let's do one thing at a time. What did you get from Roberta Ford? Was she raped by those policemen like she claimed?'

'I don't know, we didn't talk about it.'

'I suppose it would be difficult, you giving it to her and asking that.' He waited, then added maliciously to try and draw a response, 'Half the Farm's fucked her, and that college she goes to.'

No trace of emotion surfaced on Maurice's face, but that didn't mean he wasn't feeling angry with this man. The mockery was making him feel worse about the situation he found himself in. He didn't know why he didn't quit, say he couldn't do the job any more, go back to being a home beat policeman in Plymouth, to values he understood and could cope with. He suspected that he didn't want to fail the people he had chosen to spend his working life with, and didn't enjoy that suspicion that was skulking inside him. More than once last night he had been on the point of telling Roberta what he was, but had been afraid to. An opposing influence within him told him she would see it as a betrayal of the trust he was nurturing in her rather than something to celebrate. He hadn't made love to Roberta, as much as he would have liked to, nor had he tried, though he wasn't about to tell DS Tait that. She had helped clean him up and had washed the policeman's blood out of his clothes. At least they

141

wouldn't have that evidence on him, nor his trombone, which he had left at her flat, giving him yet another excuse to go back.

'The best lead I got on Del Lindo was the crematorium. Does that make sense to you?' The question was offensive, Maurice felt, and two days ago when he had first heard that the police had supposedly burned someone he wouldn't have put it. Now his perspective on his chosen people was going wonky.

'Not unless he's dead,' Tait said without missing a beat. 'What about that demo? Did you identify any of the ringleaders?'

'If the police were to change their tactics down here, we could avoid all sorts of trouble.'

'Ah, it sounds like you've fallen in love with a fucking radical, Maurice. I'll tell Chief Superintendent Barclay to change the policing methods. He'll enjoy that from you.'

'I keep hearing about the police being involved in crime. You can only ignore it so long.'

'I don't have any problem, Maurice,' DS Tait said reasonably. 'Then I don't spend my nights jammed up a police-hater who wants to do us down. Try sticking to useable facts, like most policemen.'

Maurice wondered if he gone too far. Maybe Tait was right, even though he was wrong about so much between him and Roberta. Maybe he was falling under her influence. In order to try and redeem the situation, he said, 'The demo outside the local nick is going off this Saturday, unless something happens in the Jarman murder case.'

That smile crept out of the dark corner of Tait's mind again. 'Who do they want nicked for the murder – Old Bill?'

'The feeling is that the police are ignoring the National Front, and some of the dealers who Jarman was going to blow out of the water, and a lot of policemen.'

'You're not telling us anything new, Maurice. You can tell your girlfriend we've turned over every National Front member in South London.

'Ask her where Del Lindo is – he's still our best prospect. We've got until the weekend. If a demo goes here it'll really go pop – with all those crazies in the riot squads with gas and plastic bullets. If it happens. We need that result, Maurice.'

14

HAVING MET WITH THE Chief Constable of Northern Ireland, and evidently having received his approval, acting Assistant Commissioner Jack Bentham couldn't admit to liking the man, and therefore wasn't sure why he now found himself on the plane to Belfast with six carefully picked detectives from C11. He couldn't define the reason for the feeling he had, it was purely instinctive. He had relied on reasoning when time and time again instinct had proved more reliable. His immediate impression of Sir Norman Hateley was that he had a crashing ego, but then Bentham assumed that was a prerequisite of the job. How could anyone function in that situation unless he believed what he was doing was making a difference? But that didn't make Bentham feel any better disposed towards him. It was a job, and therefore he knew he shouldn't have feelings either about it or the man he was doing it for, and he wouldn't be thanked if he quit halfway through because of a personality clash. But he couldn't avoid resenting the way in which the Chief Constable of the RUC had told him to conduct the investigation and what he'd find. Also, he couldn't avoid disliking himself for going along with that while his eyes were firmly fixed on promotion.

Bentham knew that he hadn't given enough thought to his own ego, which he knew wasn't exactly insignificant; on many occasions it was purposely inverted, something he could afford while he was doing things his way. The circumstances weren't such that he had been able to think about his position objectively; every thought had drawn him back to the prospect of being elevated to acting Assistant Commissioner – with both the authority and pay at that rank. There was currently a full quota of four Assistant Commissioners, but a time-honoured tradition guaranteed he would go into the first vacancy at that rank, unless he completely fucked-up.

Despite his misgivings about Sir Norman Hateley, Jack Bentham was determined that this was different from any other investigation only in that the eyes of a lot of interested parties would be focussed on it. The result the Northern Irish Chief Constable hoped for was, in fairness to him, no more than one would expect he would want. Bentham reflected on the reassurance he had received from both Deputy Commissioner Streeter and the president of the Association of Chief Police Officers that this was an independent inquiry, and whatever result he turned in would be the one acted upon. Perhaps they were very sure of what he would find, or he was being a bit naive; either way, it had enabled him to leap through the rank of DAC to AC, and there was no denying, even to himself, that he was enjoying the title. However, barely an hour away from London by plane, and already he had a sense of missing being near the power centre. Fortunately the shuttle in and out of Aldergrove was pretty frequent.

Travelling with only hand baggage and a briefcase, both of which he had carried with him on the plane, he was clear on to the arrivals concourse long before his men, who had large suitcases. They would be staying while he popped backwards and forwards on a weekly basis, keeping up with other developments in London. While he was waiting for the others, a uniformed superintendent approached him and saluted him as though he were a household face.

'Assistant Commissioner Bentham. Welcome to Belfast, sir. I'm sorry about the weather.'

The rain that was blustering on a north-easterly wind across the airport was turning to sleet.

'It's more like winter than spring,' Bentham said obligingly.

'It's always winter here, sir,' the superintendent said with feeling. 'I have transport to take you to your accommodation.'

Assuming a certain status would be accorded him at his new rank, and not thinking anyone here would be into game-playing, Bentham hadn't bothered to inquire about the level of accommodation for him and his men. But no way was a section house acceptable, no matter how much room they had there. It was part of the RUC training centre out in Garnerville, East Belfast, where office space had also been allocated to them. They were told it was for security reasons.

'Is it still a disciplinary matter here to have a woman in your room?' DI Neville Hodgkinson said as they surveyed the drab accommodation from the entrance hall. The rules had been relaxed back on the mainland. Hodgkinson was young and good-looking. He was university-educated and Bentham chose him for the team for the quickness of his intellect.

There was a general air of amusement about the accommodation because none of them expected to stay here. The lowest ranks among them were the two detective inspectors, and it was a long while since either had slept in a section house, where none but young new single policemen and women lived.

Bentham was aware of their expectations of him, despite their amusement. He could have turned angry and blustered, but he stayed calm. 'It's very nice of the Deputy Chief Constable to think about our security,' he said, 'but I couldn't guarantee my men would observe the house rules. I'm sure you can find us a decent, moderately safe hotel.' He looked at the RUC superintendent. 'Get me a decent room, Frank.' He handed Detective Superintendent Burroughs his bag. 'A suite where I can work if necessary. Then meet me at Police Headquarters. I'll go and see the Chief Constable.'

Whatever sparse comfort he was prepared to allow other policemen to suffer, there was no suggestion of physical discomfort in the Chief Constable's office, Bentham found. It appeared to comprise almost the entire stone house that the RUC headquarters had been extended out of – he didn't realise at the time that Sir Norman had a flat on the first floor and lived here a virtual prisoner of his own security. His large desk was lost in the expanse of thick carpet that made his prison more comfortable. Sir Norman stood in front of the bullet-proof window, which looked out on what had once been formally laid-out gardens and was now a sea of parked cars. He had his back to Bentham, the Deputy Chief Constable and Mrs Muriel Kinahon, all of whom were sitting. Mrs Kinahon represented the Northern Irish Police Complaints Commission, and she was to oversee Bentham's investigation and ensure its independence.

'I love this country, Assistant Commissioner,' Sir Norman said stiffly, and turned towards him as if the other two weren't present. 'I hate witnessing what's happening here. It's uncharitable that along with men who've done their best to hold this province together I'm being accused of doing something to harm it.' He paused, then smiled cheerfully. 'I'm sure you'll soon appreciate what a sensitive and difficult policing operation it is over here.'

'We'll try not to add to those difficulties.'

'I hope you'll be successful in your inquiry and show that the RUC has nothing to answer for by its actions. Speed is essential. There will be more damage done if it drags on. Muriel will give you whatever help you may need with facilities and so forth. Donald will lay everything else on for you. Remember, my door is always open to you.'

'Just how do you propose to conduct this investigation, Assistant Commissioner?' Muriel Kinahon said when they were in the Deputy Chief Constable's office in the main building.

There was a challenge in her tone, Bentham decided, as he looked at the plump lady with bright cheeks that competed with the colour of her hair. The cause may have been the annoyance of a ruling élite, dismissive of the abilities of anyone else. Or her question may have come out of the insecurity, the need to try and establish her own ground rules; perhaps it was simply nervousness on her part. Bentham decided to keep his distance.

'I haven't the foggiest,' he said. 'I came with an open mind, Mrs Kinahon. We'd all better read all the paperwork on those six shootings. Everything from Mr Joyce's report to the duty sheets of the officers involved.'

'Ah, that may be difficult,' the Deputy Chief Constable said. 'They were accidentally destroyed when I was conducting my own inquiry.'

A such-is-life smile started across Bentham's face and he rose out of his chair. 'Let's hope some of your men have good memories.'

Along with the accommodation he and his men had been offered, he hoped this wasn't a reflection of the RUC's intentions as far as co-operation on this investigation was concerned. He may have been wrong about that and was determined to keep an open mind. 'Mrs Kinahon, the door to our offices will be open to you at any time,' he said, slightly mocking the Chief Constable. He gave her his best smile, but received little response.

The offices out at Garnerville were open plan with steel partitions separating each of the six desks and, although by no means luxurious, they were spacious and functional. The steel desks had locking drawers and there were steel filing cabinets also with locks. It occurred to Jack Bentham that he and his men might not be the only people with keys to these locks. He considered checking that with Mrs Kinahon, but didn't, believing instead that he was working among people of basically good intentions, policemen who wanted the cloud dispersed from over them.

That belief was borne out by the superintendent from the complaints and discipline department who had been assigned to them as liaison officer. Despite the apparent destruction of essential papers, he managed to find them a lot of other papers. They arrived at their offices by the sack-barrow load. There were four such loads, with the RUC superintendent cheerfully indicating what they were. 'These are witness statements taken by the Deputy Chief Constable's investigators.'

'What the fuck are they trying to do, bury us?' Detective Superintendent Burroughs said, looking over the stacks of folders. He was a slow reader.

'Good man,' Bentham said to the RUC superintendent like he would to a dog who had fetched a stick. 'The more you can dig up that relates to anything the better.'

'If there's anything more I can be helping you with, sir.' He saluted and departed.

'The seven of us will take months to wade through this,' Burroughs complained.

'I'm asking the Deputy Commissioner to send over a couple of computer operators to get this lot on to disks. Make life a lot easier.'

Computers would be all they needed then. Bentham got in touch with Mrs Kinahon, who seemed surprised both by the call and the request. He asked for eight computer terminals.

'Goodness, I don't know if we have that resource, Assistant Commissioner. Are you all going to be working on computers?'

'No, I'm anticipating you cutting down my order.'

She laughed at that. 'Then how many do you need, Assistant Commissioner?'

'Four,' Bentham told her, and they were installed before his operators had arrived. His mind remained open, but he began to think Mrs Kinahon might be all right after all.

Jack Bentham was a fast reader, his method being to read the conclusion, then the statements in reverse order, then go through them again from front to back. He could assimilate and retain huge amounts of information, something he had learned to do when under pressure at university. But even so he was impressed by the four computer operators, two men and two women, who rattled information into the computer that had been set up in the largest of the offices. What was more impressive was the way Detective Superintendent Palmer organised the material on the computer, case by case, so that information could be retrieved by one operator or cross-referenced by another while the other two continued the input. It meant the detectives could go to work straight away. Bentham had picked Dave Palmer for this investigation solely for his computer skills; he was a difficult man to work with – introverted and often negative.

Initially a lot of mistakes had been made as the police moved into the computer age, including the choice of computers they bought, and, in the case of the Met, the way they had financed them, going into the money market and borrowing at usurer rates. In the early days, information would be fed into the computer only for them to find there was no way of retrieving it, resulting in double effort in going back to manual files. But things were changing; computer skills were developing into a fine art. That was slightly worrying for Bentham. If something came out of the computer incorrectly, it did so for one of two reasons: either it had been put in incorrectly or the retrieval questions had been programmed wrongly. It was always operator-fault. Yet, more and more, whatever came out of the police computer was accepted as holy writ.

With the case details as they were available from two of the shootings so far on the computer, and all the paperwork read by at least some of Bentham's team, they went to work.

'According to two of the witnesses,' Bentham said, sitting at the desk Detective Superintendent Burroughs was using in the main office, 'we have six RUC men at the Crossmaglen ambush, but only four statements. Why didn't the Deputy Chief Constable interview the other two?'

'I doubt if anyone asked him, guv,' DI Neville Hodgkinson said.

'Someone had better make a point of finding the other two.'

'That same thing happened with the shooting of the terrorist in that alleyway by the Divis flats,' Burroughs pointed out, his thick fingers crashing against the keys of the computer terminal as if he were trying to break them. He glanced at the green VDU. 'There were eight policemen at that incident, but only six police statements taken.'

'Is it the same two policemen who are missing?'

'I don't know.'

'Follow that up, Frank. Just in case anyone has pulled those statements for some reason. Look for other common pointers, apart from the obvious ones. Were any of the policemen at more than one of the shooting incidents?'

'Chief Inspector Paisley was,' DI Hodgkinson informed him. 'Also Sergeant Keeper.'

'That seems like a good place to start.'

* * *

148

Chief Inspector Paisley perspired with anxiety when he was called in to be interviewed by these London detectives. He wasn't sure why, and told himself it wasn't on account of any feeling of culpability. He had simply done his duty, the result of which should be neither persecution nor prosecution. He had been told there would be no action resulting from this investigation, not after what had happened to Maurice Peters and Gary Hinton. But if that was the case, why was this senior policeman over from London with his team?

He thought about Sergeant Keeper, the only other member of the SSU to be called to Garnerville police barracks with him. He had said how they might be regretting re-opening this. Terry Keeper looked confident enough, and Paisley wondered briefly if he knew something he didn't, that perhaps he shouldn't be worrying himself so.

But anxiety wouldn't leave him, and he was sure Assistant Commissioner Bentham would assume he was guilty, even though he wasn't.

'How did you know about the three IRA suspects outside Crossmaglen?' Bentham wanted to know. He attached no importance at all to this man sweating, but wasn't about to set him at his ease.

'I'm not rightly knowing, sir. From an informer, I'd say.'

'One working for the Special Support Unit?'

Giving that answer had seemed the easy way out, but now he decided it was a mistake that needed correcting. 'It came from Intelligence.'

'You mean MI6?'

'No,' he said quickly. He had been told not to involve the Security or Intelligence Service. 'From our own criminal intelligence unit.' He assumed the Assistant Commissioner wouldn't know that almost all of Special Branch's intelligence in Northern Ireland was closely tied up with the Security Service.

'They gave you time and place for the stop?'

'We reconnoitred the area as always. We decided on the place.'

'And how you'd make the stop? How many men it would need?'

'Yes. We did that the day before,' Chief Inspector Paisley lied.

'You were that certain of your information – that the suspects would be coming through there?'

'It's never certain until it proves so. We sometimes spend days waiting for something that never happens.'

That was familiar to all policemen and Bentham sympathised.

They digressed slightly to swap waste-of-time stories. Paisley relaxed a little.

'With all the planning that went into the stop, what would you say went wrong?'

'I wouldn't say anything did. None of my men were injured.'

'It wasn't the intention to shoot and kill the suspects?'

'No, sir. We had surrounded the car when they reached for their guns.'

That didn't ring true in Bentham's head, and he wasn't sure why until Detective Superintendent Burroughs passed him a witness statement, which said the police were all on one side of the road. They would have needed to be unless they were to shoot each other. 'It was then you gave the order to shoot?' Bentham asked, sliding the statement aside.

'We have a standing order to open fire in life-threatening circumstances.'

'Did the suspects open fire?'

'I'm not sure. They may have fired two shots.'

'You said they had in your original statement,' Bentham pointed out. 'You had information that there'd be three armed men in the car. You decided that six would be a big enough unit to cope with that?'

'Either we kept the number limited or there would have been no operation. We couldn't have been after concealing more men on that bend.'

'How were the men picked for this operation?'

Anxiety went another notch higher and Chief Inspector Paisley didn't answer immediately. His boss, Chief Superintendent Johnston, had advised him to keep certain parties out of this, not because they shouldn't have been there, but because their presence would be interpreted in the wrong way.

'I don't understand what you're asking, sir.'

'Is it a voluntary unit?'

'Yes, the entire unit is. But individual squads are made up by Chief Superintendent Johnston.'

'Did he ask you to run the unit that night?'

'He told me I'd be running it, I'd say,' Paisley replied, not understanding the tack.

'Who else was on the squad?'

'Sergeant Keeper. Constables Dan Grennell and William Mason, and two others I don't know.' Suddenly he felt confused about

Birchfield and Stone, whether to keep them out. He wanted to call back those words but couldn't.

'You went on an operation with two men you didn't know?'

'They were part of the Special Support Unit, of course. We draw men from all over the place. They come and go. They do so.'

'They volunteered,' Bentham said, taking a folder from Detective Superintendent Burroughs, who indicated to him that the three named had made statements, Constable Grennell mentioning the other two. 'Are these two men still in the Unit?'

'The Unit's been disbanded, sir,' Chief Inspector Paisley said, purposely misconstruing the question.

'It wasn't following that first shooting. Presumably it's quite traumatic, shooting three suspects – even though they were armed and dangerous?'

'The Deputy Chief Constable said no blame attached.'

'If it has to be done, it has to be done,' Bentham assured him. 'I'm just trying to find out what happened. Presumably the Deputy Chief Constable interviewed everyone?'

'Yes, sir.'

'There's only a record of statements, made to you, Keeper, Grennell and Mason. Were these other two men around the Special Support Unit after the shootings?'

Hesitating a moment, Paisley said, 'I'd say so.'

'There are only about forty men on the Special Support Unit. You are small and special, you've a special hut where you have your own office and briefing facilities behind RUC headquarters. You couldn't have been off having a conversation with these men, or knowing their names?'

His position perished on the rock of reason. 'One was Birchfield, the other Len Stone. There are men in the Unit I know less well.'

Bentham appeared to attach no importance to the evasion. 'Is there any reason why Birchfield or Stone didn't make a statement?'

'None I can think of, sir.'

Bentham nodded approvingly. The tiny gesture seemed to mean a lot to the man opposite.

'Back on the road when the three suspects were shot, you say no one gave the order to shoot. Who was first to see them reaching for their guns?'

'I'm not sure. We all saw it once, I'd say. Sergeant Keeper called out the warning.'

'You all fired in accordance with standing orders. How were you positioned?'

'In the hedgerow at the side of the road. Sergeant Keeper was in front of the vehicle used to block the road. Grennell was with Keeper. Mason with me. The other two were in the hedge on the driver's side of the road.'

'On Sergeant Keeper's warning, you all opened fire on the occupants of the car. Just as standing orders say – to avoid endangering any of the patrol. Did any one of you not fire?'

'I don't know, sir. Sure, it gets like a reflex action in those circumstances. You're tense, on the look-out for any sign of danger from the suspect. God, you know what might happen!' He shuddered at recalling instantly some of the situations he'd been in.

'I don't know how you people cope as well as you do like that.'

'Ah, sure, you get used to it,' Paisley responded, feeling he was being let off.

'The suspects' car was only holed with bullets on one side,' Bentham said casually, as if reading it in the statement before him.

It seemed like a sudden act of treachery that took Paisley's breath away. 'That's what the forensic report says. If you were on three sides of the car, two of you would have been shot in the process.'

Chief Inspector Paisley looked at the Assistant Commissioner as if he were a friend who had just told him he was fucking his wife.

'Would you like to think some more about that night, then make another statement?'

The Chief Inspector wanted more than just time to think about a new statement. He wanted out altogether, and would tell his boss so as soon as he was clear of this lot. He knew what the smooth-talking Chief Superintendent Johnston would say: Don't let them rattle you. He could almost smell his Homme anti-perspirant that lay over him like a coating of confidence. That was easier said than done, Paisley knew, especially when you weren't in the firing line. He couldn't see either Chief Superintendent Johnston or Mr Joyce being interviewed by the enemy.

Whether as a result of his interviews with Paisley and the one that followed with Keeper, or whether by pure coincidence, Muriel Kinahon decided to take up Bentham's open-door invitation and look over shoulders.

'These are decent men, Mr Bentham,' she said, as if she believed he had no idea of that. 'You mustn't treat them like criminals.'

'Have you ever seen the police interview criminals, Mrs Kinahon?' Bentham asked evenly.

'Yes I have, out at Castlereagh.'

'How were they being treated?'

A slight sense of panic appeared in Mrs Kinahon's eyes as she realised she had been slightly out-manoeuvred.

The reputation of Castlereagh had even reached London, but Bentham guessed she wasn't going to admit to anything other than correct behaviour there.

'They're policemen, Mrs Kinahon. I wouldn't want to treat them like criminals. You're welcome to sit in on any of the interviews.'

His reasonableness completely undermined her. Her defensiveness was deflected into questions about the shape of his investigation, as if that was the purpose of her visit to the temporary offices.

They were both still feeling their way with one another, but Bentham felt in no way threatened by her. He would conduct this investigation his own way; that had been agreed at the outset. But he knew he would be handling things badly if he couldn't manage to let her believe a lot of the input was hers.

The cars that had been involved in the ambush killings by the RUC had been brought to the police car pound opposite the fortified police station on Donegal Pass. It was there that AC Bentham went to examine them. Not because he didn't trust the forensic reports, but because he could scarcely believe that the RUC would be so indifferent to tying up their stories to accord with the evidence. What Chief Inspector Paisley had said differed from Sergeant Keeper's version and contradicted forensic evidence. He couldn't work out immediately if it was because they were lazy or stupid, or so confident in what they were doing that they believed no one would ever challenge them. But there on the pound, tucked away in the corner among the dozens of police cars, was the contradiction for all to see. The car from the Armagh ambush with holes going in only from the driver's side, with a few coming out on the nearside. That made, according to Chief Inspector Paisley's evidence, the two missing RUC officers, Birchfield and Stone, responsible. Bentham knew he could take both Paisley and Keeper back in and take their stories to pieces.

'You're lucky they're still here, sir,' said the RUC constable who was guarding the place in a flak jacket and with a Sterling machine gun. He stood watching Bentham and Detective Superintendent

Burroughs look over the car rather than for would-be terrorists. 'Didn't they go to the auctions last month. No one wanted them. Would you?'

He watched them move on in silence to the second car in which an IRA suspect had been shot dead at the traffic lights. One door looked like a colander.

'They weren't taking any chances,' Burroughs said.

'Can you blame them, Frank, in these circumstances? You get shot at and bombed like they do here, it would make you not want to take chances.'

Bentham wondered about the RUC, whether they ran scared or became more determined the more that was thrown at them. He assumed the latter, but decided it was a peculiar animal that would be attracted to the job in these circumstances, perhaps a very dangerous animal. 'I've no real objection to them operating a shoot-to-kill policy, if that's what they were doing,' he said as if to mitigate his thoughts as they walked back to their car. 'But they ought to get their fucking stories together!'

He slammed the car door, feeling angry and not sure why.

On the way back to the office he began to think the reason was because the investigation was beginning to look too involved for him to deliver the sort of result everyone seemed to want, the one that basically he'd like to deliver. There would be no real problem in doing that, only in the fact that it would look so bald that anyone who cared to would be able to see he was complicit in a cover-up.

Although computers gave his men information at fingertip demand and delivered it faster, it didn't make that work any less tedious or painstaking. After four days of cross-referencing and mapping out who was where doing what, when and to whom, a pattern started to emerge in the operations. There was nothing clear and directional, but enough to suggest who to target. There would be weeks and weeks of wading through both manilla files and data files and everyone would become heartily sick of the work, which was why Bentham also put them on to work they could relate to more readily, even though they would still have to put in all those hours of tedium.

'Chief Inspector Paisley was at three of the four shooting incidents,' Detective Superintendent Palmer said, reading off the screen. 'Sergeant Keeper was the only officer at all four.'

'Right. You start interviewing Paisley now, Dave,' he said to Detective Superintentent Dave Palmer, who was lean and effete looking and wore a thin moustache of the kind sported by movie stars in old black and white films on TV. 'Go through absolutely everything, as if we hadn't interviewed him at all.'

'It's all taking a long time, guv,' DI Neville Hodgkinson said, almost apologetically. 'It's like they're trying to bog us down with how boring it all is. They are.'

'I don't mind how long it takes. The longer the better.' Bentham knew the technique of using different officers for subsequent interviews was disorientating and the subject often changed his story, forgetting what information he had previously given. He couldn't treat policemen like criminals, nor would he want to, even if Mrs Kinahon would let him. 'What about Birchfield and Stone?'

Those thick fingers of Frank Burroughs' crashed on to the keyboard. 'They only appear not to have been on that first shooting and the one when Desmond O'Donnell died in the alleyway at the Divis flats.'

'They don't appear anywhere else?' DI Hodgkinson asked.

'No,' Detective Superintendent Burroughs said with a smile.

'Arrange for them to be interviewed next, Nev.'

'The only other officer at more than one shooting was Dan Grennell. He was at the roadblock in Armagh and the alleyway.'

'Birchfield and Stone look the most interesting,' Bentham said. 'It's almost as if someone has dropped them out. Let's go through all the police statements again looking for any inconsistencies and contradictions.'

'Have you noticed how apart from one man in his car when the IRA suspect was shot at the traffic lights,' Detective Superintendent Palmer said, 'there are no civilian witnesses?'

'What are you saying, Dave?'

'I don't know. I mean, you can understand people here not wanting to get involved. But how come no single witness to these public shootings?'

The doubts were surfacing in all of the Met detectives.

In the alleyway where Desmond O'Donnell had been shot a white cross had been painted on the corrugated iron fence, along with a message about his being a murder victim of the RUC. Someone else had tried unsuccessfully to scrub out the message, but it remained for all to read. It sent a shiver down Bentham's spine on that damp grey afternoon when he and Detective Superintendent Burroughs took Sergeant Keeper back there to go over his story. The fence painting seemed to indicate to Bentham how intractable the problem was. His thoughts jumped as he glanced over at the bleak blocks of the Divis flats. He thought about the woman who had lost her son, shot by the same unit, and recalled how difficult she had been when interviewed by the RUC. It wasn't surprising that she was. He made a note to send Bill Senior in to interview her.

'They'll erect a cross to a martyr, I shouldn't wonder,' Sergeant Keeper said. He was confused that Bentham was now interviewing him and not Detective Superintendent Palmer, who had interviewed him before, and was angry from trying to interpret what that meant. He had been interviewed once, that should be the end of it.

Bentham glanced round at him. 'Where were you when O'Donnell was trapped?'

'We didn't do anything wrong, Mr Bentham.'

'I'm not saying you did.' He would go on explaining to these men that he was merely establishing what happened.

'I was following through the compound from those flats, and over the fence. I was so.'

'Who reached O'Donnell first? Constable Stone?'

'No, he was . . . behind. At the window, I think. I'm not sure. He went into the building with me and Inspector Ross, and I can't remember who else.'

'Birchfield – I think that's who you said in your statement to Superintendent Palmer?'

'They jumped from the window after O'Donnell.'

'That was pretty dangerous – he may have turned and shot them.'

'You don't consider that in the heat of the moment.'

'You had him trapped here in the alley?'

'We did so.'

'Did anyone call a warning to him before he tried to shoot it out?'

Anger flared in Sergeant Keeper. 'This was an IRA terrorist. Do you know how many policemen they've killed?'

Bentham nodded, trying to put himself into the situation the RUC men must have found themselves in almost on a daily basis. But he could only relate to his own policing experience. 'I'm simply trying to establish the facts, Sergeant.'

Keeper wasn't placated.

'So we can have another bloody trial, so bloody public opinion is satisfied.'

'You might not believe this, but I'm not out to try and nick anyone. Just answer some of the questions that are left unanswered.'

He wasn't sure if that was true or whether he was simply trying to gain this policeman's confidence, regardless of the final result. Whichever it was, Sergeant Keeper calmed down.

'No, sir, I don't think a warning was shouted to O'Donnell. At least, I wasn't after hearing it.'

'Tell me about the other suspect who was reported.'

'I didn't see him. No one did. We were just after hearing him. The UDR were called in, but they didn't find him.'

The Met men returned to their hotel, which was styleless and modern, and made secure from the bombers of yesteryear by a smoke-filled security hut that residents and guests alike had to pass through to reach the building itself. The less-than-vigilant private guards made no one feel secure. They simply raised the barrier and waved Bentham and all members of his team on to the forecourt when they approached by car. Work didn't stop until they went to sleep. Back at the hotel, they usually met in Bentham's suite for a drink and to go over the day.

'Do you think Keeper is covering up something that happened in that alleyway?' Bentham directed the question at Burroughs and Palmer.

'Not just in the alleyway,' Detective Superintendent Burroughs said. 'There's a lot of footwork going on. My feeling is they're going to start tripping over each other before long.'

There was a long silence in the room as each of them thought fleetingly of compromising situations they had been in, but where no one had been looking to compromise them, fortunately.

'I think Keeper's shit-scared this is going to result in more prosecutions,' Detective Superintendent Palmer said. He didn't like to see policemen in trouble, and thought that within reason policemen should be exempt from prosecution.

'The thing is, I can't guarantee it won't, regardless of what we tell them.' Bentham passed round the bottle of scotch after splashing some into his own glass.

Doubt about the involvement of these men was penetrating the natural defensive barrier Bentham had developed towards police wrongdoing. So far he had resisted the possibility of the what or who that might be behind that involvement. No amount of alcohol or sleep would erase the doubt now.

15

O F ALL THE RUC policemen directly involved in the shootings to be interviewed by his team, Jack Bentham decided that Constable Maurice Peters was the most vulnerable and likely to crack and reveal something. Watching the young, thin-faced constable, whose wispy moustache made him appear still younger, Bentham's feeling about him increased, and he didn't ignore it. Every opportunity would be given to Peters or anyone else to say whatever they might want to say about anything. Maybe he was completely wrong on this occasion in his assessment, for along with his co-defendant in the Stephen McFadden killing Maurice Peters would have been under more pressure to talk than anyone, but he hadn't. Perhaps there was nothing to talk about. But that feeling he had just wouldn't go away.

'How did you come to be charged with shooting Stephen McFadden, Mr Peters? Bentham asked. 'Do you know?'

'No, sir. No one said why Gary and me was picked on.' He was standing like a soldier before his commanding officer and was surprised when Bentham invited him to sit down. 'I'd say we was the least involved, sir,' he said.

'Could that have had something to do with it?'

'I don't know, sir. We've now got disciplinary proceedings against us, which isn't right.'

'For failing to await a legal order to fire.' Bentham glanced at the summary he'd made of this man's earlier statement. 'I suppose that's why you were charged with Stephen McFadden's killing?'

'Well, you can't be trained for one thing then do another the moment someone tells you. Not in them circumstances. You're so tense. You think, God, this is it. You remember your mates what get blown away. I saw them lads raise those guns. It wasn't me what opened fire first anyway. I think it was Stone and Birchfield.'

Bentham put his summary to one side and flicked back through the thick folder that related to Maurice Peters. He found what he was looking for, and read it, keeping the constable waiting. Finally he said, 'That wasn't part of your evidence in court.'

'As it turned out, sir, it wasn't necessary. But I didn't want to lose the RUC's support.'

'Had someone warned you not to say anything?'

Maurice Peters suddenly had a feeling that this wasn't going to be as easy as he had expected.

Bentham waited a long while, but the police constable said nothing. 'You expect the same sort of result on the disciplinary charges as you got in court?'

'If they'd produced the tape-recording in court they'd have known it weren't Gary and me what fired first.'

Bentham didn't miss a beat, but said, 'It should have been produced' – sounding as if he knew all about the tape, instead of it being a revelation. 'Why wasn't it?'

'I'd say they were protecting the MI5 people.'

'It's not unreasonable to keep them out of the frame.'

'Not to put us in! Why should that be so?'

'Why didn't you mention MI5 in court?'

Constable Peters made fleeting eye contact with him, as if in a brief gesture of supplication, then fixed his gaze on the top of the desk. He didn't answer.

'Do they always record such operations?'

'I don't know.'

'How often are MI5 in on such operations?'

'Can't say, sir.'

'What happened to the tape recording?'

'They cleared all the equipment away after the suspects was shot.'

'They didn't wait around for the scene-of-crime officer?'

There was no reply. There had been no one else mentioned in the scene-of-crime officer's report.

'Where did you train, Mr Peters?' Bentham asked, changing tack.

'Here in Belfast,' Maurice Peters said, feeling more at ease now that they were on to something safe. 'I did three months with the SAS in Herefordshire for counter-terrorism training when I joined the Unit.'

'With other RUC policemen?'

'There were about twenty of us that time, sir.'

That gave Bentham another cross-reference point. With the computer system they had been supplied with his men were able to enter the personnel records held by B Department and plot who had been SAS-trained. All members of the Special Support Unit had at different times been on short training courses with the SAS, as had almost a quarter of all the other active RUC personnel.

'No wonder they shoot first and ask questions afterwards,' Bentham said, when he examined the computer analysis. 'We'd better get hold of that tape.'

That was something Jack Bentham was to find easier said than done. When he thought about it, he knew that if it wasn't out in the open and available at this point, then the likelihood was that no one had any intention of releasing it. But now he knew it existed he couldn't resist reaching for it.

Following an interview by the Met detectives, and especially one where AC Bentham took an active part, the RUC policemen in question would report directly to Chief Superintendent Neville Johnston, Special Branch number two at police headquarters in Knock Road. There the SSU men would be de-briefed and reassured.

Chief Superintendent Johnston would in turn report to his boss, ACC Peter Eglington, who ordinarily answered only to the Chief Constable; however, because complaints were being investigated and the Chief Constable might eventually have to sit on the disciplinary tribunal, his deputy, Donald Joyce, dealt officially with all matters arising. Anything of particular significance or concern, the Deputy Chief Constable informed Sir Norman Hateley of on an informal basis.

The question of the tapes from the scene of the crime being sought by Bentham was a subject of deep concern to Donald Joyce, and one that prompted a meeting between himself, the Chief Constable, the head of Special Branch and the Northern Irish DPP.

'Unless Bentham changes his tack, the attitude of the men he's interviewing is bound to change drastically, Donald,' ACC Eglington said as they came down the central stairs of the main headquarters building and stepped through to the Chief Constable's office in the adjacent house.

'I wouldn't think that's likely,' the Deputy said as he pushed into the ante-room to the Chief Constable's office. 'He was given a free hand.'

'But how free is free meant to be?'

'Sir Norman said to go right in, Mr Joyce,' the grey-haired secretary said.

Still his deputy gave a perfunctory rap at the door as he opened it.

Although he had a close relationship with Sir Norman Hateley professionally, Sir Cyril Shelldrake, the DPP, wasn't sure he was wanted at this meeting, but suspected it was simply because the Chief Constable wanted everyone involved in the machinations of state to cement some sort of loyalty out of fear. His involvement meant he lost something of his detachment when his opinion as the senior law officer of the province was required. Despite his suspicions, he hadn't protested when the Chief Constable had invited him over, assuming it was to discuss some possible prosecutions, but now he stopped himself from entering into the general discussion about the progress of the Met's investigation, unless asked a direct question.

Sir Cyril sat quietly on one of the deep buttoned sofas awaiting an opportunity to make his excuses to leave. As he sat there his mind wandered to many things: the lifestyle of the Chief Constable, even his everyday uniform was infuriatingly well cut – he had once recommended his tailor to him but he hadn't the courage to approach an expensive tailor, knowing what his wife would say. He thought about these two fat sofas, this large office, its two-way mirrors for windows – there for security reasons. There were no such security measures or opulence in his own office. Despite his resistance, the conversation kept drawing him in and he found no excuse to leave.

'If Mr Bentham is allowed to go his own sweet way,' ACC Eglington was saying, 'then I'm thinking we might not hold the line, Norman. The two officers who went on trial should have been the end of it.'

'Personally I don't mind what comes out, Peter,' Sir Norman said boldly. 'There's a part of me that wants an end to all this fucking hypocrisy. To have everything out in the open, publicly declare that these IRA murderers are getting what they deserve. More's the pity the basses didn't get it sooner. Everyone might have some peace here.' He looked directly at the DPP, noticing him fidgeting, getting ready to run. He would have liked some affirmation from Sir Cyril as to his commitment to such a course, but knew the IRA had more chance of flying the Tricolour over Stormont. His look didn't shift from the DPP, who eventually met his eyes and gave a watery smile.

'If the issue were that clear-cut, Norman,' the DPP said cautiously, 'then a solution might have been arrived at long ago. But there are political considerations that policing solutions will never satisfy here.'

'I'll have a word with Bentham,' Donald Joyce offered. 'Try and steer him away from these tapes.'

'Do the tapes actually exist?' Sir Cyril asked, as if he wanted useable information.

'That's what Bentham will want to know when he comes in later this afternoon,' Sir Norman said, not giving the DPP an answer. 'Perhaps you'd like to come along to that meeting, Cyril?'

Given the choice, the DPP knew he most certainly wouldn't. 'It might be more useful if I were to stay out of this, Norman. Perhaps instead I should offer my services to Mr Bentham as an unbiased sounding-board.'

He was surprised at the enthusiasm with which the Chief Constable took that up and worried for a long time afterwards that such an offer was a mistake. Anxiety about his being used in a way he shouldn't allow himself to be used caused that familiar tension to creep through his shoulders. He could feel one locking. Skin was beginning to flake on his pink forehead, as it did under increasing stress. He felt himself being sucked into something beyond his control, and decided he would try and take some sort of action to prevent that happening, only he was afraid to in case he was frozen out and left appearing culpable in some way.

Progress through the details of the cases was a slower business than Bentham would have liked, but there was no other route to follow if he was going to be thorough. Only then would he be sure of the case he presented, and whether charges should or should not be brought. Jack Bentham felt there was too much on the line here, and didn't care how long it took. He refused to listen to the murmurs from Mrs Kinahon about time and costs involved – their hotel rooms were expensive – any more than those that suggested he was damaging morale. What might have made him waiver was his being out of London, away from the seat of power where the intrigue that he assumed he would now be privy to abounded. That engaged him and excited him and he wanted to get back to it.

'These are the vehicles you all hid in while waiting for the suspects to collect the guns?' Jack Bentham asked in the derelict yard at Hollow Farm, where he had taken Sergeant Keeper.

Nothing much had changed here apart from the thickness of the fog and the litter. Bentham had decided to drop in on Detective Superintendent Palmer and DI Hodgkinson when they brought each of the RUC men being questioned here to go over details.

'I was in the old Hillman there so,' Sergeant Keeper said. 'Hinton and Peters were in that Ford Consul.' The hulk of the car was barely recognisable as such.

'Where were Birchfield and Stone?'

'I'm not sure – either in the van or the old railway truck.'

'And Chief Inspector Paisley?'

How many times he had been through this now, Sergeant Keeper wasn't sure, but he didn't think his story had changed significantly, if that was what they were expecting. He was a patient man, he had learned patient in his job. He told himself it didn't matter how many times he went over it, but he knew that each time some of the veneer of acceptability he had laid over this incident was cracking. If it wasn't, they wouldn't be bothering.

'Like I said in my statement, sir. He was in whichever they weren't.'

'What you didn't say anywhere, sergeant, was who he was with.'

'I don't know, sir, is why.'

'He was with someone who was recording the whole incident for posterity.' Bentham made this speculation sound irrefutable. 'Who was Chief Inspector Paisley with?'

'I don't know,' Keeper replied without hesitation. He was committed to the lie.

'Could he have been from MI5?'

When Sergeant Keeper didn't answer Bentham turned, squelched off through the mud and went into the barn. Keeper followed with the other two detectives.

'Why was this operation recorded, do you know?'

'No, sir.'

'Not privy to MI5 policy?' Bentham was still speculating. 'Or was it RUC policy?' He knew when he was reaching this man, for he didn't reply, possibly because he found that easier than lying. 'How come that once you had seen that it was two lads the order to open fire was still given?'

'It wasn't, as far as I know. That's why Hinton and Peters went for trial.'

'They say the order was given. That others fired and so did they. But then I suppose they would say that.'

'We didn't know who was to pick up the guns.'

'From your concealed positions, couldn't you see them approach?'

'We heard them. We'd no such luxury as a positive identification.'

'But it might have been anyone – kids playing, as it turned out,'

Bentham said, a little surprised. 'Did no one stop to consider that?'

'I expect someone did, sir.'

'MI5?'

Sergeant Keeper didn't answer, but wondered why he was trying so hard to keep the Security Service out of this. These policemen weren't daft.

Jack Bentham left Palmer and Hodgkinson to continue walking the RUC policeman through what happened out here, and went to keep an appointment with the Chief Constable. He wanted to pursue the apparent disappearance of Constables Birchfield and Stone, and the tape from Hollow Farm. It had been mentioned in the transcript of the trial of Peters and Hinton but not produced. It might give a clearer indication of what happened there, and who was subsequently lying.

'There's nothing sinister or mysterious about Constables Birchfield and Stone.' Sir Norman Hateley was open and charming now. 'They've both been transferred to Londonderry,' he said, revealing his origins. Republicans always called it Derry.

'With their service records?' Bentham asked.

'I doubt it. They'll be here in the computer.'

'We can't get them for some reason.' He didn't mention that Detective Superintendent Palmer had found direct access via their computer to the RUC databank, but couldn't believe they didn't know. Equally it meant that the RUC had direct access to their computer records, but then they weren't inputting anything startling, only what was already available. They would make a point of not confiding their innermost thoughts to the machine. 'We'd like to see copies of those records, and arrange to interview both of these men.'

'That's easily done,' Sir Norman Hateley said. 'When would you like to go out to Londonderry?'

'As soon as possible.'

'Good. How else can I help speed up your investigation?'

'There was a tape-recording made of the entire operation out at Hollow Farm. I'd like to hear it.'

At that, Sir Norman Hateley's attitude perceptibly changed. Bentham's, too. It was the turning point in their mutually tolerated relationship.

'I don't know anything about that, Assistant Commissioner. If there was a tape I don't know who has it. I'm sure there wasn't.'

'I'm sure there was, Sir Norman,' Bentham said, standing his ground. 'I'm trying to make headway as fast as I can, to inconvenience the RUC as little as I can, but I'm running into all kinds of resentment. I can handle that all right. I understand these policemen would resent us, I would in their circumstances. But it's beginning to feel like the obstruction is official.'

'What are you saying, Mr Bentham? This office certainly isn't hindering your investigation. I'm sure my deputy is providing whatever assistance you require.'

'Experience suggests that resistance at the bottom reflects the attitude at the top – a bit like corruption.'

'You have no experience of this province,' Sir Norman said coldly, 'and what experience you have elsewhere won't do. Here we have a high security situation, we deal with terrorists every day, both on duty and off. Of course we're going to resent outsiders coming in and telling us how we should respond.'

'I understand that. But those two lads out at that barn weren't terrorists. That isn't my conclusion. It's what your people established when they tried to find a connection.'

'Bairns here are raised to it. They're weaned from the tit to the Kalashnikov or petrol bomb. The only way to survive is to treat everyone as a potential terrorist. We don't need anyone from London telling us different. My Joyce will arrange for you to interview Birchfield and Stone, then I'd be looking for a swift conclusion, Mr Bentham.'

But no tapes. Bentham didn't push the point. That didn't seem the moment.

16

GETTING OUT OF HIS office and on to the ground to see witnesses and visit scenes of crimes made Jack Bentham feel like a proper policeman. It was a feeling he enjoyed. He went out to O Division in Coleraine, Londonderry, to see Constables Birchfield and Stone when he could more easily have arranged for them to travel to Belfast to be interviewed. Getting out meant meeting other policemen and through them he imagined he would gain some understanding of what made them function in this province. He still wasn't sure what kept people going in what to him was a hostile environment.

'This is Coleraine police barracks,' Bentham's driver said, having pulled up across the street from the heavily fortified police headquarters.

'They look like they're under siege,' Bentham said as he peered across at the police and men of the UDR looking over apprehensively at the car. 'You fancy a frontal assault?' he said to DI Hodgkinson.

They were a long while getting into the police station. Their identification was looked at suspiciously. Phone calls were made to the divisional commander, then to Belfast, to check that two such high-ranking officers had left there for this visit. They were then searched for weapons, and at that point Bentham knew that this was not a straightforward precaution, but obstruction. The resentment they felt in Belfast had spread all the way to Derry. He was prepared to tolerate this obstruction, but not the next obstacle that was put in his way.

'Neither Birchfield nor Stone are here,' the divisional commander told them when eventually they got to see him.

'I was told they were,' Bentham said patiently.

'They're both on leave, sir. They started yesterday.'

Patience wasn't something Bentham found difficult with this chief superintendent. He was built like a house, and moved and spoke slowly. He didn't appear very bright, but Bentham had no doubt that his appearance belied the fact. 'Didn't you have instructions to stop them going on leave until I'd interviewed them?'

'No, sir.'

'Fine. I'll see them at home.'

'They're both in Spain on holiday, sir.'

'What about their records? Are they here?'

'No, sir. We don't hold any records here.'

'Of course not – they're in B Department's computer in Belfast,' Bentham said with an edge of sarcasm in his tone. 'I'd appreciate it, Chief Superintendent, if you'd notify me as soon as Birchfield and Stone return from leave.'

The chief superintendent promised that he would.

Bruised by the Chief Constable and rebuffed by his subordinates, Bentham decided to pursue his natural ally on the NI Police Complaints Commission.

Mrs Muriel Kinahon lived in a pleasant leafy suburb in East Belfast. No litter filling the streets here, Bentham noticed, or burned-out houses. Several gardens had pill boxes almost instead of gnomes. RUC men with the ubiquitous Sterling sub-machine guns and wearing flak jackets patrolled out of these. Those houses were the homes of state officials and would-be IRA targets. There was an RUC man in the Kinahon garden, who watched Bentham as he walked along the path to the door, where there was a closed-circuit TV camera. There were two more on the eaves of the roof; floodlights in the garden.

Bentham immediately recognised the detective for what he was when he opened the door. There was another waiting in the hallway when he was shown into the study, which had a lot of books crammed into an assortment of book cases from a matching antique pair in mahogany to cheap MFI self-assemblies that were sagging under the weight.

'Is it that dangerous, what you're doing, Mrs Kinahon?' Bentham asked when she joined him, unsure whose target she might be. He was impressed by anyone who could function anything like normally under this level of protection. More and more it seemed to him that those who sought most to preserve the way of life here were prisoners of that endeavour.

'The detectives aren't for me, Mr Bentham,' she said with an embarrassed laugh. 'They guard my husband.'

Bentham waited, unsure if he should try and guess who her husband was.

'Lord Justice Kinahon,' she explained. She never used her title professionally.

That hit him like a bucket of icy water, and Bentham wasn't certain if he managed to keep surprise off his face. Even to him, someone who was always prepared to give policemen the benefit of the doubt, this seemed somehow unfair. Muriel Kinahon was a member of the only independent element looking at complaints against the RUC; she was married to a judge who had freed two of the RUC men he was investigating, men who helped form the predominantly Loyalist force which gave her husband round-the-clock protection. By choosing her from the eight members commissioned to supervise his investigation, someone was obviously telling him something, Bentham decided.

Suddenly this was a pointless meeting, he thought, but he told her what his problem was in order to gauge the accuracy of his conclusion by her response.

'I can't believe these two men are purposely being kept from you, Mr Bentham,' she said. 'Norman Hateley wouldn't behave in that manner.'

'Someone is. I'm not getting to see them.'

'I'll certainly pursue the Deputy Chief Constable and make sure they are available for you to interview the moment they return.' She smiled, pleased at being able to provide this service. 'Would you care to meet my husband? He's just about to go out to meet one of his colleagues. But I'm sure he'd like to say hello.'

The judge, who was twenty or so years older than his wife, had little conversation and a tight rein on his whiskey bottle. He gave Bentham a drink, the size of which suggested he either didn't want him to linger long over it or that he thought he was driving.

'They're a fine body of men, the RUC, Mr Bentham,' the judge said. 'I don't know where we'd be without them. Dead, I daresay.'

That was a pretty coloured viewpoint, Bentham thought, but didn't say so.

'Muriel tells me they've little to answer for.'

He nodded.

'But I suppose that's for you to see, Mr Bentham.'

To his surprise, Bentham found himself agreeing through his irritation.

'I must go,' the judge said to his wife; there was an edginess in his voice. 'Toby sounded in a bad way. Mr Bentham, very nice meeting you. Perhaps you'll come to dinner one evening.'

After he had gone with his detective, Muriel Kinahon said, 'Toby Hereford is our third most senior judge. He seems prone to crises, poor man. He always calls my husband.'

She seemed suddenly nervous and Bentham wondered why.

There was no worthwhile help in Mrs Kinahon, Bentham decided. What he needed to set about finding was an ally to help him circumvent the obstacles that were in his path. He thought that the Northern Irish DPP might be that person. Sir Cyril Shelldrake welcomed the opportunity of a chat, and accepted Bentham's invitation to call at his hotel for a drink after work.

The cocktail lounge in the hotel was trying too hard to be what someone obviously believed it should be: a place where Harvey Wallbangers and Moonrakers were drunk, rather than the pints or straight scotches which most of the customers seemed to prefer. Including Jack Bentham and Sir Cyril Shelldrake.

They were on their third drink, which Bentham had signed for. This wasn't an expense that he would claim for, but somehow he knew the DPP would let him pay for all the drinks regardless.

'You have to understand, Mr Bentham,' Sir Cyril said, 'that men living and working under the sort of stress these RUC men suffer tend to feel threatened by any outsider, no matter how laudable his intention.'

That sort of observation was something Bentham could get from Mrs Kinahon and her husband without buying the drinks.

Bentham noticed the DPP slip the book of complimentary matches into his pocket, even though he didn't smoke. The thought of inviting him up to his suite where he could take the soap, the shower cap, the complimentary needle and thread, amused him. 'Why do people stay under those circumstances?'

'It's home, Mr Bentham. It's what they know and care about.'

Still Bentham wasn't convinced that that was enough, and wondered if it wasn't more to do with a bunker mentality that had developed out of the policing crisis here. He thought men in the RUC were performing for their fathers and grandfathers just as much as the IRA were trying to impress their forebears, many of whom were long since dead.

'Why is everyone so ready to make excuses for policemen out here?' He was being intentionally provocative. 'I can see the policing operation has its difficulties. So does policing the black ghettos back on the mainland. No one's twisting anyone's arm to do the job.' He believed a lot of policemen were doing the job out of some over-developed sense of civic duty, but that didn't justify corner-cutting or wrong-doing. He knew it would be naive, even foolish, not to believe other than that there were rogues within the police, if only because at best they were human. Sometimes one simply had to tolerate what they got up to and ignore it, as hard as that was for some.

'What we can't accept,' Bentham said, voicing his thoughts, 'is that we can solve crime or maintain law and order by committing crimes ourselves, no matter what the pressure on us to do so. Nor can we be seen to be fair on an investigation by having a member of the PCC overseeing it who's married to a judge here.'

'They're both very decent people, Mr Bentham.'

'I'm sure they are. But I'm just as sure that about half the people in Northern Ireland would disagree with that view.'

'Are you suggesting Muriel Kinahon resigns?'

'It's not for me to suggest any such thing. I'm just pointing out what the inquiry is up against.'

Sir Cyril Shelldrake didn't respond, but surreptitiously removed the hotel matches from his pocket and slid the book on to the table.

The sound of a police klaxon filled the silence between them. It was heading in this direction up University Road, but was familiar enough not to disturb people in the cocktail lounge.

With a smile creeping over his flaking pink face, Sir Cyril said, 'The belief here is that the Association of Chief Police Officers in conjunction with our Police Complaints Commission were going to find an accommodation man to conduct this inquiry. I'm pleased to see, Mr Bentham, that something appears to have gone wrong with that plan.'

Bentham smiled now. 'I wasn't exactly sure of you, Sir Cyril.' He looked around in the direction of the police klaxon which was approaching fast. 'Is that for our benefit?'

'I expect there's a bomb scare – it's not unfamiliar. The IRA have been particularly active lately. Possibly as a direct result of this inquiry, Mr Bentham. Such procedures tend to make good men less effective. They tend to think, what the hell.'

Bentham didn't know what the answer was, but the logical conclusion was dangerous; it meant allowing policemen to set all the ground rules.

'If there's any way in which I can help you, Mr Bentham,' the DPP said, 'I'll be available at any time.'

Bentham measured him. 'There's a tape-recording of the shooting out at Hollow Farm. I'd like to hear it.'

'So would I, if indeed it exists. If it comes my way, I'll let you know.' He looked up. 'I think that alert's for here.'

The police klaxons were right outside now. Sir Cyril rose, taking his drink and the complimentary book of matches with him.

Other people in the hotel bar started to move out, most of them remaining calm enough to take their drinks. There were no hotel alarms or barked orders from staff.

The exodus met the incoming RUC officers and UDR men as they rushed towards the stairs and lifts.

Near the exit Jack Bentham stopped and looked back, reluctant to depart and take a passive role. He saw the indicator on the lift halt at the third floor. That was his floor, and too much of a coincidence for his liking. He ran back across the foyer to the stairs, where a UDR corporal stood.

'You can't go up there, sir. There's a bomb scare.' He put his rifle up to bar him.

Bentham flashed his identification, which seemed to mean little to this man.

'You still can't go up there, sir,' the corporal said bravely.

Bentham looked round for the DPP to help him past this obstacle, but Sir Cyril had gone.

'You've got a radio on your lapel,' he said to the heavy-looking corporal who had a smile etched into his face. 'Call through to your commanding officer upstairs and tell him I'm coming up.'

A full five minutes passed before word came back down. Bentham ran up the stairs. He was out of condition and by the third floor had no physical argument to give anyone.

The corridor seemed full of UDR uniforms, with RUC men going in and out of those rooms used by his men. A chief inspector caught hold of him as he came along the corridor. 'You shouldn't be up here, sir.'

'I'm Assistant Commissioner Bentham,' he said. 'These are my rooms.'

The chief inspector smiled. 'There doesn't appear to be anything dangerous here. A false alarm.'

'Who are you?' Bentham wanted to know. 'What's your name?'

The RUC man walked away without answering, and went to talk to a UDR officer and an inspector on the Divisional Mobile Support Unit.

Bentham turned into his suite but stopped as he looked in disbelief at the mess. It was as if someone had driven a tank through the place. From the way things were tipped out, he knew they wouldn't have found a bomb, even if there had been one to find. His eyes trailed over the scattered papers and clothes, realising that this was nothing to do with a bomb alert. He was feeling angry, but determined not to give any of these men the satisfaction of seeing that they might be getting to him.

'They've been through everyone's room like this, guv,' Frank Burroughs said at his side. 'I think they were looking for any evidence we might have.'

Slowly Bentham nodded, his anger slipping away to be replaced by a kind of admiration for their audacity. 'We'd best not underestimate them, Frank. They've been surviving out here for a long while, after all.'

Despite this, he would take the matter up with the Deputy Chief Constable, if only to keep the pressure on.

'I thought Met officers knew how to make a mess, especially when searching black suspects' premises,' Bentham told Harry Streeter when he returned to London the next day. 'But that lot would have something to teach us. About the only damage they didn't do was bash the television in. But then it wasn't my TV.'

The Deputy Commissioner nodded solemnly. 'It would look particularly bad if you were blown up, Jack. They have to take bomb scares seriously.'

Not for a moment did Bentham believe there had been a bomb scare, but he had got nowhere on that tack with the RUC Deputy Chief Constable. He didn't expect the same sort of treatment from Harry Streeter.

He was glad to be back in London, with the familiar, with crime he felt more able to relate to, and operational procedures he could control; he was even looking forward to picking up on the rape investigation, bringing it nearer to some resolution. Although not expecting to be welcomed back like a vanquishing hero, he was slightly alarmed to detect the change in attitude towards him from the Deputy Commissioner that had taken place. It was almost as if he was no longer the favoured protégé whose career was to be assisted. There was a reluctance about the man even to talk to him, Bentham found, and he tried to reason this out. When he couldn't, he told himself he was imagining this, that he was getting jumpy following his brief stay in Ulster.

It was fairly obvious to Jack Bentham that his boss didn't want to talk about the situation in Northern Ireland. Not the investigation nor the obstruction of that investigation nor the expectations certain people had of him. He was ready to talk about other matters. The investigation into Jarman's murder, the volatile situation that remained in and around the Farm, the complaint of rape against the police by Roberta Ford; the repeated complaints by other students of police harassment following their earlier complaints after the Home Secretary's visit to their Union. But the way the RUC policed Northern Ireland wasn't something he wanted to concern himself about. Perhaps because it was so remote, and in a sense it was, despite the interchange of manpower between mainland forces and NI, albeit mostly one-way traffic as men went west for the experience.

'Have we got some sort of problem, Harry?' Bentham said bluntly as the meeting came to an end, indicated by the Deputy Commissioner climbing out of his comfortable chair. 'Are you getting something from the RUC? Something I should know about?'

'Why would they tell me? I heard they were whingeing about what it's all costing.'

'If they were to co-operate we'd get it done a lot quicker.'

'I believe there was a sincere intention on their part to have an unbiased investigation.'

'Well, that changes the deeper we get into it,' Bentham said. 'It's looking messy. It might not come out quite as they hoped.'

Streeter farted as he stared at his carpet for a long moment, then shook his head. 'That's too bad, Jack. But I don't have any influence either way. At the end of the day you can't make people co-operate, can you? Not even policemen.'

'In Ulster there are some people you can't even get to talk to you. They're not going to behave like that, Harry, unless they're sure there are no consequences.'

'I'm sure there's absolutely no question of the rug being pulled from under you, if that's what you're thinking, Jack. ACPO recommended you because you would see the task through, regardless.'

'Even though the investigation seems to be touching people and officers far removed from those directly involved in the shootings?' Bentham said, to test his reaction.

'Such as?' The Deputy Commissioner was startled.

'The Security Service seems to be involved.'

Harry Streeter stood and thought about that, letting another little squeak hiss out of his large frame. 'I'm sure that all you need do is supply the evidence. If MI5've been doing something they shouldn't, I'm sure the Security and Intelligence Co-ordinator in the Cabinet Office would take the appropriate action. I'd have even less influence on them than I would on the RUC.'

'As you say, Harry, all I've got to do is supply the evidence,' Bentham said with an ironic smile, thinking how he'd like to try, maybe.

'Just how dangerous is Toby Hereford?' Sir Michael Newfield asked as he shuffled around his large flat in Stormont Castle in a pair of plaid carpet slippers that he had had for years and years. His mother had given them to him and he felt a great attachment to them, even though something more stylish would have been appropriate.

'We can only conclude he's very dangerous,' said Herbert Greenhous. He was number two to the Security Co-ordinator, and his closest confidant. He willingly aided Sir Michael in his bidding, not because he enjoyed his habits or shared his weaknesses, but because it gave him a feeling of supreme power, and in many ways put the Co-ordinator himself in his power. To deal with someone, anyone, with extreme prejudice, was more exhilarating than one could imagine, he found. The situation in Northern Ireland made this easy; one simply gave the right information to the appropriate Charlie Tango in either the Republican or Loyalist terror gangs and let them do the work.

The prospect of dealing with a senior judge with extreme prejudice was particularly thrilling, Herbert Greenhous reflected.

He was a small, neatly attired civil servant in his fifties who didn't show his emotions. He had learned long ago that small people didn't need to be quick or aggressive to survive. He was calm and level-headed.

'Why does he suddenly want to spill the beans?' Sir Michael asked. 'It makes no sense. He's seventy. He'll leave office and die in ignominy.'

'But perhaps with a clear conscience,' Greenhous said and sipped the sherry that was too sweet for his liking. He didn't mention this. He thought his boss had very peculiar tastes.

'He hasn't become a Catholic, Herbert?'

'Not that anyone's aware. At least he hasn't been to any of our confessionals.' A smile crept over his face. MI6 bugged confessionals in some of the Roman Catholic churches, both in Northern and Southern Ireland.

'We could leave it that the man has gone mad,' Sir Michael said, 'but that won't keep the lid on this. What about his conversation with Lord Kinahon? The judge isn't going to put it about that his colleague is a pederast?'

'He advised Hereford to keep mum for the sake of the repercussions it might have for Ulster Unionism. The boys' school is run by Unionists, after all.'

Sir Michael smiled tightly, as if going along with the pretence that he hadn't trodden the same sordid path to King's House Boys' School.

'Lord Justice Kinahon might feel differently if Toby Hereford were to suddenly go off his rocker.'

'We still don't know what prompted his need to bare his sordid secret to the world?'

Herbert Greenhous simply shook his head.

'Possibly some extreme action should be taken, Herbert. Presumably his proposed trip to London might not be unconnected with this?'

'He has made an appointment with the Lord Chancellor. I imagine to tender his resignation before telling all.'

Slowly, Sir Michael nodded his large head, giving assent to Herbert Greenhous to talk to one of his converted terrorists about Mr Justice Hereford's movements.

After his number two had left, Sir Michael went quickly to his bathroom where he retched over the loo; kneeling at the WC he vomited a vile-tasting green bile, and still felt a discomfort in his stomach that no amount of retching would relieve. The thought of Toby Hereford being prepared to spill the beans about what had been going on at King's House, regardless of the consequences, both terrified and exhilarated him. It couldn't happen of course; no one was ever allowed to be so unburdened.

When things on the investigation started to happen for Maurice Knight they happened so quickly he didn't know which way to turn.

His only experience of that was on minor investigations, but he knew that what he had to do was stay calm and work methodically. The misgivings he felt about his association with the drugs dealer Benny Soares seemed suddenly unimportant, for through one of his dealers he had found the name of one of the two young black kids who had killed Jesse Jarman. He was called Donny Jessop, and had been in the process of robbing the councillor when he had disturbed them and they had panicked.

This discovery, much to Maurice's surprise, left him feeling both nervous and excited. He resisted his instinct as a policeman to rush and tell his superiors, even though he believed it would mean him being triumphantly welcomed in from the cold. Instead, he wanted to tell Roberta, knowing he'd be home and dry with her when she learned that not only was he not a drugs dealer, but that he had discovered who had killed her close friend Jesse Jarman.

'You weaselling bastard,' was Roberta's reponse. 'You were trying to get information from me for those other shitty bastards. I trusted you.'

'I wasn't, Roberta. I swear. All I wanted to do was find Jarman's murderers.'

She laughed scornfully. 'Donny Jessop? He lives here on the Farm. He wouldn't hurt anyone. Do you know how he'd stand up to police interrogation? A black kid who's not very bright? They'd make him admit anything.'

Anger and confusion were churning around inside Roberta. She was pleased that Maurice wasn't a dope dealer, angry that he was a policeman, confused about her feelings towards him in relation to other policemen, angry that he was going to offer Donny like some sacrifice to a failed policing policy. She wanted to run away from this, not feeling she could cope with it any more. Another part of her wanted to turn to Maurice for support; yet another part told her she couldn't trust him, that his loyalty would be to his job not his colour.

'He'll be all right with a solicitor there,' Maurice said. 'There are safeguards.'

A peal of mocking laughter spiralled out of Roberta, running towards hysteria. 'Safeguards? Are you stupid? What about the safeguards that say I couldn't have been raped in a police cell? What about those?' She held his look, realising that he probably didn't believe that had happened. She turned and fled into the flat, crying.

Chief Superintendent Barclay was one policeman Maurice had

hoped he wouldn't meet again before his return to Plymouth. But carrying the news like he did, he became a part of the briefing and, if not a very important part, he could hardly pass unnoticed in a roomful of white policemen.

'There's bound to be trouble on the Farm when we go in for these lads, Mike,' a uniformed superintendent counselled.

'We'll be ready. We'll have D11 standing by with gas and baton rounds.'

Barclay was thinking about the call he would make to the DAC out at Area Headquarters. He knew this was likely to be it, the test ACPO wanted for new riot training and equipment on mainland Britain. Although he didn't relish a riot such as those in Brixton or Tottenham, in some ways he felt a sense of occasion, even that it was an honour to be the area chosen for this testing ground. This time the police would be ready, and their effectiveness would come as a rude shock to the rioters and make them think about ever taking to the streets again.

'Sir,' Maurice said, raising his hand like a child in class. 'One of the suspects is a bit simple – he seems to trust Roberta Ford, sir. If she went to get him with me . . .' He didn't know if he'd be able to achieve that even had he been given the chance.

Chief Superintendent Barclay looked at Maurice, uncertain who he was for a moment. He certainly wasn't going to let that black prat who was causing so much trouble for his Division steal his thunder, however she was connected with this black policeman.

'We'll make the arrests,' Barclay said. 'Make sure you claim all your expenses for your stay here' – summarily dismissing Maurice.

The meeting moved on physically out of the room, leaving Maurice behind. Not even DS Tait acknowledged him now. He felt crushed and angry at the rejection and wondered why he remained a policeman in the face of such shabby behaviour.

He went to look for Roberta, to try with her help to pre-empt the swamp arrests Barclay was planning. Maurice wondered if she wasn't right after all, that he was a black man first and that all he would do was unlatch himself from his culture if he tried to be a policeman first. He felt that had happened, and was uncomfortable with himself right then.

There was a strong inclination to walk away and return to Plymouth. This was no longer his problem. But he responded as a black man: he had started something that might cause a lot of strife for blacks, and he felt he should do something to stop that. Only standing, waiting on her doorstep, getting no answer from his knocking, he didn't know what he could do. Roberta arrived along the walkway, flushed with excitement and out of breath.

'I know where Del Lindo is,' she said. 'You were looking for him.'

'So what?' was how Maurice responded, and regretted it immediately. Somehow he wanted to retrieve what he imagined had existed between them. 'I've been kicked back to Plymouth.'

Roberta seemed surprised. 'Great! What if he has information that proves it wasn't Donny who killed Jesse Jarman,' she argued as if in a tutorial, rather than simply giving him what she had learned, 'but racists who the police are protecting?'

Still the words Maurice wanted to say wouldn't come. 'You know what, you're as bad as them. They won't give up; you won't give up. I mean, probably what happened in that police cell is prejudicing you. What if it was Donny Jessop and his friend – not the racists, not the dealers, not the police. No one with a grudge? What then, Roberta? What are you going to do? Find some other excuse to go on blaming the police?'

The expression on Roberta's face hardened. She didn't want to admit he might be right. 'If that's so,' she said, 'there's going to be more policing problems in this neighbourhood than the police ever knew existed.'

'And they'll just hit back even harder.'

'Do you want to talk to Del Lindo or not?'

Despite himself it was an offer Maurice couldn't refuse.

Del Lindo had been in hiding ever since he had stumbled across Jesse Jarman's body when he was supposed to meet him to give him information about police corruption. Ironically, after the initial flight from Jarman's flat, he had been hiding only two doors away, but the police were none the wiser.

As Roberta and Maurice made their way to the flat, there were signs of the police moving into the Farm in strength to arrest the two youths.

'You'd think they were purposely trying to start trouble,' was Roberta's only comment. Maurice said nothing.

'I talk to you about what I know,' Del Lindo said with a raw edge of fear in his voice. 'You do something about it, they kill me for sure, just like Jesse.' He wasn't convinced that the killing was done by those two young burglars.

'Who killed Jarman, you say – the police?'

'You're the detective.'

'Del, please help us,' Roberta pleaded. 'The police are out there now arresting Donny Jessop and Paul Marchant. Don't let it be them.'

This was a real dilemma for Del Lindo, and he didn't know which way to go. No one could help him now, and he was scared. 'The shit Jesse had on the police around here is enough to turn you white,' Del Lindo said with the laughter of someone making a final, reckless gesture. 'Dhem fuckers don't just cop off dealers. Dhey deal. Dhey buy and sell liberty; dhey burn people up at the crematorium.'

It was Maurice's turn to laugh. 'That's shit. Shit, man.'

'I'm no' shitting you, man.' Del Lindo could hardly get his words out. 'Dhey done it. Dhey fucking done it. Ask Barry Spiking or Billy Wilson, dhey fucking well got burned,' he said illogically.

'You got evidence,' Maurice challenged, 'or you about to step into court?'

'Fucking hell, man. The evidence is gone – s'why Jesse got killed.'

'Why didn't they put Jarman in the furnace?'

'Yeah, Jesse was smarter than that. I mean, he didn't have no business with the police to meet dhem at the crematorium.'

Maurice didn't want to believe this, but the rumours he had heard came echoing back at him. 'How d'you know the police ran dealers into the crematorium?'

'I watched dhem the night Jesse died. I was out dhere. I know fucking detectives. One of dhem's named Tait.'

The name jumped into Maurice's mind an instant before the man said it. He didn't know why or how. But still he didn't want to believe it. DS Tait was someone he admired for his cool professionalism. He wouldn't even want to believe what he was being told of a racist like Barclay.

'I got dheir car number written on m'car dashboard,' Del Lindo insisted, like it was the only evidence needed. 'It's down in the car park under here, s'red M-reg Cortina. You see. I writ it when I followed dhem to the crematorium.'

The car was where Del Lindo said it was. Maurice was reluctant to open the door and look at the dashboard in case the number was there. Finally he did, and it was; somehow he knew it would lead him back to Tait. He leaned against the car, not wanting to go back upstairs and admit the possibility of these shameful revelations. As he rested there in the half-submerged car park, his thoughts churning, he noticed activity near the block opposite. The Blue Berets of D11 were climbing out of their van and running into the building with CS gas and baton round launchers. Maurice suddenly felt sick. His chosen side were preparing for war over the arrests of those two lads, when a little tact and diplomacy on their part could have avoided even a battle.

Back in the flat, Maurice made a phone call to the communications room at the police station. In a matter of seconds from the car number going on to the Police National Computer at Hendon the answer was back.

'It's a police car,' the computer operator said over the phone.

'Who was it out to on the night of 2 March?' Maurice glanced over at the tense faces watching him. He hoped he wouldn't be challenged by the operator and made to look foolish.

After a few moments the operator came back. 'Who did you say you were?'

'PC Knight, on secondment to C11 from Plymouth,' Maurice said. 'I'm making the inquiry for Detective Superintendent Horsfell for the purpose of elimination.' He held his breath.

'It was booked out to DS Tait and DC Lines. They booked on the air with it at 10.37 p.m.'

Slowly he replaced the phone, and avoided the eyes that bore down on him, appreciating that no one questioned him. The next call he was even more reluctant to make. He reached DS Tait in the CID room and put it to him about the car being involved in the possible murder of Billy Wilson, a black dope dealer. He didn't mention knowing he had the car out on that night.

'How the fuck did you get the crematorium, Maurice?'

'Being undercover, you get told all sorts. Most of it's rubbish. Has that dealer gone missing, by any chance?'

'I've not heard of him for a while. You'd better forget about going back to Plymouth, Maurice. We should take a look at that crematorium.'

Maurice glanced at his watch. 'Will it be open?'

'We can wake them up. Can you meet me there? Be careful, there's a lot of activity on the street with those kids being arrested – fucking silly going in like that. 'S asking for trouble.'

It was such statements that made Maurice hope, and indeed in moments believe, he was entirely wrong about Brian Tait. But he borrowed Roberta's Renault 5 and headed over to the crematorium all the same.

'I don't know how close Maurice Knight is to anything', Detective Superintendent Horsfell said as he stepped outside the CID room with Tait, 'but he's put that car booked out to you at the crematorium the night Jarman died.'

'I'll ask him,' Tait said. 'There could be a lot of premature resignations if he gets any busier.'

'Resignations,' Horsfell scoffed. 'That'd be a real easy get-out.' He had been in the communications room when Maurice had called through with his inquiry.

The crematorium was shut tight. There was no sign of life at all, Maurice thought and smiled to himself. The large wrought-iron gates were locked. The chapel beyond was still and showed no lights. He could see well enough in the half-light of dusk, but anyone inside the building would need light, he reasoned, unless they were up to no good. He thought again about Brian Tait, and all he had discovered today, or at least what he seemed to have discovered. Still he was having difficulty believing it, despite what the evidence indicated. There was no evidence that the dealer Billy Wilson was dead, or if anyone had even reported him missing. The fact that Del Lindo had written on his dashboard the number of the car DS Tait happened to have out the night Jesse Jarman was killed didn't prove much. There was only Del Lindo's word that he saw the car at the crematorium. Tait may have had a perfectly logical explanation for being there. Or he may not have been there at all.

Why he was here now Maurice didn't know, or why DS Tait had suggested they meet here. He had no idea what he had expected to find. The thing about crematoriums was that they destroyed everything, apart from a few bones which were ground down with the remaining ash. None the less Maurice found himself climbing the gates and running across the lawn to the chapel. It was locked, and the doors weren't about to give as he leaned aginst them. The same with the door at the rear of the building. Everything was very secure. There was no one inside, he was sure, so saw no point in knocking.

A blocked-off fan in a lavatory window provided the means for Maurice to get in. The building had an eerie presence in the half-light, Maurice found, and he started at a dark blue coat hanging on a modern hatstand. When he recovered himself he moved through into the furnace room. Here he considered risking the light but didn't. There was nothing but a catafalque trolley opposite the three doors which he assumed were the ovens. He hesitated at the first, his hand stopping halfway to the winding handle.

Before joining the police he had worked briefly as a porter in Freedom Fields Hospital in Plymouth. The one duty he couldn't abide was taking dead patients to the mortuary. As a policeman he had coped with the recent dead, but the thought of them chilled in those long narrow cabinets disturbed him. He assumed the ovens would be long and narrow.

Suddenly he reached out, caught the handle and raised the metal door. A faint illumination crept into the room from the pilot light inside the oven. There was nothing in the incinerator, apart from an old newspaper and sandwich wrappings, the day's litter to be burned with the first client tomorrow. The other two incinerators were empty. Maurice left the doors open. He sat on the catafalque and watched the lights inside the long brick and steel ovens.

He waited almost an hour, his thoughts ranging over the events of the past few days, and always coming back to the possibility of Brian Tait bringing someone here and burning him. Just as he almost convinced himself that wasn't possible, rumours he had heard about the fearful doings at the crematorium crept in on him. At one point he even started thinking that Tait had invited him here to be burned too. But the fact that he didn't show up tended to make a nonsense of that.

The one serious doubt that remained about DS Tait was the question of his telling Benny Soares about him working undercover. A dealer who had given him Donny Jessop had that information and had told him Benny Soares had given it him; only one person could have told Soares, Maurice decided. That disturbed him and made him angry. He felt let down by the only friend he had in London – somehow he had turned that professional relationship in his mind into friendship. If that were true, he had put him in danger, his life at risk. It was something Maurice was determined to take up with DS Tait before going back to Plymouth.

The delay in getting to the crematorium and dealing with the problem Maurice Knight represented vanished in the fear the like of which he had never before experienced. It made him feel sick and brought an acrid bile to the back of his throat. Up until now blacks had never been a problem, certainly not on a level of personal danger. He was a policeman, and most of them were afraid of the police, especially if caught on their own; when they were mob-handed there were usually crowds of well-armed and well-protected police around, with the weight of both the law and public opinion on their side. Now there was only DS Tait and DC Lines in a car on the edge of the Farm facing a mob of black youths armed with sticks and axes and stones and petrol bombs as they swarmed from under the tower blocks. A similar swarm behind them had caused them to turn on to the Farm. Tait knew there were dozens of police around to back up the arrests of Donny Jessop and Paul Marchant, and had believed he'd be safer here than anywhere. The riot that had been threatened for so long was happening, but where were all the shock troops to lick the heads of the blacks to make them think long and hard before they tried this ever again?

DC Lines was screeching down the radio telephone that there was a full-scale riot under way. 'They're everywhere, they're fucking everywhere, we can't get out!'

Calmly the controller said, 'I'm putting you on talk-through, report your position.'

Talk-through meant that all units in the area would get the information relayed from Tait's car, only most units had their own problems, especially those that had been called back to the local police station where crowds of blacks rapidly gathered as word spread of the two youths arrested for Jesse Jarman's murder.

'Drive into them!' DC Lines screamed with the radio phone on talk-through. 'Run the fuckers down!'

DS Tait's instinct for survival was dictating all his moves. He pushed the gearstick into second gear and raced the engine, praying he wouldn't stall as he hit the crowd. It was certain none would show them mercy if he did. The mob loomed larger and angrier and denser, and he doubted if they could get out of the way even had they wanted to. It would be like hitting a solid wall. He was only yards from them when suddenly they parted, jumping every way, scrambling over each other in order to save themselves.

A laugh started out of Tait, as much from relief as at the sight of these panicking blacks. It was short-lived as a rock hurtled into the windscreen, shattering it and shocking the two detectives. Tait let go of the steering wheel. The car hit something and went up on two wheels, and at first Tait thought it was people he had hit but realised it was one of the concrete bollards that separated off a pedestrian area. The car went over on to its side and slid along the pavement to halt against another bollard. The worst of all possibilities had happened, Tait realised at once, while his colleague was shouting into the phone, 'Get us out, get us out, for fuck's sake!' The same terror touched him. But he knew they had to get out; running, they might at least have half a chance. The black mass could do them too much damage before help arrived, and if they tried to sit it out in the car they'd probably be burned out.

Pushing open the door, DS Tait heaved himself out and reached back in for his partner. The mob was recovering and regrouping in a disorganised fashion. He had barely a minute's grace.

'Come on, you cunt!' He grabbed Norman Lines and dragged him out. The DC fell down the side of the car, and ran, pulled along by Tait.

The angry mob swarmed after them, throwing stones at them, cheered by the fact that the two white men ran down the bank into the semi-submerged parking area beneath the block.

A trapped feeling engulfed both policemen as they ran deeper into the building until finally there was nowhere to run to but up the narrow concrete stairs.

An Asian family on the second-floor landing were nervously peering over the balcony to see the skirmishes the blacks were having with the police when the two breathless detectives flew out of the steps like frightened hares breaking cover. Instinctively and culturally the Asians knew that this breakdown of order was nothing to do with them, they were law-abiding, making their way in life; the lawless blacks could fight the police if they wished. But like everyone else on the estate who wasn't directly involved, they were curious enough to watch until danger was brought so close that they had to retreat into their flat. The two fleeing whites brought the danger close enough. Only they didn't retreat fast enough.

DS Tait hit the door when it was a fraction of an inch from the jamb and knocked back the man closing it. Neither he nor Lines heard the Indian's protests, but threw themselves behind the door to close it as sticks and feet rattled against it. They slammed home the two bolts.

'You got a phone? Call the nick, get them!' Tait shouted, and Norman Lines ran through the flat after the Indian.

Axes sounded against the door, which like most in the block had been reinforced both against the burglar and the police. Even so, it wouldn't withstand much of this treatment.

When Maurice tried to return to Roberta's flat on the Farm he found he couldn't. There were police road blocks on each of the three approaches. Riot police were making short forays on to the estate and were being driven back by a hail of stones and petrol bombs. Even so, they appeared not to be trying to take the ground.

Abandoning the Renault 5, Maurice approached the police line past the control van which sat behind two armoured riot vans. The mouths of policemen waiting to go in fell open in surprise, not untinged with fear, thinking they had been outflanked.

As they recovered themselves they fell upon Maurice with angry blows and what abuse they could find, 'Fucking nig-nog' being most prominent.

'I'm a police officer, I'm a police officer,' Maurice shouted, but it was a few moments before anyone listened.

Their hostility polluted everything as the serial sergeant examined Maurice's warrant card, wondering if he had stolen it, if he was some sort of Trojan Horse; were he to get it wrong he'd be in trouble. The men were ugly with anger, made worse by the knowledge that there were two policemen trapped on the Farm and they were doing nothing.

The sergeant told two constables to bring Maurice along with him as he went to check with the inspector.

'I heard there was a black undercover policeman floating around,' the inspector said grudgingly, not imagining any other black daft enough to come in here. He passed the card back. 'Don't get in our way, sunshine, that's all. We got two men trapped down there.'

'Why don't you ask your brothers to turn it in?' the sergeant said. Policemen laughed. 'Ask them nicely if we can have Sergeant Tait back?'

Maurice looked at him, but didn't respond. He felt too angry. He couldn't understand why these policemen stood around doing nothing, while colleagues were in danger. 'Why don't you go in and get them?'

'Why don't you?' the inspector said. 'We're waiting for D11 to get back here with baton rounds – fuck knows what's happened to them.'

Maurice looked beyond the line of policemen with shields to the bank of taunting black faces as the odd burning petrol bomb arced up from their midst to explode harmlessly on the street. He wondered if he could somehow get through them to Tait and his partner. He couldn't believe the police were prepared to do nothing but wait.

'Drive me on to the estate,' Maurice said, stepping up into the open doorway of an ambulance parked behind the police lines.

'There's a policeman hurt.' He assumed his lie wasn't too far from the truth.

The driver at the wheel of his vehicle with the engine ticking over was ready to go anywhere, but not until it was safe to do so.

'Not me, sunshine. That's a war out there.'

'Then I'll drive. Out!'

The surprised driver found himself sprawling on the road after Maurice wrenched him from the seat. Technically he could be nicked for assault, and for stealing an ambulance, but, like the man said, there was a war going on. He hit the klaxon switch, then revved the engine and popped the clutch, scattering policemen in disarray.

Rioters let out a spontaneous cheer at this, and pelted the broken line of policemen. Their amusement was short-lived when the ambulance bore down on them, causing them to scatter.

The frenzy of the rioters who had dragged Brian Tait out prevented them from doing him too much damage initially, they were getting in the way of each other's blows, but then someone said, ''S burn the fucker.' The cloth bung was pulled from a bomb and petrol sprayed over Tait. It stung as it went into the cuts on his face. He knew that was the least of his problems and felt heartsick that he hadn't risked jumping from the kitchen window with Norman Lines.

'It's gone over me, you cunt!' one of the rioters screamed before someone struck a match. 'It's over me!'

The ambulance coming at them prevented anything happening. They split in all directions, and Maurice swerved to avoid Tait at the last moment; he hit a rioter, then the kerb, and ploughed into the detectives' smouldering car. Maurice sprang out with the engine racing and ran back to Tait, who had staggered to his feet not knowing which way to run. He just moved his legs as fast as he could when Maurice yanked him in his direction. They ran past the ambulance and along the side of the block. Rioters came after them. They passed DC Lines, who looked as if he had been hacked to death. It was at that point that Brian Tait almost gave up, and would have, but for Maurice Knight.

There were rioters ahead of them, fighting a rearguard action as riot police from D11 bore down on them, with more police following in the wake of baton rounds and CS gas.

Maurice veered to the right with Tait, along the service road between two blocks. Just because the rioters were on the run didn't mean they were safe, certainly not with plastic bullets coming at them. They would appear to be just two more petrol-bombing rioters.

There wasn't much left in DS Tait for fight or flight, and Maurice knew he couldn't carry him. He saw a place to take refuge, in the large cupboards where four huge communal dustbins were lined up under the rubbish chutes. He dragged Tait in and pushed him tight up behind the bins, then squeezed up himself.

They could see little of what was going on from there, but they heard the screams of rioters as they were hit by plastic bullets, the thump from the guns as they were launched, the whine as they occasionally ricocheted. One hit a bin and rocked it, making Tait shake. Maurice considered him there in that darkened cupboard, and realised how scared and vulnerable this ruthlessly effective detective was. He wouldn't mind betting he had shitted himself too, but gave him the benefit of the doubt. Maybe it was spilled rubbish he could smell.

The smell that reached Maurice next was CS gas. It seeped in around him and Tait. They put clothing over their mouths and shut their eyes tightly, but couldn't keep it out. It burned the membranes of the nose and throat and seemed to suck the air out of their lungs. They coughed and retched. It was worse for their confinement. They had to get out, nothing else mattered.

'Here's some of the bastards!' The riot policeman saw Maurice's black face and the cowering figure behind him.

Four policemen fell upon them, licking their heads with their long sticks.

There was no protest they could make that the policemen would take notice of. Their burning lungs were giving out, physically they were collapsing, but DS Tait managed to reach into his pocket for his warrant card, getting his knuckles slapped several times before anyone heeded it.

'Leave off, you cunts, we're police,' he rasped from painful, gasping lungs.

Blows stopped midway. 'And him?' The policeman pointed to Maurice, who was on all fours being cracked across the back and head.

Crying and trying to laugh with lungs fit for neither, Brian Tait whispered, 'I thought the shades were gonna kill me, but I was certain you lot were.'

'We saw him,' the riot policeman said, jerking his head at Maurice. 'Fucking hell. Let's get you both out of here.'

The atmosphere back at the station when most of the police were stood down was electric. They weren't off duty, and would be in a state of alert for a day or two, though no one really expected the Farm to flare again, not after the way it had been put down with gas and baton rounds. That excited them. All those rioters treated in hospital for plastic-bullet or CS-gas injury would be charged, some of them with the murder of Detective Constable Norman Lines. That fatality was the only thing which dampened their spirits at the success of this operation, where many many more rioters had been injured than police.

Word had gone around on Maurice, and when he arrived at the police station after his check-up at hospital, policemen reached out and slapped him on the back, told him well done, offered to buy him drinks, said they were proud to serve with him. Maurice smiled. However, he wasn't done with Brian Tait yet, and these men might well change their opinion of him, but at that moment he enjoyed the warm feeling of comradeship. It made him think he had made the right choice after all, and, if only momentarily, made him forget all he had had to endure to date because he was a black policeman.

The back-slapping and congratulations continued down in the locker room where Brian Tait was supposed to be. Everyone in the room stopped when Maurice came in, then gave a self-conscious cheer. Maurice felt slightly embarrassed. He smiled and mumbled his thanks, not knowing how to respond.

His gaze fell on DS Tait, who was on a bench down the room. Tait smiled as Maurice approached. Everyone watched in silence at the expression of friendship they expected between these two. Tait rose and held Maurice's look, and then extended his hand. Maurice clasped it firmly.

No one would have been surprised if they had embraced. The observant anticipated it as Maurice reached in with his left hand and took hold of Tait and went forward to him. But the gesture was too quick. The black forehead contacted the white nose and split it open.

That might have been enough, but it wasn't. Maurice hit him with three stinging left jabs to open the nose up further, a right and another left as the policemen in the room stood frozen.

Tait went down, and Maurice followed him and hit him again and again, until at last his anger was spent. DS Tait might have suffered less if he had been left to the rioters.

Maurice climbed to his feet and looked at his painful and bloodied knuckles. Some of it was Tait's blood, some of it was his own; there was no difference in colour there. He turned and walked out. No one congratulated him now, or said a word, knowing instinctively that this was something they shouldn't become involved in.

When he was almost at the door, someone behind Maurice said, 'Black cunt, ought to be nicked.'

Maurice turned and looked, but his challenge wasn't taken up. Somehow Maurice knew that DS Tait wouldn't be pressing charges.

17

EVERY NEWS BROADCAST carried a statement by the Home Secretary roundly condemning the riot as a monstrous attack on the fundamental liberty of our great and tolerant nation; his praise of the police for the valiant way in which they had swiftly and effectively dealt with the situation in the face of savage provocation was fulsome. Their response was a vindication of the law and order policy that demanded harsh situations be dealt with by harsh methods, even though it was to be regretted that CS gas and baton rounds had ever had to be used on mainland Britain.

Jack Bentham found no fault with any of that. Where he wanted to part from the official line was over the death of Detective Constable Norman Lines. It was being called a savage and brutal murder, the belief being that he was set upon and clubbed to death with a degree of savagery that defied the comprehension of compassionate people. No one at the top of the Met was rushing to tell the Home Secretary that DC Lines was dead before the first blow was struck, dead from a massive heart attack, and it was doubtful that he wanted to hear that anyway.

'It's an ill wind that blows no one any good,' the Commissioner said to the Deputy Commissioner, Bentham and the Territorial Operations AC when they met in his sixteenth-floor office to consider the provisional post-mortem report. There was propaganda mileage to be had, but they weren't about to mention that to anyone, lest it diminish the impact of Lines's death.

On the traditional morning-after walkabout of the riot area, now made secure by the high-profiled District Support Units and members of the Blue Berets, with their gas grenades and plastic-bullet launchers, the Home Secretary stopped at a particularly prominent piece of devastation. The burned-out cars around the burned-out ambulance made an ideal backdrop for his pronouncement to the media circus. His entourage of senior policemen – including the Area Headquarters commander, the

DAC, the operational AC, and Jack Bentham – and civil servants stayed out of frame. This was a politically right moment, not to be shared.

'Seeing the level of destruction here today only leads me to reinforce my statement to the Association of Chief Police Officers earlier this month. We will continue to strengthen both the law, and the law-enforcement bodies to make them one hundred per cent effective against this sort of lawlessness. There is no price too high for the security and peace of mind of the general public. The police are an exemplary body who are prepared to pay the highest price of all to provide that security, as was witnessed here last night.'

The cameras had stopped turning and the sound mikes were off when the Home Secretary, striding on ahead with his PPS, said, 'As tragic as this is, there's every indication of it helping our popularity.'

A tight little smile creased the corners of his PPS's mouth. His northern parliamentary seat had become marginal at the last general election; he was acutely aware of the need to court popularity.

AC Jack Bentham's ringside seat came about by accident rather than design. He was over from Northern Ireland and happened still to be operational head of C11, despite leap-frogging DAC Doc Holliday in rank, and detectives from his department happened to be on the ground in the area. But he had nothing of significance to add to the meeting that took place at the local police station after the Home Secretary's departure.

'What is of paramount importance,' said the operations AC chairing the meeting in the conference room next to Chief Superintendent Barclay's office, 'is that we claim every last bugger who laid into DC Lines. I mean every last one of them. There's to be no token trade-off in order to keep the peace. We've shown them how effectively we can keep the peace, if they fancy another hiding. Jack, the local CID are going to need as much help down here as they can get. Your undercover people were a big help in finding those lads who killed that black politician.'

'That lad's a non-starter now,' Bentham said. 'He's had his cover blown.'

Bentham listened to the proposals from around the conference table, most of which were swamp procedures, backed up by gas and baton rounds. The policemen were cocky for having succeeded, and believed they could do so again. Probably they could, but the problem that Bentham foresaw was in the sort of mentality they were developing whereby they believed that that was the only policing option, the policing of confrontation. He was almost back in Northern Ireland, where elements of an alienated community knew how to hit back at the police with brutal effectiveness. The problem was that the day would come when this community being confronted continually with armed police would find the means of arming themselves other than with clubs and stones. He said nothing about that, for his colleagues weren't in the mood to listen. There was the death of fellow policemen to avenge, even though the people who were aggressively being sought didn't actually kill him.

'What about when word gets out that DC Lines died of a heart attack?' Bentham ventured, and brought a murmur of confusion from those who didn't know.

'That hasn't been confirmed, Jack,' the operations AC said curtly. 'Let's wait for the full post-mortem.' He meant the second post-mortem that would hopefully disprove the first finding. 'The Commissioner wants these bastards charged with murder. I don't think he's in any mood to see it changed to criminal attempts.'

There Bentham let the matter drop.

'I've had some fucking complaints in my time,' David Loughton, the ACC from Merseyside said to Bentham at his next meeting that morning, 'but these fucking students. There's barely one of them will co-operate.'

That wasn't Bentham's problem, except in how it could affect the complaints inquiry into the alleged rape of Roberta Ford. He was looking for some conspiracy among the students whereby they put her up to it to discredit the police. But Bentham wondered if such a motive hadn't more likely started out of her black politics. She wasn't one of those charged so far following yesterday's riot, but was certain to be near to the centre of it in view of both the position she held in that community and the touch-paper her complaint against the police represented.

'There are forty-odd students being prosecuted from that demo.' Bentham couldn't believe none of them were co-operating.

'They're collecting their own statements from each other,' Loughton said. 'Personally I'd nick the fucking lot, if only we could find their names.'

'What's been adding to our problems, Assistant Commissioner,' said a Merseyside superintendent with a sallow complexion and a cigarette never out of his mouth, 'are their complaints of continual police harassment.'

'Is there any substance to the complaints?'

'Of course there's none,' ACC Loughton interjected.

'None that we can establish,' the superintendent said, like a man who had learned to tolerate his unthinking boss. 'We did establish that two of the students central to the complaints, Stanley Scone and that black lass you're following up, had been stopped. But for legitimate reasons. The officers concerned were identified.'

'It was Stanley Scone who put up the suggestion about students taking their own statements, sir,' DS Denis Marsh said. He was acting as Bentham's aide on this inquiry and kept him in touch with developments. They had once been on the Regional Crime Squad together.

'He's complained of being stopped repeatedly,' the Merseyside superintendent said, 'but he hasn't kept any details such as vehicle registration, identification or collar numbers. The same with Roberta Ford. She said it's always detectives who've stopped her, but she didn't see their warrant cards.'

'What did they approach her about?'

'Trivial matters apparently, or for no reason at all. But she claimed they threatened that she would either end up like her friend Jarman, or be nicked just as she was about to sit her final exams.'

'Pretty heavy stuff,' Bentham commented.

'Some of these fucking students are into pretty heavy stuff,' ACC Loughton said. 'Fucking anarchists, most of them. That black woman needs a psychiatrist more than she needs a solicitor.'

Bentham nodded slowly, but didn't comment further. He made a mental note to ask Harry Streeter to talk to the vice-chairman of the PCA about having Loughton replaced. They might find a little more willingness on the part of the students to co-operate with the inquiry then.

After more than thirty identity parades of policemen and women, Roberta Ford managed to identify only two. There was a possibility that all the policemen and women involved in the demo hadn't been paraded, Bentham reflected as he left the Yard to resume interviewing policemen, but no more than a possibility. What was in less doubt in Bentham's mind was the fact that someone had been in that cell with Roberta Ford. What's more, whoever it was knew they had been, and was covering up, either for themselves or someone committed to a lie; the longer that situation continued the more difficult it would be for whoever to backtrack and admit the original deception, even if the primary accusation had no foundation. All of which made him more and more inclined to believe there was substance to the original complaint.

Perhaps the only way to find those responsible was by putting a lot of external pressure on those in the job who were helping in the subsequent cover-up. However, that sort of publicity and pressure would have to come from the top, and he didn't think the Commissioner would be in any mood for that sort of witch-hunt following so closely on what had happened on the Farm yesterday.

Birchfield and Stone, the two RUC men whom he had so far failed to locate and interview, slid obliquely across his mind as he sat in the small over-heated interview room with PC Kevin Pratley went through his statement. Perhaps a similar cover-up was going on here as seemed to be happening in Belfast. There were serious discrepancies between what PC Pratley said in his written statement and what he had previously put down in the questionnaire the inquiry had used to plot the movements and actions of the policemen at the demo. However, many such discrepancies had appeared in most of the subsequent statements.

'Of the three-hundred-odd policemen who were paraded,' Bentham said in a not unfriendly manner, 'why do you think Roberta Ford picked you out?'

'I dunno, sir,' PC Pratley said with the right sense of injustice. 'I mean, she didn't at first, did she? She picked the lad next to me. I definitely wasn't in that cell. I wasn't, sir.'

'That's not what WPC Winder said,' Bentham tried. She had been picked out of the line up too. 'She said you were. Isn't it better to get it over with? We're not saying you raped her. Only that you were in that cell.'

'No, sir,' Pratley insisted, his face going red. 'I swear to God. Honest.'

Bentham's manner became heavier. 'You lying fucker, you were there. What's more, you know who else was, Kevin.'

Silence filled the small room as the young PC held his ground, save for a tic he couldn't control in his left cheek.

'Come on, Kevin,' Bentham cajoled now. 'Let's not fuck around. It's time to let the Met off the hook. There's a cloud hanging over every one of those policemen on duty around the Students' Union that night. Tell us what happened in that cell. Give you a lot of stick, did she?'

The corporate guilt that was weighing on the police seemed to affect PC Pratley not at all. Perhaps he was only imagining it affected anyone else, Bentham thought, as he listened to this young constable repeat his denial. He closed the folder in front of him and gave an appreciative nod.

'Fine, thanks for your trouble,' he said, letting the PC go. He saw Pratley's disbelief that he was unable to check immediately. It didn't lead Bentham to any conclusions.

'They'll be hard nuts to crack, Den,' he said to DS Marsh, who was his own age. He would have felt it unnecessarily formal to address him by rank or surname. He wouldn't have objected to this DS or most other policemen he worked with using his first name, but rarely did any of them do so at work. 'In our day a young PC would have put his hand up to anything an Assistant Commissioner put to him. Sign of the times.'

'Could be he wasn't in that cell, guv.'

'Someone was. Whether they raped her or not, someone put her down there.'

Bentham followed the students' trial taking place in Bow Street Magistrates' Court only in the newspapers. Those that had been heard so far didn't exactly vindicate the police. They were winning and losing at about an even fifty per cent. Officially the police tried to distance themselves from what happened in court, maintaining that the results were no reflection on them. In theory, the police were as separate from the courts as the courts were from the law-making executive, but in practice they were interdependent, one being impotent without the other.

Bentham knew that the case the Crown Prosecution decided to go with was only ever as good as the evidence the police put together, and with that rate of acquittals the police had evidently been lazy, incompetent, arrogant, or all three. The consequence was that while the rank and file became further demoralised, as their superiors failed to learn from their mistakes the quality of leadership deteriorated and the effectiveness of policing at the sharp end diminished. Bentham made a note for the conference of chief officers to debate the situation. The plank of his argument would be that it was better for far fewer to be taken before the courts with a huge improvement in the quality of the evidence. He could see what would happen on the prosecutions of the black rioters from the

Farm. The police would go at it in anger and frustration, without the ends neatly tied, and the same problem would arise; more acquittals than there should be. There would be a heavy reliance on police propaganda to impress the court.

The dismissal of the case against Claud Fentiman, the deputy president of the Students' Union, for allegedly using threatening behaviour wasn't going to help Assistant Commissioner Bentham with his investigation of the alleged rape of Roberta Ford. It was after going to aid Fentiman that Ford had been arrested, and she had given evidence on his behalf in court. The stipendiary magistrate had chosen to believe her when she said Fentiman hadn't been using threatening behaviour; that tended to put Roberta Ford in a similarly credible light. For her trouble in aiding a fellow student she ended up in a police cell and was allegedly raped. From her evidence in court she didn't seem like the kind of loony who would make up such a charge. Indeed, Jack Bentham tended to believe her story even before her appearance as a witness. He wondered also if there wasn't substance to her complaints of police harassment. There would be every reason to suppose it could happen with the sort of lifestyle she led on the Farm, without what she alleged had happened in the police cell.

He said none of this at the meeting in her solicitor's office, where he went to interview her again. Instead, he listened to her tirades about the police raids on the Farm, how they had used a battalion of police in the most provocative way possible to arrest two young black boys.

'If you feel there's substance for a complaint in those arrests,' Bentham said patiently, 'I would advise you to make it.'

'After what happened? Do you think someone's going to care? All they're thinking now is how those savage blacks killed that poor policeman,' Roberta said angrily. 'Nothing about how that particular policeman was dealing in drugs on the estate. How he might have been responsible for burning a dope dealer called Billy Wilson. If you want to know, ask the policeman from Plymouth you had working undercover. Maurice Knight knows.'

'The public have short memories,' Bentham said, making a note to pursue Knight.

'Of course, until the media resurrect it all in favour of the police. I've already made one complaint. The police don't want to believe that.'

'I believe it, Miss Ford,' Bentham told her. 'I'll go on treating this as a rape inquiry until I prove otherwise.'

'I'm impressed. You're such a high-ranking policeman, but still nothing gets done.'

'There's a lot of activity, I promise you.'

'What about the policeman and the WPC who Roberta identified?' Martin Potter, the solicitor, said. 'They must know who else was there.'

'Only WPC Winder was positively at the station at the time,' Bentham said, opening the file he'd brought. 'She admits to seeing Miss Ford in the cell. She brought her up for release, and according to her statement remarked that she was looking a bit groggy.'

'She held me – she helped them! The truth is no one wants to find them because of what it means.'

'I want to find them, if they exist,' Bentham said, 'regardless of the cost. The policeman you picked out of the line up wasn't at the station. He was at the Union building.'

'He was in that cell. He certainly was.'

'I am going to continue looking. What I need is something to go on.'

'What about the police car that followed Roberta home from college on Tuesday? And the Monday before last?' Martin Potter asked.

'Assistant Chief Constable Loughton is looking into that. His inquiries haven't established they were policemen.' Bentham hesitated, wearying of the assault from this woman and her solicitor when he was only able to repeat himself. 'You're an attractive young woman. That might have something to do with your being followed.'

'It wasn't,' she shouted. 'The police are trying to scare me into dropping my complaint. They won't succeed. Certainly not after what happened on the Farm. I'm going to get those bastards behind bars, I promise you!'

Anger suddenly flared in Bentham. 'Do you really think police officers would behave in that way? They're there to protect people – what you're saying is so bloody offensive. But me, I'm a decent, fair-minded bloke and I will go on pursuing this.'

'They think they can get away with anything,' Roberta said, on her feet now and shouting at him. 'Well, you're not going to, they're not!'

She fled the office in tears, feeling both foolish and angry that someone like this had brought her to tears.

After a moment, the solicitor said, 'I think the interview is over, Assistant Commissioner.'

'I'd say so.' Bentham passed the folder back to DS Marsh. 'We'll go on looking.'

'The other matter I'd like to raise is the question of the statements given to Assistant Chief Constable Loughton's team ending up with the prosecuting solicitors in the student trials at Bow Street.'

'They weren't given to the prosecution by policemen, Mr Potter,' Bentham said lamely. 'By the Police Complaints Authority.'

'It doesn't alter the fact that the prosecution is getting information students gave in confidence. They had been assured of the investigators' independence. They didn't expect it to be used against other students. It means complainants can't trust the words of policemen investigating their complaints.'

'I hope not,' Bentham responded automatically as the police politician. 'When a policeman takes a statement, that becomes evidence. Of course it will be used if it relates to a crime. Were they promised otherwise?'

'The three students I have as clients were assured it was confidential.'

'So it is – confidential to the police, the PCA and the Crown Prosecution Service.' He felt like telling the solicitor he was being fucking naive, but he was learning the diplomacy of high office.

The feeling of unease Bentham had about Harry Streeter evaporated when they met before his return to Northern Ireland to talk about removing ACC Loughton from the inquiry. The Deputy Commissioner's impromptu invitation to lunch had a lot to do with it.

As they stood in the entrance of the restaurant near Scotland Yard waiting to be shown their table, Bentham said, 'The hostility I'm meeting here on that alleged rape complaint is worse than what I'm getting in Ulster.'

'I wouldn't be surprised. You going to be there much longer?'

'It needs something to get us on the plane. I can understand the RUC's resentment, it's similar to the feelings of those policemen I'm looking at here, but I am becoming very pissed off with it.'

'You could always come back,' Harry Streeter said with a smile. Despite the smile, an edge to the remark made Bentham wonder how casual it was.

'I don't think so, Harry,' he said. 'The way to crack the RUC is by keeping the pressure on – they feel the government is making them scapegoats. Once the pressure slackens we may as well all come home.' He wanted to see what the response was, but the waiter arrived with a twelve-inch smile that looked as if it was worn by a dead man.

'Your table is ready, Mr Streeter. This way, sir.'

'The last time I had a meal in here it was paid for with luncheon vouchers.' A DI on the RCS had paid for the meal.

'Bent, were they?' Streeter assumed that was the case. Then added, as if to reassure Bentham that he could have what he liked now, 'This one's on the house.'

The waiter left them menus and departed.

'What about Merseyside?' Streeter said, glancing up from the menu and adjusting his glasses. 'You fancy they should be replaced?'

'Only the Assistant Chief Constable. He's so prejudiced it's clouding his judgement. I'm not surprised a lot of the students aren't co-operating.'

The Deputy Commissioner nodded solemnly. Then that smile that made Bentham wonder earlier what he was up to darted across his face. 'You'd better take over that inquiry. I'll have a word with Jonathan Entwistle.'

'I could probably manage to oversee Loughton's deputy, if he ran it.'

'No.' Streeter shook his head, dismissing that. 'A busy man always finds time to take on more, Jack – an old Met proverb.' He went back to the menu.

Bentham wondered if the idea wasn't to keep him so busy that the RUC investigation might slip. He said nothing, but was determined that it wouldn't happen. 'I'd better get a fucking telescope to take back to Ulster.'

18

STEPPING OUT OF THE spring of London and back into the winter of Belfast, Jack Bentham was welcomed at Aldergrove Airport by Detective Superintendent Burroughs with good news. It was good news for a detective conducting a difficult and complicated investigation, as good as it can be when something breaks on an intractable-looking case; but bad news for a senior policeman who was supposed to have a political overview. The two parts of him were in conflict. Possibly he hadn't been senior enough for long enough. His instincts were still those of a detective and that was the direction he was being pulled in.

'Good flight, guv?' Frank Burroughs said, reaching to take Bentham's bag.

'Not bad. I could have pulled one of the stewardesses, but you're terrified of AIDS nowadays,' he joked. He'd received a friendly response from her, but hadn't asked her for a phone number, wondering when he would fit in such a diversion.

'That's not stopping any of our lot,' Burroughs said with a grin. He enjoyed being away from home.

There were armed RUC men wandering around outside as the two policemen walked to their car, which Frank Burroughs hadn't been allowed to park by the exit. 'They even make me jumpy,' he said, seeing his boss's glance at the armed men.

'Back home people are being reassured by their appearance,' Bentham said ironically, thinking how politicians pandered to what they saw as the popular drift and endorsed the police's firearm tactics.

'That was nasty out at Greenhill Farm.'

'The tragedy of it is, Frank, that the whole fucking episode could have been avoided. Some of them seem to have learned fuck-all from Brixton or Tottenham.' He fell silent, thinking about the meeting he had had with PC Maurice Knight, and the unofficial version of the events that had led to the riot. It was depressing if a quarter of all that the black policeman told him was true about the level of corruption, and Bentham knew he'd have to decide what action to take.

In the car Detective Superintendent Burroughs said, 'We've had a real break with one of the witnesses – the kid who survived the shoot-out at Hollow Farm. Bill Senior gained his confidence. The lad told him Stephen McFadden said he saw the IRA suspect killed in the alleyway by the Divis flats.'

Frustration suddenly flared in Bentham. 'Shit, shit, shit!' he said, trying to suppress it. 'I fucking well hope not, Frank. I dearly hope not.'

A whole series of consequences following that possibility sped across his mind in an instant, the basis of which was a widespread conspiracy to murder involving both the RUC and the Security Services. The tapes of that shooting incident recorded at the time suddenly took on even greater importance and Bentham began to understand why they hadn't appeared and why they never would. That wouldn't stop him doing his best to get them.

Bentham and Burroughs went straight out to meet DI Bill Senior, who was at the children's hospital on the Falls Road. The detective had taken young Kit to play in the meagre recreational area within the hospital grounds, where Bentham and Detective Superintendent Burroughs found them. They watched the frail figure of Kit McMahon in a thin brown anorak and slightly too short jeans on the roundabout that was being turned by Bill Senior. Kit looked like an old man who was suffering from emphysema.

'I want to get off now,' he said.

DI Senior slowed the roundabout and let him down on to the earth-worn grass where puddles of water from the earlier rain had collected. He took his hand. 'Mind the puddles, mate. You get your feet wet, you'll catch cold.'

They went across to the swings, Kit deciding the direction. He didn't attempt to get on the swing. He had no interest in anything.

'Kit,' DI Senior said, gaining his attention, 'tell us how Stephen knew those guns were in the barn.'

A troubled frown formed in the deep lines on Kit's face as if starting off a tortuous thought process. He glanced quickly at Bentham, then looked away, the thought flying.

DI Senior glanced anxiously at his boss, as if concerned about wasting his time. He knew you couldn't hurry kids if you were to get the best out of them, especially not when they were damaged, but he knew Jack Bentham had no children, and assumed he didn't understand them. 'What do you say, mate? Can you tell us?'

Kit moved his lips as if about to say something, but the thoughts that dragged him back to that barn made him catch his breath and sob instead. Bill Senior put his arm around his shoulder. 'You'll get to it when you're ready, won't you, mate?'

'We wanted to play cowboys,' Kit whispered. 'Steve said they were there.'

'Did someone tell him about them?'

Catching his breath again, Kit said, 'The man tol' me not to tell anyone. He tol' me.'

Jack Bentham suddenly felt a claw at his throat breaking through the velvet glove of the hand that had been there since the start of this investigation.

'What man was that, Kit?' he said in a well-modulated tone reminiscent of political leaders trying to win friends.

'The man came and he said I shouldn't never tell . . .' Fear rushed out of Kit on an hysterical fountain and his need to recover his breath fought his need to sob. Bill Senior picked him up and held him, talking gently to him all the way back to the ward.

Bentham watched them, envying Senior that empathy which very few policemen retained.

'The boy was badly traumatised by the whole shooting,' the young psychiatric registrar said as if delivering some profound clinical observation.

They were in the sister's office, watching Bill Senior as he sat talking to Kit on his bed along the ward.

'I'm not saying he won't recover. What we don't know is how quickly.'

Bentham was moving on from Kit's psychological problem; Bill Senior was better able to cope with that anyway. 'Who interviewed him after the shooting?' he asked.

'We don't keep those sort of records,' the doctor said pompously, as if defending the patients' rights against state interference. He checked the file anyway. 'It was a month or so after the shooting before he could even recognise anyone.'

'Only his family have been in to see him, apart from the priest and the RUC men,' the ward sister said. 'And Mr Senior, of course.'

'What RUC men?'

'I don't remember. They might be in the ward diary.' She

stretched across the desk for it, her starched bodice pulling tightly against her breasts and her frock skirt riding up, showing a sewn ladder in her tights. The lady wasn't particularly pretty but had an attractive, helpful manner, and Jack Bentham had been thinking quite a lot about sex. He had made no progress in that direction with the Deputy Commissioner's secretary. But it was spring and the earth was warming even in Northern Ireland. He suspected Bill Senior had made a move in the ward sister's direction, and he felt irrationally jealous.

'You don't know how long ago we're talking about?' She glanced up from the page as Bentham shook his head. 'Here! It doesn't say who. Just RUC officers to see Kit.' She showed Bentham the book.

'You're not suggesting that these police officers have done something wrong?' the doctor said. He was part of a counselling group to the RUC and had nothing but admiration for them, particularly for the way they coped with stress.

'We're just trying to piece the story together.'

'We're rather weary of our policemen receiving this sort of shabby treatment when they're doing such a grand job!' That was as emotional as this doctor got, and too emotional for him to handle in public. He strode out of the office and disappeared off the ward.

The ward sister ignored his departure and continued to flick through the diary. Finally she was rewarded. 'Here's something – a note to call Superintendent Johnston at Knock as soon as Kit McMahon is able to respond.'

'Was it Chief Superintendent Johnston who came to see him?'

'I don't know. I'm thinking two men came. One not in uniform.'

Conspiracy to commit murder. The possibility bounced around in Jack Bentham's head, refusing to leave him. It was ridiculous, he told himself, and for that reason it stayed with him. There it resonated with what Roberta Ford had said back in London about policemen being responsible for burning a dope dealer, and with what PC Knight had told him. He wanted to believe that this was no less ridiculous, but it stayed with him also. Both were part of some malicious fantasy that a malignant worm in his brain was feeding for no other reason than to prevent him making that successful transition from high-ranking policeman to the third highest office in the Met, and perhaps higher. But if that were so, it was only something he must identify, challenge and overcome if he was to go on and up. It was the detective in him. That side of his character that made him good at what he did, that made him enjoy what he did;

only when he had opened up these ideas, laid them out flat for rigorous examination, only then would he be able to let them go.

'Let's suppose it was Johnston who went to see the boy,' Bentham said, pacing his hotel room with a drink in his hand. This was the only place he felt relatively at ease about opening his thoughts. 'Let's suppose it was him who told the boy to keep quiet. Why?'

'The only reason I can think of,' DI Senior said, glancing at Detective Superintendent Burroughs, not wanting to speak out of turn, 'is if they set Stephen McFadden up at Hollow Farm.'

'That's a bit strong,' Burroughs argued. 'Unless we have something pretty fucking substantial to back it up, it could slaughter these policemen.'

'Understood. But we're in my hotel room, Frank, having a drink, talking. It's going no further, is it?'

Once the ground rules were established, the detective superintendent nodded, agreeing to go along with it. He wasn't ordinarily cautious, but then he wasn't ordinarily investigating other policemen. 'Stephen told his friend he saw the shooting in the alley. It was near his flat, of course. But he was a bit simple, liked to play cowboys and indians.'

The ground rules set for this very private meeting were something Jack Bentham would readily change whenever the moment was right – and he knew from the start that he would interview Chief Superintendent Johnston. What he didn't know was that their conversation was being listened to by mechanical means. In a room on the opposite side of the U-shaped hotel sat a man from MI6 with a Sony recorder transmitter and a tapedeck, and a camera with telephoto lens set up and focused on Bentham's windows. The transmitter was voice-activated and the field officer's physical presence wasn't strictly necessary. The concern of his boss, Mark Howellet, the security liaison officer, was that someone might stumble on it accidentally or otherwise. He listened with interest now. A boring duty had suddenly sparked with life. He took photographs of the three men in the room opposite, but doubted if the quality would be much good.

'Suppose he did see the shooting,' Bentham was saying, 'and that somehow the RUC got to know. Suddenly we have something that we may not fucking well like, but we might have to live with.'

'But he was just a kid,' Detective Superintendent Burroughs said indignantly. He had pulled plenty of strokes in his time. 'I mean, that's not fucking on, is it? No matter what.'

'I hope not, Frank,' Bentham said, meaning it, 'but I think we'll have to put it to Johnston all the same.'

When the conversation moved on, the listener in the room opposite made a phone call to Mark Howellet, who would come over to hear the tape himself.

The warning Chief Superintendent Johnston received made him feel angry and vulnerable, and the subsequent call from Detective Superintendent Burroughs to arrange for his boss to interview him made him feel more so. The feelings didn't go away when he refused to be interviewed. That was only round one. Round two would probably be to Bentham. The chief superintendent didn't know what was causing the situation to deteriorate like this. That wasn't part of anyone's scenario.

He couldn't concentrate on the game of basketball he was coaching in the gymnasium out at Garnerville. The players were all over the place and he was doing nothing to correct their problems. He continued to ignore Jack Bentham where he stood near him on the sideline with his aide, but the London policemen was thick-skinned and wasn't to be put off.

Finally Chief Superintendent Johnston rounded on him and said, 'I'm a loyal and hardworking policeman, for fuck's sake. I've been working like Murphy for this province. I won't be hauled off like a criminal to be interrogated about killing the McFadden bass. You talk to the SIS instead. You have to have some understanding of this province before you can police it. Ask any of these.' He indicated the policemen who had stopped playing ball and now stood watching the proceedings, none of them amused by the Met men's presence.

'We'd better conduct this interview in private, Chief Superintendent.'

'I've told you my answer,' Johnston said through clenched teeth, trying to get back the lost rag. 'I'm not a criminal. I'm a policeman. As God's my witness, everything I do here is for the good of this province. So fuck off and leave good men to do good work.' He turned away and blew his whistle, bringing the players back from their own personal confrontations with these outsiders.

Bentham nodded, and turned away, knowing this argument was going to have to be carried to a higher level.

Neither the Deputy Chief Constable nor Mrs Kinahon enjoyed the interview Jack Bentham forced them into with Sir Norman Hateley any more than he did. He wasn't expecting to win any popularity contests in Northern Ireland, nor even to be thanked, but he had no plans to let them make a complete prick of him. Sir Norman Hateley tried to put him off, and then kept him waiting in his ante-room at Knock with the Deputy Chief Constable and Mrs Kinahon. They had a long wait with nothing to say to each other.

'I'm very busy, Mr Bentham,' Sir Norman said when they were eventually shown into his office. 'I'm sure Donald and Muriel can deal with any problems you have.'

'I don't have any problems – you do.'

'None that we haven't been able to deal with ourselves quite adequately.'

'There comes a time when the rubbish tip gets full up.'

'Oh, I don't think anyone's been burying anything, Mr Bentham,' Muriel Kinahon said defensively.

'Why don't you say what you've got to say, Mr Bentham. We don't go a lot on nasty innuendoes here, however much you might prefer them back in London.'

'To be perfectly honest,' Bentham said, refusing to address the Chief Constable by rank or title, 'I would just as soon resign from this inquiry and go back to the mainland. I can have all the aggravation I want there in comfort.'

Sir Norman gave a wintry smile. 'Then you'd surely go back to the rank of commander, Assistant Commissioner.'

That got to Jack Bentham more than anything, because he knew it was true. To resign here was to fuck up, and in that event Harry Streeter had told him he wouldn't be confirmed in the rank of AC. There was a lot of pressure on him to acquiesce to the external demands of this inquiry, but pride wouldn't let him.

'That I can live with,' he said boldly.

'You're going about things in entirely the wrong way. You can't treat the men here like criminals.'

'The fuck I can't.'

'There's no need for language with a lady present.'

'Thank you, Norman,' Mrs Kinahon said. 'But that's quite all right.'

With no more than a glance at her, Bentham reached into his pocket for the miniature microphone he had found in his room and threw it on the desk. 'That suggests that I can treat the RUC like fucking criminals. It was in my hotel room. What I didn't discover was where it led.'

He had guessed that Johnston had somehow been warned when he went to interview him, and not by either of his two detectives. They had found the microphone and transmitter sewn into the top of the curtains.

'Maybe you gave someone permission for this to be planted in my room, or maybe the Secretary of State did. Or maybe no one at all gave permission. But it doesn't make for a position of trust. I want to know who put it there, because I want to know who warned Chief Superintendent Johnston.'

'I don't know what you're suggesting, Assistant Commissioner,' the Chief Constable said, 'but I advise you to tread carefully or I'll have your whole circus on the next plane out of here.'

'And I'll have the whole fucking story on the front of every newspaper,' Bentham threatened, knowing there was no turning back now. The time for that was when he found the bug, and before he demanded to see Sir Norman Hateley. To make his point he added, 'Fuck the traditional silence of senior officers.'

The two men instinctively glanced at the woman who was present, then glared at each other across the vast desk, each hating and fearing the other equally for what they suspected the other could do to him.

The Deputy Chief Constable shifted his weight from one foot to the other, knowing there were going to be no winners here, only losers. If Bentham hadn't been there he would have advised Norman Hateley to back down, and hoped that somehow Muriel Kinahon would do so with her silent presence.

'I can assure you I know nothing about this, Mr Bentham. But I'll certainly have it looked into.'

Turning to Bentham, Muriel Kinahon said, 'I'm not sure that you can ask any more of the Chief Constable at this stage. Equally, Norman, I think Donald must arrange for Mr Bentham to interview Chief Superintendent Johnston at his convenience.'

'Of course,' Sir Norman Hateley said. 'Of course.'

'And the person who went with him to the hospital,' Bentham put in.

Had the Chief Constable gone along with that, Bentham might have let go his conspiracy theory. But Sir Norman might almost have been willing him to run it until it died.

'No,' he said forcefully. 'There are grave security considerations here. As a result, I say who you can interview in my force, Mr Bentham. In future, Mr Joyce will want a list of all the questions you need to ask any of my men.'

Disbelief caused Jack Bentham to laugh. 'That's not possible.' He appealed to Mrs Kinahon with a look, but she refused to meet his eyes.

'A policeman as resourceful as you, Mr Bentham, you'll find it so. Or you don't interview them.'

The thought of trying to find someone more powerful in order to neutralise the Chief Constable still appealed to Bentham, but he didn't know who that might be, or even who might help him to find such a person. Harry Streeter was a doubtful prospect, so too was the chairman of the Police Complaints Commission. For security reasons both would go along with Sir Norman Hateley. It was the Minister of State, if not the Secretary of State for Northern Ireland himself, that Bentham needed. But at this stage he wasn't sure if an approach to either would be at all wise, not knowing what their feelings were about this investigation, or who had their ear. He wondered if he might seek the help of Julian Brind, who was an undersecretary at the Home Office. They had been at university together. Julian himself wasn't the man to help directly. He was a behind-the-scenes manipulator, and hadn't the weight or power to get into horn-locking; in any case he was in the wrong department to make any noise on Bentham's behalf in the Northern Ireland Office. Reluctantly Bentham decided that challenging the Chief Constable was wrong-headed. For the time being he would accept his terms, but change them as he went along – if he could.

In the interview room at police headquarters where he was obliged to see Johnston (a room he suspected might be bugged – although he didn't bother to look), Bentham, accompanied by Frank Burroughs, started off with the prepared questions, and received guarded answers. His sixth question departed from the text.

'Who was the officer who accompanied you to interview Kit McMahon?' he asked, as if reading from the text before him.

'I don't have to answer that,' Chief Superintendent Neville Johnston said quickly. 'I don't so.'

'Why not?' – innocently, as if there were no ground rules.

'It's not on the questions to the Deputy Chief Constable.'

'It's just an oversight. I can't think why there would be any objection to it, can you?' Both knew that was the purpose of the prepared questions. Bentham waited but received no response. 'You're not afraid to answer?'

No response from Johnston.

'Have you something to hide that the identity of the second man might expose?'

'I'd say not,' Johnson said tersely.

'Then what's the reason for not answering? You're a policeman, the same as me; the truth interests us both.'

Johnston remained unmoved by reason.

'Was it a member of the Security Service?' Bentham speculated. 'Let's assume that it was. Even so, what are you protecting him from? Is he up to something dirty? What branch was he? MI5? MI6? SMIU?'

'I never said it was Security with me.'

Bentham smiled. 'Your covering up tells me that.' He was chinking this man's resolve not to talk. 'MI5 wouldn't want to show their hand – that's understandable. But then, fuck it, I'm a senior policeman, a keeper of secrets. Why keep this knowledge from a keeper of secrets? What's your guess, Frank?'

Detective Superintendent Burroughs considered the RUC man. He was irritated by his attitude, and if he had been a regular suspect he might have hit him by now. But he was a policeman and they couldn't give him the treatment; not that he wanted to, he'd sooner not have the information. 'MI5 was at the barn for sure, guv. I'd say they were either doing something they shouldn't have been doing at the hospital, guv, or trying to cover something up.'

'Let's suppose Stephen McFadden saw the killing in the alleyway behind his house, then Special Branch found out and told MI5, as they naturally would. A witness might not be good news, even one who's retarded. So, they set him up, easy enough – in the same way they set up O'Donnell. But this lad's got a friend who survives the shooting. Now, suppose we visit the hospital with a friend in the Security Service . . .?'

'You cunts! This is ballocks.' Chief Superintendent Johnston flew out of his chair, barely stopping his fist at Bentham's face. 'You fucking lot are going nowhere with this investigation, I promise you.'

A forced smile stretched across Bentham's face, his breath became shallow as his chest tensed. He could feel his legs trembling with tension. It wasn't fear, at least he told himself it wasn't. 'You might have the umbrella protection of your Chief Constable, but I bet he couldn't get in here in time to stop me breaking your jaw.'

With a feinted right hook, which Johnston foolishly followed, Bentham unexpectedly head-banged him in the face, sending him sprawling across the room. He went after him simply to help him up, but the Chief Superintendent thought there was another one coming, and scrabbled away like a crab.

'Mind how you go,' Bentham said consolingly. 'The floors are slippery.' He and Burroughs pulled Johnston upright and watched him take a handkerchief to his cut lip and nose. 'I'd say that all we need to do is locate this non-existent Security officer you hang around with, and you could find yourself in the dock on a murder charge. Not much of a prospect, even if you do go and get a result at the end of the day. It's there on your record, blighting your career. What you've got to ask yourself, Mr Johnston, is this: Would you want to stand in the frame for something either the RUC or the Security Service or both are possibly responsible for?'

The prospect brought the RUC man no comfort at all.

As they were leaving the main building to walk to their car that they were forced to park in the visitors' park outside the security net around headquarters, Frank Burroughs said, 'They might try and nick you for bumping him like that, guv.'

'Some fucking chance with you as the only witness, Frank,' Bentham said collusively and laughed, enjoying the action he had taken. 'But to be perfectly honest, I don't give a fuck.'

The thirty-two women in the aerobics class moved in unison to the music, each keeping to their own space on the sprung ballroom floor. They were all fashionably dressed in leotards or body stockings or shorts and tops that showed off their slim or well-shaped bodies. There were no fat ladies among them, and Jack Bentham gained the impression that any woman coming to this group would only do so after she had first got herself into shape. Leading the movement at the top end of the room was Maureen McFadden, who was wearing a white body suit with large shoulder pads and white tights. He could have arranged to see her elsewhere, but couldn't resist coming here.

Standing at the back of the room where mahogany folding doors bisected it, Bentham's eyes took in everything like a greedy child in a sweet shop. Only he wasn't about to make a grab for anything. He was aware that everyone was curious at his presence and it excited him a little to think that some of these women might be putting something extra into their exercises for his benefit. So absorbed had he become that he barely noticed the music slowing down. Finally it stopped.

'OK, relax a moment,' Maureen said. 'Everyone take a deep breath. Let it go. Take another one. I hope everyone's feeling in good shape, not too many aches.' She had a warm, easy manner that the dancers responded to. Some with groans. ''Bye, everyone. See you next time. Don't forget your exercises.'

As the group started to disperse, Maureen glanced along at Bentham as he pushed the doors open wider for the women to pass through. It was a needless self-conscious gesture; they had all come in through the gap. She went across and unplugged her stereo cassette player, then stepped into the top and bottom of her white tracksuit, aware of his watching her.

Bentham didn't move as she came along the room with her stereo machine.

'Is this a paid job?' he said, with a slight awkwardness that might not have been present had he seen her under any other circumstances.

'Do you get paid for what you do?' was her sharp reply.

He stepped back instinctively. 'It looks a lot nicer than what I do. I'm Assistant Com . . .'

'I do read the papers, Mr Bentham.' She went out past him. 'As I told one of your detectives, I don't have anything more to say to the police.'

He followed her out of the rambling hotel on the north-eastern outskirts of the city, where she approached an old Ford Escort. He waited while she unlocked it and put her belongings on the back seat.

'The RUC murdered my son,' she said, rounding on him. The anger and hurt she had tried to bury were perilously close to the surface. 'No way will I be convinced it was a mistake – but I was only his mother. He was a simple lad who never harmed anything. The police had their inquiry, as we knew they would, and put some policemen on trial before a single Unionist judge without a jury. It's all an unjust conspiracy. So why am I supposed to feel reassured by another set of policemen who come to conduct another inquiry at the invitation of the Chief Constable? Tell me that.'

Slowly Bentham nodded, seeing how quickly emotion was overwhelming her. He found it a little frightening; like so many men, he was afraid of his feelings. 'I understand how you feel, Mrs McFadden.'

'I doubt it,' she said in a whisper. 'I doubt if you do, not unless you have children who make you sick with worry every time they go out, every time you notice them getting more and more hardened to the violence around them, anxious in case they become caught up in it.' Shaking with emotion, she wrenched open the car door, climbed in behind the wheel, and slammed it closed. She tried to pull herself back from this precipice on which she found herself dangerously near the edge. 'Go away, Mr Bentham. Leave me alone and let me forget. Please leave me alone.'

There was no way, suspecting what he did, that he could not interview her. He thought about letting this go for now, but knew it would be the same next time. Standing by the door, he watched the tears roll down her cheeks. She wiped them away with her hand before trying to start the car. With too much choke and too much carbon on the points, she only succeeded in flooding the engine. It whirred pathetically as she tried again and again. Finally Jack Bentham opened the door. 'Move over.'

'It's all right. I can manage,' she insisted. She hated the idea of men stepping in and taking over as if they always knew best. She had managed without them for a long while.

'You can't drive like that. I'll drive you. Move over.'

Finally she gave in, despite herself, telling herself that the girls would be worried if she was late home.

There was no conversation in the car, apart from the most perfunctory directions of how best to get to Divis Street avoiding the control points. By the time she reached her front door and put the key in the latch, all sorts of feelings were going through her. Curiously she found she appreciated what this man had done rather than resented it. Then she immediately recognised the trap and realised she had almost fallen for his ploy to gain her confidence; she felt vulnerable bringing him here like this, and not a little anxious for him – neighbours had noticed their arrival.

'I'm not going to change the way I feel, Mr Bentham,' she said, trying to distance herself. 'I don't expect anything of the police, it doesn't matter where you come from. I really would like to forget. If you want to know anything, read my statement.'

With that, she closed the door. He almost said he had read her statement, and that it didn't tell him what he wanted to hear; he might have told her he was inclined to believe her – if only to spite the RUC – but thought it would be pointless then.

Glancing around at the block, with its visible signs of abuse and neglect – the graffiti, the litter, the boarded-up or burned-out flats – he wondered about Maureen McFadden living here. She travelled to the more prosperous eastern sector to work at a middle-class job, and lived in what was approaching a slum. He wondered what the inside of her flat was like, whether it reflected the style she showed in her aerobics attire.

His driver had followed him from the hotel, and when Bentham returned to the car he was looking around anxiously. 'I was a bit worried about you going in there, sir,' he said. 'The Divis flats are no place for a policeman on his own. We had an officer killed in there the other week.'

'Wouldn't that solve a lot of problems,' Bentham said, but thought at once he was being churlish in the face of this man's concern. 'I appreciate your waiting for me.' He wanted to come back and pursue Mrs McFadden and wouldn't want his driver insisting they came back only with an RUC armoured Land-rover. Her rejection was fairly resounding, but he had laboured against greater odds before now.

'Superintendent Burroughs's been through, sir,' the driver said. 'He wants you to meet him and Inspector Senior at the hospital.'

The news there was getting better. Kit had managed to describe the man who had visited him with Chief Superintendent Johnston.

'You ought to go on to the payroll here, Bill,' Bentham said where they sat at the meal table in the centre of the ward with Kit and Frank Burroughs. 'You get these sort of results.'

'Kids get hurt,' DI Senior said. 'A bit of affection, they start to respond.' He didn't tell his boss about the crummy home life the boy had to put up with, where hostility was in disproportion to affection and praise as scarce as physical resource.

'Maybe we should start treating villains that way.' Bentham rose, touching Kit's head in an uneasy gesture.

'Villains? What are they?' Detective Superintendent Burroughs asked.

Reluctantly Chief Superintendent Johnston agreed to come out to the Met's base at Garnerville, not to be interviewed, but for an informal chat. Basically policemen, when the subject of an inquiry, were no different from anyone else, Bentham found; they would talk for their own reasons. Johnston may have agreed to the visit because he was scared of him physically, but it was doubtful. What had almost certainly happened was that common sense told him that this investigation had to run its course to some sort of conclusion; what happened then was another matter.

'It's good of you to come at short notice,' Bentham said in a friendly way when Johnston was shown in. 'Have a seat. Do you want a drink?'

Neville Johnston was suspicious as he watched his antagonist open a filing cabinet and pull out a bottle of Bushmill's whiskey and some paper cups, yet paradoxically he was reassured by this human frailty.

'This is about the only thing that doesn't get touched when your people go through my drawers.' Bentham smiled at the stony face opposite; the lip and nose had lost their puffiness. 'In your position I'd probably do the same. What offends me is that you think us so stupid we'd leave anything around nowadays.'

'I don't know why you've asked me back, sir,' Johnston said. 'I'm fairly busy.'

Bentham paused and considered him, then extended the paper cup of whiskey. When the RUC man made no move for it, Bentham withdrew the offer and drank it himself.

'You probably won't believe this, but I am on your side. Most policemen are. Certainly the Police Complaints Commission. But you're making it a lot fucking harder for us to progress to a satisfactory conclusion.'

In spite of everything Jack Bentham knew that was what he wanted when he pushed aside the irritation he felt; to lift the RUC out of trouble and catch the plane back to London. The prospect seemed a long way off.

When Johnston made no response to the offer, Bentham said, 'We know who the other man was who went with you to the hospital. We have a detailed description. What I'm doing is giving you an opportunity of helping us, and at the same time helping yourself.'

Still there was no response from the man opposite.

'Fine,' Bentham said with an air of finality. 'Thanks for coming.' He watched Johnston rise and start out before saying, 'It's only a matter of time before we find him.' He allowed the threat to hang in the air between them.

The Security Service, where Bentham started looking for the second man, was no more helpful. Laurence Payne, one of the Security liaison officers at Knock Road, did things correctly and referred him to his boss, Sir Michael Newfield. Although resident in Stormont Castle, Sir Michael agreed to see him out on an army shooting range in Lisburn.

Perhaps it was to impress him, Bentham thought as he watched what resembled a large, slightly overripe pear using a rifle with a telescopic sight. Bentham's eyesight was good enough to know he was hitting the target with a high score, but wondered for what purpose. Was he ever going into the field again to use that skill?

Sir Michael lowered the rifle and raised the binoculars from the stand near him and checked the sight. He climbed awkwardly off the ground and dusted only imaginary dross off his clothes. 'Two off-centre,' he said and collected the rifle off the floor and handed it to a captain who was with him. 'There was a time when all six would have gone in on top of each other.'

'Looks pretty good to me,' Bentham said. He had failed as a police marksman when he had done shooting as part of the CID training course.

'It would no longer get me to Bisley. Thank you, captain.'

'My pleasure, sir,' the army man said. He was acting like this was the Prime Minister on a visit. He glanced at Herbert Greenhous, who was with them, and started away.

Sir Michael walked off the range, expecting Bentham to follow. 'You're making a bit of a nuisance of yourself, Commander,' he said.

A smile wrinkled in Bentham's mind, and he refused to be diminished by this obviously intentional demotion. 'Life would be easier if MI5 would co-operate . . .'

'There's no reason to allow the Security Service to be sucked into this.'

'They are in it already. I'd like to interview them.'

'Have you any evidence of that?' he asked, rounding on Bentham and making him shorten his stride. 'Apart from some vague description given by a disturbed ten-year-old, and the RUC's understandable reluctance to co-operate. Do you suggest we hold an identity parade of some sort, Commander?'

'I paraded three hundred policemen in London, trying to find a suspected rapist.'

'Security officers are working in the most sensitive and dangerous theatres possible,' the Ulster Security Co-ordinator said. 'What you suggest is nonsense.'

This argument was going nowhere, Bentham realised, and would go nowhere with a man who was a personal friend of the Prime Minister's and would probably go that high, if, in the unlikely event, he found he needed to in order to win. If he wouldn't let him try and identify the second man from the ranks of MI5 and the SIS there was nothing he could do about it, but even so, Bentham resented being talked to in this way. 'It's not a public event that I'm selling tickets to,' he said. 'I'm a senior policeman.'

'Then for fuck's sake start behaving like one, Mr Bentham, as if you know whose side you're on in this war.'

With that, Sir Michael strode away with his number two, moving like a woman moved, Bentham noticed, his hips arcing in a circular movement with each step, making his ample buttocks roll.

The frustration Jack Bentham felt on the work front was counterpointed by what he felt sexually. Whenever his thoughts strayed in that direction now, they seemed to find Maureen McFadden. He had a clear image of her in her white body suit with the shoulder pads, the curve of her tense, slender body, the slight mound at her crotch. He saw her reaching and stretching to aerobics music.

It was those thoughts unclearly focussed – other than in some unworked-out fantasy – that led him to Anderson and McAuley's department store and the first-floor lingerie department. He believed that he had been kept under observation at various times since arriving in Northern Ireland, but the feeling had increased since his meeting with the Ulster Security Co-ordinator, and he told himself this department was a good place to identify such a tail, if he had one. Only two women came into the department while he moved around to the rack of silk underwear and watched the escalator discharge shoppers. There was another man there, but with a woman, and both had the tense, burred faces of people who live in an inhospitable climate.

After staying longer than he dared without being challenged, and with the overcoat he had hardly taken off since coming to Northern Ireland hiding his erection, he took some white silk French camiknickers with three buttons at the crotch to the till where stood an elderly sales assistant.

'You realise it's silk, they are, sir? They're £39.95,' she said.

'I saw it on the label,' he replied brusquely, covering his slight unease. He glanced around at the other customers, thinking maybe he had imagined the tail.

'They are very nice, of course.' She put the camiknickers into a brown and orange bag. 'We'll change them if they're not quite right if you keep your receipt.'

The fantasy had expanded to Maureen McFadden dancing in that ballroom at the hotel on her own in these camiknickers.

He masturbated in the shower back in his hotel suite with that same image in mind, but felt worse afterwards, not relieved. The telephone ringing got him out of the shower. It was Harry Streeter. Somehow he had been expecting a call, but thought it would come from someone at ACPO.

'Jack?' He paused. 'How's it going out there?'

'Like wading through mud. They spend so much time tapping our phones and keeping us under obo,' he added, as if to cut the ground from under the Deputy Commissioner.

'I wouldn't have thought so, Jack,' Streeter said quickly. 'Not at your rank,' as if it made some difference.

Bentham didn't argue, seeing no point. 'We're inching forward. We've had a couple of good results. But unless they firm up, we might as well come back.'

'Any idea when that will be? There's a lot going on here.'

'When isn't there, Harry? About three to four weeks we'll be looking at a provisional report.'

'Good,' a lighter note coming into his voice. 'Roy Genders looks like turning in his papers . . .' He let the statement hang like a carrot. The resignation of the Assistant Commissioner with responsibility for specialist operations would provide Jack Bentham with the opening he needed, provided he didn't fuck up here. Bentham knew exactly what was being said, and the Deputy Commissioner could have put the phone down at that point.

'I've had the people from Curzon Street House on to me.' A smile crept over Bentham's face. 'It looks like they've got good reason.' Now he knew they had.

'I can't control that element, Jack. Nor can ACPO. Do yourself a favour. Just go around MI5.'

'Of course I will,' he said obligingly.

They were going to have to find somewhere else to hold their briefings, Bentham decided when he put the phone down. He didn't want to tell his team to look for Security Service connections with any of the shootings while he was in the hotel suite or at their offices at Garnerville, in case they were still bugged. The bar, or the dining-room, where they all met up over breakfast, was a likely place. But looking down at his naked stomach and the fat on his thighs he thought a jogging session in the park might be a safe place.

He wanted to see Maureen McFadden again; he needed to talk to her professionally, or at least someone on his team did, and that gave him an excuse. He wanted to see her in the aerobics class again. Frank Burroughs found out when she held them.

Bentham thought he definitely should take up jogging, as he waited at the back of the class. These females not only excited him, but made him feel unfit. He would be ashamed to take his clothes off in front of a woman as he was at the moment.

His eyes flitted across the girls who were in the class, not daring to linger in case his thoughts were too clearly perceived by Maureen McFadden, who occasionally looked his way. There was nothing inviting in her look.

At first she pretended he wasn't there, but found his presence more and more intrusive. Although men were welcome in the class, they were unwelcome spectators.

Finally Bentham's presence wore her down. 'Keep moving,' she said to the class. 'Keep jogging for a few moments.' She walked around the edge of the room and past the policeman, who stepped through the gap in the sliding door to join her. 'I told you the other day, Mr Bentham,' she said in an angry whisper, 'I don't have anything to say to you. I want to be left alone.'

'I can't do that, Mrs McFadden; I'm sorry if it's painful. But there have been things going on here that I can't penetrate. You might be the only one who can help.'

Shaking her head, she said with an air of finality, 'I can't. It's done. Nothing will bring Stephen back. Please go away.'

She turned back into the class, trying to shut the doors after her, but they required more than a casual gesture to close them. By the time she reached the top of the room, she noticed Bentham had gone. She felt relieved and anxious at the same time, wondering if she perhaps shouldn't try to help this policeman; perhaps he was genuine. Finally she decided it was the best that she didn't go back over that painful ground when it would almost certainly achieve nothing. She slipped back into the movements to the beat of the music, but her concentration wouldn't return. She noticed the concerned expression of her youngest daughter Angela, who joined the class once a week, and smiled at her. Kathleen, her elder sister, was also looking troubled, and Maureen smiled at her too.

On leaving the hotel with her daughters, Maureen saw the policeman waiting in the car park, and an involuntary smile started across her face. She checked it as he came to meet them. 'You're very persistent, Mr Bentham.'

'I practise. Are these your daughters? They look a lot like you. Angela and Kathleen,' he said addressing the wrong girl.

Angela eagerly corrected him.

'Why don't you wait in the car,' Maureen said quickly, seeing what would happen. Her daughters responded too readily to interesting men.

'They're very pretty,' Bentham told her as he watched them go.

She resented that tack. 'You should have told them, they'd have been eating out of your hand, they would so.'

Marshalling what sincerity he could, Bentham said, 'I realise you've no reason at all to feel good about the police. I don't know if I can convince you this is different. Perhaps I can't.'

'Or perhaps you're kidding yourself, Mr Bentham.'

'Maybe. I can't be that different. I went through the same conditioning – different circumstances, is all.' He knew that if he gave something of himself, the chances were he would get something back. It was always a gamble, but worth taking.

Nothing came back from Maureen McFadden.

'The truth is, I'm in trouble, Mrs McFadden,' he said, opening himself up some more. 'I'm under increasing pressure to find the sort of result everyone out here wants. That's going to be hard to resist unless I can make a big jump forward with my investigation. I believe the wrong men might have been put on trial for shooting Stephen – oh, those two were there, of course.' He hesitated. 'Maybe you can help connect his death to the killing in the alley behind your flat. I think there might be a connection. I don't know what it is.'

Hearing someone say those words took her breath away, and she began to shake her head out of an instinct of self-preservation, but stopped as confusion flooded in on her. Tears were pushing up behind her eyelids and she used the heel of her hand to massage between her eyes to stop herself crying. She quickly walked away.

Bentham stopped himself going after her. He felt he had almost reached her, but perhaps hadn't give quite enough, or didn't appreciate just how deep the hurt was for a mother who had lost a child. He watched the scene in the car as the two girls comforted her with words and slightly awkward gestures. Their glances his way made him uncomfortable, but he refused to retreat to his car. Perhaps in future he should send Bill Senior to talk to this woman; he might be more successful.

Finally, Angela climbed out and ran across to him. At first Bentham thought she was going to attack him. 'We talked about it, what you want, that is,' she said. 'Mum said she will help if she can.'

'That's good, Angela. That's good.' He gave her a warm smile, and felt like putting his arms around her.

Their flat, the part he saw, was a pleasant surprise, Bentham found; a sparsely furnished but good-looking oasis in a desert of destruction. Angela made him some tea and brought it to him in the sitting-room with some sponge cake she had made earlier.

'Now I know it's all right,' he said, and glanced around at Maureen McFadden, as she came in, having changed and wearing a dress. Kathleen followed her. They sat on a rug on the floor.

'Do you need to be very fit to teach aerobics?'

'It makes you pretty fit.'

'Do you have any men in the classes?' He hadn't seen any.

'It's not macho enough, I'm thinking.'

'Probably.' He wouldn't have minded joining such a class when he was in shape. There was a silence as he ate some cake and drank tea. 'Kit McMahon told us Stephen saw the shooting out there.'

'Kit couldn't talk, his Mum said.' Kathleen was surprised. 'How did you make him?'

'Twisted his arms – the usual police torture methods.' He smiled at their surprise, then told them about Bill Senior and his interest in the boy.

Still Maureen held back, until her younger daughter came to her side. 'Tell him, Mum. We did decide.'

'We did so,' Maureen sighed. 'My daughters have taken a liking to you, Mr Bentham. They think you can be trusted. I hope you won't let them down.'

Obviously, Bentham thought, he hadn't given enough. More of himself was required, and perhaps more than he could deliver.

He smiled. 'That's nice. But I don't know if I can always. What I'll do is try. If I find a connection between what I think Stephen saw and what happened to him . . .'

'I didn't want to think about that,' Maureen said, and caught her breath. 'Stephen did see the shooting – least, he said so. The poor soul lived a lot in his imagination, he did so. But he didn't tell lies.'

'This wasn't some fantasy?'

She shook her head. 'He would tell me about those again and again. He only told me this once when he was watching the news. He said it didn't happen as they showed on TV, that the man didn't have a gun. That upset him, that they'd got it wrong on the news.'

'He meant Desmond O'Donnell, the IRA man?'

'Yes. After the shooting, Stephen claimed the police chased him and that he hid in the flat. That made me wonder – until a neighbour here told me the police did come into the block looking for someone else.'

Bentham didn't disbelieve what she said, but he was disappointed because her information was hearsay and so unusable. He couldn't produce her as a witness. They needed something else. 'Why didn't you tell anyone, Mrs McFadden?'

She closed her eyes, and said, 'I was scared – if it were true, if he had seen it like he said. Then I was scared he wouldn't be able to keep quiet about it.'

Kathleen interrupted with, 'We talked about it and decided we'd best tell someone.'

Maureen smiled grimly and touched her daughter's arm in appreciation for that shared responsibility.

'Who did you tell?' Bentham asked.

'We went to see a solicitor. He told us it would be a terrible ordeal for Stephen, and that no one would believe him anyway. He told us to forget the whole thing. I couldn't have wanted to hear anything better.'

'A solicitor actually told a material witness to a murder to forget what he'd seen?'

'Stephen had a mental age of eight, Mr Bentham.'

Bentham nodded. 'Eight-year-olds sometimes make perfectly reliable witnesses, Mrs McFadden.' Suddenly his investigation was up and running. 'We'd better have someone interview this solicitor.'

19

OFTEN WHEN HE HAD seen people jogging in London, Jack Bentham had thought it a pointless waste of time, especially as the exercise appeared not to be sufficiently vigorous to be of any value physically. However, when he bought a tracksuit and running shoes and began jogging around Ormeau Park, which lay along the east side of the river Lagan, he had a definite purpose; it was to keep information away from the RUC and MI5. As he ran at a lumbering gait with calf and thigh muscles stinging and lungs burning, he began to appreciate just how physical it was and how unfit he had been. But something this painful had to be beneficial, he decided, and he wouldn't seem such an out-of-condition lump in the presence of aerobics dancers.

His men weren't similarly disposed to train, and avoided running at their meetings in the park; at first, Bentham welcomed the break to stop and talk with them, but soon he started running on past and made them keep up.

Detective Superintendent Frank Burroughs prised himself off the bench and quickly fell into step as his boss approached with no obvious intention of stopping. It was harder work trying to catch up.

'I interviewed that solicitor, guv,' he said, having plenty of breath for conversation at that point. 'He denies ever seeing Mrs McFadden, with or without her son.'

Bentham glanced round at him, not losing his stride.

'He said he doesn't know the woman. It's what he said.'

'Did you think he was lying, Frank?'

'He's a solicitor – that's the first thing they're taught in law school, isn't it?'

The Detective Superintendent's breath was going, and Bentham slowed down to a bench up ahead, where he did tendon-stretching exercises as he had seen other runners do.

'You gonna do this often?'

'I've bought all this gear, I may as well get fit.'

Frank Burroughs groaned; having accepted the original idea, he was not enjoying it day after day. 'I should think you must have fallen in love – myself, I'd sooner have a pint.'

When Bentham put Edward O'Dwyer's denial to Maureen McFadden as she was preparing to begin her aerobics class, she paused midway through pulling her jumper off and looked at him, anger appearing in her face and making her subsequent movements jerky.

'He's lying – Jesus, he is,' she said in a tightly locked-down whisper. 'I went there with Stephen, I did so.' It hadn't occurred to her before now that the policeman might not believe her.

'Why would he lie?' Bentham wanted to know. He could speculate, but preferred her to.

'How would I know?' She turned away and busied herself with the cassette player. Then suddenly she stopped and became calm. 'I'd say he's afraid, like most people. He had to go on working here, living here, poor man.'

'Poor man? That's big of you.'

'Anyone who's afraid, for whatever reason, is poor in spirit. All your fear does is add to the power they have over you.' The priest she had talked to soon after Stephen's death had said that to her. She agreed with the sentiment and remembered it. She didn't know who 'they' were and it didn't matter. 'I certainly was in his office in Chichester Street,' she insisted, wanting to be believed. 'Didn't we sit there looking at the maroon carpet with a great wear hole in the feet space under his desk?'

'Anything else about the room I can challenge him on?'

Maureen smiled, feeling a sense of relief, and sent her mind back to that shabby law office to retrieve what details of it she could.

They were all correct, Bentham found, when he sat opposite the desk in the solicitor's office. Probably in the same chair she sat in. The large picture of a rural scene, cottage and horsemen; the view of the green control-sector gates from the window behind the desk.

'I'm unable to add to what I told Superintendent Burroughs, Assistant Commissioner,' O'Dwyer said weaselling, leaning forward, his hands together on his desk as if in prayer, as he glanced nervously at DI Senior. 'I don't know this poor soul. I've never spoken to her son.'

'Is it possible she might be confused with some other visit here? – it would be understandable in the circumstances.'

'I don't think so.' He sounded sure of that, disguising the anxiety that was rising in him like bile. He remembered his meeting with Martin St James, his cousin, out on Shandon Park Golf Course after the meeting with Stephen and his mother, and telling him about what the boy allegedly saw. Although Martin was an assistant chief constable in the RUC, he believed the boy's death shortly afterwards was no more than a coincidence. But even so, he believed he was best kept out of it, whatever this policeman now believed.

'She did describe your office, right down to the hole in the carpet,' Bentham was saying, still avoiding any accusatory tone. 'Maybe she came to see you or someone about something else? – I'd like the loose ends cleared away before I write my report.'

Edward O'Dwyer sat back now, the wheels turning in his mind, slipping on the slurry of lies he was spreading. 'It's possible,' he ventured cautiously. 'I don't remember all my clients – not the blow-ins for one-off consultations. When was this again?'

'Back in February, around the twenty-fourth.' He knew precisely.

'I've no recollection of any meeting. Just a moment.' He rose and went through to the ante-room and came back at once with the large diary, in which his secretary kept appointments. He flicked through the pages, shaking his head doubtfully. 'I can't see anything around that date, Assistant Commissioner.' He went on looking, as it was easier than meeting the eyes of either of these policemen.

'But she's so insistent, Mr O'Dwyer. From her description, I'd say she has been in this office at some point.'

'Ah! Ah, here's something.' He extended the book. 'On the First of March a Mrs McFadden came to see me. Is that possibly her? She came to see me about a housing problem.'

'It doesn't sound like she came with a backward son.' Bentham was preparing to leave.

'I would have remembered. Especially if she came for the reason she claims,' the solicitor said, feeling satisfied. 'The poor soul is obviously confused.'

'What do you think, Bill?' he said to DI Senior as they walked towards their car that was waiting on a restricted zone adjacent to the control sector. He felt the need to ask because of his uncertainty about his own feelings towards Maureen McFadden, rather than uncertainty about her story.

'If he wasn't a brief, guv, I'd say have him down to the nick.'

Bentham smiled. He didn't always accept the opinions of his men, but nor did he ever ignore them. 'Run a check on him, Bill. See if there's any reason for him to lie about that meeting.' He saw DI

Senior's look. 'Other than getting his knuckles rapped by the Law Society. Look at family connections, business associates, school governing bodies, PTAs, the lot.'

Welcoming any opportunity that took him to see Maureen McFadden, Bentham called at her flat, but found only Angela there. She told him where her mother was. His driver took him back to the city control sector, where Bentham pursued her to a shopping mall on the edge of North Street. She emerged from a wholefood shop with a bag and started along the covered arcade. Even here, shops were boarded up as business had vanished from the city. He told her about the solicitor.

'He was either lying or mistaken the first time, Mr Bentham – why would he change his mind? He's lying if he says I went to talk about a housing problem. At the Divis flats? I'm more likely to go to the housing executive.' She started away from the shop. 'How did you know I was here?'

'Angela told me – every shop. Even what you were going to buy. Can I carry that?'

It was a long while since he'd carried a woman's shopping bag, and reached for it. Being even longer since she had had a man carry her bag she was embarrassed and confused and pulled away, dropping one of her woollen gloves. Bentham settled for retrieving it.

'You've made a big success with Angela,' she said, admonishing him.

'More than I have with her mum.' He tried on the glove, pulling it away when she reached for it. It didn't go too far on to his thick fingers.

'Were you expecting a success, Mr Bentham?'

He stopped and gave her a boyish smile. 'I wouldn't mind taking you out to dinner.'

'Why?'

Her bluntness startled him. 'Well, I could pretend I need to ask you more questions – I might think of some. Like how you got into aerobics. Why you stay in Northern Ireland.'

'I'd probably say it's none of your business. May I have my glove?'

As she took the glove, her eyes fell on the window of the pet shop on the corner of the arcade and North Street. She had passed it hundreds of times, thinking the same thing each time she saw the window half-full of birds.

'What do you think those wretched creatures have done to deserve

225

their life sentence, Mr Bentham?' She offered this as a challenge. 'I have an ambition to one day set all of those birds free.'

'Would they survive outside their cages?' he asked, gauging the ground.

'Would it matter much? That brief flight of freedom is probably better than imprisonment.'

'Why don't you do it?' She reminded him of someone else he knew who would do such things, and worse, for animals.

After a moment, Maureen said, 'They might be frightened – they've been imprisoned so long.'

Bentham nodded, knowing which way to go now. 'Maybe they could be coaxed gently.'

'Yes, maybe.'

They started along North Street, past an electronic bingo palace that looked as jaded as the half-dozen or so lives that were eked out in front of their score cards.

'That looks like a good night,' Bentham said. Maureen glanced in at the depressing room with its permanent pall of cigarette smoke, but didn't comment. 'Would your daughters like to have dinner with me? – with you along to chaperone them.'

'That's not a good idea.'

He thought it an excellent idea.

'If you're lonely, Mr Bentham, there are lots of women in Belfast who would go out with you. Try the bars.'

Irritation was beginning to reach him now, and was making him more persistent, even reckless. 'What about you?' he asked. 'Do you get lonely?'

'I'd say it was none of your business.'

'Sometimes it gets that I don't know what is and what isn't. But I try to keep the rule I have about dinner always being off-duty.'

'You are very persistent.' She wasn't giving ground.

'You'd better believe it,' he told her.

He returned to the police barracks in Garnerville with no more than a determination to pursue the solicitor, Edward O'Dwyer.

'Guv,' Detective Superintendent Burroughs said, coming into his office, 'we got a call from a solicitor with a client in the Maze who wants to talk to you.'

'What about? Did the solicitor say? – it's not O'Dwyer?'

Burroughs shook his head. 'I've set a meeting up.'

'Any sign of those two missing RUC men, or are they on extended leave now?'

'Dave tapped into their computer again,' Detective Superintendent Burroughs said, nodding towards Detective Superintendent Palmer, who was now acting as collator. 'He came up with a complete blank. They've either sacked them or buried them, along with their service records.'

'Or perhaps they never worked for the RUC,' Bentham said intuitively, thinking that they might have belonged to the Security Service. 'They're somewhere, Frank. They're not a figment of our imagination. I'd better have another go at the Deputy Chief Constable.'

The phone call he made got him as far as the ante-room to Donald Joyce's office and there he sat for an hour. Although he read through two thick files, he'd rather have been elsewhere. He looked pointedly at his watch as the secretary emerged from the inner sanctum, tightly closing the door.

'Is there any prospect of seeing your boss today?'

'He is terribly busy, sir,' she said, without looking at him. 'I did say I would be trying to get you in to see him, sir.'

'You did,' Bentham said, rising. 'I can't wait around here any longer. I'll leave him a message. You'd better write it down because I want him to get it right. I need to interview Constables Stone and Birchfield, who I assume are back off leave. I also want copies of the tape made out at Hollow Farm – '

'I don't know if I can, sir,' she started to protest.

'I do. Either I get them, tell him, or I'm going over both the Deputy's and the Chief Constable's heads.'

With that he marched out, not having the foggiest notion who he would go to, or if he found someone whether that person would have the guts to go against the Chief Constable. Sir Norman Hateley ran the RUC like a personal fiefdom where his was the last word, and any price was paid, it seemed, to keep the fragile peace that his forces on the ground held. The price seemed far too high, Jack Bentham decided, the deal that was struck for the politicians and the law officers, and most of all the taxpayers, was piss-poor. But he had no real expectation of securing anything better for anyone.

Approaching the Maze prison was like walking into a brick wall, the atmosphere was so heavy. The grey inner walls enclosing the H-blocks were twenty feet high, topped off with green fencing. Despite the arrangements that had been made before their trip out to Lisburn, Bentham and Burroughs were confronted by a soldier from the Staffords with an Armalite. The prison officer on the first checkpoint was no less helpful. He went on collecting the playing cards from prison officers as they came off duty. These were exchanged for the internal pass at the main gate. Eventually an assistant governor was fetched and they were admitted as far as the main gate. Finally, they were given special security passes and admitted through the security Portakabin.

Momentarily, Jack Bentham was able to forget what the inmates might have done and to almost feel sorry for them, as he and Detective Superintendent Burroughs were led across to the secure visitors' block. It was a fleeting feeling that passed as he adjusted to the initial shock. He had visited many prisons in similar circumstances but none as awful as this, and none with such a smothering blanket of fear and loathing lying over it, holding in the rank smell of bodies and minds and spirits decaying without hope. That was something peculiar to prisons holding men serving natural life. What the whole of the prison system represented, and what the Maze epitomised, was a society that had little compassion for those that offended against it.

James Naughtie, the Nationalist prisoner who requested to see Bentham, was forty and had spent a little more than half of his life in one institution or another and was now looking to break from that by securing for himself some sort of early parole. However, what he had seriously misjudged was both Bentham's power and his effectiveness in this situation.

He watched the departure from the visiting room of the two prison officers who had escorted him there and waited for them to slam and lock the door.

'They go outside like the polite gentlemen they are, sure enough,' he said mockingly. 'But I daresay they got the room bugged.'

'I shouldn't worry about it, Mr Naughtie,' Bentham told him, enjoying this prisoner's name.

The smile disappeared from Naughtie's face. 'They'll be after knowing about me.'

'There's a good chance they do already. So don't let it inhibit you.' Bentham hadn't been in a prison where there was so much electronic surveillance. Cameras were mounted on every wall. There were two in the drab cream visiting room that was rank with the smell of stale tobacco smoke.

James Naughtie wasn't sure now. He glanced between the two policemen, looking for some encouragement. The cigarettes Bentham had remembered to bring with him seemed to be it. Naughtie leaned across the table to light one and said quietly, 'Will I get some remission for my information?'

'It would be the easiest thing in the world for me to say yes,' Bentham said. 'Wouldn't cost me a thing. If the information is helpful, I will approach the Minister of State and put your case.'

That seemed to satisfy the prisoner. Here was someone who cared enough to come out and see him, at least. He nodded his agreement. 'It's about Stephen McFadden, the lad shot out at Hollow Farm. Now, how did the RUC know those guns were going to be in that derelict barn?'

'I've got to confess, Mr Naughtie,' Bentham said, suddenly wondering if this man was a bit stir crazy, 'that's something I've been unable to find out. Can you tell us?'

'I can't, of course,' Naughtie said sharply, and smiled. 'What I can be after telling you is that I was cleaning the corridor on our H-block yesterday and I heard two of the prisoners talking – one was Kevin Lampard. He was saying how the RUC had been to see him and asked him to say he was the source of the information about those guns in the barn. It would be worth his while.'

'Did he say who the RUC men were?'

'He did not. And I couldn't ask! But there can't be that many came in to see prisoners.'

Bentham smiled. 'We might just be in business.'

It was a promise, but depending on what came of this he would try to help Naughtie.

The second assistant governor was keen to help identify the visiting RUC men, even without fully knowing the purpose. He knew why Assistant Commissioner Bentham was in Northern Ireland, and was young enough to believe that it was a good thing basically to sort out the rot wherever it appeared, but he wasn't experienced enough to know it wasn't always expedient to do so.

'There'll be a record of the visit at the gatehouse, sir,' he said as he led them across the windswept yard, overlooked by the security towers, where soldiers stared coldly down at them. 'I seem to recall it was Superintendent Corbin of E4 who telephoned to organise the visit.'

Inside the gate office the principal officer in charge saluted them. 'Afternoon, sir. Five souls released today, sir,' he informed the assistant governor. 'Nine arrived.'

'Ah,' the assistant governor sighed. 'We can't even pretend the prison system is working, Mr Toynbee.'

Bentham wasn't sure if this was their own oblique sense of humour. He found the gate office as oppressive as anywhere, and never before had he felt that the prison officers were as much captives as the prisoners. 'Who were the policemen who came to see Kevin Lampard the other day?'

The principal officer folded open the large day book which contained all movements and ran a thick finger down the columns, where various inky spiders had crawled. 'I hope everything is in order, sir,' he said as his finger stopped. 'One was Chief Inspector Paisley. The other didn't leave his name.'

'Was he RUC?' Bentham asked.

'Don't believe he was, sir.'

'Why didn't he leave his name? Isn't that the drill?'

'It is, sir. I believe the gentleman in question was from the Security Service. We don't push them for their names in the circumstances, sir.'

'What makes you think he was with the Security Service?' Bentham asked.

'You get to know the look, sir, the way they deport themselves. He's been here before.'

'Do you know who he was?'

The principal officer looked at the assistant governor and hesitated, suddenly cautious of this outsider. 'No, sir,' he said categorically.

Bentham didn't even get angry.

Driving away from the Maze, feeling as if he were driving out of a bad dream, he said, 'Unless we start getting more co-operation around here, Frank, we might have to try and nick one or two – we won't be any worse off. Perhaps Johnston and Paisley.'

'Any chance they'd go, guv?' Detective Superintendent Burroughs said.

Glancing at his driver and wondering how much he would carry back, Bentham said, 'I'd put money on it.' He thought about the situation, and where they were going and if they would get there. Everyone couldn't be involved in a cover-up. The thoroughly worked-out conspiracy that made the so-called Left so jumpy never existed. Almost always conspiracies came about by chance, in answer to someone's need to survive, and there were always ends that weren't tied in, that could be caught hold of, however tenuously, and pulled until the whole weave came undone. He refused to allow himself to become paranoid. These policemen were simply looking to survive like any policeman in trouble, and were improvising the cover-up as they went. They had yet to find the loose strand that would unravel everything, Bentham decided, but they would in time, and he would pull it. 'Let's go back to the beginning on everyone. Everyone with any connection with those shootings. Have them in and question them all again. Someone knows who's involved besides the RUC.' He glanced at the back of his driver's head again, then added, 'Put some pressure on Constables Peters and Hinton, and on Sergeant Keeper.'

Letting this go back via the driver was the beginning of that pressure. But whether it would have a result, Bentham couldn't guess.

20

THE BUNCH OF FLOWERS and bottle of wine he was carrying made Jack Bentham feel self-conscious, and slightly foolish; self-conscious because this wasn't the usual way to approach a witness, and his driver was probably wondering what was going on; foolish because Maureen McFadden wasn't expecting him and had previously given him little reason for believing she would be anything but hostile to this approach. He wondered fleetingly how she might respond if he offered her the camiknickers he had bought, and still had fantasies about her dancing in them.

'Will you be wanting me to wait, sir?' the driver said when he pulled on to the rubble-strewn parking round between the Divis flats.

'Well, there's a question now, Joe,' Bentham responded, as if to a man who had been in a similar predicament. 'I daresay you don't want to hang around here.'

'God, if they knew who I was. By rights, sir, I shouldn't be leaving you off on your own here.'

'Why don't you go and get yourself some dinner? I'll phone my officer if I want you to come back.'

Bentham watched the car roar away before he turned and walked into the graffiti-scarred entrance. There a feeling of nervousness crept over him, not because of where he was, for despite policemen getting killed in NI – and two had since his arrival – the possibility still wasn't touching him. He felt himself only distantly connected to the RUC and their troubles. His fear now was of the prospect of rejection. The whole notion was ridiculous, he told himself, turning up here like this; it was arrogant to assume she might feel anything for him other than a cold forbearance, allowing him the benefit of the doubt, waiting for him to confirm her expectations of all policemen. However, he was determined not to turn tail, even though he was unsure of his feelings.

The door was opened by a surprised Kathleen. 'Mum's in the bath.'

'That's nice,' Bentham said, but realised the girl didn't connect with his thoughts.

They stood awkwardly on the threshold. Kathleen noticed the flowers. They were white freesias; the perfume from them was heady.

'Is she expecting you? She never said.'

'You're never expecting the police, or you're always expecting them.' He stepped inside.

Kathleen and Angela were cooking supper, which seemed to make his mission even more difficult, and he regretted not having phoned first. He regretted bringing the flowers and wine as they closed off the possibility of retreating into business to save face.

'Are you coming to supper?' Angela asked cheerfully, as she sprinkled flour into a frying pan of vegetables.

'What are you cooking?' he asked, avoiding the question.

'Leek and mushroom pie. We're vegetarians – we don't eat meat,' she explained.

'That's a vegetarian for you!' he said.

She misunderstood his joke. 'Oh, it's all right. You get enough proteins and amino acids and stuff.'

'I know. I used to be vegetarian.' He had been converted by a lady who he had spent a lot of time with. It had been easier than trying to find some argument for eating meat at every meal. Finally, he had come to the view that eating the corpses of other species was a bizarre thing to do. Yet, with that lady's influence gone from his life, he had quickly slipped back into bad habits. Being a policeman gave you all sorts of bad habits. But he often ate vegetarian food from choice now there was a choice in most restaurants.

'Why did you give it up?'

'It gave me up, I think, Angie,' he said. 'Is your pan all right?'

Angie turned back to her cooking, as her mother came along the hall in her bathrobe, got from the bath by Kathleen.

'How can I help you, Mr Bentham?'

Jack Bentham felt more awkward now. There was no retreating. Having presumed as much as he had, all he could do was press on. 'It's dinner time. I was hoping you'd have dinner with me.'

'No. I can't.'

Her manner was brusque, defensive. She was curiously flattered but at the same time resented the intrusion, the way men seemed to think they could take over the moment they arrived on the scene.

'That's a shame. I booked a table at Oscar's – I heard it's good.'

'No, I'd rather not – I'm vegetarian.' The excuse sounded feeble.

'He used to be!' Angela said, as if by way of an apology for him. The girls were awaiting developments.

'We could go to a vegetarian restaurant, if you know one?'

'There's Zero's – it's brilliant,' Angela told him.

Still Maureen resisted, despite Bentham's promise not to behave like a policeman.

'Oh go on, Mum,' Angela urged. 'You never go out.'

'Angie!' Maureen went quickly to the stove to stir the pan of vegetables, grateful for something to distract her. 'That's getting too thick. It'll burn.'

'Why don't you go, Mum?' Angela asked, puzzled.

'How can I?' her mother responded quietly, arguing with herself now that she was over the shock of Jack Bentham's unexpected arrival. She glanced at the policeman, who waited so uncertainly, then at Kathleen, who nodded enthusiastically in response to her silent question.

Maureen tried to hold back her smile. 'We've always done things democratically in this family – they seem to think I should.'

The two girls jumped around excitedly, as if it were their special treat. Bentham felt relieved, if only to be able to relinquish graciously the flowers and wine.

'Were you that sure I'd go out with you?' Maureen asked guardedly when they were eating their meal in Oscar's. Zero's had closed early. Her feelings were like the cloudy waters of a dam that the cranked-open sluice gate was stirring up, trying to get out in turmoil and confusion.

'I wasn't sure at all,' he said candidly; then smiled. 'I was planning to arrest you if you didn't.'

'But you brought flowers and wine.'

'I'd have taken them back.' He found himself on the defensive.

'It seems a wee bit old-fashioned, giving a woman flowers.' She didn't really want to say that, but it was such a long time since a man had given her flowers.

'Flowers feed the soul. I'd say all our souls are vegetarian, wouldn't you?'

Maureen stopped eating and looked at him, unsure whether he was mocking her. 'You don't expect policemen to talk about souls.'

'I could say you don't expect people living in the Divis flats to,' he came back at her with.

234

She stared at him. 'Some of them are good people – for the Republicans, most of them are.'

'So are some policemen, believe it or not.'

She shifted the ground. 'Why did you stop being vegetarian?'

'Laziness, I suppose. I used to go out with a woman who was vegan. Heavily committed to animal rights – I had to arrest her,' he joked, laying that relationship safely to rest. 'That isn't why you're vegetarian?'

She shook her head and shivered as a ghost walked past. 'Stephen made me stop eating meat,' she said. 'He wouldn't, even as a baby. He said, Mum, it's dead animals. He got on with all animals.'

She fell silent, remembering things that were painful to her. Bentham wanted to reach out and touch her hand, but didn't risk it.

'We won't turn back, for his sake . . . excuse me.' She struggled against tears that she believed had long been washed out of her and left the table.

Bentham asked for the bill and paid while he waited for Maureen to return. 'Why don't you let it all out? Just let go,' he advised as they walked along the pavement from the restaurant. His car, which he had telephoned for, was following them, the driver happier about waiting on Bedford than on Divis Street.

Maureen was staring thoughtfully ahead, worrying about what might happen next and was startled by his words. 'What?'

He caught hold of her and stopped her, but she avoided his eyes, fearing she would cry again if anyone looked into them and recognised the pain.

'You suffered shock, then anger, hatred, loss – you probably made yourself terribly busy to avoid all that.'

'I don't know what right you have to intrude like that,' she said, jolted to anger as a defence.

'None – but I might as well say it now. You seem so screwed down that you want to scream. Well, go ahead, scream why don't you? Scream and scream if it'll help.'

'Thank you for dinner, Mr Bentham,' she said with a forced calm. 'I can do without the counselling.'

She turned and hurried off along the street. Bentham went after her and caught her by the shoulder and turned her. She tried to fight him off, but then burst into tears. Bentham simply held her and let her cry. People passing looked at them as they would a deformed person, quickly averting their eyes. Two drunken youths made some crack but he let it go.

After a moment, he said. 'Come on, I'll take you home.'

The girls had gone to bed when they got back and Maureen offered him coffee. He waited on the small, slightly broken-down sofa in the sitting-room, sensing she wanted a moment or two alone. He wanted to consider his next move, whether there was one, other than returning to his hotel. He was unsure.

'Do you feel better now?' he said when she brought the coffee.

'I'm fine. It doesn't make the loss any less.'

She sat lithely on the floor opposite the sofa and, although the room wasn't very big, she seemed miles away. 'Are you any nearer to understanding what happened to Stephen?' she asked suddenly.

'The deeper we get, the more muddy the water becomes.'

'I don't hate those people,' she said reflectively. 'Only what they did.'

Bentham said nothing, but realised how close that was to his feelings about his job, or at least how he liked to believe they were. He didn't hate criminals, and some he even believed he felt sympathy for, but he often hated their crimes.

'I came past the pet shop in North Street this afternoon,' she said. 'Most of the birds have gone from the window. Someone bought the less exotic birds and let them go.'

'Someone beat you to it.'

'It was you,' she said speculatively. 'It was, wasn't it? It sounded like you. I questioned the shopkeeper.'

'Maybe you should have been a detective.'

Still Jack Bentham didn't admit what he had done. He thought about the shopkeeper's surprise when he told her what he had wanted to do, only to be told that some wouldn't survive. He had bought the twenty-eight birds that could survive. There had been curiosity from other shoppers when they took them into the street, and reluctance on the part of the birds at first to leave their cages. But finally all had soared.

Now he thought perhaps all he had to do was admit this and he would be made. Yet somehow he thought that would be taking advantage.

Glancing at her, then avoiding eye contact, he said, 'I'm forty-five, and I've forgotten how to get from A to B.'

'It's been such a long time, I don't know either. Maybe you should think about going – your poor driver.' That wasn't what she wanted to say.

'Yes, I suppose I should.'

He set his mug on the table and rose stiffly, his muscles not yet having found their level from jogging. He started out, then turned back suddenly as she came after him. 'Maybe we can . . .' he began. She was close to him. He took a chance, reached out and put his hands on her shoulders. She was still uncertain. The first kiss was hesitant and a bit clumsy. The second was less restrained. Her emotions became more cloudy, not less.

Kathleen, with her ear pressed to the bedroom wall, followed their progress to her mother's bedroom next door. She hadn't been able to sleep since going to bed for the excitement over what might happen.

The bed creaked in the next room and she started as Angela came into her room.

'What's happening, Kath?' she said.

Her sister shushed her. 'He didn't leave at all, he didn't.'

'Grand,' Angela said. 'That's grand.'

The news of the murder of Mr Justice Hereford and his wife from a culvert bomb as they came through the border post at Newry on their return from England via the Republic deeply shocked the security forces in Ulster and sent them into a tailspin. The outrage, for which the IRA claimed responsibility, was as deeply shocking to Jack Bentham. However, it affected him only inasmuch as the members of the RUC had more excuses not to heed his requests, being too busy with new security arrangements for all those people they were giving protection to, and for the fact that Muriel Kinahon was under heavy sedation following the news, and wasn't available either to supervise or support him.

Although as a policeman he felt concern for any policeman killed or injured on duty, and anyone like judges who were at risk by what they did, Jack Bentham didn't feel there was added risk to himself here because of what had happened to Judge Hereford. He decided there would be little progress to make with the RUC until after the funeral of the judge, where security would doubtless be intense. He thought about going back to London until he could freely interview policemen here again. But he wanted to see Maureen McFadden again.

They pressed on with their investigation.

The calling-back and re-interviewing of RUC men from the Special Support Unit was a particular irritation to most – they seemed to think Bentham should have the decency not to make waves at this particular time; to some it was a source of anxiety. It brought further complaints from ACC Peter Eglington, who was head of the RUC Special Branch, from the Deputy Chief Constable, who told him his timing was in bad taste. He had asked when would be the right time, and had no reply.

The number of complaints Bentham received from the men he interviewed again were, he decided, a barometer of the likely results. However, he knew there was a limit to the number of times he could interview someone without progressing before they also recognised that. Which was the point they were reaching with Chief Inspector Paisley, who had twice refused to come for an interview on account of what was going on by way of funeral security arrangements. When eventually he was persuaded to come out to Garnerville, Bentham attempted to irritate him and goad him into saying something stupid. He made a point of keeping him waiting as he himself was kept waiting when he went to see the Deputy Chief Constable. There was little else he could do that wouldn't bring about his removal from the inquiry. Paisley didn't have the nerve to refuse to wait. Although he was supported by senior officers in the RUC, he didn't know how far they would go along with insubordination, even to an outsider. Some rules were inviolate.

'Is he going to be much longer?' Paisley said across the room to Detective Superintendent Burroughs, and looked at his watch yet again. 'I have a briefing with the UDR this morning. There are a lot of important people over.'

'He won't keep you much longer. I know he particularly wanted to interview you himself.'

'There's nothing else I'd be after telling him.'

Bentham emerged from his office in time to hear this. 'We're both wasting our time then, Mr Paisley.'

'I'd say we were, sir. It's all in my statements.'

'What you didn't get to, because it hadn't happened, is why you went to the Maze and talked to Kevin Lampard.'

Paisley stared back with unfocussed eyes at the short, wide detective in the pale grey woollen suit. Externally he stayed in control, but he felt as if he had been punched in the stomach. He had come here feeling confident, secure, even superior in the knowledge of the whisper Chief Superintendent Johnston had given him this morning. Bentham was a-whoring with one of the witnesses. They all knew what that meant: questionable judgement – if only for her being a Catholic.

238

It was all he could do to stop himself blurting that out now. Instead, he said, 'You're mistaken, sir.'

'Either I am, or the gate officer is, or the prisoner who overheard your conversation with Lampard.'

Lampard himself had denied any such visit had taken place when Detective Superintendent Burroughs interviewed him. The principal officer in the gatehouse at the Maze might have a change of heart about who called to see that prisoner, but fortunately the day book where the visit was recorded had sequentially numbered pages and one being removed would look odd.

Detail by detail, they put together what looked like a case against officers on the Special Support Unit, both for the shootings – which seemed increasingly like cold-blooded acts of murder – and the subsequent cover-up by senior officers and possibly members of MI5. But Bentham knew that so far none of it amounted to anything that the DPP here would act upon. They still needed something to help them ground the imaginative leaps they were making.

Possibly Bill Senior was luckier than a lot of policemen, or was more painstaking, or approached people in such a way that got the best out of them. Whatever it was, he came up with results. On checking the background of Edward O'Dwyer, he discovered that he had a cousin by the name of Martin St James, who was an assistant chief constable in the RUC; further, out at Shandon Park Golf Club, where they were both members, he learned that they had played and had lunch together two days after Mrs McFadden alleged she went to see the solicitor with her son.

'We can take it she did see O'Dwyer with Stephen, Bill, for deffo,' Bentham said, leaning back at the metal desk in his office. Whenever doubt about anything Maureen McFadden said or did was raised, he found himself dismissing it. He was aware he was doing it, and cautioned himself to stop. 'This could be why he might be denying that visit.'

'It's a good result, Bill,' Detective Superintendent Burroughs conceded. But then, as if echoing what was in everyone's mind, 'It's a bit of a fucking jump – from their game of golf to St James doing the biz.'

'We have to make that sort of jump, Frank, if we're going to crack this.'

The chasm yawned dangerously before Detective Superintendent Burroughs. He didn't like to think of the one opening before these RUC officers. He looked to DI Bill Senior, as if with some notion that he of all people might share his doubts. He averted his eyes. DI Hodgkinson shrugged non-committally. 'I mean, fuck me, Jack,' Frank Burroughs added. 'You know what we're saying?'

'St James could have mentioned it to the Branch,' Bentham argued, wondering why Frank Burroughs was being so cautious. Then it occurred to him that maybe it was him being incautious. This wasn't after all an investigation of minor corruption by the RUC, but he refused to acknowledge that Maureen McFadden might be influencing him. There was no denying the boy had been shot dead, and that he had probably witnessed Desmond O'Donnell's killing; equally probable was his visit to O'Dwyer two days before the solicitor's game of golf with ACC St James.

'I'd better interview St James,' Bentham said. 'What would be handy is the person who told Stephen the guns were in that barn.' He looked at Senior hopefully.

'That would be very handy, guv,' Senior said. 'I called in to see Kit earlier. He's getting quite talkative' – like a proud father telling of a son's achievements. 'Something we ought to look at, we get time, guv, is that boy's home he was in, King's House. He said that teachers used to arrange for men to come out and bugger the kids.'

Bentham looked startled. Everyone's attention was on Senior; a phone rang unanswered.

'He said that?' Bentham asked.

'It didn't come out like that. But that's what it amounts to.'

'Sounds pretty nasty. D'you think he's making it up?'

'It could be to keep my attention. But I don't think so. It might be worth a look.'

'It's really something for the RUC, not us,' Bentham said. He saw Senior's disappointment. The DI had a good sense of a ramp, he knew, and acknowledged it. 'Give it a look if you get time. But for fuck's sake don't let's upset this lot any more than we are.'

DI Hodgkinson cupped his hand over the mouthpiece of the phone he had finally answered and said, 'Guv, it's that caller again. He still won't give his name.'

The anonymous caller had rung when Bentham was out, but refused to talk to anyone else. Bentham reached for the phone. Everyone in the room waited, curiosity aroused.

'Bentham. Who am I talking to?'

'I'll not say on the phone,' the heavily diguised voice said. 'But I want to talk to you about the RUC's shoot-to-kill policy, if you'll meet me.'

'Of course I will – if you can persuade me this is not a get-up.'

There was a silence down the phone, then the caller said, 'Keep looking for Birchfield and Stone. They're not RUC men.'

'You'll do,' Bentham said calmly. 'Who do they belong to?'

'When we meet. You'll be coming alone?'

'Alone?' Bentham wondered immediately when he was given details of where to meet if his phone was tapped, and if it was, how he might handle this. One thing was for sure, if the RUC showed up he'd know it was. Then he wondered about the RUC appearing there to spring a trap. The RUC wouldn't dare set him up, he told himself, and they'd be the only ones who'd want to. But he wasn't entirely convinced.

21

D RESSED IN TRACKSUIT and running shoes, Jack Bentham emerged from his hotel for an evening run at a gait which suggested he had been jogging for years, only his calf and thigh muscles still told him otherwise. He jogged no farther than his car, which would take him to meet his mysterious caller. Detective Superintendent Burroughs went with him, not dressed for running and uneasy about the whole enterprise.

'This is fucking mad, guv,' he said, as if it were some new and persuasive statement he was making. 'Going on your own like this. It's a million to one it's a set-up.' He was thinking how as the next most senior officer on the team he'd cope with this investigation. It would grind to a halt and then be disbanded. The whole thing was getting perilously close to being stopped now, as difficult as that might be politically. 'You're not even shootered up, for fuck's sake,' Burroughs argued. 'I mean, all it needs is for someone to have tipped off the IRA. Do you think they give a fuck that you're Met?'

Bentham didn't want to think about that. 'Have you noticed how fast I am in these now?' he said, indicating his expensive, well-cushioned running shoes.

There was no help Detective Superintendent Burroughs could give when his boss climbed out of the car on the Ravenhill Road entrance of Ormeau Park and set off up the slight incline past the running track. A sense of anxiety slid over him as Bentham disappeared into the dusk. He thought about what would be said to him back in London if anything did happen here. Ironically, he might be held culpable for not asking the Security Service or the RUC to provide cover. No one would appreciate just what was going on here or why that wasn't possible. They were policemen after all, and policemen didn't behave in that way towards policemen!

Sergeant Terry Keeper smiled as he watched the Assistant Commissioner jog over the crest of the hill past the disused tennis courts. He came through the ornamental rose garden, where roses pushed out new growth in defiance of the weather. He went around the octagonal shelter and turned back, waiting for contact. A man walking his dog approached from the opposite direction. Keeper was hidden like some flasher in the shrubbery close to the path. He had a pair of infra-red nightsight binoculars.

'Looks like the man with the doggie,' Chief Inspector Paisley said, at his side. 'Do you recognise him?' He wondered if this location known as a homosexual pick-up was someone's idea of a joke. He hated homosexuals.

'No, I can't say so. I'd not say he was a policeman.'

That was the expectation from the phone conversation.

Paisley looked at him sharply – there were no homosexuals in the RUC!

Bentham passed the man with the dog again. The caller hadn't said anything about a dog, only that he would recognise him. The man was glancing behind him, pretending to be interested in what his dog was doing as Bentham ran back to him.

'I'm Bentham – Assistant Commissioner . . .' – noticing the man had make-up on.

'I'm just walking my dog!' came the hysterical response. 'Is there a law against it? Why do you always pick on innocent people?' With that he was off, dragging his dog. Another jogger went past, taking an interest but not stopping.

Bentham had done quite enough running for one night and decided that his contact wasn't going to show. He hoped more than he believed that this outing was in some way a test.

There was more trouble with the present tack of the investigation when ACC St James refused to be interviewed unless the questions were first submitted to the Deputy Chief Constable. Bentham made a point of being at RUC police headquarters on Knock Road the following morning, waiting for St James to arrive. He caught him as he came up the open stairs to his office on the first floor, but St James remained adamant about not answering questions unless first submitted through the proper channels.

Following him uninvited into his office, Bentham said, 'You may not be a detective, Mr St James, but you're still a policeman. You must know we can't reasonably progress that way. What the fuck is it you people want me to put in my report – that you don't want this inquiry to progress to a satisfactory conclusion?'

'That's not the situation at all,' St James retorted angrily.

'You're Edward O'Dwyer's cousin.'

'He's my cousin, right enough,' he said, suddenly calm. 'You know Edward?'

'You know I do. I'd say you also know I know he told you Maureen McFadden came to see him about the O'Donnell killing at the Divis flats. What I don't know yet is who you told about that and how that relates to Stephen McFadden's death.'

'That is totally offensive, Assistant Commissioner,' St James said, his anger flaring again. 'I'll not be talked to like this.'

'How the fuck should I talk to you – like you're a helpful witness? Are you saying you didn't have a conversation with O'Dwyer about what McFadden saw?'

'Indeed I am. I am indeed.'

'If you go into the witness box with that, the evidence will show you're a liar and a perjurer.' Bentham smiled despite himself. He wasn't enjoying this man's discomfort, even though it was helping him relieve some of his frustration.

'You'll make a bloody fool of yourself, and the RUC into the bargain. Be very careful, Mr Bentham, because you're making a lot of enemies here. If you're wanting to interview me further, submit your questions to Donald Joyce and make an appointment. Now you'll excuse me.'

'I'm getting pissed off with being shouted at by a bunch of bullying fucking bigots. The next time I interview you, it will be under caution.'

ACC St James blanched at the prospect of that – whatever the final outcome – and had difficulty remaining silent before the short policeman opposite him turned and marched out.

No word was forthcoming on either of the two missing RUC men, Birchfield and Stone, and Muriel Kinahon of the PCC, who was barely emerging from her librium stupor following the death of Judge Hereford and his wife, wasn't able to help. Bentham knew she would only get her reassurances from the Deputy Chief Constable anyway. They came no closer to identifying either the MI5 man who went out to the hospital with Chief Superintendent Johnston to talk to Kit McMahon, or the man who went to the Maze prison with Chief Inspector Paisley to proposition Kevin Lampard. Bentham suspected they were one and the same. Small and neat was the description he had, and thought it might fit the Deputy Security Co-ordinator, Herbert Greenhous, though he doubted that man would become involved at that level.

Whatever anyone thought of his sense of objectivity, Jack Bentham was seeing more and more of Maureen McFadden. Usually he tried to find a reason connected with the investigation for such meetings, and maintained that façade even with his colleagues. It went some way to armouring him against what he found himself feeling for her, and he told himself that as a result he was able to maintain objectivity. He never considered he might be in danger physically from going into the Republican Divis flats. The RUC would almost certainly believe that he was in danger, but hadn't warned him.

'What we badly need,' he told Maureen over lunch in Zero's, 'for our investigation to get anywhere is a solid connection between Stephen seeing that shooting and being told guns were in the barn. I'd say the two are connected. I know it's painful, but are you sure he didn't mention anyone telling him about the guns?'

Slowly Maureen shook her head. Her feelings had changed towards this man, who had been at first a painful reminder of just how futile life was at times. Now she wanted him to change, to stop being a policeman who imagined he could only impress her by solving problems and being strong, instead of behaving like a normal human being who was vulnerable and could be hurt.

'What does it mean, Jack, even if you find some connection?'

'But, Mum,' said Angela, who had come along too to the restaurant. She sensed her mother's mood and felt insecure because of it. 'Don't you want to get them? The people what killed Stephen?'

After a moment Maureen sighed. 'I don't know. It won't bring him back. It won't even change anything, will it? Will the killing and violence stop, Jack?'

'It's never going to stop all the while people can walk.' Bentham responded like a policeman, ignoring the historical perspective that told him retribution wasn't a deterrent. 'If no one's prepared to say, Fuck it, you've gone too far this time. They have, haven't they?' He glanced at Angela, not thinking of her as a fifteen-year-old, but as a mature woman.

With difficulty Maureen met his look, wanting so much for him not to be a policeman, if only for this meal time. She said nothing.

Then suddenly Bentham was human, still a policeman, but open and a little vulnerable. 'I'm in trouble, Maureen,' he said. 'It looks as if my masters are not pleased – I'm not doing what I'm supposed to do. It would be easy to find no charges to answer, take the plane, launch into the work waiting for me back in London. All I need is a little encouragement not to.'

'What do you want from me?' she asked, scared of her feelings.

'For you to say it's important. If it's not important to you, then who is it important to?'

She found herself on the horns of a dilemma, fearing the commitment he wanted right then, but knowing that without it she might never make the commitment she wanted. She said, 'I'm sorry, Jack. I can't tell you what's important, what's the right decision. You have to make it for your own reasons.'

With that, she stood abruptly and opened her bag to find some money, having difficulty taking it out of her purse.

'That's silly,' Bentham said, as she put the money on the table. 'I paid when we got the lunch.'

Without replying, she dived down the narrow stairs beside the kitchen. The mostly student clientele glanced up and went back to their own conversations. Angela half rose, feeling torn between these two people, afraid the man might not come back if she left too.

'Go after her, Angie,' he said. 'It's all right. I understand how she feels.'

'Shouldn't she be glad you're going to catch Stephen's murderers?'

He smiled grimly. 'We'll have a go. Come on, then, I'll give you a lift back to school.'

He stopped abruptly at the head of the stairs to the first-floor restaurant and turned back to see a man on his own in a booth at the end of the small L-shaped room. He was watching him and trying to get out and finish his food at the same time. The man looked suddenly caught out. Bentham had no recollection of having seen him around, but his face was familiar, having seen it every day of his working life in those alert watchful features of the detectives he worked with. His smile said all he needed to say to him without approaching.

'There was a call-back from that informer,' Detective Superintendent Burroughs told him when he arrived back at the office. 'He said the RUC were around at the last meet.'

Not for a moment did Bentham doubt it, but wondered how they would overcome that problem at the next venue, a telephone box on Central Station on East Bridge Street.

The one he had chosen was the first of four pods nearest the ticket barrier on the modern central concourse. Bentham stood outside the travel and information centre and glanced casually about the station, trying to spot any obo detail. A woman approached the phone pod but Bentham smiled at her and said, 'It's out of order. It won't take coins.'

She went off to look for another vacant box as the phone started ringing. Bentham stepped across to it and lifted the receiver. He waited.

'Mr Bentham?' the same diguised voice said. 'Are you alone?'

'I doubt it in view of last time. We didn't set you up. The phone must have been tapped.'

'I expect this one is too. Put the receiver down and go across to the phone on the wall. D'you see the one I mean?'

There could be no mistaking it. Bentham did as instructed, glancing about the black and red concourse for watchful faces. The phone was out of order, but it rang as he got to it. Had he been conducting this operation, he'd have tried to anticipate such a move by tapping every phone in this line. C11 often tapped phone boxes near villains' homes, and had had some good results that way when the target popped out to use a 'safe' phone.

'The car park on Great Victoria Street behind the Europa. It'll take you a few minutes by cab. There's a cab rank down the steps where the buses turn. I'll give you ten in case anyone follows you. I'll be on the top deck. If I'm not it's because you didn't lose your tail.'

Finding a black cab waiting on the rank when he reached the bottom of the steps, Bentham told the driver to go up and around the road and meet him up on the bridge. It might have been an everyday occurrence for the driver, who didn't question it. Bentham then took the escalator back up to station level as two men came hurrying down the fixed stairs, and half-broke their stride when they saw him, but didn't turn back.

Conventional wisdom said the black cabs were Republican and car cabs Loyalist. Bentham didn't care. He was glad to see his cab waiting on the bridge.

'Is it followed, you are?' the driver asked as Bentham looked from the back window. He was sure he had lost his tail.

'In this city how would you know?'

'Right enough. Nowadays there's no one here except a few businessmen.'

Before Bentham got out the driver offered him his card to arrange for his cab to the airport when he was leaving.

Sergeant Keeper watched over the rim of the car windscreen as

Assistant Commissioner Bentham came through the car park, avoiding the rain puddles in the uneven tarred surface, where once a warehouse had stood. He reached for his S&W .38 on the seat beside him and pushed it into the small holster tucked into the top of his belt and pulled his coat over it. He opened the door and slid out, as Bentham reached the wire at the rear of the car park and turned back.

The sound caused Jack Bentham to turn again sharply. Sergeant Keeper was in the car park that backed on to this one from the adjacent street. He wasn't surprised to see him and didn't think he was there as part of some surveillance team. 'My guess was a policeman.'

'Yes, some of us even have consciences, Mr Bentham,' he said through the diamond-wire fence.

'Just as well. Fewer and fewer punters seem to – even in the straight world.'

'It seemed the right thing to do at the time,' Keeper said, justifying himself. 'Eliminate all the terrorists who bomb and shoot their way into the headlines, you eliminate all the problems.' He remembered the briefings they had had. Plausible-sounding people full of reason and integrity and concern for the greater good had gone over the arguments. Only a long time afterwards did he realise that none of them had any identity whereby they could be re-questioned. 'When that lad was shot . . . Something like that makes you stop and think. You think, where do you draw the line? You do so.'

'Was he set up?' Bentham asked directly, thinking how Maureen would react to this.

'If I thought that, Mr Bentham, I'd be shouting from the top of police headquarters.'

'I might take some convincing.'

Sergeant Keeper nodded. 'I'm thinking you don't care much about this province or its police force. I contacted you because I want to see you finish your inquiry, so we can get back to proper policing.' That was his object, and Sergeant Keeper didn't seem to consider any of the obstacles that might be in the way. Least of all Bentham's feelings.

'Summarily executing known terrorists?' he said.

Ignoring what the Assistant Commissioner had left unsaid, Keeper replied, 'I'm thinking they won't continue with that policy,' but didn't offer a reason for that opinion.

'How much are you prepared to tell me?'

Having made his decision, the RUC man saw no reason not to tell all he knew. 'I'm not prepared to go supergrass or make a formal statement. Nor will I talk to anyone but you. If you want to ask me about something, get in touch and I'll tell you, if I know.'

'Let's start with what you know about the RUC's shoot-to-kill policy.'

'I don't know much about it – we were at the sharp end. I don't think the RUC dreamed it up. It was the Security Service. We just made it more respectable.' He started in alarm, and was ready to run as a car swept towards them through the car park Bentham was in and turned at the last moment. 'We'd better not stay here. Can you climb over the wire? I've a car here.'

Bentham climbed the fence with difficulty.

They considered driving around the city as they talked, but Sergeant Keeper was distracted, fearing he might be seen and recognised by the numerous RUC personnel on the streets, and ended up feeling not much more secure in Victoria Park walking around the edge of a poorly attended football match.

'What can you tell me about Birchfield and Stone – why have they disappeared?'

'First, they're not RUC men,' Keeper said, wanting to distance himself from them, recognising from the first that they were dangerous men with guns. 'They're either Security Service or SAS. I'd say probably SAS – they liked the action too much for MI5. The SAS does a lot of training for the RUC – MI5 are part of that. They get you in the classroom over in Hereford and put the fear of God into you about the consequences of not defeating terrorism after you're back from a night or two on the Brecon Beacons, shagged out. It's no wonder lads step forward for this lot like they do. A lot of RUC men are ex-paras. They do a truncated training here with us. The trouble with those sort is either they're basket cases or their first loyalty isn't to the RUC. You go out with them, half the time you don't know what they'll do or who they might be taking their orders from.'

'They're a force within a force?' Bentham said, thinking of the firm within the firm that was the CID, and the firm of Freemasons within the police at large. There too you never quite knew where first loyalties lay.

'They're now a large part of the RUC, and the UDR.'

'Did Birchfield and Stone have different orders from anyone else?'

'God knows. We all went to the same briefing, we did so. They might have had another.'

'Who conducted those briefings?'

'Mr Johnston usually. Sometimes ACC Eglington. He was mostly at the de-briefing after an ambush.'

'How were the targets selected? Where did the information come from?'

'From our intelligence unit, E3. Some of it came from military intelligence. Or from SIS, if it was across the border. They do a lot across the border. It's reckoned they got someone in every Garda station in the South.'

'Is that where the intelligence about the arms in Hollow Farm originated – the SIS?'

Sergeant Keeper took a long time answering. He turned his gaze to the footballers bogged down in the mud on this chill damp afternoon.

Bentham waited, following his gaze.

'Brian Paisley said it was MI5 being where that came from. There's a lot of needle between MI5 and the SIS, they try to score off each other. They put up jobs to show the other outfit in a bad light. But if anything goes wrong the SSU bears the brunt.'

'What has gone wrong?'

'Those two lads of ours standing trial. That should never have been.'

'Did you know that Stephen McFadden had seen O'Donnell killed?'

'Not at the time.'

'Did MI5 know?' Bentham asked, happy for this man to speculate as he wasn't going to be a witness in any subsequent trial.

'I'm not privy to what MI5 does. I only know what I am told.'

'Isn't that a remarkable coincidence? He sees a shooting, then the same unit accidentally shoots him?'

'I'm no' after thinking it was anything different, sir,' Sergeant Keeper said sombrely, the veneer of self-delusion he had created giving him little protection.

'I'm not sure I believe you.' Bentham sensed his vulnerability and was seeking to exploit it.

'I swear to God it's so, sir. Didn't I tell you I'd shout it out otherwise?'

There was a sense of desperation about Keeper that impressed him. But an emotional man was no more truthful because of his emotion, Bentham knew from experience. What seemed to be wracking Sergeant Keeper was what he didn't know, rather than what he did.

'Where are Birchfield and Stone now?'

'God knows. They left us soon after they shot those lads,' Keeper said. 'I heard they went to the RUC holding centre at Castlereagh.'

'Not for interrogation?' Bentham said lightly. Castlereagh was what MI5 used as their Northern Irish interrogation centre, and the departure of Birchfield and Stone there for whatever reason – Bentham believed there was no such thing as coincidence – was one more indicator of MI5's involvement. 'They shot those lads,' he said, 'not Hinton and Peters?'

'They shot them first, I'm sure of that.' Keeper looked at someone among the spectators, who turned and glanced at them as they passed, then quickened his pace. 'I've got to go,' he said. 'Try the SAS at Hereford. My guess is they're back home by now.'

He had no idea if they were in fact; that was simply what the MI5 Security liaison officer Laurence Payne had told him to say.

22

'MR BENTHAM, COULD WE meet for a wee chat?' Muriel Kinahon said down the phone, surprising him with the call.

'Of course. Are you recovered now?' Being charming cost him nothing.

'One never fully recovers from these things, Mr Bentham. But one can't stay sedated all one's life.'

At that moment, she reminded him of his mother, who also had enjoyed being the martyr.

He invited her to lunch, and took her to Zero's, which she didn't even know existed. She glanced around apprehensively at the long-haired men and women in protest T-shirts, trying not to stare openly.

'Are you a vegetarian, Mr Bentham?' she asked in a low voice as if it might be something he needed treatment for.

'More or less,' he said, immediately enjoying that moral high ground. He chose this restaurant because a tail was easily spotted in here.

'The food is very good.' She was pleasantly surprised.

'What was it you wanted to say to me?'

She looked around, apprehension entering her look. She hesitated. Bentham waited. The bean stew grew cold. 'It's not really related to the investigation, Mr Bentham. But I didn't know who else to turn to.' She hesitated again, and put her knife and fork down, no longer able to face food. 'It's about the death of Toby Hereford – my husband doesn't know I'm here, but I'm afraid he might be the next target.'

'The RUC have tightened security – that's the reason I've had such difficulty calling in some of their officers.'

'I'm not convinced the terrorists were responsible – they're not that clever or well organised. They'd have had to penetrate the Garda or the RUC or both . . . Toby Hereford told my husband he was going to resign – he went to see the Lord Chancellor. He's been

252

involved in . . . it makes me feel ill to talk about it. He was involved sexually with children at a community home . . .'

'King's House Boys' School'. Bentham said intuitively, startling Muriel Kinahon.

'You know about it?'

He grimaced as if he did. 'Why don't you tell me what you want to tell me.'

'I don't know what more there is to tell. He deeply regretted it. I'm sure he wouldn't have any of those children harmed.'

With difficulty, Bentham refrained from laughing. He wondered what sort of life she led, and whether she viewed wrongdoing by the RUC in the same way. 'Why did he suddenly have an attack of conscience? Do you know?'

'He told my husband he was being blackmailed by a security officer.'

'He didn't say who it was, or what he wanted?'

Muriel Kinahon shook her head. She was clearly shaken to the core by what she had just revealed. It was as if it had knocked the foundations completely from under her. What puzzled Bentham was, in view of their relationship, why she had told him. He thought perhaps both the shock and the librium she had taken had made her vulnerable.

'Who do you feel was responsible for Judge Hereford's death?'

'Oh, I'm sure it was the IRA who planted the bomb, just as they claimed. I can't bear to think how they might have got the information about his movements or who helped them place it there unchecked.'

It was Bentham's turn to be shocked. This was a member of the NI Establishment. 'Are you seriously saying it was someone in the security force who helped them?'

She hesitated again. 'I know it's extraordinary when put as baldly as that. One wonders if one has suddenly gone mad. I've been through this again and again – I even thought the best thing to do was simply go on taking the librium and keep it all at bay.'

'Why would the Security Service want him dead if he was resigning anyway?'

Without looking at him, she said in a low voice, 'I haven't got the answers to give you. I only wish I had . . . There have been rumours about King's House School for a while – somehow it was easier to ignore them.'

Bentham understood that at once. It was almost always easier to ignore what you feared rather than confront it. He felt that as a society we made an art form of that; the police as a microcosm of society did when it came to corruption, violence, racism. 'What kind of rumours were they?'

'Oh, that certain important people had been provided with sexual favours.'

'Had there been complaints of any kind?'

'From an ex-pupil, I believe. They were supposedly investigated by the RUC, who did nothing because of Orange Lodge connections.'

'You don't know who these important people were?'

She shook her head. 'I'm sure they're just rumours. I don't know why I mentioned it. I didn't know who else to tell. I know it's something the RUC should come to grips with, but they are so closely involved with the Security Service.'

'Is your husband in danger because of what Judge Hereford told him? Is that what you think?'

'Ernest hasn't said as much, but I believe he is. All judges and such in Ulster are targets, of course. My husband copes with that very well. He believes that what he does is right. But ever since Toby's death he's been terribly nervy and irritable. Close friends have been killed before; it tends to strengthen his resolve to go on.'

'Couldn't be he's facing the same dilemma you are – what to do about what he has been told?'

'Toby's dead. Whatever we do won't bring him back to life. Certainly not talking about his sordid little habit.'

'The thing is, Mrs Kinahon, what do you want me to do about it? I would have to talk to your husband.'

'He wouldn't talk about it – I would prefer you didn't.'

'Then all we're doing is talking?'

'I suppose I hoped it might somehow form part of your inquiry. Apart from that, I just don't know what you can do.'

At that precise moment Bentham didn't know either, but one or two notions were forming. One thing was certain, he'd tapped something too important to the whole concept of security in Northern Ireland to simply ignore what she had told him.

Having Bill Senior start over with what Kit McMahon had told him was the first thing Bentham did. A meeting with the Northern Irish DPP was his next move.

His office, adjacent to the Royal Courts of Justice, was as threadbare as the man himself and his denial of ever hearing any rumour about King's House School. Bentham was as certain of him lying as he was of anything in his life. His belief wasn't that Shelldrake was necessarily involved, but that he had at least heard rumours. It wasn't this that had ostensibly brought him to this meeting, but the inquiry that they were marking time on. Now he was sure that he was tapping into a seam that would change the whole completion of the investigation, and give him the initiative for the first time.

Although Jack Bentham didn't for a moment imagine Sir Cyril Shelldrake was sufficiently powerful politically to help facilitate his inquiries, he suspected he was close enough to the Chief Constable to counsel him in the wisdom of some sort of trade-off. Not that Jack Bentham had any set intention of honouring such a deal necessarily, even if he got that lucky.

The DPP was edgy, and it wasn't simply that he was impatient to sneak off to the races – a pursuit he had successfully managed to keep secret from his wife.

'We're finally getting to the question: do I go on with the investigation in its present form, or do I broaden its scope?' Bentham said as they left the Royal Courts of Justice on Chichester Street. 'Either way, the RUC must know they're on a hiding to nothing. No one wins, whatever the outcome, but either you investigate the complaints or your reputation suffers, as you nod towards the Left's police state.'

'Of course one must conduct such inquiries,' Sir Cyril said boldly. 'What's more, one has to be seen to do it vigorously. Norman Hateley understands that. I'm sure he'll want anything that's germane to your inquiry investigated.'

'I want to go on believing that. But I'm not convinced.'

'He's only human, Mr Bentham. You have to allow for a certain amount of resentment.'

'I do. I resent those fucking students in London complaining about the Met,' he said, offering a little of himself. 'But I'm not wilfully obstructing the Merseyside police.'

Sir Cyril thought about that, wondering how far he could go in defending the RUC and still maintain his credibility. 'I can't believe Sir Norman Hateley's being wilfully obstructive. It's probably some sort of damage-limitation.'

'Based on the information from our "Deepthroat" out at Knock, I believe there will be charges to answer. But it's pointless making those sort of recommendations and doing the police here more damage if no one's willing to act on them.'

'I'm certainly willing, Mr Bentham,' the DPP said in a kneejerk response, 'assuming the evidence is sound. I can't make a commitment until I have had an opportunity to consider the evidence.'

The procedure Jack Bentham was obliged to follow, having completed his report, was to deliver it first to the Chief Constable with a copy as a courtesy to the Police Complaints Commission. It was for the Chief Constable to involve the government's law officer in Northern Ireland, taking his opinion as to whether a *prima facie* case existed. Only if he refused would the Police Complaints Commission insist. However, Bentham knew he could fall at either of those fences and wanted to arm himself with Sir Cyril's advice on evidence, ahead of the field. Then at least he would know how difficult the going was.

'Is this supergrass you've found at police headquarters willing to go into the witness box? They've been thoroughly discredited over here with their retractions, I'm afraid.'

'Our man is not offering to go to court. His information seems accurate,' Bentham said. 'It's corroborating what we're getting elsewhere.'

Panic suddenly crossed Sir Cyril's face as he stopped at the bottom of the steps to the court with its mock colonnades and looked around at his detective who was behind.

He moved away towards his car, which was waiting along with an escort car full of armed RUC detectives. Lowering his voice, he said, 'This is off the record – make of it what you will. If need be I will deny it – this is my home, Mr Bentham, I have to go on living and working here, conducting the intercourse of life with these people, most of whom are decent and whom I respect.' He paused and glanced again at his own RUC detective, who provided round-the-clock protection, wondering what he would make of this, whether he would see it as a betrayal. He would hate to be thought badly of by this man. 'From the very first I've suspected a shoot-to-kill policy here, one that was orchestrated by the Joint Intelligence Committee in the Cabinet Office via the bods in Curzon Street House. The charges that arose out of it were ill-prepared and doomed to failure. I must take some part of the blame. There was a lot of pressure to deflect the sort of inquiry that you're now conducting. Despite one's independence of the executive, it's not always possible to avoid coercion in this climate. The reason I'm saying this, Mr Bentham, is so that you have a crystal-clear understanding that subsequent charges against these men will have to be backed by rock-solid evidence. They will so.'

Bentham was uncertain whether to thank him for his advice. But didn't finally, probably because he suspected he'd not be able to rely on him to fight his corner. He was just too much a part of this establishment for that. 'I'd need to interview some RUC officers under caution', he said. 'Without submitting the questions to the Deputy Chief Constable. I'd like to interview MI5 officers in the same way. I don't think the Police Complaints Commission is going to help me in that.'

'Let me catch a glimpse of your evidence, Mr Bentham,' the DPP said, 'then I'll tell you what help I might give you.'

'Fine. First I need to interview the elusive Birchfield and Stone, and see their service records. They're not RUC men.'

Sir Cyril Shelldrake talked to the Chief Constable about Birchfield and Stone, but didn't get far. Sir Norman Hateley still denied that they were other than *bona fide* members of the RUC, but didn't offer them up.

'How dangerous do you think this informer of Bentham's is, Cyril?' Sir Norman asked from the deep armchair in his sitting-room in his flat at police HQ. The armed policemen that surrounded the area served more to remind him of the prison he was in than to reassure him about his security.

'I haven't seen his evidence. But if it's someone here at Knock, you must expect him to have a high damage potential.'

'What a loathsome creature it must be,' Sir Norman said with vehemence but no sense of irony. He wasn't even giving so much as a nod in the direction of all the supergrasses the RUC had bludgeoned physically and emotionally out at Castlereagh, or the convictions that had been secured in the Diplock Courts on their dubious evidence; those the Security Service had used; those the SIS was still turning within the IRA, the INLA, the UDA.

'If I'm to remain credible to Mr Bentham,' Sir Cyril said, 'possibly I should persuade you to allow him to interview Birchfield and Stone.'

'Of course,' Sir Norman agreed. He knew the DPP wouldn't have the stomach to insist this happened. 'He won't get far with either of them, I'm sure. He no longer seems to trust Muriel Kinahon, so *you* should try and dissuade him from broadening the scope of his investigation to take in rumours about King's House School. There's nothing there, of course. There's hurt for everyone and benefit to none if he does.' He was uncertain if Shelldrake was playing a sort of double game, or simply keeping on the right side of Bentham and trying to create some distance between himself and any messy scandal that might erupt. 'If you can't, Cyril, we will have to find some other means.'

Sir Norman was reluctant to bring on the heavy artillery at this stage by asking the Association of Chief Police Officers for help in dealing with Mr Bentham. It would be an admission of failure, and he wasn't about to admit that. But he wasn't such a fool as not to stop Bentham in any way he could – that was publicly acceptable – should the need arise.

Simple precautions such as locking all drawers and desks and filing cabinets, and windows, and doors to offices, and not leaving anything revealing lying around, were sufficient to deter ordinary burglars. Indeed, the fact that the target offices were in a police barracks which were enshrouded in armed security would have been enough to put off any intruder. However, those that went into the offices assigned to Bentham's investigation were no ordinary burglars. They worked with well-fitting keys on a completely deserted corridor in the full glare of all the security lights, and unhurriedly. They stole nothing, but purposely damaged papers and left files out and drawers unlocked as if they wanted to leave a calling card. They also ran all the discs through the computer and erased them.

In the absence of AC Bentham, who had returned to London for a few days, Detective Superintendent Frank Burroughs complained to the Deputy Chief Constable. He listened, amused, then more or less told the London detective he was mistaken, that they didn't have break-ins on police property, saying this was obviously an 'own goal' while smiling the whole time like a Cheshire Cat.

The feeling of frustration was such in Frank Burroughs that he misdialled Jack Bentham's number twice before he got it right. He could still see the Deputy Chief Constable's smile and it brought back all his irritation.

'The cunts,' he said down the phone, not caring who might be listening in or who it might get back to. 'These fucking Mick cunts, I'd nick the lot of them. They break into our offices, fuck everything up and then try to tell us we did it – they got some fucking front.'

'Was there anything left behind that could drop them in it?' Jack

Bentham was in a meeting in his new office on the fifteenth floor at Scotland Yard, an office more in keeping with his rank, though he still held his other job running Criminal Intelligence.

'The cunts are too slippery for that. They obviously wanted us to know they'd been.'

'Did they wipe every tape, Frank?' Bentham said over the phone, glancing back at the three men and his secretary at his long conference table.

'They didn't find the dupes – the cunts.'

'Good. Get them copied. Put them back in the same place. I can't see any value in my complaining, but don't take too much of their shit.' He was thinking about the harassment allegedly going on around the students' complaints inquiry, and wondered fleetingly if they shouldn't give more serious consideration to the new complaints about harassment from unknown policemen. 'Did Birchfield and Stone materialise?'

'Did they fuck. Do you want me to go back to the Deputy Chief Constable about that?'

'Save your breath. We'll do them up with what we're getting on the King's House Boys' School. I'll see you in a day or so.'

Bentham put the phone down and returned to the briefing table, where Chief Superintendent Gordon Campbell from Merseyside sat with his deputy on one side of the table and with Detective Superintendent Alan Horsfell and DS Denis Marsh on the other. Bentham didn't really want to sit at the head of table but chose that rather than to appear to be lining up on one side against the other.

The investigation of alleged wrong-doing by policemen rarely, if ever, went smoothly, and this was no exception. Animosity flared into hostility on occasions and as he listened to reports of it Bentham had found himself more and more in sympathy with Campbell, the outsider, rather than his own men. He would sooner not be supervising it.

The trials at the magistrates' court of all the students arrested around the demonstration against the Home Secretary were over, and the results far from encouraging. There was a 52 per cent discharge rate, which in no way helped the police case in the complaints investigation.

'These policemen don't deserve any sort of result after the sloppy way they brought their evidence together,' Bentham concluded. He wasn't a policeman who mourned the passing of that age where a suspect was convicted simply because a policeman got into the witness box and said he did it.

'Policemen had copied each others' notes and read them in court,' Chief Superintendent Campbell said. 'The trouble with that this time was that the original note-takers had made some serious errors. The magistrates had the similarities pointed out to them time and again by the defendants' solicitors.'

'Have any of the students found guilty withdrawn their complaints?'

'Only one,' Campbell said. 'We've been concentrating on those officers who were criticised in court, hoping they might feel under pressure and want to make a deal. I'm surprised how tight they're staying.'

'I'm not,' Bentham responded, thinking of the RUC. 'Have you tried tapping their phones? You won't need warrants for phones in police stations. I don't even think you'll need them for their homes.' On this point, he saw no parallel between this investigation and what was happening in Northern Ireland.

'Up to what rank should I go, Assistant Commissioner?' Chief Superintendent Campbell asked for clarification, not wanting to reach too high on his own initiative.

'Everyone who was involved with policing the demo. I'll inform the deputy chair of the PCA.' He didn't want to believe there would be anything worthwhile to be had from anyone beyond the divisional commander; it was possible that the Area DAC was defending the actions of his men and manoeuvring to make them secure from disciplinary action. Anything was possible, he now realised from his own recent experiences, but he didn't wish to pursue it. He sensed he was pissing off enough people in high office already. 'What developments are there on the harassment Roberta Ford and Stanley Scone are supposed to be having?' he said, turning to Detective Superintendent Alan Horsfell.

'Not a lot. The officers who made the stops have been seen, guv,' Horsfell said. 'Scone was stopped three times, the woman twice – they're stops we can trace. They were genuine.'

'So you're saying there's no police harassment?'

'It doesn't look like it, sir,' Horsfell said crisply, responding to Bentham's irritated tone. 'The stops were recorded, the reasons noted down. It was different officers each time.'

'But the students are alleging it's happened more than five times to each of them.'

'What they can't say is who it was, if it was Old Bill at all. Roberta Ford say they were CID, but they didn't produce their warrant cards.'

'She ought to know CID when she sees them.'

'The phone taps might pick up the anonymous phone calls they claim to have received – if we've got the right nick.'

'What about the alleged rape? Are we near to identifying the other officers in that cell?'

'We keep covering the same ground there, boss,' Chief Superintendent Campbell said.

'Well, let's see if some pressure will produce them,' Bentham said. 'Start treating every officer on that demo like a suspect.'

'We're just gonna accept that she was raped?' Detective Superintendent Horsfell said, surprised and angered by that. He kept a hold of his feelings.

'Why not?' Bentham said, seeing greater damage from this the longer it went on. 'I'll talk to the Deputy Commissioner about everyone facing disciplinary charges for withholding information.' He glanced around the table at the surprised faces. It had never been done before and it would look like the thin end of the wedge for a lot of policemen, all those supposedly good and straight policemen who did nothing about their colleagues' wrong-doing but went along with it by their silence. He was no longer in the mood for endless, painstaking re-examination of details that took them further from rather than nearer to a solution. 'Someone in the job's withholding information.'

Harry Streeter was surprised at the course Bentham wanted to take on the alleged rape complaint. They all wanted a result, of course, if there was one to be had, but he wasn't sure the prize was worth the candle. He even began to wonder if he had been right about the calibre of this man that he had pushed so hard for promotion. There was no doubt but that he was a clever policeman, as results had shown. But that alone didn't necessarily make him a good police politician. What he was proposing would offend as many senior officers as it would rank and file. They had not only come to expect more support than that, but demanded it. This move, combined with the feedback he was having from Ulster, was causing the Deputy Commissioner to have serious second thoughts about Jack Bentham.

'I hate to think what might get thrown up with taps on all the phones in E Division, Jack,' Harry Streeter said over lunch in his favourite restaurant near the Yard.

'We'll need to be selective in what we pull out,' Bentham said, suspecting what was on the Deputy Commissioner's mind.

'Thank fuck for that. For a moment I thought you were trying to usurp CIB-2.' They frequently tapped station telephones.

'With everyone under threat of disciplinary action for withholding information, we'll get a result.' He put his hand up and caught the waiter's eye for their bill.

'We might get a lot of resignations, too. Is this the time for such a move? They won't let you pay, Jack,' Harry Streeter told him. 'Don't embarrass them by trying.' He rose and the waiter appeared at once to ease the table away to let the large frame of the Deputy Commissioner escape.

'Did you enjoy your lunch, Mr Streeter?'

'Very nice. Thank you.'

Bentham would have been happier paying, but said nothing about the perk they had taken, that most policemen learned to take as of right when they first went out in uniform; he didn't even say thanks to the policeman who had arranged it.

'The problem here, Harry,' he said as they walked back to the Yard, 'is a bit like the one I've got in Northern Ireland. It's the same on any investigation of the police that suggests endemic corruption.'

'Fuck me, Jack, you're not suggesting we don't conduct such investigations,' the Deputy Commissioner said ironically.

Bentham looked at him. 'There's a choice between the wholly intolerable as far as we're concerned, or the plain unacceptable as far as the public's concerned.'

'We usually have to live with it, either way.'

'Maybe it's time for a change, Harry. God knows, they've got problems in Northern Ireland, but the RUC's not helping. They need something to shake their arrogant belief that whatever they do is for the greater good. We know more or less what levels of corruption the Met can tolerate, what you let go, what you draw the line at. But there – it's out of control. They're a law unto themselves. They're getting away with murder. The question I ask myself is this: Why is it tolerated?'

'The original problems both there and here are not dissimilar, Jack: anarchy from students, a worse kind from the IRA. They'd both have society on its knees if we let them. The RUC has been raised on that sort of policing. Just as we're now getting a generation of policemen who have never experienced consensus policing. Policeman are bound to hit back at times. It's only human.'

'I know that,' Bentham said. 'But it wasn't a few pissed-off RUC renegades killing those IRA suspects.'

'The IRA kills indiscriminately. A lot of their victims have been policemen. Here as well as in Ulster. You might remember that, Jack.'

'I know. But Stephen McFadden wasn't remotely connected with any terrorist organisation.' Bentham stopped at the kerb in Victoria Street. He glanced sideways at Harry Streeter, who had a comfortable look on his face. 'It looks more and more like he was set up.'

Harry Streeter nodded thoughtfully, then said as they crossed the road, 'There are stories about you doing the lad's mother, Jack.'

'What?' Bentham was surprised – mostly at this being raised here in London. 'Who the fuck's saying that?'

'Not me, Jack,' the Deputy Commissioner said with a quick defensive parry. 'What you do out of the office, so to speak, is up to you – within reason. I don't need to tell you where to draw the line. I'm just warning you, Jack, in case your judgement is called into question.'

'Is it?' Bentham wanted to know.

'The Chief Constable would be happy to be rid of you right now. He's been talking to the Association about that. He wants you replaced by someone more . . .' He stopped, trying to choose the right adjective, but couldn't find anything kinder than 'Amenable.'

They walked along the Broadway to the entrance of Scotland Yard in silence, Bentham wondering how he might retrieve the situation. Not for a moment did he consider his judgement was at fault, though he could see that some might use that to cut the ground from under him. He had done everything he should do and nothing he couldn't do. On reflection he knew that was surprising to policemen like Harry Streeter and his former boss, DAC Doc Holliday; like the RUC chief, their expectation was that he would support the status quo. Why he wasn't doing so, he didn't know, but told himself it wasn't because of Maureen McFadden.

'I doubt if the Association would interfere, Jack. But it's not beyond them to have a word with the PCC over there – that wouldn't do your prospects much good.'

Bentham laughed, despite the seriousness of the situation. He wondered what ACPO could say to the Police Complaints

Commission in Northern Ireland, or rather Muriel Kinahon, now that she had approached him like she had. In its independent supervisory role, the PCC could quite easily decide that he wasn't being effective and have him removed from the inquiry. Yet Muriel Kinahon was selling him as some sort of white hope.

'I'm sorry, Harry. I was just thinking how messy things are getting out there. But thanks for the warning.'

He wasn't sure if it was a warning of imminent danger, or one with sufficient time for him to change course if he chose. His problem right then was that he didn't know if he wanted to.

The thought of policemen's phones being tapped made Detective Superintendent Alan Horsfell more cautious than usual about the phone he used, especially for what he had in mind. He had no reason to expect that the phones on the fourth floor of the Yard were being listened in to but, like the phones in all police stations, they were subject to random checks. The public phones across the street in Broadway would be safe enough and, using the number he had taken from the Met's internal directory, he dialled the direct line to a detective superintendent he knew whose phone would be tapped.

They had once done business together, but Horsfell wasn't about to renew the acquaintance when the man answered his phone. 'This is to warn you that taps are being put on the phones of everyone involved in policing that demo at the Students' Union,' he said, disguising his voice.

An edge came into the voice down the phone. 'Who is this? I'll have to report this conversation to CIB-2.'

Detective Superintendent Horsfell smiled, knowing the detective had got the message. He had been given short warnings about dangerous situations in the past and was glad to do it for fellow policemen. He wasn't thinking that his action might prove an impediment to finding the alleged police rapists, but that business casually conducted on the phone coming on top would do no good for anyone.

He hung up, his duty done. Whatever the detective superintendent did with the information, there was no doubt but that word would spread, policemen would be more cautious.

Feeling beleaguered, even besieged, every time he went out in his car now, Stanley Scone hunched tensely over the wheel of his Renault 4, searching around as he drove, studiously keeping to the speed limit, giving all the correct signals. He was using his car more and more reluctantly, as in it he was so easily identifiable and vulnerable; he was late for a tutorial, where he was going to discuss his thesis at length. He was terrified of being stopped by the police, even though he wasn't doing anything to be stopped for. The uniformed police weren't so bad: officious, intimidating, but at least identifiable. Other people in the street could see them, as if somehow that made him safe. The detectives who would suddenly appear out of nowhere, wanting to know who he was, what his movements were – they were scary.

Concentrating hard on doing what was right and strictly legal, Stanley Scone didn't notice the white police car that slipped in behind him. His reflex was to brake, as if believing they were flashing him to stop. But they weren't. They followed him for a couple of minutes first. Of all the times to get stopped this was the worst, and he hesitated about responding. He thought instead about making a dash to the college, where at least he'd have sympathetic witnesses, perhaps even the protection of his tutor. That was daft, he told himself. He would just be asked a couple of pointless questions. It would mean being a little later still. All he had to do was stay cool.

'Are you Stanley Scone of 18A Lyham Road, Brixton?' the policeman asked as he came to the car. They knew he was.

'Was I speeding? I'm sorry, I didn't think I was,' Stanley apologised, jumping out now.

'Got your driver's licence, have we, sir?' The policeman smiled tolerantly.

Fumbling in his pocket for his wallet, Stanley passed over his licence.

The policeman studied it. 'You haven't signed your licence, sir. Did you know that's an offence?'

'No. I must have forgotten,' he said in a panic, imagining himself being taken to the station. 'I'm sorry. I overlooked it.'

'Easily done, sir,' the policeman reassured him. 'We won't take any action this time. I should sign it if I were you, sir.' He handed it back.'

'Thank you. Thank you very much,' Stanley said as the policeman turned to walk away.

When he climbed back into his car, Stanley found himself trembling. He realised then that he hadn't taken the policeman's collar number or the number of the car as the guy from the local police monitoring unit had advised him. He was too scared to look around in case the police took exception and decided to stop him again. Instead, he started the car, gave the correct signal and rejoined the traffic.

When he dared to look in his mirror again and noticed what car was behind him, he almost steered into stationary vehicles parked at the side of the road. It was the maroon Montego. Oh, Christ, he thought, oh dear God, help me! He didn't know what to do and felt sick with panic. The Montego, with two men in it, did nothing, just followed. It was a coincidence, he told himself, it wasn't the police. This was an ordinary sunny afternoon and he was on his way to talk through his thesis with his tutor. Nothing else was going to happen to him.

Panic started to subside. He was going to be all right. His speed crept up, putting noticeable distance between him and the Montego. Another car overtook and crept in between them. Relief flooded through Stanley and his breath came easier; he started to laugh. Then stopped abruptly as the maroon Montego overtook the intermediate car and drew alongside him. The passenger looked at him, then indicated with his finger for him to pull over.

When he failed to do so, the driver of the Montego pulled in front of him, causing Stanley to jam on the brakes. The two men leaped from their car, ran quickly back and opened the driver's door of the Renault.

'Why did you do that? – I nearly ran into you,' Stanley protested.

'We signalled you to stop. Are you Stanley Scone?'

'Yes.' His mouth was dry and he could find no saliva. 'I've just been stopped by other police officers,' he said as if to give himself credibility. He assumed these were detectives but didn't think to ask to see their identity cards. Fear and panic were making him forget everything.

'We'd like you to come with us to the police station,' one of them said.

'I'm going to my tutorial – I'm a bit late.'

'Professor Rollings won't hold it against you – we won't keep you long.'

'How do you know . . .?' Stanley began, startled that they knew who he was going to see.

'There's not much we don't know about you, Stanley.'

'Are you arresting me? I mean, do I have to go?'

'If you'd sooner get dragged out of bed at the crack of sparrow's fart and held for seventy-two hours, you just blank our invitation, *sir*.'

'We won't keep you long. We need to ask you some questions.'

'I don't want to be difficult, but I am getting a bit fed up with being stopped by the police.'

'You'd best tell the duty officer at the station, sir.'

The duty officer didn't materialise. In fact, surprisingly, Stanley didn't see a single uniform officer there apart from one who was getting into a car in the compound as he was taken out of the detectives' car.

'You were at the demo against the Home Secretary back in March,' the detective, Lefty Morgan, said, sitting opposite the student in the small green-painted interview room.

'Yes, I was . . . I've answered questions like this a dozen times.'

'You helped organise it.'

'No. I just went to have a look. I don't have strong political views. I don't.'

'Don't you think students should get bigger grants from the government?'

'Well, yes,' Stanley conceded. 'I mean, who doesn't?'

'I don't – so, I'd say you were against the government's educational policies.'

The second detective came in without a word and stood behind Stanley, making him feel uneasy, afraid to glance round at him.

'Not really – I hadn't thought about it.'

'It's the government that's stopping your grant being increased.'

'Yes, I suppose so,' Stanley again conceded, finding that easier than trying to argue around corners.

'You must find their policies pretty mean – unfair to students?'

'Yes – look, I'm going to miss my tutorial.'

'That's all right,' the detective behind Stanley said. 'Professor Rollings said not to worry, he'll hang on till you get there.'

'Oh. Oh, I see,' Stanley Scone said, feeling reassured. 'He said he'd wait for me?'

'You're not a member of the Socialist Workers Party, Stanley, are you?'

'No.'

'But you know students who are – who were at that demo.'

'I suppose so. I hadn't thought about it.'

'The SWP is helping organise the students' complaints against the police,' Lefty Morgan said.

'I wouldn't think so. I don't know.'

'We do. Why are you helping organise against the police if you're not in the SWP?'

'I'm not. I told you I wasn't.'

'You are trying to bring the police into disrepute.'

'Well, it's wrong what they did at the Union that night, that's all.'

'What, protecting a democratically elected member of Her Majesty's government? Upholding the rule of law?'

For a moment he doubted these men were policemen and panic rushed him again. 'Look, do you think I could see the duty officer?'

'Of course.'

The detective went out, leaving his colleague who was behind Stanley to do the questioning. He came around to the other side of the table, and Stanley noticed how badly pock-marked his face was, as if he had once suffered from a skin disease. The detective took him over the same ground again and again until he grew tired and confused and frightened, and again asked to see the duty officer. The second detective left him to find the first.

Time crept by and Stanley grew anxious about his tutorial, whether the detective had in fact spoken to his tutor. Then he thought about getting up and walking out, and his pulse rate increased alarmingly. But fortunately he realised in time that this was what they wanted so they could pounce on him for trying to escape.

Finally the door opened and the two men returned, smiling.

'The duty officer's coming now,' Lefty Morgan said.

'Are you going to drop your complaint against the police, Stanley?'

Stanley hesitated and looked between these two, realising now what this was all about. He regretted not simply saying yes. But maybe they wouldn't have believed him. 'Is that why you brought me here?'

'Not really. We suspect you deal drugs to other students.'

'That's ridiculous.' He was further confused by this sudden tack. 'I've been here for over an hour – you've never mentioned drugs before.'

'That's how we work. First things first. Take your clothes off.'

That startled him. 'What? I mean, I don't have to without . . . Look, I'd like to phone my solicitor.'

'And warn him about your drugs stash? Don't fuck us around, Stanley.'

268

Without warning, Lefty Morgan grabbed the student around the neck and wrenched him out of the chair and ran him up against the wall. 'We suspect you've got dangerous drugs shoved up your bum. So take your clothes off so we can conduct an intimate body search. The quicker we get it done the quicker you're on your way, if you've nothing to hide.'

Barely able to keep himself from vomiting with fear, Stanley managed to say, 'It's supposed to be done by a doctor.'

'Come on, Stanley,' the apparently more reasonable one said. 'Do as you're told.'

The searing pain in his back passage made it difficult for Stanley to walk as he left the police station. It was a raw nerve-tearing pain that felt worse with every slow step along the road. He felt sick and his head throbbed as he pressed back the tears. He wanted to run to get away faster, but couldn't: he would have preferred to stand still and hold on to something but didn't dare, in case the police came and dragged him back into the police station. He gulped in breath when a police van slowed as it passed, the occupants in uniform watching him. One smiled and said something to his colleague and the van picked up speed.

When he got back to his car, he saw the windscreen had a notice stuck to it, warning him not to attempt to drive the car as it had been wheel-clamped. He wasn't aware that the clamping service and retrieval was operated by a private company for the police, and assumed this would mean more contact with them. He burst into tears. That thought was more than he could take.

23

JULIAN BRIND WAS A RUNNER, in addition to being an under-secretary at the Home Office. Not one of the peculiarly cautious breed the Home Office raised, he was prepared to take a chance, hold opinions, make decisions beyond his immediate authority, raise his head above ground in the confidence that he was right in his particular endeavour. That confidence and self-assertiveness had caused him to rise faster and higher than might otherwise have been expected for a red-brick university entrant; the fast stream was designed by and for Oxbridge graduates. Brind had the ability to do and get right whatever he had the confidence to push himself into. He had a shrewd brain for working out the political ramifications and enough self-assurance and common sense to leave the chest-thumping to politicians, who claimed the attention for anything only half well done through others' efforts.

There was a competitiveness in this man that Jack Bentham hadn't noticed before, but did now as they ran together out of the bottom end of Green Park to dodge through the traffic on the Mall. He almost regretted inviting him out for a run. A couple of times around St James's Park while they talked was all Bentham had had in mind, not a complete circuit of Hyde Park, Kensington Gardens and back to St James's Park. That sort of run was hard-going on his lungs, to say nothing of his legs, and there was little space for conversation. Pacing him made Brind lengthen his stride, determined not to be overtaken.

As they leaped the low railings to St James's Park, both put on a spurt across the grass, each instinctively sensing this was the final stretch. Bentham found the oxygen somehow, gave it all he had, but Brind sprinted on to the bridge ahead of him.

Jack Bentham was breathing hard and his lungs and legs were burning, and he might have thought nothing of second place and accepted instead the benefits such exertion would bring, had he not seen that Brind was breathing easily and smiling, looking like he had done no more than run up a flight of stairs.

'I didn't realise you'd be quite so fit, Jack,' he said spitting into the pond. 'Senior policemen usually get out of condition.'

'Like senior civil servants, Julian.'

'Not with all the running around we have to do. I don't remember you running at university.'

'I had to work,' he replied with a self-deprecating grin. He did, but didn't regret that. 'I took it up in Northern Ireland.'

'Nothing else to do on those damp evenings.'

Bentham laughed, his breathing becoming easier now. 'You've obviously not listened to the gossip.' He waited, but Julian Brind was equally practised at that. 'Word is someone wants me removed from the RUC inquiry.'

'Word is you're not digging in the right places, Jack,' the civil servant said, imitating the language of the policeman. Brind made a point of informing himself about most politically sensitive policing issues, even when they fell outside his bailiwick; those were what policing was increasingly about.

'Who is making the ground rules?' Bentham wanted to know. 'The Northern Ireland Office? The PCA? The Chief Constable?'

'In a sense, you are, Jack. You have to give a respectful nod in the direction of all those offices. Along with the Association of Chief Police Officers, and the Security Service. What they're all mostly concerned with is maintaining the status quo.'

'Wouldn't it be nice to be an old-fashioned copper again, feeling the collars of villains you know are guilty – if only because you put the evidence on them.'

As soon as he had said those words, Bentham realised how far he had moved from that position. Chasing villains may have been exciting in its time, but in truth he knew it was boring compared to the heady stuff he was into now. What worried him, of course, was that he might not be up to what was expected of him, much less what he expected of himself. As willing as he was to learn, there might not be time. At the deep end, everyone assumed everyone else could swim.

'Off the record, Jack,' Brind said, as they set off at a comfortable pace towards Birdcage Walk, 'I believe there might have been a shoot-to-kill policy in Ulster based on Sir Frank Kitson's scenario – probably the Brighton bombing prompted it. There are a lot who would like to go further.'

Bentham didn't mention having been told that before – off the record. This man was better placed to know its source. 'With the approval of the government?' he inquired innocently.

A smile crossed Brind's face, not at the audacity of the question, but at the fact that, despite his answer being non-attributable, the policeman still had to ask. He decided to answer anyway, thinking it would help Bentham with an overview, a political perspective that would allow him to make the right moves in Northern Ireland.

'Let us concede the Security and Intelligence Co-ordinator,' Brind said. 'Sir Lionel Savory and his secretariat would certainly have tasked this. But, having mandated this policy, it's doubtful whether the PM would want to hear day-to-day details. Though, being a good friend, Sir Michael Newfield . . . I expect all his briefings are off the record, Jack.'

'Renegade RUC officers shooting terrorists out of hand begins to look like an easy option,' Bentham said soberly.

'I wouldn't have thought so – least of all for the officers concerned.' That would have resulted in more prosecutions; none were expected as a result of the inquiry.

They walked in thoughtful silence for a moment. Traffic locked along Birdcage Walk as it tried to squeeze out through Great George Street into the greater congestion of Parliament Square was releasing clouds of carbon monoxide, which both runners imagined was undoing the benefits of their run.

'Northern Ireland has become a testing ground for so much of tomorrow's policing. The basis of our Public Order Act comes from the tried and tested NI (Emergency Provisions) Act,' Brind said.

'I knew a lot of our people went over to study counter-insurgency and riot control.' Bentham didn't say that he thought it the unacceptable face of policing. He didn't know why he held back; this was a friend from what now seemed comparatively untroubled university days of the sixties. It was an off-the-record conversation. 'You know the RUC comes over to Herefordshire to train with the SAS?'

'It makes sense. Even your so-called straight villain is becoming more and more politically motivated. Not simply the animal liberationist. Consider the political statement there is in a deprived black going on a mugging binge.'

'I'm not sure, Julian. Most of their victims are other deprived black kids.'

'That's not a statistic that suits the current political climate. Law and order is football, never more so, and no one understands that better than the Commissioner, or the Deputy Commissioner for that matter. You're now a political policeman, Jack, whether you like the label or not. You're a policeman who can go as high as you choose to. But what you can't change through your profession is government policy. If that's your aim, become an MP.'

'What I'm after, Julian, is doing what's right.'

'Most of us settle for what's expedient. If the policy is right, and we assume it is as our masters have formulated it' – making no mention of this formulation being based on policy submissions from the servants – 'then we're better appreciated if we help expedite that policy.'

'Historically the policy's only ever right if you don't get found out, and innocent people don't get hurt.' He didn't add that the government had now been found out, but the thought hung between them in the exhaust-laden air.

'Both you and I know the historical perspective tends to change according to who wins. There's no doubt about who's going to emerge the victor in this, Jack. It can't be any other way.'

They walked up through Queen Anne's Gate to the Home Office building, where they stopped and Julian Brind looked at the senior policeman and smiled to soften the impact of what he was about to say. 'You would come perilously close to making a fool of yourself if it transpired that Mrs McFadden and her son had the remotest connection with terrorism.'

Bentham met those smiling eyes, which were showing only concern, he thought, and looked away, revealing none of the emotion he was feeling then. Long ago he had learned to disconnect his facial muscles from all channels of emotions.

'Let's have dinner before you return to Northern Ireland. Thanks for the run.' Brind smiled and turned into the Home Office and was gone.

One of the benefits of his rank was a bathroom in his suite of offices, one he shared with another Assistant Commissioner, but a luxury still. Especially to be able to shower at the end of the day and change clothes. He worried about what Brind had said as he stood under the shower, wondering whether the civil servant was warning him off or warning him about something that had yet to happen, if somehow the RUC Special Branch were suddenly going to find terrorist skeletons in Maureen McFadden's cupboard. It could be made to happen, and he thought about how he might protect her.

He dialled her number on his private line as he finished dressing and listened to it ring out, glancing at his watch, wondering if she was at her aerobics class, when she answered.

'Maureen, it's Jack Bentham,' he said a little stiffly. 'How are you?'

'I'm fine, Jack Bentham,' she replied, mocking him. 'Why wouldn't I be? I was just out of the door to my aerobics class.'

'Am I keeping you?'

'They won't begin without me. Are you coming over soon? – Angie was asking' – not daring to make that commitment herself.

'I'll be back in a couple of days, after I've . . .' He stopped himself going into any detail about his work, what he had to do in relation to her now. 'It doesn't matter.'

'Is there anything wrong, Jack?' For a moment she wondered if he was coming back at all.

'No, I'm fine. I wanted to say hello. It would be nice to see you.' He avoided saying he was missing her, not feeling sufficiently in control of those sorts of emotions. He wanted to ask her about her past, but knew a phone call with her halfway out of the door wasn't the time. He wanted more than anything to simply accept that there was nothing, but knew Julian Brind would consider that naive of him, if not negligent and unworthy of the office he was holding. 'Give Angie a kiss from me.'

'What about Kathleen?'

'Yes, of course . . .' he laughed.

There was a silence on the phone, neither being able to say what they wanted to say.

'I'd better go, Jack.'

After replacing the phone, he thought about Maureen and his feelings towards her, what they might be and why he couldn't speak to her about them; if he would ever be able to now that Julian Brind had raised such a spectre in his warning. Bentham wanted to dismiss that entire prospect as nonsense, telling himself he was a shrewd enough judge of character to know that she was sound. But the doubt wouldn't recede and he found himself punching out their office number in Belfast to talk to Detective Superintendent Burroughs.

This was his routine daily call, he told himself as Frank Burroughs answered and they talked generally about the investigation: the level of resentment they were still encountering; and his grass, who had called.

Bentham told himself there was no need to worry about Maureen, but then at the end of their conversation as if with no will of his own he found himself saying, 'I want you to look as closely as you can at Maureen McFadden and her family, Frank. Right back to before she was married, where they lived, where she went to school.'

'What are we looking for, anything in particular?'

'I don't know. Any connection with terrorist activity or proscribed organisations, however remote. Even if she just gave one of them the time of day. Her children as well, most especially Stephen.'

'The RUC reckons he had none – apart from that nonsense with his friend's Dad.' Kit McMahon's father had a Special Branch tag on his police record for threatening someone after a drunken brawl with getting his Fenian friends to kneecap him. There were no such friends as far as anyone could tell.

'I want to be two hundred per cent certain, Frank. So there are no nasty surprises sprung on us.' He knew they could adversely affect his investigation, let alone his relationship.

Bentham had expected to return to Ulster before the weekend, having brought himself up to date with all the investigations he was overseeing, and had a meeting with Jonathan Entwistle from the Police Complaints Authority to discuss where they were going. He expressed himself more satisfied than Bentham was.

The new complaint from Stanley Scone that he was taken to a police station and anally assaulted by two unidentified detectives delayed Bentham's departure after an agitated phone call from Jonathan Entwistle. The complaint had been made by Scone's solicitor, and to make the investigation more difficult Scone himself had gone into hiding out of fear. The *Guardian* newspaper ran an in-depth analysis of the complaints following the Home Secretary's visit to the Union, with details of the alleged police harassment of students.

'That looks great,' Bentham said to the meeting of relevant senior officers in his office. 'Whatever the truth, whatever the final outcome, we're made to look like sadists and sexual perverts.'

'It's fucking nonsense, sir – with the greatest respect,' Chief Superintendent Mike Barclay said angrily.

He was the divisional commander and Bentham remembered him as a nasty bigot. 'Every policeman on duty that afternoon has been questioned. No one saw these detectives, no one saw Scone at the nick.'

'That accords with the student's story, Mike,' Chief Superintendent Campbell said. He had been dealing with Stanley Scone's solicitor.

'It's not possible to come in and out of the nick, shove your finger up a suspect's bum and have no one see a bloody thing.'

'Quite,' Bentham said pointedly. 'It's uncannily reminiscent of the Roberta Ford case. Both claim to have been harassed by the police since.'

'There is forensic from this complaint,' Chief Superintendent Campbell said.

'What's that, a fingernail in the rectum?' Chief Superintendent Barclay responded drily.

'He's undergone surgery for an anal rupture.'

'So do lots of homosexuals, Gordon,' said the Area DAC, under whose control this Division was. 'Some of the objects they shove up each other, bottles, the lot.'

'That possibility did occur to us,' Chief Superintendent Campbell replied.

'Let's have an all-out effort to get this sorted, for fuck's sake,' Bentham said, feeling as hurt as any policeman by the *Guardian* piece. 'I want a special squad of detectives put together to work on this. A couple from down here, the same from E Division, and two of your squad, Gordon. All they do is investigate those two alleged assaults. Is Stanley Scone homosexual? – even if he is, it doesn't necessarily rule out the assault he claims was committed. See if we can put some sort of photofit pictures together of the policemen involved. I really want some action on this; too much damage is being done to our credibility by having it drag on.'

'If there's no evidence forthcoming,' Jonathan Entwistle said, when Bentham went to see him in his office adjacent to St James's Park, 'you might look at the possibility of there being some sort of orchestrated campaign against the police by a dangerous, politically motivated group of students.'

That was a possibility Bentham had considered, but was reluctant to pursue. But if the *Guardian* piece signalled that the gloves were off as far as the media were concerned, then he would have to. Bentham knew, and very evidently Jonathan Entwistle did, that if the police lost the propaganda war, then all was lost.

*　　*　　*

When the ACPO meetings were concerned with the developments of computer technology, moving the police nearer to the new age of the master computer syndrome – in which not only all police computers were interactive, but all computers of major institutions such as the Tax Office, data banks, the DHSS, commercial banks – Julian Brind would sometimes attend, this being his speciality at the Home Office. In fact the road that was leading the police towards the master computer syndrome – where even such things as people working in the black economy could be checked up on and caught out, because they would have nowhere to put their 'anachronistic' cash – was constructed by Brind. Senior policemen who had started their careers with notebook, pencil and truncheon and the physical ability to lay a finger on a collar were a bit in awe of him, and the direction he was helping them to go in.

It was prior to such a meeting on the eleventh floor at the Yard that he took the opportunity to speak to the Deputy Commissioner and allay some of his concern about the direction Jack Bentham was allowing himself to be drawn in.

'He was being a little naive in his approach to the Northern Ireland question', Brind said. 'I no longer believe he's dangerous, Harry – and I never thought him unreliable in his independent viewpoint.'

'Could be he went up too quickly from being a copper's copper,' the Deputy Commissioner said, feeling some relief. He liked Jack Bentham, and trusted Brind's shrewd assessment more than his own. 'That fine sense of what's expedient sometimes takes time, Julian.'

'Bentham's a quick learner. We all pay our dues finally in our own way. Despite his somewhat unnerving approach, his final analysis of the situation will, I'm sure, set everyone's mind at rest.'

'Thanks, Julian. Some of the Association members will be pleased to learn that.'

As indeed was Sir Norman Hateley when he had word from Roger Gannett, the president of ACPO. He didn't do a U-turn and lay the entire Royal Ulster Constabulary at the feet of the Met investigating team, but a conscious spirit of co-operation entered the men of the RUC, although they maintained some of the natural reserve of inhabitants of that northerly state and that caution which had been developed over their years as policemen. Their insularity had made them always wary of the outsider and that couldn't be pulled away overnight, even had anyone felt the inclination to do so.

'Whatever it was that was told to Bentham, it seems to have had the desired effect, Norman,' the Deputy Chief Constable said, as he and his boss went up the stairs together to the dining-room at the Knock headquarters. 'They are now concentrating most of their efforts on the McFadden family. Looking for terrorist connections.'

'If they were to find such a connection, wouldn't that shift the whole centre of this inquiry?'

'I've given them an assurance of our full co-operation in this area. Anything we have they are getting.'

'Good,' Sir Norman said with a confident smile. 'Let's hope they're successful.'

'I've a feeling they might be so.'

The chief inspector who ran the computer end of the RUC's communications and computer services didn't know what had brought about the change in attitude towards the Met's investigation, but the chief superintendent in charge of D Department said to give them all the information they had relating to the McFadden killing, even that flagged by the Special Branch. Ordinarily they would clear that with the Branch, as it was information that they hadn't even been able to obtain by tapping directly into their computer; that information was filed under its own entry code separate from ordinary RUC traffic. The chief inspector had given word to the inspector, who had asked the sergeant, who oversaw the ten operators working there, to dig out the information and pass it through.

Despite the close relationship that existed between Special Branch and the Security Service, the piece of information about the observations MI6 had made, and which were recorded in the computer, made the operator hesitate.

'Is this information about MI6 to go across, boss?' he said turning from the VDU.

The inspector came along the arc-shaped bench and checked the screen. 'If it shows he was a terrorist suspect.' The identity of those keeping the observation on Stephen McFadden suggested that. 'Print it.'

The information that was considered fairly low grade by the RUC might have slipped by had not Detective Superintendent Palmer been using an analysis program similar to that used by C11 for collating any rumour, however vague, and laying it alongside any other rumour that bore generic relation.

'What the RUC call low-grade information,' Detective Superintendent Palmer said excitedly as he tapped into the keyboard while Bentham looked over his shoulder, 'is suddenly looking like something, guv. First it's MI6 keeping obo on McFadden. Next we get the date it started.'

Bentham was reading it faster than the detective superintendent was saying it. 'The day after O'Donnell was killed in the alleyway.'

'The day we have the solicitor Edward O'Dwyer together with ACC St James at the golf club,' Palmer added.

'There were no observations prior to that?'

'Not that we've been given. It looks like the RUC had no knowledge he even existed before then, or any of his family. Even though they've details of more than 40 per cent of all males over twelve years of age, and 74 per cent of all Catholic males.'

'Stephen met both those criteria,' Bentham said thoughtfully.

'Why are we suddenly getting this?' Detective Superintendent Burroughs said. 'Do you think these slippery cunts are trying to point us to something, or away from something?'

'My guess is they think we're trying to deflect public opinion over Stephen's death. Possibly they want us to see him as a terrorist rather than an innocent bystander.' Bentham felt himself getting angry, not at this situation, but because he couldn't make all the connections. 'It's circumstantial, but let's read it like they put him under observation to establish his movements. Not to find a terrorist, but to set up a witness. He played at the barn regularly. How difficult to entice him out there with the prospect of some guns?'

'That's a fucking sickening prospect, guv,' Detective Superintendent Burroughs said. What was worrying him was the possibility of making that leap.

'I know,' Bentham said resolutely.

24

THERE WAS NO SIMPLE WAY of meeting up with Sergeant Keeper other than by calling him into the office for another interview, when the rest of his team would know his identity along with the RUC or Security Service who might be listening in. Instead, Bentham went through the complicated, time-consuming process that ended with them both feeling reasonably safe walking around Ormeau Park, paying attention to the athletes who were practising there. Bentham felt some affinity with them because he was continuing with regular exercise.

The first thing Jack Bentham asked Keeper was what he knew about King's House Boys' School.

Sergeant Keeper broke his step and looked at him. 'What do you know about that?'

'Enough to know that what's going on there touches some raw nerves here,' Bentham said, as if he knew more than he did.

Sergeant Keeper hesitated, confused, uncertain how this was connected with the shoot-to-kill policy and whether anyone would want him to say anything about that. 'It's only rumours I've heard. I'd say the headmaster gets a lot of protection through the Orange Lodge he belongs to.'

'From the RUC?'

Sergeant Keeper stopped and stared pensively out at the athletes. 'I'd say so. Anyone who has connections with the Order would help cover it up.'

He had no hard information that would take Bentham further in that direction and he felt more frustrated. He moved on. 'Why did MI6 have Stephen McFadden under observation?' he wanted to know.

'They did? I didn't know they had so.' Keeper was surprised. 'It was established that he had no terrorist connections.'

'The obo started after the O'Donnell killing.'

A low groan came out of the RUC man, as if denying something unpleasant, like the death of a cherished belief. 'Didn't I suspect that shooting at Hollow Farm was a set-up?' This was the first time he had articulated his suspicion and now felt a curious sense of relief about what he was doing with this detective. 'They recorded it. You should be getting those tapes, Mr Bentham.'

Bentham looked at him and nodded, as if deciding to take his advice. 'Who took charge of them?'

'The MI6 man with Chief Inspector Paisley.'

'Do you know who he was?'

'His name is North. Roger North. I don't know his rank. There were tape recordings made of each of the shootings following the one at Hollow Farm,' Sergeant Keeper told him.

Ironically, Roger North, the field officer with the SIS, was only two hundred yards or so from the two men in the park, a camera with a telephoto lens trained on them. Tailing details were only as successful as the amount of effort put into them, and the more cautious the quarry the more difficult and labour-intensive the detail. After the debacle at Belfast Central Station when they had lost Bentham and failed to identify his informer, no effort had been spared. He pressed the shutter release again as Bentham and his companion turned in his direction and took a series of six photographs in rapid succession and decided to call it a day. There was no doubt about the identity of Sergeant Keeper, and no point in risking exposure by getting too close; however close he got he wasn't going to hear their conversation.

The result of that conversation was to make Jack Bentham more determined to find a clear line through this investigation, whatever the conclusion was, or however embarrassing it might prove politically.

Bypassing the PCC and the Deputy Chief Constable, he went directly to Sir Norman Hateley's office and was surprised that the Chief Constable was available to see him. He hadn't yet got a lever on the Chief Constable and didn't know how he would prise the tapes or anything else out of him if there was no will to do so.

It was in these circumstances, and perhaps for the first time, that he realised just how powerful, just what a law unto themselves, senior policemen were. Who could make Sir Norman Hateley do anything he didn't choose to do? Not the PCC, the DPP, nor the Secretary of State in these dangerous times. Only in theory could they bring him and his men to book. It was less to do with the fact that the RUC were above the law, more that there was no one to check them while the political will was lacking, and it would remain so all the while they were holding the line against anarchy.

'Either I have those tapes, Chief Constable, and get to interview Birchfield and Stone, along with the MI6 officer who was out at Hollow Farm, or we go home.'

The threat clearly didn't impress Sir Norman. 'Quite frankly, Mr Bentham, I'm astounded that you're still pursuing something that I have no evidence of even existing. I don't understand why you're trying to connect the Special Intelligence Service to these killings in some sinister fashion. It's as if you're trying to undermine the security of this province.'

If Jack Bentham had been given to demonstrative responses, his jaw might have fallen open. 'The tape recordings do exist. They are material to my investigation.'

Suddenly the Chief Constable changed tack. 'Yes, they do exist, Mr Bentham,' he confessed. 'I have listened to them, and I assure you there's nothing on them that will assist you with your investigation. Forget about them, and any MI6 connection. There is nowhere for you to go along those lines. Even if there were, you ought to know better.'

'It's what you called me in for,' Bentham said feeling exasperated.

'No, sir!' The Chief Constable rebuked him like a stern teacher. 'You were brought here to prove there wasn't a shoot-to-kill policy. I'd like you to get on and do what you're here to do. Concentrate on proving the terrorist connection with the McFadden boy. That's the most constructive thing you can do.'

'There is no connection,' Bentham argued. 'I repeat, I want those tapes, and I want to interview the MI6 field officer. Then you can have my provisional report.' He could have left it there, but he was angry and wanted to strike back at this man in any way he could. 'I'd like to broaden my inquiry to look at King's House School – there's a possible connection with homosexual acts and the Security Service . . .'

By this time, the blood had drained from Sir Norman's face, and Bentham thought the school worth raising just for that. However, this tack was a mistake, he realised.

'There is no question of you looking at anything that isn't directly related to your investigation. For your information, we investigated complaints about King's House, and found no case.' That closed this avenue as far as the Chief Constable was concerned. His word was the last word.

There was nothing more Bentham could say to the man without becoming involved in personal insults, so he turned and walked out.

The raised profile of the RUC Special Branch detectives who were following in the footsteps of Detective Superintendent Burroughs and DI Senior wasn't how they normally worked. But their intention was to not allow the Met detectives, who were checking the McFadden family background for any terrorist links, to steal a march. It was fear that if they found such information they might choose to bury it in order to protect AC Bentham. Chief Superintendent Johnston planned not to give them the opportunity.

No matter how carefully a background investigation was conducted, there would often come a point where it couldn't be kept from the subject, unless it was based solely on a computer search. Once friends and acquaintances of the subject were questioned, the nature of the operation, if not its purpose, was out.

When the proprietress of the hotel found Maureen McFadden and told her about the visit she had received from detectives asking about her movements and those of her children, Maureen guessed at once what was going on. It confirmed the distance she believed she had detected in Jack Bentham's manner since his return.

She felt sick with anger as she ran to the hotel reception, where she grabbed the phone and dialled Bentham's number. The hotel proprietress followed her and waited.

'Assistant Commissioner Bentham,' Maureen said into the phone, barely able to speak.

The voice down the line told her he wasn't there and invited her to leave her name. She slammed the phone down and caught her breath, determined not to let herself cry, to push the hurt, the betrayal, aside, to deny to herself that she felt anything at all.

'I told them you didn't know any terrorists, Maureen. For heaven's sake. Why would you? You never know if policemen believe you' – despite living in Loyalist East Belfast all her life.

'No. Nor should you ever believe them,' she said, her feelings coming under control as she went back to the ballroom to prepare for her class.

Jack Bentham was waiting by her car when she came out of the hotel an hour later, and she wasn't sure if she could face him, but knew she couldn't run back into the hotel. Her response to him was flat, but she told him there was nothing wrong when he asked the reason.

'My days here are numbered,' he said. 'I had another row with the Chief Constable.'

'Because you're getting somewhere, or not getting somewhere?' she asked pointedly.

Bentham looked at her but didn't answer. He reached for her hand and pushed distractedly at the cuticles that revealed moons at the base of her nails. 'When I go back will you go with me?'

She wanted to ask cruelly if that meant she had passed her test, but simply said, 'I don't think so.'

He nodded, as if expecting this rejection, and tried to withdraw from the vulnerable position he believed he had put himself in. 'I'd like to think I'd salvaged something from all this.'

Getting to it was difficult, but she did finally. 'Why didn't you tell me you were checking up on us? Why didn't you say?'

Bentham hesitated, as if caught out on a lie. 'You knew I'd have to do that. That's part of the job.'

'The Special Branch had done it. We were cleared by the RUC. I told you Stephen wasn't a part of any of that. I told you, Jack.' She was becoming upset despite herself.

'We had to be two hundred per cent certain.'

Staring at him, not liking what she saw, liking less what she heard, she said, 'It was for you, Jack. Your sake. You didn't dare trust yourself to trust my word.'

'I want someone to go for Stephen's murder – not just scapegoats. I'm having a relationship with you – I had to be more than sure.'

It sounded reasonable to him, but not to her.

'All the more reason to take my word,' she responded, with female logic based on trust and love. 'Or was it you were after suspecting me of trying to influence you against your better judgement?'

'It was for the best, for all of us, Maureen. Believe me.'

Slowly she shook her head, feeling icy detachment now. 'I told you it was best to forget what happened. It was stupid allowing it to be resurrected.' She strode around the car, climbed in and slammed the door. Although she told herself she felt nothing, she didn't trust herself to drive. When she saw Bentham walk around to her side of the car, she pressed the door plug to engage the lock, not wanting the discussion to go on, not wanting to hear the excuses in case she found herself weakening.

Bentham glanced back at his driver, who gave the impression of not following this, but he knew he wasn't missing a single detail. 'Maureen, let's talk,' he said quietly. 'Please.'

She shook her head, started the car and drove off the forecourt.

Bentham watched her go and didn't attempt to pursue her, but he knew he would at some point.

Right then he felt like getting drunk, but knew it wouldn't help resolve the predicament he found himself in, and would leave him not being able to function the whole of the next day. So instead he returned to the office.

It was there that the MI5 security liaison officer, Laurence Payne, found him alone. Payne, with his rangy, military bearing, his brogues, brown cord trousers and waxed coat, looked like a young fogey off duty. He wandered the corridors of the Garnerville barracks unchallenged. He walked into Bentham's office without knocking, then, before speaking, looked into the adjoining office to make sure it was deserted.

'Mr Bentham. We haven't met, but it might be worth our while talking.' He smiled tightly, uncertainty making his boyish face tense.

'I'll talk to anyone if it brings me nearer my objective.' He noticed the gun tucked into the man's belt as his coat parted. 'Who are you?' he asked.

'The SIS have almost certainly bugged your office,' Payne said. 'We might talk elsewhere.'

'Shy about being recorded?' Bentham asked and rose from the desk. He had no intention of going too far with him, even though he had given him information he didn't know. He assumed Special Branch was listening in for MI5, not MI6.

They went to the canteen where they could only get tea from a machine at that time of the day. Both seemed reluctant to drink it.

'Your trek towards an MI5–RUC connection in these shootings is quite close, Mr Bentham,' Payne said, and smiled tensely again. 'Yet paradoxically entirely wrong. You'd be more productive looking at the SIS.'

Bentham waited, feeling he would need little prompting.

'They've been struggling for supremacy in operational intelligence ever since MI6 was brought into Northern Ireland by Edward Heath's government in the early seventies.'

'Who was causing them problems?' Bentham asked for information.

'We were,' Payne said, and saw the question in the policeman's face. 'MI5. Army Intelligence at that time was totally amateurish, and the RUC Special Branch unreliable – they were too attached to

285

the historical position of the RUC. That's how MI6 came to be here – up until then, they only worked outside the UK. Of course, they seized that opportunity with both hands, but found themselves slightly constrained by being under the control of MI5's chief. Is this familiar, Mr Bentham? Say if you wish to skip the history lesson.'

Bentham said nothing. He wanted to hear whatever Payne was willing to tell him. He would judge it afterwards.

'Most of the cock-ups here have come about as a result of the conflict between the SIS and MI5, with Special Branch shifting loyalties according to where their best interests were served. The situation didn't improve when our man was replaced by Sir Michael Newfield as the Ulster Security Co-ordinator. MI5 simply found itself on the defensive with the SIS making the running.'

'Are you saying the shoot-to-kill police was an MI6 strategy?'

'It was, and quite impractical.' He smiled again, the tension on his skin slackening. 'If you are going for the "final solution", then you must deliver the final solution. We argued that at the time. You have to bring in the SAS and take out all the gunmen from all the various factions at once, and all the men behind the men with the guns. You can imagine how that went down with the RUC. Sir Norman might have agreed had we talked about taking out all of the IRA and INLA people, and might even have gone along with the SAS doing it. The RUC currently favours MI6, preferring their *agent provocateur* style of operating – infiltrating the IRA, the INLA, the Garda Siochana; that way they can control the information and the action that results.' He met the Assistant Commissioner's eyes briefly and saw the question. 'We collect information across the board, no matter what its antecedents.'

'You seem to suggest the RUC doesn't move against the Protestants?' Bentham challenged, having evidence to the contrary.

'Not at all, Mr Bentham,' Payne said. 'I'm saying they're highly selective when it comes to those targets. MI6 has been working directly with the Special Support Unit, excluding me as security liaison officer from a lot of the stuff they receive from across the border. They seconded the paras into the units for operations.'

'Birchfield and Stone,' Bentham said, assuming there were more than those two.

'I'm sure Sergeant Keeper told you how you'll seek those two here until hell freezes over. You won't find them. They're back in Hereford with their regiment.'

Every time he heard something about Birchfield and Stone, they were somewhere else and Bentham even began to wonder if they existed. But whether they did or not, it was this man knowing about Keeper than Bentham found shocking. He hoped his surprise didn't show on his face.

'My feeling is that Birchfield and Stone might be more informative than Keeper,' Bentham said cautiously. 'You seem to think otherwise.' He wondered if he had been set up in some way with Keeper, even though he had given details of things they didn't know.

That caution caused Laurence Payne to smile, but there was uncertainty in his look that suggested he may have committed himself to something that wouldn't pay off. 'I persuaded Keeper to contact you, Mr Bentham.'

'Why?' Bentham asked, sipping some of the foul tea as if to indicate only a passing interest.

'Oh, the man was troubled both by his conscience and the pressure you were putting on him. But quite simply, sir,' Payne said candidly, even earnestly, 'we want the SIS–RUC axis to collapse. We told the RUC that the plan wouldn't work right from when it was first proposed by Sir Frank Kitson. We made sure the Joint Intelligence Committee knew our opposition to it when the whole notion was resurrected after Mountbatten's murder.'

'What persuaded the Security and Intelligence Co-ordinator to task this operation in the face of MI5's opposition?' Bentham asked.

'The Brighton hotel bombing had a lot to do with it. Sir Michael believed the effects in terms of public opinion and terrorist reprisals could be controlled.'

'It looks like he'll lose anyway and MI5 will gain the control out here. Why do you need me to bat for you?'

'Sir Michael's control is pretty tight. He's not going to go down in a blaze of publicity. The area where he is at risk, no one in the media will dare touch,' Payne hinted darkly. 'It doesn't matter what outrage is perpetrated by the terrorist, Mr Bentham, retaliatory acts by governments that put innocent people at risk are doomed to a bad press. Unfortunately, we can't control every media outlet.'

'All I need to do is get the Security Co-ordinator to confirm this, in the absence of any hard evidence,' Bentham said sarcastically.

Reaching into his inside jacket pocket Payne removed two folded xeroxed sheets and passed them over to Bentham. There was a deadly intense expression on his face now and Bentham realised why when he skim-read the pages. It was a memo from Rupert Mower, an undersecretary at the Northern Ireland Office, to the Security and Intelligence Co-ordinator in the Cabinet Office summarising a meeting at Stormont Castle between the Ulster Security Co-ordinator, the Minister of State, and the Chief Constable at which the final solution for terrorism was agreed on a selective basis through the RUC.

Reading that, then re-reading it to make sure of what he had read, and keeping in mind the possibility that this was a forgery – but also bearing in mind the worse possibility that it wasn't – Jack Bentham felt cold and angry at the same time; both elated at this evidence and disappointed at what it meant.

Laurence Payne rose from the table, leaving the xeroxed memo with the Assistant Commissioner. 'You can get me through the security liaison office at Brooklyn. Make sure you're as cautious in your approach as you are in contacting Sergeant Keeper.'

Bentham didn't confirm anything about Keeper, but knew the relationship couldn't be other than as Payne said it was. He watched as the other man walked out of the canteen, then rose himself, knowing the first thing he had to do was check the authenticity of the memo. What worried him more than it being a fake was what, having found that it was genuine – as he knew deep inside it was – he would do next. Laurence Payne had no doubt that he would use it.

The most obvious person to approach was Sir Cyril Shelldrake, Jack Bentham decided, having discussed the development during a walk in the park with Detective Superintendents Burroughs and Palmer. Without taking an overview of any kind, they were excited at this breakthrough, seeing the investigation coming to an end and their catching the plane home. Wrong-doing had been done, and by a bunch of policemen they scarcely related to at times; it was identifiable and indictable as far as they were concerned. They were ready to see the report written and the collars felt. Those were the basics to police work, and it was at that level that these two policemen functioned.

The question that confronted Bentham was how independent were the police of the executive? In theory they were, but that theory would be sorely put to the test if this evidence was correct, for the executive had sanctioned the wrong-doing. The obvious answer was to feel a collar, but Bentham wasn't so sure that was the right move now. The Northern Ireland DPP was even less sure when Bentham told him he had evidence of the shoot-to-kill policy – who was involved, how it came about. Bentham didn't say what it was, or where he had got it from, but he had satisfied himself that the memo from the Northern Ireland Office undersecretary was genuine.

'You're satisfied that the McFadden family have absolutely no connections with terrorist organisations?' Sir Cyril asked, diverting the conversation away from the involvement of the SIS and the Northern Ireland Office.

'We couldn't be more certain,' Bentham replied, sitting across the desk from him in his Royal Courts of Justice office, sensing his disquiet at these revelations.

Suddenly he knew that this man wasn't going to be of much use to him, especially if he tried to take the line that his two superintendents expected him to take, rather than one moderated by a political overview. Here they were merely having a discussion about the possibilities of his provisional report, and already he was running scared. 'We've checked and double-checked the family. There's nothing held by the RUC, the army or the Security Service to suggest any links,' Bentham said.

'That's perhaps as well in the circumstances, Mr Bentham,' the DPP said, without meeting his eyes.

A smile almost started across Bentham's face at what the DPP left unsaid. He hadn't even the courage to mention what he had evidently heard of his relationship with Maureen McFadden, so what chances was there of his being brave enough to pick up the political time-bomb Bentham had presented him with and run with it?

'I'm satisfied that it's a sustainable fact,' Bentham said. 'Someone should go for Stephen McFadden's murder. That's going to be part of my provisional report to the Chief Constable. I'd expect the Police Complaints Commission to support it.'

'Are they supporting this, Mr Bentham?'

'Partly,' Bentham replied. He believed he could strike a bargain with Muriel Kinahon over his looking at King's House School. Though possibly she too might prefer to live with the uncomfortable knowledge of a cover-up than the results of a messy scandal. 'What Mrs Kinahon is having difficulty with is my recommending the suspension, with immediate effect, of three senior policemen in Special Branch. Then, I suppose if you sew on buttons for RUC men in your spare evenings it's to be expected.'

Jack Bentham had no expectation that his recommendations would stop there. It could do if he were agreeable to some effective damage limitation, but he thought the RUC had too many deep and fundamental problems for him to want to go along with that. The force was sectarian, bigoted, violent, and needed radical changes; that wasn't part of his brief when he came out to Ulster, but then he never really expected to find a shoot-to-kill policy that led all the way back to the Cabinet Office or a police force so steeped in hatred for another section of society that such a policy could be implemented.

He thought briefly about the racism that existed in the Met, and which existed in most other police forces, and knew it was time someone got to grips with that. Perhaps it wasn't possible to do anything about either problem by attacking the structure of the institutions within which it existed, perhaps only when there was a fundamental change within society would it be reflected in the police. Despite that awareness existing on a plane beyond intellect, he was determined to try and do something to change the situation both here and in the Met, now he was in a position of influence, a position to give a lead. The three suspensions he was recommending here would be the springboard. All he needed to do was find someone brave enough to care.

'Write your report, Mr Bentham,' Sir Cyril said. 'If the evidence is there, well, we'll do what we can. Sure we will.'

Bentham was surprised and grateful.

As he sat in his office out at Garnerville police barracks, transcribing the provisional report himself directly on to a typewriter as detectives sieved, collated and summarised statements, Jack Bentham became more and more convinced that the evidence was there and usable. The report ran to eighty pages and took him two days and most of two nights to type. When he left the office to eat or sleep, the report went with him. All that was needed, he believed, was the political will to act upon it.

That quite definitely wasn't present in Sir Norman Hateley, even though Bentham found him in a philosophical mood when he answered the summons to the Chief Constable's office following the delivery of the report. The large man with the expensive taste in clothes paced about his comfortable office and pulled at his spiky eyebrows as he reflected on his time as a policeman in Northern Ireland, and all the difficulties the statelet had been through, how without the RUC it probably wouldn't exist. For a while he sat there in the heavily brocaded chair, listening without speaking. Bentham thought perhaps the Chief Constable was about to tell him that, despite all this hard work and the good intentions, he had failed in his job as chief of police in Northern Ireland, as Bentham's report had showed, and that he was therefore going to resign. Jack Bentham couldn't have been more wrong.

Stopping by the two-way mirror window that looked out over the police headquarters car park, Sir Norman collected his thoughts rather as a runner might his breath, then said, 'There's no end in sight to the war that's going on in this province. It grieves me to see this land that I love being torn apart with such ancient weapons as stupidity and ignorance and bigotry. It's as if we're none of us capable of learning anything from our past. The men who hold this province together, RUC men, are brave souls, heroes. Every one of them achieves feats of heroism each time he steps on to the street and faces the terrorist bullet; each day he looks at his family and knows that they may not be there tonight. If there weren't enough problems for these brave souls to contend with from that enemy without, they have had to endure a worse enemy within, suffer the betrayal by a brother. They've been subjected to this low form of attack from men they should have identified as friends, kindred spirits, but instead they have had them weaselling around, trying to do what the terrorist bullet has not done. Now the protagonist of this perfidy has the audacity to recommend that three of my senior men who have been in the front line against terrorism should be suspended while he himself dallies in sexual contortions with the mother of a terrorist.'

Bentham rose slowly out of his chair, feeling there was no point in continuing with this meeting. 'It's good to know you kept such a fatherly eye on us,' he said mockingly.

'I'm only interested in saving this province from a total breakdown in law and order,' the Chief Constable declared.

The inclination to say 'Even if it means breaking the law to do it', was something Jack Bentham resisted, not wanting to give him that warning. Instead he said, 'I'd say I'm better able to keep my personal feelings out of my work than a good many here.'

'You've not been under fire or lived with the prospect of dying at any moment of the night or day. These brave souls that you want suspended have.'

'You've had my recommendation. It stands. Assistant Chief Constable Eglington, Chief Superintendent Johnston and Chief Inspector Paisley should be suspended pending the completion of my investigation.'

'Your investigation is completed, Mr Bentham,' Sir Norman

bellowed at him. 'When I've deliberated on your report I'll respond, as I've no doubt the PCC will.'

Bentham wasn't listening at that point, but was on his way out, considering as he went the possibility that the Chief Constable was mad, and should also be suspended.

Bentham received his biggest surprise when he was at his office sorting out papers. It led him to think there was hope here yet.

It came out of Muriel Kinahon's visit to him with the chairman of the Police Complaints Commission. Both were lawyers, and as such responded to the report as they knew the DPP must. They saw no alternative but to press on now.

'Your report makes depressing reading, Mr Bentham,' the chairman said. 'We would prefer your visit not to have been necessary. But now it's started we would like to see it finished.'

Bentham looked at Mrs Kinahon, as if expecting her to contradict this.

She avoided his eyes and nodded. 'There are none so blind, Mr Bentham . . . We feel you should broaden your inquiry now to include such earlier investigations as complaints about King's House Boys' School.'

That was obviously very painful for her, and Bentham admired her courage in being prepared to see it go public.

Now he was on his way home with a not very satisfactory conclusion, but more hopeful that the investigation would be concluded, that the radical action he deemed necessary for the sake of the RUC would be taken. Before he departed he had one call to make in order to try and bring a satisfactory close to the emotional involvement he had found himself in here. Having managed to distance himself from Maureen McFadden, more as an emotional damage limitation than to protect his career, he still felt he had a lot to say to her. The fact that she hadn't taken any of his phone calls since he had been back in Belfast didn't help. But at least he had something to give her now.

Although he wasn't about to admit it when he went to the hotel where she was holding her aerobics class, he was seeking Maureen's approval. He wanted to redeem himself for the sin he somehow felt he had committed against her. He had intruded into her life both as man and policeman, while she had wanted to forget both; he had caused feelings and memories to surface that she had wanted to remain buried. Not having helped her resolve either, he felt culpable.

Watching her car arrive at the car park and stop, he caught the hesitation in her look when she saw him and for a moment thought she would start the car again and leave. Instead, she went quickly towards the entrance without acknowledging him. He went after her and took hold of her.

'Maureen. There's a lot we should talk about.'

'I'm late, Jack,' was all she said.

'I've delivered my report – I'm going back to England for a while.'

They were standing on the steps under the hotel portico out of the rain.

She didn't respond, but didn't attempt to pull away.

'I'd like you and the girls to come with me.' He hadn't intended saying that and it was said out of desperation. Not a good move. It got no response.

Maureen didn't know how to answer. A part of her felt curiously flattered; another part made her dismiss such an overture. She shook her head wilfully. 'I can't trust you, Jack. I'm sorry.' She sounded hurt, but wasn't any more, she told herself. 'I suppose senior policemen never expect to be trusted, or loved, when they have such heavy responsibilities, such important priorities.'

Suddenly he felt angry, as if it were impossible for her to concede that he might have feelings too. 'You're being naive. Checking into your background was absolutely necessary if I was to get some convictions for Stephen's murder.'

'What if you had found some terrorist link, Jack? What then? Would you have dumped us as too risky?'

Bentham didn't answer because he didn't know the answer.

'The damage is done, Jack, and you can't undo it, because you can't ever be sure, despite all your inquiries. Only I know for certain whether I had such a dangerous connection.'

'They're saying that the guns found in the barn and Stephen showing up there to get them was the connection,' Bentham told her. 'I'm saying the RUC planted them, and MI6 sent Stephen there to get them.'

A woman with a duffle bag ran up the steps. 'Am I not late?' she said. 'I thought I was.'

'I'll be right there, Mare,' Maureen said after her as she continued into the hotel. Then she turned back to the policeman without looking at him. 'I've got to go.'

'I'm going to nick everyone involved in Stephen's murder' – it was a final desperate offering – 'no matter how high it goes.' He wondered if she recognised the doubt behind those words.

Her eyes met his and held his look. 'Don't do it for me, Jack. I told you, I would rather forget.'

There was an air of finality in her words. She turned and went into the hotel.

Bentham felt disappointed, despite telling himself that what he had done wasn't for her at all. But done it was and there was no turning back.

25

RISING LATE ON THE FIRST DAY of his leave and taking a leisurely wet shave rather than one with a rash-inducing electric razor in the car as he drove to work, was a nice feeling, Terence Keeper found. It made him feel reasonably human, rather than edgy and under pressure. His thoughts strayed to the coupling that had taken place with his wife a short while ago. To stay late in bed for that on a Wednesday morning with the kids safely away to school was real luxury. Afterwards to drink strong tea his wife had made him, and eat hot toast with cunt-smelling fingers added to his pleasure. Now he could smell breakfast cooking down in the kitchen. His wife would be frying his eggs until they were hard and putting tomatoes into the same pan until they were soft, serving it up on thick slices of toast with more dark tea. Right then he considered himself fortunate indeed.

Work was behind him for three days, along with most of the worries about what he was doing with Laurence Payne to sort out the problems the SSU had been running into. Chief Superintendent Johnston had said at worst the Special Support Unit might be disbanded as a result of the Met's investigations – and re-emerge under another name when the fuss had died down. He had heard that the chief superintendent was on the Met's hit list. It was only a rumour and he didn't want to think about it, or that it may be the result of the information he had given Assistant Commissioner Bentham. He felt no compunction about that, no sense of betraying his colleagues or his country. His conscience was clear in the belief that it was for the greater good, just as he had been convinced that what they were doing on the Special Support Unit had been for the greater good.

Going down to breakfast feeling relaxed in his brown towelling dressing gown, he was thinking about taking his missus back to bed after breakfast and the idea was making him stalky again. That increased his pleasure; within an hour of making love he was getting another erection.

The doorbell startled him and he looked at his gun hanging on the hallstand, but didn't for a moment think he'd be needing it. Mornings were the time for checking under the car for a bomb as he did before each journey; the sort of house calls to get jumpy about usually came in the evening – the thick Micks never learned. The thought made him smile.

'I'll get it,' he called to his wife as she emerged from the kitchen.

She stood in the kitchen doorway, tension contorting her red face, as she was reminded of the stark reality of a policeman's life in Ulster. She screamed the moment she saw her husband's instinctive move for the gun as he tried to shut the door. Both barrels of the sawn-off shotgun blasted into him as one of the visitors kicked wide the door as it opened. The other, holding a handgun, blasted bullets into the writhing, screaming bloody mess on the floor where the shotgun blast had carried him. He screamed for a full minute before he died. His wife went on screaming and screaming as the two men retreated down the path to their car and were gone before the UDR unit that regularly patrolled the Castlereagh district responded.

Bentham was back in London, a feeling of anti-climax surrounding him, awaiting a response from the NI Chief Constable to his provisional report, when he heard the news of Sergeant Keeper's death. It disturbed him more than the death of a policeman ordinarily did; he knew the risks out there like most policemen, but Bentham couldn't help feeling Keeper's death might be in some way connected with his relationship with him, despite the IRA claiming responsibility. He was still functioning as acting assistant commissioner, but he felt at a distance from his senior colleagues and was looking for an excuse to go back to Belfast to pursue Maureen McFadden. Now, he resisted going over. Instead, he used Sergeant Keeper's death to pursue the SAS men Birchfield and Stone. They were in his report, they existed, and it would have been up to someone else whether they appeared. For all his independence, he hadn't been able to conjure them up. Maybe the executive hadn't been actively interfering with the police in the pursuit of crime, nor exerting influence on others to resist him, but they had done nothing to facilitate his investigation.

He was driven in the back of a black Ford Granada to the sleepy little market town of Hereford, and had lunch with his driver in a hotel that pretended to be something it wasn't; then talked about what had been on television last night, but the conversation was one-sided, as Bentham hadn't seen any television. The town, he observed as they walked back to their car, seemed to be in the process of transformation to one of those soulless, modern shopping centres that would suffer commercial death at its perimeter, and vandalism at its centre, acknowledging nothing of its past as it grabbed at some economic future. In its wake would follow the social violence that the town's non-planners were trying to hold off. It depressed Jack Bentham slightly that no one seemed to take lessons from recent history.

Bradbury Lines, where the SAS was located, was an unwelcoming low spread of red-brick buildings over a flat track of neatly trimmed grounds, on the south-east outskirts of the city. They were reluctant to admit even such a senior policeman, as he wasn't expected; Bentham had seen no point in warning them. The Ministry of Defence police came out from their office by the gate and were obviously impressed by his rank. He persuaded the sergeant of the guard to call the adjutant, who came across to the guardhouse and escorted Bentham through the camp to see the colonel. He was perfectly proper in his response to this equivalent, if not higher ranking, officer, but beneath the surface civility there was seething anger at being questioned as if he were harbouring criminals.

The colonel was fifty and had risen through the ranks by his practical application to soldiering, but felt slightly disadvantaged when dealing with university-educated adversaries. He had been in the army since he was seventeen and had learned to accept orders and carry them out or see they were carried out, and was respected for this by his superiors. He was shrewdly capable of identifying the danger men within their ranks, those who would question and challenge and sow the seeds of doubt. He clearly recognised Jack Bentham as someone who had probably never accepted an order without questioning why it was given, and it disturbed him that such a man could rise so high within the civil authority.

'I'm not underestimating the importance of your investigation, Assistant Commissioner,' the colonel said, having listened patiently to the reason for his visit. 'If you had telephoned I could have saved you a journey. Neither Sergeants Birchfield nor Stone are on the base.'

'Where can I reach them, Colonel? I am going to interview them.'

'I can't give you any information as to their whereabouts. They're not in the UK at present.'

'Can you confirm that they were in Northern Ireland during the period in question?'

'No, sir. Not without clearance from the Ministry.' He had the authority to give such information, knowing that even the SAS weren't above the law. However, he believed the task for which they had been seconded to Northern Ireland should be outside the law, and not subject to the ambitions of a clever policeman.

'It's a matter of record that they were there,' Bentham said, realising he wasn't going to get anywhere.

'I can't confirm it without MoD approval' – believing someone higher in the chain of command should stop this man.

'The DPP thinks there's a better than even chance these soldiers will stand trial for murder with RUC men,' Bentham said.

The colonel was unimpressed. He smiled as he rose. It cost him a lot. He reached across the desk to shake Bentham's hand. 'I'm sorry I can't help you further.'

The intelligent thing to do, Bentham knew, was to give it up at this point, let the Police Complaints Commission decide the next course of action based on his provisional report. Meanwhile, he ought to clear up the loose ends on the students' complaints inquiries and the inquiry surrounding the alleged rape of Roberta Ford, and then get back to the area of police work he preferred – intelligence. But a perverse streak to his nature defied both intellect and the sensory receptors in his brain that told him he was being hurt by the process he was refusing to relinquish. It led him to what he thought would be a showdown with Harry Streeter, although he wasn't sure that it would help him achieve his objective.

'It's fucking outrageous, Harry. This is a murder inquiry and I can't get to witnesses.' He was walking up Queen Anne's Gate, heading for St James's Park with the Deputy Commissioner to meet with the president of APCO. It was a warm, sunny day, and he thought little more of the meeting in the park than that it would be more pleasant than on the eleventh floor of the Yard.

'If they're on sensitive anti-terrorist operations in the Middle East,' Streeter said, refusing to be drawn, 'you can understand the MoD's reluctance to fly them back here.'

'What you're saying, Harry, is that it matters less what you're doing than who you're doing it for.'

'I'd say so,' Streeter said simply. That was practical policing, and he didn't want a philosophical discussion. He was a practical policeman, after all.

'Why does Roger Gannett want to meet in the park?' Bentham said shortly. 'Is he worried about the Security Service bugging his office?'

'I wouldn't be surprised – he would know better than most what the Security Service was like from his time as head of Special Branch in Northern Ireland.'

Bentham glanced sideways at his boss, surprised at his casual acceptance of that information. He was aware that, like most chief constables, Roger Gannett had moved around before his appointment to Cumbria, but not that he had been an assistant chief constable in Northern Ireland. Bentham knew then there was no reason to assume the man would be other than impartial.

'Is Sergeant Keeper's tragic death going to affect the outcome of your inquiries, Jack?' Roger Gannett asked as they strolled along the edge of the pond, causing the birds to fly up before him.

Bentham hesitated, wondering at Gannett's assumption that it might, whether he knew the RUC sergeant was more than he appeared in his provisional report. Until then he hadn't questioned the fact that it was the IRA who had killed him. He had no reason to; they had claimed the shooting after all. But then anything could be made to happen in Northern Ireland. He tried to tell himself that he was being unnecessarily jumpy, but he recognised that he was becoming more and more isolated in the position he was taking. Such thoughts seemed totally bizarre on this warm early summer morning in that popular London park.

'He was more than just a witness,' Bentham told Gannett. 'He was our deepthroat.'

'One wonders how long such sickening violence can go on without the complete collapse both morally and spiritually of the people of Northern Ireland,' Gannett said. He often made pronouncements about things moral and spiritual.

'It might depend whose side you're on and who's getting killed,' Bentham replied.

Harry Streeter wasn't particularly enjoying this walk in the park and didn't want to prolong it. He would sooner have met over lunch. 'Jack's concerned that he might have inadvertently been part of some sort of cover-up, Roger. I've told him it's ballocks.'

'That was the Chief Constable's impression of my role. He was a bit pissed off that I wasn't co-operating.'

'I can't say I blame him, looking at your report. Whatever you think Norman Hateley's expectations might have been, this wasn't a cover-up. I'm sure you're wrong about him. He wants the cloud of suspicion lifted from the RUC. Your provisional report is uncompromising, but it's not something he can give a kneejerk response to. After they've all deliberated on it, and its consequences for Northern Ireland . . .'

At this point Bentham stopped listening, believing he had got no further in finding out the true purpose of his being sent out to Northern Ireland. He knew he had to think long and hard about his next move.

On the investigation of complaints of police harassment against students from London University, more had been done in terms of man hours worked and witnesses interviewed, but this brought them no nearer a solution. While the alleged rape still defied reasonable explanation – the two police officers who had been picked out from the identity parades continued to deny their involvement and the other two, imagined or real, hadn't been forced out by the contempt of colleagues. That disturbed Jack Bentham and frustrated him. Had the two protagonists in this particular drama, Roberta Ford and Stanley Scone, been people they could have dismissed as mad, then Bentham, along with most other policemen involved, was getting to a point where he'd settle for that. Only they weren't mad. The photofit pictures based on Scone's description of the two detectives who supposedly anally assaulted him had produced nothing but abuse scribbled over the posters in the stations in which they were put up.

Bentham didn't want to give up and take the easy way out, but he was reluctantly coming to the possibility of these students having invented their stories to discredit the police. Considering Roberta Ford's background, that was an increasingly attractive proposition, and one his colleagues would have picked up and run with, had he let them. He could understand that happening while the trials of the other students had been going on at the magistrates' court, but not now; there would have been little prospect of the judges at the appeals of four of those found guilty being impressed. Everyone knew judges didn't read newspapers anyway!

The unpleasant conclusion that Detective Superintendent Horsfell came to about Stanley Scone was that his damaged anus was the result of anal intercourse. 'Anal ruptures happen almost every time they have sex. The lining of the rectum is so thin. That's why they get AIDS so easily.'

'Is he homosexual?' Bentham asked.

'He's flagged on the PNC as being homosexual,' Horsfell informed him. But not how the student came to be on that listing.

All offenders with a criminal record who were known to be deviant in any sort of way were similarly flagged, even though their so-called deviancy wasn't in itself criminal. Stanley Scone didn't have a criminal record as such, but had recently acquired his listing on both the Criminal Intelligence computer and Special Branch's computer.

'Merseyside's inquiries around the university haven't revealed any girlfriends.'

'That doesn't make him homosexual, Alan. But then again it might,' Bentham conceded.

Stanley Scone had the same solicitor as Roberta Ford, and that alone was enough to condemn him in some policemen's eyes, as Martin Potter was newly acquiring a reputation in south-east London as a lawyer who didn't mind tangling with the police. Lately all his cases seemed to have as their main defence plank a complaint against the police; that alone might have caused some to doubt his credibility, but Bentham knew that once a solicitor gained a reputation for standing up to the police, there was a path beaten to his door with similar complaints.

Bentham was reluctant to go and see the solicitor because of the scant progress they had made. Potter wouldn't want to believe the reason was because there was no substance to the complaints and, as regrettable as that might be to the solicitor, Bentham knew that was what he was preparing him for. Potter wasn't about to admit that his client was homosexual and sustained his injury through a homosexual act.

'There's even less evidence to suggest a policeman did it, Mr Potter.'

'There has been a conspiracy of systematic harassment of both Stanley and Roberta. Who do you suggest could be doing it, if not the police?'

'We've got to the point where we're seriously looking at the possibility that they're doing it themselves,' Bentham said evenly.

'I can't believe this.' The solicitor was exasperated. 'I really can't.'

'You give me a motive, I guarantee I'll find you a criminal. The police don't have a motive for terrorising those students.'

'The police want them to drop their complaints, Assistant Commissioner.'

'Do you have any idea of just what's required to organise that sort of conspiracy, Mr Potter? Not to have anyone talk or anyone identified at the end of the day? It's ludicrous even to suggest it.'

'I can assure you my clients are not going to drop their complaints,' the solicitor said with absolute conviction.

Bentham matched it in his assurances that the police would go on looking in order to try and bring the inquiries to a satisfactory conclusion.

Before he left the office around eight that evening with a bagful of papers on the Northern Ireland shoot-to-kill inquiry, he had heard from Chief Superintendent Horsfell that as a result of another supposed incident of harassment, including threats of what would happen to him during an impending visit to the hospital for further surgery to his back passage, Stanley Scone had withdrawn his complaint against the police unreservedly.

At home, going through the computer analysis of reports from Ulster, piecing together a pattern of the Security Service involvement, a thought occurred to Jack Bentham about what was happening to those two students. He called Detective Superintendent Burroughs, who – despite the time – came into town from Sutton to meet his boss at his flat in Hammersmith. Frank Burroughs assumed this was about their going back to Northern Ireland. He had had a good time there socially, despite the RUC, and was keen to go back.

'It remains to be seen whether we will be going back, Frank,' Bentham said, without rancour. 'I expect everyone's looking for a way out before that happens.' He wasn't about to expand on what had been troubling him. 'Do you have anyone who's reliable in the Branch?'

'There's a DI who I overlooked a couple of things for when we were on division. I don't know how much I'd trust him, but he owes me. What did you have in mind, guv?' Burroughs asked, staying the right side of familiarity even with a drink in his hand and no one else around.

'I got Dave Palmer to make a computer analysis of all Security/ Intelligence involvement in our inquiries in Northern Ireland – if my contact in the security liaison office is to be believed.' He reached for some of the printed sheets open on the floor. 'Look. Nowhere do any of them actually come to the surface.'

'Of course not, you've got the Branch fronting for them. We know they do. No one denies it. It keeps the Security Service at a discreet distance.'

'It's the same here, Frank. The Security Service tries not to crawl out of the woodwork. They're less interested nowadays in counter-espionage than they are in subversives – trade unionists, left-wing journalists, organisations such as CND and the Animal Rights movement, also students in universities. Who operates at that level?'

'The Branch,' Detective Superintendent Burroughs said.

'There's no way MI5 is not keeping tabs on these students, especially the likes of Roberta Ford. I'm wondering if we've been looking in the wrong place for the policemen harassing those students. Talk to your DI in the Branch. See if you can get the names of any Branch officers who might have been operating at that level.'

'Is this official, guv?'

'Not until I know they were involved. If they are, I'll parade the entire Branch if need be. Perhaps Stanley Scone might think again about withdrawing his complaint.'

'Of course we've infiltrated the Union at the University,' Detective Inspector Dennis Grove-White said as he lifted his glass of Guinness and drank. It was a taste he had acquired while doing a short stint in Northern Ireland. 'We have most of the university unions. MI5 has dossiers on worthwhile students from when they first raise their profile. There are Branch flags in the PNC on a lot of them.'

'I know that from tapping into our computer, Dennis,' Detective Superintendent Burroughs said. 'There are a lot of people flagged but they're not necessarily active.'

'We look closely at whatever activity there is when senior politicians visit the universities. MI5 has been making the running at London themselves. I think they're looking to discredit some of those students who they feel are getting too much street cred. That's about all I know.'

Detective Superintendent Burroughs nodded solemnly. It was enough.

26

THE SHOES DEPUTY COMMISSIONER Harry Streeter was wearing had cost him a hundred and sixty pounds in Jermyn Street – expensive comfort on his feet was something he had promised himself when as a young constable he bought cheap boots advertised in the back of *The Job*; now sand was getting into those soft tan shoes and tar was sticking on to them as he trudged along the windswept beach at Scarborough, thinking this was taking reasonable caution a bit too far.

With him were Sir Norman Hateley, Roger Gannett, the president of the Association of Chief Police Officers, a reluctant Jonathan Entwistle from the PCA, Sir Peter Friar, HM Inspector of Constabulary, and Clive Salaman, the Chief Constable of Lancashire. Harry Streeter could understand Roger Gannett, who had called the meeting, not wanting it to take place in a hotel room where someone might easily record it, while all present might perhaps be too polite to question if that was happening. But was the beach chosen so that the wind and the crashing sea would preclude the possibility of a recording, without the need of mistrust raising its head? If that was so, Harry Street couldn't help speculating which of them walking along the beach, in anything but an inconspicuous manner, was likely to try and record such a conversation and for what purpose.

'However this matter is resolved,' Sir Norman told them forcefully, raising his voice to compete with the elements, 'one thing is certain, I am not going to allow the RUC to be scapegoated for the repeated failure of government policy in Northern Ireland. Especially not now they've all but sold out to the Dublin government.'

Such a categorical position left little room for manoeuvre and threatened the tenuous accord they had found; unless they held the line all might be lost. No one wanted to meet the Northern Ireland Chief Constable in a head-on open confrontation, but they were all of equal rank and didn't want to be seen to be bullied either.

'I don't believe that's what anyone expects, whether from accident or design, Norman,' Roger Gannett said, feeling embarrassed for his colleagues. 'Scapegoats don't solve the basic problem.'

'There is no problem,' Sir Norman said; not the way he saw things. 'The RUC should never have been involved in such a policy. Only to point out terrorists. The SAS should have been brought in and done the job properly.'

'What should have been done, and wasn't, won't change the situation. We do find ourselves with a difficult situation as a result of Jack Bentham's report. What are your views, Harry?'

'There needs to be some nifty footwork for Norman's lot to get out from under,' Harry Streeter said, meeting Sir Norman's hostile look. 'If we risk pulling the rug from under him, there could be other policemen falling over as well.'

'You told me he was one hundred per cent reliable, that he would do the job that was expected of him,' Sir Norman carped.

'I told you no such thing. I said he was thorough and efficient; acutely intelligent and ambitious,' Harry Streeter argued.

'This is no way to fulfil his ambitions. The man's a renegade; I wouldn't have him in the RUC,' Sir Norman said.

'As I understand it, the Police Complaints Commission in Northern Ireland is encouraging him.'

'That's unlikely. Muriel Kinahon clearly recognises the problems Ulster faces, and what the solution is. Potentially Bentham's exposed a lot of people who can't be exposed for very practical reasons that affect the security of the province.'

'One can hardly roll back the stones Mr Bentham has disturbed,' Jonathan Entwistle said carefully, thinking about the tenuous image of independence the PCA was promoting, and just why he had agreed to come to this meeting. The more he heard, the less he liked what he heard, despite what he already knew, and what he could reasonably speculate about.

'We had all the disturbance that was needed with the trial of the two RUC officers. They were acquitted. It should have ended there.'

'Then why did you call for an outside investigation?'

'There was hardly an objective choice. Who can withstand such pressure? What I'm not sure of is how it was so well orchestrated.' He suspected MI5 had a hand in that, but no proof.

Someone was needed to blame, and everyone avoided eye contact lest it be seen as an accusation.

'There's no value in arguing among ourselves,' Roger Gannett said. 'Practical solutions are required, not criticism.' He turned to Sir Peter Friar, HM Inspector of Constabulary who had once been an assistant chief constable in Northern Ireland. 'What are your thoughts, Peter?'

'Clearly the investigation has to proceed,' he said deliberately. 'Clearly it can't go on unchecked. All investigations are inevitably finite affairs, lest everyone is eventually implicated in some gigantic conspiracy. Clearly a satisfactory conclusion is required at the end of the day. It would be a sound decision to replace Mr Bentham.'

'For what reason?' Harry Streeter wanted to know.

'The fact that he's indispensable to the Met could be a reason,' Sir Peter Friar said.

'That's not a good enough reason,' Harry Streeter argued.

'Also, it would downgrade the subsequent investigation', Jonathan Entwistle pointed out, glancing at Clive Salaman. He knew of some plan; seeing it work out was the difficulty.

'I tend to agree,' Sir Peter Friar said. 'Clearly we must consider Mr Bentham's judgement to be unreliable in view of his relationship with Mrs McFadden.'

'It's still not a sound enough reason, Peter,' Sir Norman said.

'If we're not careful he could defend his relationship with her and become an heroic figure in the general public's eyes. I'm in favour of Clive coming across and taking over the investigation. But it needs Bentham safely disposed of.'

'Short of having him step under a bus,' Harry Streeter said, 'what do you suggest?'

'His career has to be squashed as flat, I'd say,' Sir Norman said. 'It does so.'

There was a long moment when no one spoke but listened to the wind and the sea as if they might be offering them the answer.

The Lancastrian Chief Constable, Clive Salaman, kept quiet. He knew what Sir Norman had in mind but it wasn't for him to raise it in view of his expecting to go out to Belfast to take over the inquiry. He knew Norman Hateley well as they both sat on the North-West Regional Conferences of ACPO and, despite his outspokenness, he trusted him to make the right decisions. Even allowing for the distortions by the left-wing media, when they took things out of context, Clive Salaman accepted that decisions such as that being made here today were always for the greater good. That was why he had agreed with alacrity to go out to Northern Ireland when he had been approached. He couldn't understand why men of this calibre were hesitating. It wasn't the time for recriminations, but for action to get the job done.

'Possibly the proposal Sir Michael Newfield put forward is the most practical,' Sir Norman said quietly, as if out of reverence for it.

The members of the cabal leaned closer, as the wind grabbed his words and threw them up the beach to smash into the promenade wall. No one picked them up, and for a moment he thought perhaps no one had heard them. The truth to tell, no one wanted to endorse them.

Harry Streeter was thinking about the ACPO conference in the hotel across the promenade that each of them was ostensibly here to attend, and what those policemen would make of this conspiracy. Would they be outraged to hear of plans to suspend an Assistant Commissioner from duty pending an investigation into allegations of corruption against him? Or would they recognise the expediency of the move? Somehow he knew they would be outraged, as he was, and would then accept that it was expedient.

'I daresay there is something in each of our pasts,' he said, 'that doesn't bear close examination. Jack Bentham's a good copper. I'll be sorry to lose him.' It was but a token protest.

Roger Gannett acknowledged the protest. 'If you have a more practical solution, Harry? Of course we can't afford to lose policemen like Bentham, but there are more important issues at stake than the survival of the individual.'

The Deputy Commissioner didn't question what, he merely let it go. There was another moment before Sir Peter Friar caught Jonathan Entwistle's eye and said, 'We'd better talk to the Home Secretary.' The deputy chair of the PCA nodded curtly. 'We might need something out of this. I'm not sure what, but something.' He was thinking that policemen elsewhere might have to be sacrificed for the sake of the Authority's independence.

Friar and Entwistle were chosen to do ACPO's bidding, as the corruption which Jack Bentham was involved in would concern the Police Complaints Authority, while the effects of his fall would reverberate within the Royal Ulster Constabulary, for which Sir Peter Friar had some responsibility.

As a matter of courtesy, the Secretary of State for Northern Ireland was invited to the meeting in the Home Secretary's seventh-floor office at Queen Anne's Gate with Sir Peter Friar and Jonathan Entwistle. But he was otherwise engaged and asked the Minister of

State, Timothy Faligot, to go. Brian Churchward, the undersecretary from Ulster, came over for the meeting, which was also attended by Julian Brind and the permanent undersecretary at the Home Office. No one truly wanted to hear the painful details of what the deputy chairman of the PCA or HM Inspector of Constabulary had to say, but everyone listened carefully. Without a word of it being mentioned in that large comfortable room, everyone knew that the alternative to relieving Assistant Commissioner Bentham of his duties was the government's guts hanging out from Whitehall to Belfast.

'It seems a pretty drastic measure to take, Jonathan,' Timothy Faligot said in response to the PCA's proposal to suspend Bentham.

'The situation calls for drastic measures, I'm afraid. I personally liked Mr Bentham. His forthright manner is refreshing. I felt one knew where one was with him. I'm particularly sorry that he won't be continuing his investigation of the alleged rape in police cells.'

'You're not proposing that the Chief Constable of Lancashire takes over that investigation, Peter?' the Home Secretary said.

'No, just the Northern Ireland investigation', Sir Peter Friar said.

'After he's completed investigating the allegations surrounding Bentham?'

'That would seem to make sense. Clearly he would give that investigation priority.'

'There is no doubt that he is culpable in some way?' Timothy Faligot asked. 'Setting aside one's feelings about the man, I wouldn't want this to be seen in any way as nobbling the investigation in Northern Ireland.'

'That does worry me slightly, Timothy,' the Home Secretary said.

'We're bound to get an element of that in any event,' said the permanent secretary. 'It's something I think we will have to live with.'

'How substantial is the evidence against him?'

'The Association of Chief Police Officers passed details to us of his involvement with a London businessman who has a criminal record. He was being paid, it seems, to pervert the course of justice,' Jonathan Entwistle said. 'It needs thoroughly investigating.'

The Home Secretary looked along the table to Julian Brind, who was the youngest there and perhaps the brightest.

'The police will be in a no-win situation if Bentham is suspended,' Brind said, thinking more practically than out of any misplaced sense of loyalty to Jack Bentham. 'The sort of charges that suspension follows would be damaging both to the policeman in particular and the police in general. We might think in terms of some sort of damage limitation. Possibly Bentham might be invited to take extended leave while investigations were under way.'

'That would be most unusual, Julian,' Sir Peter Friar said. 'Is there any precedent?'

'Is there for suspending an Assistant Commissioner? The usual way is to have them quietly resign. I somehow doubt that he would.'

'And if sufficient evidence is found against him?' the Home Secretary wanted to know.

'One still has considerably more room to manoeuvre,' Brind said.

'On reflection, suspension at this stage may be hasty,' Sir Peter Friar said. 'I'm sure ACPO wouldn't want to be seen to be in any way vindictive. As long as he's removed from his current investigation.' He knew that, whatever the outcome of this, Jack Bentham wouldn't be returning to the investigation in Northern Ireland, and Sir Norman Hateley would feel the situation had been pulled back from the brink.

Everyone in the room began to breathe more easily, not because a resolution of a difficult problem had been achieved, rather because it had been deferred, with real options still available in the event of the worst possible contingency; that was what political decision-making was all about.

No one told Assistant Commissioner Bentham of this decision, but he should have read the signs. He couldn't make contact with the Northern Irish DPP, and was informed that Sir Cyril Shelldrake had been ordered by his doctor to take sick leave; none of his deputies were available. Bentham wanted to discuss some points in his report with the DPP. He couldn't get hold of Muriel Kinahon or the chairman of the Police Complaints Commission on the phone. He left messages for both, but they didn't ring him back. Finally he rang Mrs Kinahon at home and her husband answered.

'I don't think my wife is available to come to the telephone, Mr Bentham,' he said curtly. 'Can I give her a message?'

Bentham hesitated, considered mentioning King's House Boys' School to the judge, but finally didn't. 'Can you ask her to ring me? I'm coming back over to Belfast and I'd like to arrange a meeting.'

There was a brief silence down the phone, then he said, 'I will give her the message.'

He decided that travelling to Belfast would give him an opportunity to see Maureen McFadden, whom he was missing. He warned Detective Superintendent Frank Burroughs and DI Bill Senior they would be going too. But then he got a call from his secretary to tell him that when she had requested their air tickets through the Supplies and Services Department, she was told there was an embargo on any such purchase.

'Who issued the embargo?' Bentham wanted to know.

'The instruction came from the Deputy Commissioner's Office, sir.' She was obviously embarrassed.

'Fine. I'll follow it up,' he said, thinking there was some crude action being taken now to block his investigation.

'There are some letters to go off to Sir Norman Hateley and senior RUC officers I want to interview,' he told his secretary as he went through the ante-room on his way to see Harry Streeter.

The Deputy Commissioner wasn't surprised when Bentham arrived unannounced at his office, but was reluctant to have a meeting with him.

'What's going on, Harry? You cancelled my trip to Northern Ireland.'

'You're not going back there.'

'Why's that? There's still a lot to come out.'

Harry Streeter nodded, as if agreeing with him. 'Clive Salaman will find it, hopefully. He's replacing you on the investigation, Jack.'

'He's about as bright as a one-watt bulb,' Bentham said calmly, his outward appearance belying what he now felt. 'I suppose he's reliable,' he conceded; then angrily, 'You stood the prick, Harry, if you've let that cunt from Ulster pull such a stroke' – misreading the situation. Internal rage was distorting his judgement.

'It's out of my hands, Jack,' Streeter said, avoiding looking at him. 'I did warn you, but you wouldn't fucking well listen, would you? Now you've had all this down on your head like a ton of wet shit.' This anger helped him to deny guilt.

'All what?' Bentham said cautiously.

'You're being looked at, Jack – with a view to disciplinary proceedings, maybe criminal proceedings. It was all so unnecessary!'

'Oh yes? What the fuck is that all about, Harry? If I'd done it their way there'd be no problem? What kind of ramp is that?' He was shouting.

'I'm not saying there wouldn't have been a problem, Jack – I don't know what you may or may not have done. All I'm saying is no one would have gone looking. The PCA has received a complaint against you that they consider warrants serious investigation.'

'I bet they find the right person for it, too.' Bentham was dismayed, less at the situation he found himself in, more at the fact that he hadn't anticipated the possibility, and somehow forestalled it. 'Where did the complaint come from?'

'You know better than that, Jack,' Streeter said as if unaware of his hypocrisy. He caught a look in Bentham's eyes as his gaze glanced off him. It caused him to pull himself up sharply. He hesitated. 'It came via the Association – if it had come to me, Jack . . . Well, there's fuck-all I can do now. You're to make yourself available to be interviewed by the Chief Constable of Lancashire.'

That truly surprised Bentham. 'He's investigating me as well as taking over my investigation in Northern Ireland? I don't believe anyone's got that much front, Harry.'

'Like I said, it's out of my control.'

Streeter informed Bentham that he was to take extended leave. It meant he would still have access to the building if he wanted it, and could approach other policemen if he so chose – actions forbidden to policemen who were officially suspended.

If there was anything to be grateful for in this, Bentham was grateful for that, even if it did sound like a consolation prize.

'We've all got things in our past that any of us could be pulled up on, Jack. It depends how badly anyone wants to pull us up.' Streeter was thinking about what this man may have had on him. 'I had no part in this, Jack, believe me. I think the Security Service is behind it – that's off the record, of course.'

Nodding solemnly, Bentham said, 'The Security Service or SIS?'

'Same difference,' Harry Streeter said. 'Sir Michael Newfield.'

That showed how little he knew about the situation in NI.

Jack Bentham's thoughts were seeking out his next move.

Julian Brind was a mine of information, and the fact that he rang him three times and didn't reach him or get a call back suggested to Bentham that he was either involved in this, or knew about his trouble and couldn't help. He wasn't about to jeopardise their friendship by trying to force a civil servant to deliver something he obviously couldn't.

The slight advantage Bentham's low profile gave him by being on leave rather than suspended was removed when someone took the trouble to tip off the press. In a generous moment he decided it was probably a lowly press officer at Scotland Yard who owed a reporter a favour, rather than someone directly involved. But the level of interest from the media said it was someone directly involved. He found reporters camped on the doorstep at the mansion block in Hammersmith, where they pestered neighbours about his movements and waited for his rubbish to come down the chute. He felt besieged; being famous, even for a day, wasn't a feeling he enjoyed; nor was being asked questions he couldn't answer, because there was a code of silence that he, like most other senior policemen, adhered to. What made it worse for him was that his silence made him appear guilty.

'They're out there again, Mr Bentham,' the porter of his mansion block said as Bentham came out of the lift.

Bentham hesitated and thought about the reporters outside, hating them at the moment, and fearing them a little. He was going to see his solicitor and wondered if he should get the solicitor to come to him.

'Why don't you go out through the boiler room and up the back area steps?' the porter suggested.

Bentham was grateful for that, and felt elated as he walked away along the street, seeing the reporters waiting in vain.

But for saying nothing he still found himself in the headlines and on the radio and TV news the following day. Someone was stoking the story. Someone was giving them information about him and his erstwhile investigation with the right amount of incorrect facts to direct everyone away from the source. Interest in the reason behind Bentham's removal from the Northern Ireland inquiry flared for three days, to be rekindled by the weekend, and eventually forced him to reconsider his position.

His solicitor advised that the best course of action was a press conference, which was held at Scotland Yard's briefing room on the first floor. Charles Spiller, who was a partner in one of the most prestigious firms in the City, read a short prepared statement to the assembly.

They wanted more, which he wasn't about to give them. 'I repeat, there is no substance to the allegations against Mr Bentham. In fact, no charges have been put to him. My client welcomes an early interview with the Chief Constable of Lancashire to answer all questions put to him.'

Listening to this and the rapid, urgent, often inane and mostly repetitious questions that came from the pack of reporters, Jack Bentham felt as though he was cheating them. They had come for a story, and had received a standard denial. At that moment, with this much attention, with the media apparently behind him over the injustice he was suffering, it would have been easy for him to believe that he could have taken on the Establishment over Northern Ireland and won.

Support from the press, of course, would have been there only for as long as their interest and the public's interest in the story held, so he resisted the temptation of being a media hero for a day. That sort of exposure might be no better than the hierarchy deserved for putting him in this position. If enough media pressure could be sustained, it might bring him through, back to reinstatement, but no one would thank him for arguing his case in public. His career would stagnate, slip sideways, then downwards. He preferred to do what he could his way.

'Mr Bentham,' a reporter said, 'is your suspension related to your Northern Ireland investigation?'

'I can't say,' Bentham said patiently. It wasn't the first time the question had been asked.

'Is Mr Salaman taking up where you left off?'

'You'll have to ask him that.'

Most reporters seemed to ask a variation of the same questions, as if their own approach would elicit a more expansive answer, or had to be asked by that particular journalist to justify his writing the story.

The press conference lasted over an hour, and just when Jack Bentham thought it was over a reporter said, 'Is it true that the Northern Irish Chief Constable questioned your judgement over your relationship with Maureen McFadden, the mother of one of the victims . . .?'

That shocked Bentham, and he couldn't but react, 'Where the fuck did you get that?'

A buzz went around the room like a charge of electricity.

'Is it true, Mr Bentham?'

'I demand to know what weaselling wretch fed you that?' Bentham persisted foolishly.

Questions came like stab-wounds. He wanted to plunge off the rostrum and hit the woman from the *Star* for that.

'Leave it go, Jack!' his solicitor counselled, his hand on his arm.

Bentham clenched and unclenched his fists and finally heeded the advice.

Profiles of both his career and Maureen McFadden's life followed on the news broadcasts and in the newspapers, along with speculation about what he had found in Northern Ireland; how he had rowed with the RUC Chief Constable and crossed swords with the Security Service. What startled Jack Bentham were details of a relationship he had with a Hampshire businessman, David Dalgety, who had a conviction for tax evasion. He felt incensed at that, and talked to his solicitor, who ventured the opinion that the report might be actionable. But after his initial anger passed Bentham decided not to pursue it, not least because he had done favours for Dalgety, and had been offered some shares in return; he suspected insider trading might have been involved, but hadn't asked. He knew that the moment he responded to the press report he made a story; if he ignored it, then tomorrow or the next day, perhaps the day after, media interest would move elsewhere, leaving him, hopefully, with post-press-attention depression.

Meanwhile, he was working on his own behalf, finding policemen who were loyal to him and prepared to help.

One of the few he could really trust was Detective Superintendent Frank Burroughs, but he wasn't entirely sure of the basis for that trust; they were both good thief-takers, both practical men, and, he supposed, needed little in common beyond that. He guessed that Burroughs knew that if he could go like this, then anyone could at any time.

Frank Burroughs was keen enough to help to put on a tracksuit and trainers and run round Kensington Gardens, despite being convinced it was seriously damaging his health. 'God. I hope you're right about being under obo, guv,' he wheezed as he met up with the similarly attired Jack Bentham. 'I should hate to think this was for nothing.'

'It'll make you fit, Frank, or kill you,' Bentham said. Having kept up his jogging, he could go around the park a half-dozen times without any problems. He didn't regret getting fit.

As they walked along the side of the Round Pond, he said, 'Too many of my moves are known for someone not to be keeping watch on me.'

'I talked to that DI in the Branch,' Burroughs said. 'He reckons the original complaint came from Alan Horsfell.'

'Oh yes,' Bentham said, shocked. 'What's supposed to be involved? Is it David Dalgety?'

'No. You remember that Bermondsey haulage firm we had under observation most of last year? They were suspected of hauling stolen motor spares across to the Continent.'

It was one of many intelligence jobs that produced nothing but those involved had been under observation long enough for Bentham to remember.

'Doug Raymond, the managing director of the firm, is supposed to have given you money for us not to have moved against them,' Burroughs said, avoiding looking at his boss. He chose not to believe it, but knew it could have happened because it did all the time; paradoxically, that was partly why he didn't believe it. Such an allegation was too easily put together, and Jack Bentham was too bright to take that sort of deal.

The last person Detective Superintendent Horsfell expected to see on the fourth floor of the Yard was Jack Bentham, and the moment he caught sight of him in the C11 office he knew why he was there. He wanted to run, but there was nowhere to run to. He thought of telling him to fuck off, but reasoned that if Bentham could not only gain access to the Yard while under suspicion – that's what he assumed – but to this, one of the most sensitive areas, then perhaps his position wasn't as vulnerable as he had been led to believe.

Pulling him into the DCI's empty office, Jack Bentham felt like punching this man. But he was more angry with himself for having done nothing about him when the suspected corrupt moves he was making had been brought to his attention.

'They had a gun to my head, guv,' Horsfell said by way of both explanation and apology. He looked around at the door. Not wanting to go on with this. 'They had details of some business I'd done with a drugs dealer we were looking at.'

'Who was putting pressure on you?'

Alan Horsfell's expression changed rapidly from one of anxiety to that of surprise, then regret, wondering if he had said something he needn't have said. 'It was the Branch.'

Bentham nodded, satisfied. 'I suppose the only thing you should ever do with a bent copper is turf him out – however good a thief-taker he is' – still regretting his mistake.

'Great,' Horsfell said defiantly. 'Who the fuck would you have left?'

Bentham thought about that as he measured the man opposite him. He was tall and rangy, but Bentham still had the inclination to punch him. 'Who's the Special Branch contact?' he asked.

'I don't know. They came with DCS Sissons from CIB-2.'

There was more than one favour owed him by the deputy assistant commissioner who ran the Complaints Investigation Bureau, and Jack Bentham intended to collect.

'I'm going to survive this ramp, Alan. That's bad news for you.'

He enjoyed issuing that threat, but wondered afterwards as he crossed the Thames to Tintagel House on Albert Embankment if it was quite the cleverest thing to do. It might make Detective Superintendent Horsfell equally firm in his resolve that he shouldn't survive, as his own existence would depend on that.

DAC Ron Hazell wasn't exactly warm in his response to Bentham's impromptu visit. He had no reason to be other than irritated at the events surrounding Jack Bentham's departure from office, as CIB-2 had been left out of the subsequent investigation; however, he was enough of a police politician to know there was more involved here than simply a complaint of perverting the course of justice. He didn't like the smell of it, but there was nothing he could do about it.

'You know what the complaint is, Jack?' DAC Ron Hazell said.

'I haven't had any charges put to me. I know it involves a haulier from Bermondsey,' Bentham said. 'I've never met the man. C11 were looking, that's my only connection.'

'Is that right?' DAC Ron Hazell said. 'He knows you. They have a photo of you together at a Masonic function at the Hilton. I didn't know you were in the Brotherhood, Jack.'

The tone of the DAC's statement caused Bentham to say nothing. He didn't know Ron Hazell was a Freemason until then. Not that that fact made any difference to him, but his believing he was might cause something to be imparted.

'Doc Holliday was in the photo with you, Raymond and a couple of others at a Lodge function.'

The gathering at the Kensington Hilton was to raise money for a boys' club in Hammersmith. Bentham remembered it clearly, but not the people he had been introduced to. He recalled a conversation Doc Holliday had had with him some months afterwards about the observation they were keeping on Doug Raymond's firm. He had urged him, purely on economic grounds, to call in the Serious Crime Squad and initiate a move against Raymond's firm or let it go. There wasn't enough hard evidence to have the Serious Crime Squad go after him. But never once did Doc Holliday give any hint that he knew the target. What Jack Bentham also remembered about that fund-raising evening at the Hilton was that Detective Superintendent

Alan Horsfell was there too. He shared the same Lodge as Doc Holliday and was senior there to the DAC, holding Grand rank.

The picture that slowly emerged was becoming clearer and clearer to Jack Bentham, but still he wasn't sure he could do anything with this information to turn the tide his way.

There was no way Doc Holliday wanted to talk about these things in his office when Bentham returned to the Yard to see him. They went instead to a café in nearby Victoria Street.

'I don't believe they'll proceed with charges against you, Jack,' the DAC said confidently, as if he was doing him a favour. 'I never believed it for a moment.'

'They shouldn't have gone that way in the first place,' Bentham responded, holding his anger down. 'It was a get-up, the whole bloody thing based on something Alan Horsfell told CIB-2 and Special Branch under duress.'

'It doesn't matter a fuck what the evidence is, Jack, does it?' Doc Holliday paused and lit a fresh cigarette. 'The fact that it's been put to you, and you've been dropped out of Northern Ireland, that does it. All you have to do is sit back and let that wally from Lancashire interview you. He'll stumble around Belfast asking all the wrong questions, doing no harm to anyone.' He seemed to be under the impression that this was what Jack Bentham wanted to hear.

As they sat in the café drinking not very good tea and eating stale Danish pastries tarted up in a microwave oven, Bentham reflected on what he had said to Alan Horsfell about the only thing ever to do with a bent copper was turf him out, and the Detective Superintendent's words echoed back: Who would you have left?

Who indeed? Bentham wondered. He knew he had to take some responsibility himself for this situation, particularly on two counts, both of which had nothing directly to do with Northern Ireland. One was not going after Alan Horsfell; the other was not making sure of Doc Holliday. On an earlier investigation of his, into widespread corruption within the Met – one resulting in the resignation of hundreds of policemen, including an assistant commissioner – Doc Holliday had been found in the bag, but his Masonic connections had not only pulled him clear, but had restored him to office. He was definitely a survivor, for he should have been dead from lung cancer years ago.

'You know Clive Salaman and Norman Hateley are in the same Lodge,' Doc Holliday said conversationally. 'What can you do about something like that? It makes no difference offically. But he wouldn't be much of a Mason if he didn't help one of his own.' He gave Bentham a measured look. 'There's nothing you can do about all this now, Jack. The damage has been done. Just keep your head down. You'll come out all right. No one wants to see you come to grief. You're too good a cooper.'

Slowly Bentham nodded and then rose from the table. The damage was done, but he didn't believe it couldn't be undone, for they had picked the wrong ramp. One where he was wholly innocent. Right then, he was determined to use whatever means he could to retrieve the situation, but he knew he had to go about it cautiously.

27

I T WAS THE FOOD he had eaten at lunchtime that had made him sick, not the information the duty officer had brought him about Assistant Commissioner Jack Bentham arriving back in Belfast; that added to his discomfort, of course.

Sir Michael Newfield tried to tell himself it was something disagreeable in the fish that was the problem. Possibly a little of the increasing amounts of untreated fecal matter that was finding its way into the fishing grounds around the coast and inevitably into the fish and those who fed on it. But it was the third time he had been sick this week, and although each occasion had followed a meal he wasn't convinced they were all responsible. Increasing occurrences of nausea had finally compelled him to visit a physician, who had arranged for him to be seen by a consultant physician at the City Hospital.

Meanwhile, whatever he might tell himself about his nausea being caused by eating unwisely, or by the unwelcome visit of a senior policeman, whose presence could only mean trouble, he knew that once he had been to the hospital his deadly secret would be out. That the consultant would tell him he had AIDS, he was sure, and equally sure that not long afterwards the whole world would know. Pity was a contemptuous feeling, Sir Michael found, and that of his fellow creatures for his plight would be as unwelcome as the hostility of a larger section of the population who would know him immediately for what he was.

The sick feeling recurred as Sir Michael turned his thoughts back to the problem Jack Bentham represented with his presence in Northern Ireland. Clear, unbroken thoughts wouldn't come easily as he sat at the Louis XIV table in the sitting-room of his flat at the top of Stormont Castle. Distracting him was the acidy bile rising through the sphincter from his stomach into the oesophagus, and he had to constantly remind himself not to be sick or he would find himself rushing to the bathroom. He had an abhorrence of illness, and a worse fear of people knowing he was ill.

'What does he want back here?' Sir Michael asked, wondering immediately if the information he had received about Bentham's investigation effectively being stopped was somehow wrong. 'Do we know why he's here, Herbert?'

'There was nothing on the intercepts from London,' Herbert Greenhous, the Deputy Security Co-ordinator, said. 'He is growing daily more cautious about where he holds conversations. If he's planning a rearguard action, we don't know about it, I'm afraid.'

'It would be foolish to assume he is here solely to see Mrs McFadden.'

'There was a report from London of his meeting with Superintendent Horsfell,' Herbert Greenhous said. Then, seeing his boss's look, 'The corrupt policeman instrumental in Bentham's difficulties with the Police Complaints Authority.'

He went no further, but let the implication in his words hang between them. Sir Michael was someone who could extract reams from the slightest hint or innuendo. He made imaginative leaps that set him apart from other Security chiefs Greenhous had worked with.

'Let us assume Mr Bentham managed to persuade his corrupt colleague that his safest course would be to back him in this affair, rather than an outside agency,' Sir Michael speculated. 'If that's so, then obviously Mr Bentham would feel it was necessary to take action to remove the threat this outside agency posed. He would come here to do something about that threat, because he would guess that this was where it was given life.'

'But what could he do?'

'That's the worry, Herbert. We could be arrogant and decide our position is unassailable. Possibly it is. But should we take such a risk with Mr Bentham? He's a powerful policeman, after all; one who hasn't been stopped by the complaints procedure.'

Anxiety closed in on Sir Michael. Bentham was a real threat, he decided, not because he was a high-ranking policeman with access to hitherto unattainable places – offices that were conducted in secret would remain closed regardless of who came a-knocking on the door, or the secret records destroyed long before the knock at the door – but because he was a high-ranking policeman who failed to understand what was required of him.

'Perhaps we need to take more extreme action, Herbert,' Sir Michael said, squashing the slight feeling of nausea as it rose in him again.

'If we were to talk to one of our Charlie Tangos. Perhaps if it were to be known that Jack Bentham is part of British Intelligence, whose investigation is simply a cover.'

That was all that was needed to stop Bentham. It was a desperate action, but these were desperate times, and there was too much at stake to trust to the traditional silence of senior policemen.

The assumption that he was being kept under obo, and the decisions he took as a result, made life easier for Jack Bentham on his visit to Belfast this time. He moved around the city without bothering to lose his shadow or even try to identify it. Although making the contacts he needed to make was difficult for, even if he wasn't concerned about his tail, one in particular of the other parties most certainly would be.

Neither Sir Cyril Shelldrake the DPP, nor the chairman of the Police Complaints Commission would care about his being seen to go to their offices, as neither was available to speak to him. Bentham knew both were in fact in. Muriel Kinahon was at home when Bentham went out to her house near Stormont, but she was very agitated by his unexpected visit and didn't invite him further in than the floral-decorated front hall with a fifties look to it. The armed RUC officer was right outside the door. Another was in the garden and a third in the street.

'I can't speak to you, Mr Bentham,' she said curtly. 'We have nothing to talk about.'

'I'd say we have a lot to talk about, if only you were brave enough.'

'That's rather impertinent of you, but I'll ignore it in the circumstances. You're suspended, and it would be incorrect of me to discuss a case with you.'

'I can't believe this sudden change. You came to me with your suspicions about King's House School and the Security Service's involvement in Judge Hereford's death.'

'I think you're mistaken, Mr Bentham. I certainly was if I said anything of that nature.'

'Someone's been putting pressure on you – who?'

'That's quite enough, Mr Bentham. I'd prefer you to leave.'

There was no going back with this woman, Bentham clearly recognised that in her. Whoever applied pressure to her had been very effective. He left, hoping his next contact would be more successful.

Leaving the Europa Hotel on Great Victoria Street, he walked to the City Hospital on Lisburn Road, which was less than a mile away. At the hospital shop in the brightly lit ground-floor corridor of the modern tower block, he bought a bunch of scarlet roses that were wilting slightly but would pick up, the flower-seller assured him. There was nowhere else to get flowers at that time of night, and he hadn't thought to buy them ealier. He then moved deeper into the hospital building, following his own sense of direction rather than the signs that pointed to the post-graduate centre. He found an exit that brought him out on the opposite side of the building, and walked into Donegal Road. He hailed a black cab that was heading off to Ballymurphy and took it across to Divis Street. The cab smelled of stale tobacco smoke after a long day of ferrying shoppers across West Belfast; not in a long while had he encountered people who smoked as much as they did here.

There were two light bulbs smashed from their holders on the walkway to Maureen's flat and, with the evening closing in, Bentham decided that the ill-lit balconies might help his as yet vague plan to succeed. He rang the doorbell and waited, turning as he did to look down into the alleyway where Desmond O'Donnell was killed. It seemed like a long time ago. He could still make out the scrubbed-off painted cross on the corrugated fence marking the spot.

Maureen was surprised when she opened the door. She stared at him without inviting him in. She had been unhappy about her name being linked with his in press reports, but it seemed unimportant compared with his troubles now.

After a moment, she said, 'I saw the news. They said you were suspended. Is everything all right now?'

He shook his head briskly. 'Not for them,' he said with more bravado than conviction. 'Can I come in?'

She hesitated, then stepped back from the door, closing it after him. Conversation was difficult, as if they were complete strangers now, with nothing to say to each other. Possibly he only imagined they had had anything to say to each other before. The flowers were received with restrained thanks, as if from fear of some commitment. A meal was offered like a ritual to a traveller who stopped there. He declined it, even though he hadn't eaten anything since breakfast, apart from a greasy shortcake on the plane with a cup of bad coffee.

He accepted an offer of coffee, which Angela hurried to make as if welcoming the excuse to leave the room.

Bentham had hoped things might have been different between them, but didn't pursue the thought to any logical conclusion.

'Will you be able to prove you're innocent so they give you back your job?' Kathleen asked in response to his brief explanation of what had happened.

'I doubt it,' he said, wondering why he was burdening them with this. Because he cared, he decided, both about them and what they thought of him, and because he realised how he missed them. All the feelings that he had forced himself to bury when Maureen turned her back on him were being resurrected, but he was determined not to let them become random. 'I'll only be reinstated if it's finally decided by someone that either I'm safe to keep the information I have, or the situation that I have information about ceases to be dangerous.'

'Is it you who are safe at all with that information?' Maureen asked. This was Northern Ireland and she knew well enough that anything could happen to anyone.

He tried to detect concern in her voice other than the basic concern of one living creature for another. Until then he hadn't truly considered his own personal safety. When did policemen of his rank get killed in the line of duty?

'The irony is I don't have the information they think I have. Or at least what I have right now is not complete enough for me to use it. What's happened has effectively stopped me getting it.'

'Wouldn't it be better for all concerned if you just let things take their course?' she asked.

'It might.' He didn't want to remind her what the outcome of that would be, or remind himself of the compromise he would have to live with. 'I feel the need to take some action to try and determine the outcome. Maybe I'm kidding myself.' Maybe he was, he thought.

He had to leave for another meeting he had arranged, but he didn't want to and wished now he'd accepted the offer of a meal. He thought about asking for more coffee, knowing the longer he was here the more chance he'd have of rekindling something he believed had existed between them. But he let that opportunity pass too. A silence crept in between them; he wanted to reach out and touch Maureen, hold her, smell the perfume in her hair. Instead, he asked the girls how their examinations went; neither responded with enthusiasm.

323

'Dunno,' was Kathleen's reply, but she was self-effacing.

Another silence.

'I've got to go,' he said.

Neither he nor Maureen could quite bridge the chasm between them.

'Can I come back later?'

Maureen closed her eyes. She knew he would.

The girls avoided his eyes.

Bentham smiled grimly, and said, 'Can I leave via the bathroom window?'

All three of them were puzzled by that request.

'Leave? How?' Maureen asked.

'Up the waste pipe, and on to the roof,' he explained matter-of-factly. It might have been the normal back way out.

'Oh my God – someone's following you? They're watching the flat! Are they watching the flat, Jack?' She held her breath, hoping he wouldn't answer, not wanting to hear that he was possibly in more serious trouble than she thought, and not wanting him to lie to her. For the truth was she cared about him more than she wanted to admit.

Bentham didn't reply, but looked at the urgent, anxious faces of the two girls.

Angela said, 'Let him, Mum. You must.'

Kathleen nodded her agreement.

Bentham smiled, thankful for this democratic household.

There could have been no time that he was more grateful for getting himself reasonably fit than when climbing out of the darkened bathroom window and reaching across to the four-inch cast-iron soil pipe that ran the length of the building. He stood on the short horizontal spur that came from that bathroom loo, and paused to consider the twenty-foot climb to the roof. He didn't want to think about the forty-foot fall to the ground, and the wreckage he might fall on to. Moving hand over hand as he gripped the pipe, he cautiously started upwards. Both tension and exertion combined to cause sweat to flood out of him and he thought his hands were going to slip on the pipe, and might have but for the rust-pitted surface, where housing executive painters had missed the back of the pipe.

He was trembling on reaching the next horizontal spur from the loo of the flat above, and almost slipped, he was so startled when the light went on in the bathroom. He stood still, even though he doubted he could be seen through the frosted glass. The WC flushed, the light went out, and he continued on his way as quickly as he could. The second stage of the climb was no easier than the first, and attempting to get himself over the parapet on to the flat roof caused him more than a few anxious moments. He trembled as he pushed himself out in an arc off the wall to clear the overhanging ledge of the parapet. He had to let go the pipe with one hand and reached over the parapet to grip the far edge. He couldn't reach it and returned his hand quickly to the pipe, for his left arm was trembling violently under the exertion as muscles close to exhaustion were ready to give up.

He knew that the longer he hung there, the worse the situation would get. He wouldn't recover, he would become more exhausted. Inching up the pipe, he came closer under the rim of the parapet and let go one hand again and reached recklessly over the top, found the top wet with a slimy lichen and could find no purchase until his fingernails scraped at the surface in a frantic effort to stop the rest of him slipping back. He paused fractionally and thoughts of plummeting to his death assailed him. He shut them out and moved his hand and got his fingers over the far edge and tightened his hold, then threw his other hand up, gripped the edge with that, and hung off the wall. He could feel his arms trembling with exertion again, and suddenly thought what stupidity this was. What was he doing here? What did he expect to achieve? He could be comfortably back in London with his unexpected extended leave, enjoying some time off. Surviving – the answer came in a flash.

Kicking forward furiously, he gained some purchase on the smooth concrete surface which helped him as he pulled himself up. With one tremendous effort he hauled his chest up on to the flat parapet and lay there unable to move, his legs dangling. He was resting now. His weight was over the roof. His arms twitched violently as the muscles searched for glucose to repair the damage. Slowly he lifted his leg around and hooked it over the edge, then levered himself into a sitting position. He suddenly felt elated, his recent fitness régime had made him this capable physically, and it led him to believe he was going to achieve what he set out to achieve.

It was a few moments before his breath returned to normal and he decided to move off. He brushed the moss and lichen from his coat as he went along the roof and across the metal catwalk that connected this building to the next block of flats. He moved over to the courtyard side of the flats to try and identify the car that would have a couple of Branch detectives in it keeping obo. He couldn't see it, but didn't for a moment doubt they were there.

Bentham hoped he had gone far enough from them to get clear when he dropped through the access hatch on to the top of the communal stairs and went down into the far side of the yard. He waited, looking out carefully for any watchers before slipping away out past the end of the corrugated fencing.

Laurence Payne was waiting in a booth in the first-floor bar of the Europa Hotel, and didn't seem at all surprised by Bentham's less-than-immaculate appearance. He showed no anxiety that the Assistant Commissioner might have been followed there, and simply assumed that he wasn't.

'You did well to elude your watchers, Mr Bentham,' he said with a tense smile. 'They're making quite a number out of keeping track of you.'

'Why are they being so heavy? What are they afraid of?'

Another smile stretched the young man's face. 'What we're all afraid of: being made vulnerable.'

'Someone has me by the short and curlies, and I'm not enjoying the experience.'

'Perhaps you'd like the means of reversing the situation?'

'I'm not interested in revenge, Mr Payne. I simply want to get this sorted out.'

'Honourably? Or any way you can?' There was a suggestion of mockery in his tone.

'So I'm left feeling not too fucked over.'

Laurence Payne's tight face creased uneasily into a smile. It was a defence mechanism rather than his finding the situation amusing. 'You can easily reverse things. Just by doing what you obviously do so well,' he said. 'Doing what we can't be seen to do at any price.' A silence slid between them as each gauged the likely cost while he sipped his drink.

'You hardly need reminding that you failed to question the Security Co-ordinator about the policy of bringing terrorists to the final court of justice. But there's no disgrace in that, Mr Bentham. Sir Michael Newfield isn't vulnerable to frontal assault. However, he does have an Achilles heel.' He waited, not encouraged by the policeman's emotionless expression. But he wasn't about to turn back. Too much was at stake. 'He's a pederast – well, even in this age of AIDS we all try to be tolerant. He has a penchant for young boys. A dangerous predilection for someone in his position, you might think. But he has an ever-ready supply to meet his needs at King's House School for wayward boys.'

The proposition was outrageous, ridiculous, but more than a possibility in view of what info was finding its way back to him on that school. He certainly couldn't dismiss the statement.

'How do I know this is not another mud-pit I'm being steered into?' Bentham asked.

The MI5 man laughed, enjoying the metaphor. 'It's certainly very mucky, sir. Maurice Humphreys, the headmaster of King's House School, was an active member of the UDA. The Special Branch intelligence unit E3(B) found him – they deal with Protestant activities. We managed very nicely to turn him. He was giving us all sorts of useful information about the Ulster Defence Army's activities, and a number of arrests were made. Then Sir Michael pulled his file and had MI6 run him. Soon after that, we found that Humphreys was being used to another purpose – namely, to pimp small boys from the community home he runs.' He paused and waited for a reaction. There was none. But then he supposed it was pointless expecting a policeman like Bentham to be shocked.

'I was planning to investigate that when I was stopped. Who else goes out to that school?'

Payne hesitated, trying to assess how much Bentham knew. He wanted him to know nothing more than was necessary to damage Sir Michael Newfield and MI6, not threaten the status quo of Northern Ireland. 'You obviously know more than I anticipated.'

'I know Judge Hereford among others visited the school for sex with boys.'

Slowly Payne nodded. 'None were as threatening to Sir Michael as Toby Hereford. He was going to peach – conscience, I suppose. Whether he would have named others . . . one presumes he knows others . . . I daresay Sir Michael didn't know that when he had one of his Charlie Tangos set the judge up – but possibly he did.' He smiled again. 'As you say, Mr Bentham, a veritable mud-pit we're all wading around in.'

'How much does the RUC know of this?'

'Individually or collectively? They've been helping the Security Co-ordinator cover up for a long while – not for his sake but for the other bum bandits involved.'

Bentham almost smiled at the quaintly old-fashioned expression, but didn't feel like it. He didn't feel anything. His thoughts were teeming as he schemed on how best he could use this, whether he could in fact use it at all; what the effect might be.

'How much credibility would it have if my name were on the report in my circumstances?' Bentham said. 'The evidence would have to be absolute.'

'Oh, it is. The whole situation's like an overripe boil. It matters not who squeezes it. The result is just the same. I'm sure Maurice Humphreys would need very little squeezing to be persuaded to talk to you.'

The two Special Branch men were unobtrusive where they sat in their rusting eight-year-old Renault 18, parked within sight of the entrance to Maureen McFadden's flatblock. There was enough going on around the Divis flats that sufficiently aroused their suspicions for them to have acted, had they not been on this observation detail. The two young men who were trying car doors on the opposite side of the parking area were, they speculated, attempting to steal a car to use for luring the RUC into a trap. The fact that they weren't inhibited in front of them indicated how successful the two Branch detectives were. The people that hurried on by as if not wishing to be caught out at night were almost certainly involved in something illegal, something that a few pointed questions would have brought to light. Both men conceded that the game they were playing might have been the result of boredom; there was nothing more boring than this sort of detail, or more galling when they knew the subject was comfortably tucked up in bed with a woman, and that they would have to stay here with the cold and damp seeping in until he decided to move.

The man who walked past was one of theirs, they simultaneously thought the instant they saw him. He didn't have Special Branch blazoned across his back, but there was something familiar about the way he moved across the litter-strewn area – alert, ready for trouble; but not alert enough, for he had missed their car! He turned back.

'I walked past it purposely,' he said when finally he stooped to the window. 'Just testing you in case you were asleep or playing with yourselves.'

'It's enough to make you, just thinking about him in there with her.'

'Still there, is he?'

'He is. He'll probably not move now. Would you?'

328

'It makes no odds. The observation's cancelled. Report back to Brooklyn. It's 10.57,' he told them, looking at his watch.

Neither of the men in the car challenged the change of plan. Changes not infrequently occurred. Only the duty officer with some sort of overview knew why. He would tell them or not tell them when they got back; probably he wouldn't, but neither would feel he had failed.

A little over an hour later, Maureen woke from a light restless sleep. She had not been long to bed, having sat up half-expecting Jack Bentham to return, and secretly hoping he would, without once admitting that was what she wanted. He was as decent as anyone she knew, she decided, and quite human despite the façade that suggested he couldn't be affected by anything. She knew she had both hurt and affected him and thought she was hurting herself more by holding on to her hostility. She would tell him what she felt for him if he came back. She would even think seriously about going back to England with him, if that was what he wanted. The girls' education would survive the upheaval, probably even benefit from it. What had awoken her she didn't know, but assumed it was the precursor to the noise she heard in the flat now. She had left the bathroom window open but didn't believe a burglar would come in that way, nor did she expect Jack to return through it.

'Jack?'

She reached across the bed for the lamp but didn't get there. The bedroom door flew open, as if kicked, and two men in masks raised their pump-action shotguns and blasted at the bed. They assumed there were two people in bed because that was what they were told, but hadn't been about to ask them to identify themselves. Without checking, they turned and ran, taking their guns with them. They didn't shut the door to the flat and didn't stop running until they reached their car that was parked outside the flatblock opposite with the engine running. The whole episode was concluded within four minutes. They were a long four minutes both to the two men who went in and the one who waited behind the wheel.

The security forces were never far away from Divis Street, which ran west–east right to the edge of the city centre. An army patrol of a lieutenant and four soldiers was the first to arrive. They had been just north of the incident, on Shankill Road in an armoured personnel carrier, when they heard the talk-through about the shooting.

The RUC were the next to arrive in their grey Land-rover. Then came an ambulance, which was of no use at all. RUC Branch detectives were the next to arrive. Then neighbours ventured out, not knowing what had happened, but fearing the worst and believing how it might have been any of them, and thanking God it wasn't.

There was a crowd gathered by the time Bentham arrived in a black cab, not confident about the sort of welcome he would get, but hoping her feeling of missing and needing was similar to his. He wasn't at all concerned about the obo detail seeing him go back in now. He was amused by the confusion it might create in them.

'Some poor soul's got a packet of trouble, I'm after thinking,' the driver said as he stopped the cab on the perimeter of the activity.

A feeling of anxiety grabbed at Bentham's throat and he couldn't reply. His mouth had gone dry. He tried to push away those thoughts that were crowding in on him as he made his way towards the flatblock. Suddenly that was the last place he wanted to go, frightened of what he might find, but trying to tell himself he would find nothing that would directly affect him. That this was trouble fallen upon some other poor soul. But fearful thoughts assailed him.

He quickened his pace across the forecourt of the flatblock, having identified the floor where the activity was. He tried to convince himself that Maureen was on the next floor up, but couldn't. Running up the stone stairs, he was challenged by the RUC constable at the top, but Bentham just pushed him aside without bothering to explain. The constable came after him, levelling his gun. His shouted warning brought Branch detectives to the flat door. One of them produced his pistol to stop Jack Bentham, then lowered it immediately on recognising him.

'She's dead, I'm afraid,' the RUC man said with a familiar softened edge to his voice, like he had broken similar news before.

Jack Bentham had known from the moment he arrived back here, and now that it was confirmed he didn't know how to respond. He wanted to blame someone, to hit out in anger at this outrage that had touched his life. How could people behave in this way, and take it with the unconcern that these RUC men seemed to show? Was it just another Catholic bastard who was blown away? He hated them irrationally just then, held them responsible. They were all helping perpetuate this atrocity. He tensed his fists as if about to pound them into the cruel, insensitive faces standing in the hallway.

The feeling didn't pass. Instead of violence to others, Jack Bentham started retrieving his emotions, allowing them back into the deep pit he was opening up in his psyche. He penetrated the flat, ignoring the policemen who gave him bits of information about this being thought to be the work of the IRA. By the time he turned into the bedroom he had so many protective layers smothering those emotions that he felt nothing. His eyes surveyed the scene almost clinically, trailing across the blood-soaked sheet that covered the body lying askew on the bed. He had slept in that bed – the thought jumped at him as he paused before moving his gaze to the blood-spattered wall. His glance moved on to the scene-of-crime officer.

'What have you got?' Bentham asked evenly.

'Not a great deal, sir. Part of a footprint on the door where it was kicked open. It was well planned and executed.'

It would be, Bentham thought. 'Where was the Branch observation detail that was on this flat earlier this evening?'

The RUC sergeant said he knew nothing of any detail.

Bentham turned away and saw the two girls in the bedroom at the end of the hall. They were sitting on the bed wailing inconsolably as they clung tightly to one another. He thought about what he might do for them, but told himself there was nothing he could do. If Bill Senior were here, he would have had him go in and talk to them. Feelings struggled to get out of that pit into which he had cast them, to share some mutual loss with the girls, but he refused to let them for fear that he would be in there crying with Angela and Kathleen. In that case, he told himself, he would be of no use to himself or anyone else. It was that notion he clung to like a piece of floating wreckage, distancing himself from the emotional turmoil he was afraid of being sucked into.

Closing his eyes briefly against their devastation, he turned and walked out of the flat. The feeling that followed him was one of terror. He knew that he was expected to have been in that bed. At first he tried to deny the thought and ignore the feeling. When he failed, he tried to drown both in the hotel bar.

The Chief Constable gave no sign of surprise when Bentham showed up at police headquarters the next morning and demanded to see him. His head ached from too much whiskey, and still he had too clear a memory of the events last night. Someone had obviously briefed Sir Norman about his being at the Divis flats and of what had happened.

'Who took the observation detail off Maureen McFadden's flat last night?' Bentham asked bluntly.

'What detail is that, Mr Bentham?' he replied. 'I know of no such police observation. What reason would we have for watching her?'

With difficulty, Bentham looked steadily at him. His head was going to burst, he needed to sit down, he wanted someone to share his loss, but refused to give this man the satisfaction of seeing him in need. 'It was me they were watching. It was organised by the SIS.'

That provoked a surprised response from the Chief Constable, but he soon recovered himself.

'They set her up,' Bentham said. 'Thinking I was in the flat.'

He was guessing. As devastating as that conclusion was, it had set firm when he was in his cups last night, and it was that as much as Maureen's death that had caused him to take to drink. He could only guess at who he was such a terrible threat to and why. He knew that threat still existed.

'You have my condolences over Mrs McFadden, sir,' the Chief Constable said. He sighed heavily. 'It's a fact of life the RUC lives with every day – our loved ones killed and maimed by terrorists as they try to render us less and less effective. It's of little comfort, but we will do our best to track down these murderers.'

For a moment that seemed wholly reasonable and Bentham might have accepted it. He would have prefered that and left it there. But he couldn't, if only to prove to himself that he wasn't a part of their process.

'The men behind the men with the guns set her up,' he said, anger entering his voice. 'Your creepy pals in the SIS. Your fat pederast friend who you've been covering up for so long.'

'Your emotional involvement with Mrs McFadden has clouded your judgement. I'll not hold that against you – we all occasionally make fools of ourselves over women. But I must tell you, Mr Bentham, you made a bad choice. You're not welcome here. Go home. Forget your fantasies about the SIS, and everything else. Leave us to clear up this mess. Believe me, we're better able than you.'

Bentham considered the man, hating him for his cool superior manner, hating him for the fact that he may just have been right about his judgement.

'If you don't leave Ulster,' Sir Norman warned him, 'I'll have you put on a plane back to England. Not a pleasant prospect for a senior policeman, but you will leave me no choice.'

Jack Bentham took the first option, preferring to be left some room to manoeuvre, however slight. He left the police headquarters and immediately took the British Airways shuttle back home.

28

THE FUNERAL OF Maureen McFadden was a quiet affair at which there were more Security Service personnel than real mourners. Having established the time and place, Jack Bentham didn't go to it himself for fear of being sucked back into that emotional turmoil from which he was managing to gain some distance. The gesture would have benefited no one, even though he was sure the Chief Constable would have made some concession over his returning for that. Instead, he asked Detective Superintendent Burroughs and DI Senior to attend. It was planned throughout as a private visit and one they were both willing to make on his behalf. He paid their air fare and hotel accommodation.

Passing through the airport, neither of them knew whether they had been spotted by anyone interested in their arrival; the chances were that they could slip in unnoticed, and a funeral in Belfast was always a plausible excuse. They purchased a decent wreath, but at the last moment didn't go to the funeral at Milltown Cemetery, sending the wreath by cab instead.

They took another cab in the opposite direction, out across the Lagan into East Belfast, and on to King's House School for Boys. The headmaster wasn't expecting them but became alarmed at their presence. When they walked into Maurice Humphreys' study and confirmed the reason for their presence, it soon became apparent that he had been expecting such a visit for a long time. He laughed and blustered, threatening to call people in the RUC who belonged to his Orange Lodge. When he saw the two policemen weren't intimidated by this, and having by then overcome the initial shock, he seemed curiously relieved, and cried and cried with shame at what he had allowed to happen.

Paranoia continued to swirl around Jack Bentham, affecting him as much as those responsible for it. He didn't arrange any meetings that could interest anyone that they might be able to record.

Where he stood in the observation niche on Hungerford Foot-bridge over the Thames, he couldn't help wondering how things might have been different for Maureen McFadden had that meeting with Maurice Humphreys taken place earlier. There was no guarantee it would have made any difference, and he refused to dwell on it further or live the regret now. That was a futile exercise. Equally, there was no guarantee that the information Frank Burroughs had brought him would change his predicament one jot. But it might, it just might, and Bentham knew he had to go that way.

Detective Superintendent Burroughs waited for a train to pass as it rattled across the railway bridge immediately behind them and into Charing Cross Station. Then he said, 'I couldn't believe what we'd get when we went into that headmaster. The poor sod literally shit himself when we put it to him about pimping boys for Sir Michael Newfield, Judge Hereford and the others. He had to go out to the lavatory. I mean, we couldn't say no with shit running down his legs. We thought he was doing a runner or trying to phone someone, he was gone that long. But we found him in the lavatory; he'd tried to hang himself with his belt.'

Bentham nodded solemnly as if it was nothing more than he expected.

'Bill should have been a psychiatrist or a therapist of some sort,' Burroughs said, smiling as he remembered how his colleague had handled the would-be suicide. 'He coaxed him back, helped him clean himself up, took him back to his office, made him some tea. It all just poured out of Humphreys then – more shit, different sort. We could barely keep up.'

'Did you get him to sign a statement, Frank?' Bentham asked, anxiety causing him to treat Frank Burroughs like an inexperienced policeman. He would pursue the tack he had planned anyway, but a statement would help.

Reaching into his jacket pocket, the detective superintendent removed a wad of typed sheets folded into three and gave them to Bentham. 'We had him sign the written statement, too. Just to make sure we didn't miss anything' – he opened his briefcase and pulled two cassette tapes of the interview and passed those over. 'Do you think that's going to do it for you, guv?'

'If it doesn't, Frank, I'm fucked if I know what will.'

The situation Jack Bentham found himself in when he took the train north to Preston, then a cab out to the Lancashire Constabulary headquarters at Hutton, was a familiar one of late; however, his experience had been entirely from Chief Constable Clive Salaman's side of the table. Possibly it would be enlightening, to sit on the wrong side in an interview following a complaint about corruption. He felt buoyant now, for not only did he know the whole episode of the complaint against him was a get-up to stop him, he believed he had the means to reverse the situation. The information he had wouldn't clear him of the charge against him as such, but then he felt it was incumbent upon them to do that.

'Is your legal representative not going to be present, Mr Bentham?' Clive Salaman asked stiffly, surprised that he wasn't.

He was visibly less comfortable than the interviewee, and might have preferred a solicitor there to give him distance from Jack Bentham.

A smile started across Bentham's face, not at the thought of his strong position, or anything the Chief Constable said, but at the expectation of him having his brief in at the interview. Any other rank was afforded no such luxury, and CIB-2 even resisted policemen having a Federation representative with them when questioned on disciplinary or criminal matters. It was almost as if they didn't want to damage him too much, Bentham thought.

'I'm sure we won't need him. The fewer people who know about this interview the better.'

The observation puzzled the Chief Constable and panic sped across his face as he glanced at his staff officer, a superintendent. He feared that Assistant Commissioner Bentham would prove as unpredictable as he had proved unreliable.

'I have served you with notice of the questions to be asked of you at this interview,' he said, trying to bring it back to its structured course. 'This is in accordance with Regulation 6 of the Police (Discipline: Senior Officers) Regulations, 1985. You have had a copy and have read the questions?'

'I have.' Bentham knew the regulation was to restrict rather than fully explore investigations involving senior policemen.

'It is now 10.03 a.m.,' the Chief Constable said, observing the letter and noting down the time they were starting. The staff officer did the same.

With a sudden feeling of impatience, Bentham said, 'You can note this down, and it can either go into your report or not, just as you please. What I want to say is this, I was fitted up over my alleged

335

past deeds by MI6. Which is something I think you know about, Chief Constable.'

'I know nothing about it at all, Mr Bentham,' Clive Salaman said quickly, as if not wishing to dwell upon those possibilities. 'If we can come to the first item on the notice, your relationship with one Douglas Raymond, a haulage contractor from Bermondsey.'

'My relations with villains, real or made up as in the case of Doug Raymond, has fuck-all to do with anything,' Bentham argued from a feeling of confidence. 'The Association has pulled this up from somewhere. They may have directed the evidence through the Police Complaints Authority, but that makes it no less of a get-up. The truth is, I could go through your past relations with villains and come to any conclusion I wanted to about your being complicit in corruption. Any policeman conducting a complaints investigation can make it come out any way he wants it to come out.'

'Can we just get back to the questions on the notice?' the Chief Constable persisted, choosing not to challenge Bentham's assertion. Bentham stared at the two men across the table. Both seemed embarrassed by his steady eye-contact and looked away. He flipped open his briefcase and removed a yellow document wallet.

'I don't even think you're an innocent party here, Chief Constable,' he said, being deliberately offensive. 'At one point I'd have given you the benefit of the doubt. You were chosen for this job because of your relationship with Ulster in ACPO. You and Sir Norman both sit on No. 1 (North West) Regional Conference. Also, you share Masonic connections.'

The nerve that hit was raw. 'I advise you to be careful in what you say about such matters, Mr Bentham,' the Chief Constable said angrily. 'It's obviously something you know nothing about.'

'Are you saying you're not a Freemason, and don't have connections with Sir Norman?' Bentham asked, pulling from the yellow folder a sheet containing all those details that Bill Senior had found out. 'Or that you weren't chosen for these investigations because of it?'

'I'm here to ask the questions, Mr Bentham, all of which you've been given notice of,' Clive Salaman said, feeling himself losing control of the interview.

'Of course,' Bentham responded, with an exaggerated sense of injustice. 'That's how it will come to whatever conclusion you want it to. I'd like this investigation to let the truth out. Personally, I've nothing to fear, and I've got fuck-all to lose, as my career of this

336

moment is in ruins. Think about it before you commit yourself to something you can't easily back out of.'

Clive Salaman said nothing, which Bentham saw as a favourable sign. It suggested he was being undermined. Bentham took from the folder a copy of the lengthy statement made by the headmaster of King's House School. 'Before you get any deeper into the mud you're wading through, you'd better read this. It's a statement from Maurice Humphreys, a UDA member working for the Intelligence Service in Northern Ireland.'

Accepting the papers stiffly, Clive Salaman said, 'Are you offering this statement as a rebuttal of the allegations against you?'

He was truly shocked by Bentham's response.

'Don't act the cunt, Mr Salaman. I'm giving you details of sexual relations the Ulster Security Co-ordinator, Sir Michael Newfield, has been having with young boys in a remand home in Northern Ireland, along with members of the judiciary and the Civil Service. Now, scandals can't come much seamier than that, nor is there anything more likely to cause the Northern Ireland Office or the Intelligence Service profound embarrassment. We're not talking about some low-ranking pederast who can't forget his public-school ways. This is the former head of the Secret Intelligence Service; judges buggering boys whose fathers they're sending to prison; civil servants close to the Prime Minister.'

He paused, but neither of the two uniformed officers opposite said anything.

'Buggery in high places is nothing new, of course, and it's not even very shocking. But this looks particularly worrying because of who's involved. This doesn't relate to any allegations against me or my supposed involvement with Doug Raymond. What it does relate to is the fact that I was about to expose what MI6 were up to in Northern Ireland.

'They were using the RUC's Special Support Unit to wipe out the middle stratum of terrorists who they couldn't turn into Charlie Tangos, to use the parlance – converted terrorists. They were dispatching people with extreme prejudice – more parlance – when they threatened their existence, as Mr Justice Hereford did.'

The truth to tell, Bentham didn't know if that was the real scenario as confirmed by Security Liaison Officer Laurence Payne, or whether it was more the mindless, unresolved rivalry between MI5 and MI6 – with the victims simply the means by which one faction tried to discredit and undermine the other – and that the judge's death really was the work of the IRA. But right than he didn't care. And as to the killing of Maureen McFadden, he didn't raise the spectre of him being the intended target. He didn't want to even think about it because if he did, he knew he would have to try and take some action for her sake, regardless of the consequences. Deep inside him, in another pit, like that in which his feelings were buried, a craven instinct for survival told him there was nothing he could do about that killing, other than to sacrifice himself in some futile gesture that would be soon forgotten. What he could do, and what he thought was sustainable with evidence, was reach out to stop Sir Michael Newfield. That he would follow through in his calculated bid to survive

'The question that still intrigues me, Jack,' Harry Streeter said as they stepped along the sixteenth-floor corridor to the conference being held in the Commissioner's suite, 'is would you have used that information about Sir Michael Newfield if the PCA hadn't dropped the charges against you?'

Without hesitation, Bentham said, 'Of course not, Harry. I'm a senior policeman. You don't do those sort of things, do you?'

'No,' the Deputy Commissioner said. He knew that, but wasn't entirely convinced Jack Bentham did yet.

Still, there remained a faint question mark over Bentham. He had been welcomed back to his office after the Police Complaints Authority had decided there was no evidence against him following the Chief Constable of Lancashire's swift conclusion to his investigation. The sop to their independence was the prosecution of three policemen on the student demo against the Home Secretary. Sir Michael Newfield's resignation on health grounds was incidental to any decision that was made about Bentham's career. It was found that Sir Michael had cancer of the colon, which had metastasised in other sites. Jonathan Entwistle, the deputy chairman of the Police Complaints Authority, was delighted with Bentham's reinstatement, as it had meant he could conclude the investigation into the alleged rape by policemen on the black student Roberta Ford.

Although Bentham functioned back in office, and indeed had been confirmed in his promotion to assistant commissioner following the retirement of AC Roy Genders, he hadn't the freedom generally accorded policemen of that rank. The Deputy Commissioner had decided to keep track of what he was up to, at least until the investigation of the RUC now conducted by Chief Constable

Salaman was complete, when it was expected that no further charges against anyone in the Special Support Unit would be necessary. The telephones in Jack Bentham's office were tapped and his instructions and orders were counter-checked.

All of this Bentham wasn't unaware of, although he didn't believe that Harry Streeter knew that he knew. As he remarked to Detective Superintendent Frank Burroughs, he could use the lavatory in his office suite, but someone counted the number of sheets that went missing from the loo roll, and he couldn't order a new one without that order being diverted via the Deputy Commissioner's office. All of which put pressure on Jack Bentham to resign, and all of which he withstood surprisingly well in the circumstances, or at least thought he did.

'I would like to have gone back there, Harry,' Bentham said wistfully, as they walked along the carpeted corridor. 'It would have been nice to have finished what I started in Northern Ireland.'

Harry Streeter hesitated, and glanced sideways at Bentham, wondering if he was being serious. 'That's not possible, Jack, even if Norman Hateley would let you back. Clive Salaman will finish the investigation.'

'Of course he will . . . Of a fashion.'

With a chuckle, Streeter said, 'As you say, of a fashion.'

The jury would remain out on Jack Bentham, at least for a while.

The conference chaired by the Commissioner was held in the deep armchairs set out in a semi-circle in his main office. In addition to his deputy, it was attended by the four assistant commissioners, three of the DACs from central squads, including Special Branch, and the two DACs from Area 7 and Area 3. It was districts within those areas, namely E Division and M Division, that were the focus of Jack Bentham's provisional report following the conclusion of his investigations into the allegations of rape by policemen in a police cell, and complaints against the police by students of London University.

Carefully and succinctly, Bentham outlined the circumstances based on information to hand from C11, Special Branch and local intelligence units that led to the policing operation at the Students' Union. The men around the room had most of the details and weren't about to challenge what he said. Although he didn't wish to bore them by repeated information, he couldn't take it for granted that they were all familiar with all of the facts of the cases involved. He was aware of how much of a test this was for him.

No one dropped off to sleep as he spoke and, apart from a couple of points, it wasn't so abstruse that items needed to be gone over. When he began to summarise his conclusions, he noticed an extra alertness in those around the room. They stopped prodding at their noses or ears.

'There is no doubt,' Bentham said, playing to his audience, 'absolutely none at all, about there being a good deal of violence from those officers who policed that demonstration. According to what is happening in our ranks, and indeed in the country as a whole, we often take the line that violence by the police at any level and in any circumstances is unacceptable. So it is, when we have a reasonably stable society. Indeed, in those circumstances the profile of the police becomes lower and lower; consensus policing becomes the norm. In less stable social conditions, a physical, sometimes violent response by the police is both necessary and reasonable. No one would argue against that in our response at pickets at Wapping or black rioters or black rioters in our inner cities.'

No one argued with his juxtapositioning of the most violent demonstrations against the police with those that took place at the Students' Union. It was that frequent and skilful use of imagery by the police that created strong impressions in the mind's eye of the general public, and led them to believe that all demonstrations required large numbers of police because all demonstrations were *de facto* violent.

'On the evening of 4 March the police met a great deal of violence from the students, most of it instigated by those among them belonging to the WRP. The police retaliated with force, but no more force than was needed to restrain and arrest those demonstrators who were being most violent.

'There were forty-nine arrests, mostly under the Public Order Act. Twenty-seven of those charged were found guilty at the magistrates' court; seven appealed against sentence. All but two had their sentences upheld. The fact that it was a relatively poor showing at court is as much to do with the failure of magistrates to understand the complexities of public-order policing and the immense pressure on the policemen involved. The expectation that policemen can make some sort of contemporaneous notes is ludicrous, and I think it is incumbent upon us to convey this to the Magistrates' Association. It would be too easy to blame it on the incompetence of the police in general or the laziness of policemen in particular, although some policemen are at fault and must be dealt with by the courts.

'Between the officers from Merseyside, who were brought here to conduct the complaints investigation, and detectives both from CIB-2 and C11, who I used on the rape allegation inquiry, four hundred and seventeen statements were taken. We've lost track of the man hours involved – to say nothing of all the unpaid overtime that policemen put in. I can say without fear of contradiction that no stone has been left unturned; not only that, all those stones were seen to be turned. My conclusion as a result of all this activity is that in all but three cases, there is no substance to the complaints against the policemen at the Students' Union demo. That is my recommendation to the Police Complaints Authority. Some policemen might regret that, perversely feeling it might be better to suffer self-flagellation rather than risk what might look like a whitewash. That's ballocks. We'll have to live with name-calling until someone finds a better way, a more efficient way, a yet *more* independent way of dealing with police complaints. I know how thorough it was. I don't believe any investigation could have been fairer to the complainants.' He only reluctantly gave the name of the policeman charged with assault of a student on the steps on the Union building to Jonathan Entwistle.

'There were two particularly nasty complaints following from that demo, Jack,' the Commissioner said, feeling reassured if not satisfied. This would be the last such inquiry during his term in office and he was pleased to be going out on a high note. 'I want us to be seen to be scrupulously fair.'

'So do I,' Bentham responded confidently, sensing how those present were feeling about what he had said, and how it reflected on him. 'What I'm not prepared to see is the police whipped merely for the sake of public opinion. If I believed there was substance to the complaints from either Roberta Ford or Stanley Scone, then policemen would be toeing the line. Consider for a moment what it would mean if this woman had been raped in a police cell by policemen. It would mean that no woman would ever be safe when taken into custody. If we covered that up and pretended it didn't happen, we'd all be holding our breath until it happened the next time. What I believe we're dealing with is a politically motivated black activist who would do anything to show us in a bad light. She was closely involved with the local politician who was murdered.

341

This really looks like some sort of vendetta. First she blames the police for his death – Jesse Jarman was digging up dirt on the police to continue his propaganda war – then paradoxically she blames us for finding his killers. Unfortunately for the political ends she serves, the killers happened not to be racists or policemen but a couple of black kids who panicked while caught by Jarman in the act of burgling his flat. That was a piece of police work we can be proud of, especially in that it resulted from a dangerous stint of under-cover work by a particularly young black policeman. I am pleased to say that, unlike most of us, he won't have to wait until he gets to heaven for his reward. He's being put up for the Queen's Award for Bravery.' Bentham had made the recommendation.

There were murmurs of approval from around the room.

'There were repeated complaints of police harassment from these two students, but neither Roberta Ford nor Stanley Scone ever managed to identify a single policeman involved or take down a single car number that could be traced. Scone's original complaint having been taken to the police station by two unidentified detectives, who allegedly assaulted him, leading to an anal rupture, is unsubstantiated. Following exhaustive inquiries, it was concluded that no such assault took place but that Stanley Scone was a victim of his own sexual preference. He's a known homosexual and is likely to have suffered damage to his rectum from one or other of his sexual pursuits.

'Scone has since unreservedly withdrawn his complaint against the police and has fled the country. However, because of the particularly vicious nature of both these complaints, and the excessive expen-diture in police manpower, to say nothing of the damage in both public relations and police morale, I feel we should look to prosecute these two for maliciously wasting police time.'

Finally, when Bentham stopped and lowered his notes, he glanced around the room at the thoughtful faces. Some were nodding, none were disagreeing. He looked at Deputy Commissioner Harry Streeter, whose responsibility it would be to take action on these recommendations. There was a broad grin of approval on his face. Bentham knew that he wasn't simply saying yes to the prosecution of a couple of vindictive students, he was welcoming him back to the fold. Jack Bentham knew then that he had passed whatever test he had unknowingly been put to. He felt pleased and relieved and grateful. He liked being a policeman. He wanted to go on being an effective policeman.

It was a nail-biting time for Herbert Greenhous and Laurence Payne as they sat in the Security Co-ordinator's office in Stormont Castle, awaiting news of their latest venture. With the departure of Sir Michael Newfield, his deputy, now acting as co-ordinator, had quickly read the wind and realigned with MI5, seeing them as gaining the ascendancy. The enterprise they were awaiting news on was a joint MI5/SIS operation that, if successful, could wipe out an entire IRA cell in Armagh. One of their well-placed Charlie Tangos was instrumental in organising the cell to launch an attack on the magistrates' court at Castleblaney in Monaghan. They were planning to ram it with a mechanical road-digger with 1,000 kilos of explosive in its shovel. The destruction of the court building would be a powerful gesture, both symbolically and physically.

As he sipped the malt whiskey Greenhous had given him, Payne reflected how skilfully the Acting Co-ordinator operated, and he wouldn't be unhappy to see him appointed co-ordinator. However, he suspected that that depended more on political fidelity than ability. Whatever the outcome, this new spirit of accord was a pleasant respite, however short-lived it might prove.

When the green telephone rang, Herbert Greenhous set his drink calmly on the coaster he had on the desk to avoid marking the brightly polished wood, adjusted the length of his cuffs and reached for the receiver and simply said, 'Greenhous.' He listened without speaking, his index finger stroking his neat moustache.

Laurence Payne waited, holding his breath, watching alertly for any sign the Acting Co-ordinator might give. He gave none.

'What casualties did our people sustain?' He paused. 'I see. Thank you.' Greenhous replaced the phone, rose and took his glass to the whiskey decanter, where he glanced at Payne. 'Can I get you another, Laurence? Not champagne unfortunately.'

A smile crept across Laurence Payne's tight face. He waited.

'All nine members of the IRA cell were shot by the SAS as they tried to ram the court house.'

'Nine?'

'Yes. Our Charlie Tango was shot also.' There was no regret in his tone. 'Two SAS men were wounded in the exchange of fire.'

'Quite a successful operation.'

Herbert Greenhous stroked his moustache. 'Certainly a lot more effective than the RUC operating some half-baked shoot-to-kill policy. Congratulations, Laurence. A first-rate idea well executed.'

He smiled for the first time that evening, the smile in anticipation of things to come.

Epilogue

REMEMBERING THE FEELING he had had while walking through the locker room at the local police station after having pulled Detective Sergeant Brian Tait out of that riot at the Farm, having other policemen, white policemen, slap him on the back and congratulate him, Maurice Knight had truly felt one of them, like he belonged. At that moment he hadn't been a black man with racial and cultural roots elsewhere, but a policeman belonging to that unique community of men and women who first and foremost took care of their own. He was glad to belong, and it was that expression of comradeship from those white policemen, many of whom had given him hassle before – before knowing he was one of them, before knowing he was other than just another black face looking for trouble – that helped him decide not to leave the police force.

Only afterwards did he get angry, but mostly at himself for going along with this, for keeping quiet about DS Tait. He had done so, he told himself, because the circumstances didn't seem right to bring up what Tait was. But deep inside, Maurice knew that the real reason was because, having been brought into the warmth of fellowship, he didn't want to be cast out into the cold of minority isolation again. Then he had refused even to think about his justification, much less the reason for it.

That feeling of belonging recurred when posted in *Police Orders* was notification of his being awarded the Queen's Gallantry Medal for bravery of a particularly high order. That preceded the listing of his name, rank, nature of the award and deed in the *London Gazette* with other recipients of awards who were going to the Palace for the investiture by Her Majesty the Queen. There could be no surer confirmation that he belonged. He felt immense pride at seeing his name in print like that, and a slight sense of shame about his even considering the possibility of leaving this outstanding body of officers, who not only made the country safe for decent folks to live in but also kept the traffic moving! His parents, along with his extended family in and around Plymoth, shared his pride; so too, he was sure, did his brothers up and down the country. This was their award too, he imagined. He had heard about Roberta Ford and was angry that she had been trying to make trouble for the police, and now simply regretted the fact that it reflected badly on his people.

Listed also was Brian Tait, who was to receive the same award. Seeing his name there brought back the feeling of anger that had driven Maurice to attack the detective at the police station. It was there in the lists as if to mock him and degrade the honour he was to receive. He had thought about refusing it at that point, but knew it would only serve to make him look foolish and disappoint his parents. That certainly wasn't the time to take a stand on Brian Tait. He should have done that long ago if he intended to. When his anger subsided, he began to think that perhaps he was wrong about Tait after all. Now being a detective himself, Maurice began to take a completely different perspective. In the CID, things were never quite as clear-cut as they seemed in uniform. Tait was possibly no more than a hard-working detective who used sometimes unorthodox but necessary methods. Maurice found he could live with that viewpoint, and therefore with Tait receiving the award too.

Maurice's mother had been up and bustling around the house since five o'clock in the morning, getting the day started early to reach Buckingham Palace for her son's investiture at eleven o'clock. She and her husband were going as Maurice's guests. They saw this not only as their son making it in his chosen profession, but as their acceptance at long last in the country they had come to in the fifties as a nurse and carpenter, when both skills were in short supply. She was now a district nurse and her husband taught carpentry for the local education authority, but even so they still found on occasions that they didn't fit in. Now it would be different.

She posed for the local press photographer on the doorstep of their house in her dark floral print dress and hat, bought especially for the occasion. Maurice and his father were both in hired morning suits; they could have gone in dark lounge suits but wanted to do this right. The photographer asked the men to put on their grey top hats, and Mrs Knight made minor adjustments to them before she let them be photographed.

The taxi from Paddington Station took them as far as the gates of Buckingham Palace. The policeman on duty saluted Maurice when he showed him the formal invitation to the investiture. Maurice liked to think he recognised him as a brother officer, and almost wished he had gone in uniform. Being in the CID now, he wasn't obliged to wear a uniform for formal occasions.

Investitures were held in the Palace ballroom, and the Knight family, like everyone else who attended for the first time, was curious and at the same time disappointed as they were shown through the Palace by a liveried attendant. Fabulous and fairyland it was not, but slightly frayed and worn in parts.

If any of them were asked what the most memorable moment was they would have said the excitement that was generated by the four hundred or so people at the investiture, and the silence that fell when Her Majesty the Queen entered unheralded with the Master of the Household in his vice-admiral's uniform and secretaries trotting behind. Following her entrance, murmurs started up again. The light music continued throughout from the ten-piece ensemble in the gallery as the Queen positioned herself on the throne.

The hundred and twenty recipients at this, the second ceremony in November, entered from the antechamber in order of status of the award they were receiving. Their guests were seated in gilt and red chairs across from them in the ballroom, all craning their necks. Inevitably Maurice Knight was alongside Brian Tait, who told him that he had been promoted to detective inspector. Maurice felt slightly outdone, but not resentful, for he saw himself rising as fast, now that he was in the CID.

Jack Bentham received his award before either of these two policemen. He would make a point of speaking to them afterwards, and congratulating them. He had had the press officer at the Yard organise newspaper photographers to get the black and the white policeman together, to show that ethnic minorities prospered among their ranks the same as white policemen. He had recently been awarded the Queen's Police Medal for outstanding professionalism, but ironically that wasn't part of the Queen's investiture. The recipient of that award was recommended to the Home Secretary by the Commissioner; the Home Secretary made the appropriate recommendation to the Central Chancellery for the Queen's approval. Then the Commissioner of Police made the award. It had been one of his last acts before leaving office and having the Deputy Commissioner take over.

Bentham was here today to receive a CBE for outstanding services to policing. If ever there had been any doubt before about his position in the police hierarchy, there could have been none now.

Although he had no intention of speaking to ACC Peter Eglington of the RUC, he felt no rancour over his presence at this ceremony, even though he had recommended at one time that he be suspended over the alleged shoot-to-kill policy. Jack Bentham did note with satisfaction that he was below him in line, receiving only an OBE.

When Brian Tait reached the Queen there was a smile set into the DI's face so deeply that a hammer and chisel would have been needed to remove it. This ceremony told him he could literally get away with murder, and that was something to smile about.

'For your outstanding courage in the face of a furious and violent assault by rioters,' Her Majesty the Queen said, having been briefed about this recipient by the Master of the Household, who handed her the medal. 'Such courage cannot be commended too highly. Well done.'

'Thank you, ma'am,' Tait said, making a half-bow as he had been shown to at the briefing. 'It was mostly my partner's effort, I must admit,' he said, but the Queen seemed unimpressed by this gesture of generosity – he might have been telling her someone had got something wrong.

He moved away to stand with the other recipients.

'The act of bravery for which you are receiving this medal,' Her Majesty said as she shook hands with Maurice Knight and passed over the medal, 'speaks well of our future as a racially integrated nation. Your people have every reason to feel very proud of you, Constable Knight.'

That was one more of the patronising, racist insults that Detective Constable Knight had learned to let slide off his broad back. He felt like saying in best pidgin, which he'd heard his cousins use when mocking a whitey, 'What mean you, Queen boss, I'm you people.' But he didn't. Instead, he looked beyond the gracious lady to his parents, both of whom were smiling and weeping with joy.

'I understand you play the saxophone' – just having been incorrectly briefed by the Master of the Household.

'Yes, ma'am,' Maurice said compliantly, without correcting her. 'Jolly good.'

Maurice grinned and made the expected half-bow before the Queen.